Inhibited

Cerynn McCain

I Love you
and miss you ♡
- Cassandra
Mullins

Inhibited

To Phil,

who didn't know that,

with one phone call,

you chose this.

Thank you for your expertise.

Inhibited by Cerynn McCain

Cover: Drop Dead Designs

Map: Inkarnate

Publisher: Yeir Publishing, Chelan, Washington

Editor: Cassandra Sparks

Creative Consultant: Bethany Stanley

ISBN: 978-0-9988563-2-2 (Second Edition)

ISBN: 978-0-9988563-1-5 (Kindle Edition)

Library of Congress Control Number: 2019908114

Questions, Comments, and information on book purchases email:
inhibitedbooks@kjsparks.com

By the power bestowed unto me by The King himself, before he was banished from this world, I hereby authorize this Àraid Scribe to record the events that transpired, and dramatize them in order to make them readable to the human race in this world. May the events occurring worlds away serve their purpose to this world, and whomever reads these accounts. I authorize that these events occurred as the Scribe says.

-Elder Pïlű̃л

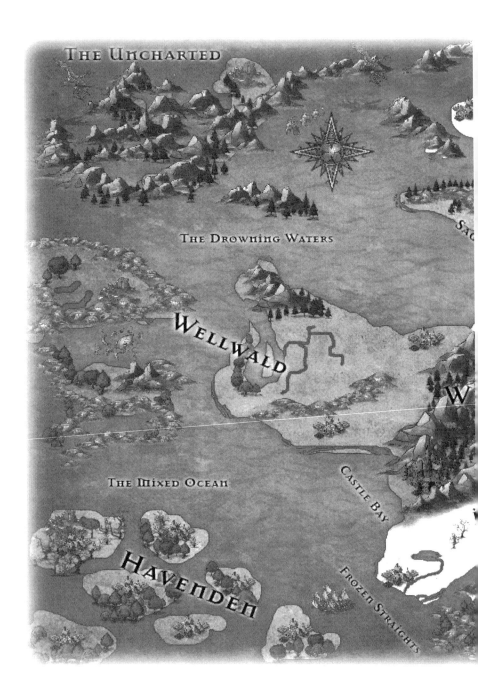

Prologue

Outside the gates

32nd Day, The Season Of Death, 749-PW

"The darkness is coming."

That phrase keeps running through my head.

Who said it? What is the darkness? Has it come yet? Maybe the

darkness passed. Maybe I missed it.

But if it already happened, why won't those words leave my head?

The Captain said writing might help me regain my memories, but

it's not.

I only remember The General. And pain.

But I forgot something important.

What?

"Alice?"

I slammed my journal shut, and glanced at The Captain.

"Is it helping? Do you remember anything?" Hope shone in The Captain's eyes, but faded when I shook my head and pressed my lips together. He took my journal from me, and handed me a blank piece of parchment.

"I'm going to see if I can find the city. You stay here. Don't light a lamp. Don't wake the lacelights." He pointed at the bugs sleeping on the windowsill. "They're looking for any sign of life out here. Don't give them that sign."

How long will you be gone? I scribbled on the page, and held it up for him to read.

"I need to find the city. It can't be far from here."

How long? I dug the quill into the parchment to emphasize my question. Fear choked me as I thought about being alone in here.

My eyes danced around the dark cabin, but refused to settle on the three bodies in the corner. The Captain said we didn't have time to bury them.

"The darkness is coming, Mommy. I cannot save you." My daughter's voice echoed in my head.

The Captain held up his pocket-watch.

"I swear I won't be gone more than four hours."

Four hours? Could I just come with you?

"That's not safe. If he finds me out there, he assumes I'm looking for you just like all his other guards. But if he finds you out there..." He trailed off, and traced the bruises circling my neck. "I can't let him find you. Not again."

May I have my necklace back before you leave?

He touched his pocket, and shook his head.

"I don't want you to lose it before we're safe. Okay?" He kissed my forehead, and disappeared into the night before I could protest. I locked the door behind him, and went over to the bodies in the corner.

Tears ran down my face as I looked down on vacant eyes. I should've closed them earlier.

The youngest of the trio, only three cycles old, took an arrow through her neck as we escaped. She died in my arms as we ran. I couldn't leave her behind. The Captain said I should have left her.

Her sister was four, and already sick when we escaped. Without a healira, her illness turned deadly. I did my best. I tried to remember what herbs would help her, but nothing worked. Both deaths were tragic, and unnecessary, but they weren't the ones that scared me, because The General didn't know these girls were dead.

The oldest child was seven when he died. I feared him the most.

He didn't escape with us.

My son, Collin, took on too many of his father's traits. The Captain insisted I leave him behind. Three days after we escaped, Collin collapsed on our porch. I let him in, and held him in my arms as he fought for one breath after another.

His father sent him as a message. He sent him to show me he knew where I was, and he didn't mind killing to get to me.

We're not safe here, Captain. I could barely scribble as I wept over my son.

"Of course we are, Baby. The General won't go near the haunted forest unless he has proof you're here. He's just guessing right now. He doesn't know for sure." The Captain's breath hissed through my hair as he tried to calm me.

Haunted?

"Legend says an uncollected Àraid soul remains inside

that forest. The city should have starved out cycles ago, but they're still there. The Àraid are dead. The only explanation is a haunting."

He thought we would be safe if we found the city, but no city would let me in without registration.

I crouched on the floor beside my son. I knew he was dead, but I couldn't accept it. It didn't feel real. It wasn't right. I brought them with me to keep them safe. Now they lay dead at my feet.

My fault.

It was always my fault.

"It's your fault, you know. Things could gone well for you if you'd played my way." The General's whip bit into my back. My son watched, eyes wide, as I swayed, but refused to fall. "What are you trying to prove? Why are you still fighting?"

I wrapped my arms around my knees, and shivered. My fingers pressed into my temples as I tried to block out his voice. My mind hid almost all my memories from me, but not him. It never forgot him.

I pulled Collin into my arms again, and rocked him. Maybe if I rocked him long enough, we would wake from this nightmare.

A knock rang out through the silence, and I froze. Dread knotted my stomach, and I strained to hear The Captain's comforting voice on the other side of the door.

But it wasn't his voice that filtered through the decaying wood.

"Open the door, Dear. I know you're in there." The General sang.

He found me. All that running. All that death. He still found me.

"Did you really think a haunted legend would keep me away from you?" He shoved his way through the fragile door, and smiled when he saw me. "There you are. You've been quite problematic, Dear. I liked your son. It's a shame you forced me to kill him."

He found me.

I would never be free. No matter how far I ran he'd always find me.

"I think maybe the Àraid ghost story isn't the one you should worry about." The General grabbed my shoulders, and my hands glowed bright blue. Pain seared through my body, and the world spun around me. Bright blue light wrenched itself from me, painfully ripping at my core, and sank into my son's still form. I threw my son's body from me as his eyes blinked open, and he gasped.

Collin stood and faced his father, waiting for a signal. His fingers changed to claws, and he turned toward me. I scrambled away from him, but the small cabin didn't allow me to escape.

"Come here, Baby. I'll protect you." The General held out his arms, and I ran to him. He won. Again. I was right where he wanted me. I hated myself for caving in so easily, but only he could stop my son. "You haven't served your sentence yet." His voice changed from kindness to anger as he drove a knife below my ribs. I collapsed, and tried to protect my unborn child from his knife. Bright light flooded the room, and I shut my eyes.

"You should have believed the ghost story, General." Hot hands pulled me into warm arms.

"Leave her alone. She's mine." The General spat through clenched teeth. I squinted against the light, but only made out a cloak of coals. Flaming hair shot sparks into the dark room.

"Living souls belong to no one." The burning man hissed at The General, and his fire lit the cabin around us. "She's not yours to own."

"She belonged to me the moment she drew breath." The General lunged at the flaming man, but he dodged the knife. Fire poured from his hands, and consumed The General. Fire wouldn't kill him, but it slowed him down. The

General's eyes met mine as his sick laugh rose over the flames.

"You will be mine. I found you once. I'll find you again."

His laughter faded as the earth opened beneath the man on fire, and consumed us both.

Christa

A few days earlier, inside the city

"**D**o you need help with the dishes?" My husband wrapped his arms around my waist, and pressed my hips against the sink.

"No, I can do it. Go get the kids ready for bed." I smiled up at him. His embrace lasted a moment longer, and then he lumbered up the stairs. Squeals of happy laughter, and playful growls, soon drifted down the stairs after him. If I focused on the laughter upstairs, and not the packed bags by the door, it almost felt like a normal night.

Four knocks sounded on the back door. Code. My mother. I dried my hands as I picked my way through makeshift toys. I begged the kids to pick up, but Willic never enforced my rules. I cracked the door, and made sure it was only my mother waiting on my doorstep, before I pulled her inside, and re-locked the door.

"What is wrong, Mother?" I frowned. "You should stay away. It is not safe."

"Someone was asking about Willic down at the mail drop." She twisted her hands and glanced through our curtained windows.

"Who? Did you recognize him?"

"It was a Rak guard." Her voice trembled as much as

her hands.

"Not The General?"

"No, but someone in town talked. The General is on his way." Her fingers danced over her necklace. "You need to leave, Christa." Tears danced in her eyes as she scurried around my kitchen, hastily packing whatever she found.

"Ms. Avens, I didn't know you were coming by unannounced tonight." Willic lumbered back down the stairs, and frowned at my mother. She froze, and stared at my husband.

"The Raks know where you are. You need to leave."

"Was The General in town?" Willic stifled a yawn.

"No, but they sent him word. He's coming."

"From Nalaise. Unless he has a dragon, he won't get here until tomorrow night. We have plenty of time and you know it. Why are you so worried?"

Mother pressed a hand to her mouth to stifle a sob.

"I'm sorry. I didn't want to tell them."

"You told them?" I gasped.

"They were very persuasive. I'm so sorry." She pulled down the neck of her dress; revealing a ring of bruises around her neck. "I only revealed Willic, though. They don't know about you, or the children. It might be safer to split up."

"That won't be necessary." Willic put an arm around me. "I can keep my family safe. Goodnight, Ms. Avens." He pushed my mother back out the door, and locked it.

"We need to cut ties with her. She's not trustworthy." He sighed and cupped my face in his hands. "Go get ready for bed. I'll be up in a few minutes." He pressed his lips against my forehead.

"Are we not going to leave?"

"We have time, Christa. No sense worrying the children. We'll leave after breakfast tomorrow." He turned to the dishes in the sink, and I went to check on the children. Jaycobe and Ginny slept in one room, and Cerynn slept *across the hall. I checked the hidden room off Jaycobe and Ginny's room.*

Unlocked. Ready for two little children to hide. Just in case.

Across the hall, Cerynn flipped through a picture book Willic drew for her. I did not tell her to stop. She loved books.

"Goodnight, Cerynn." I whispered. She waved her small fingers at me, but did not look away from her book. I left her door ajar, and hurried into my own room. Willic finished cleaning the kitchen tonight, which meant he had expectations of me.

I unbuttoned my dress, and exposed my chest to the mirror. My fingers traced my stretch marks. Willic hated my marks. My body changed a lot after three kids, but I had time to get better. I was only sixteen. My marks would fade.

"What are you doing?" Willic's words thudded into my mind. I quickly covered myself, and faced my husband. He glared at my exposed marks.

"I was just check-"

"Don't undress with the lights on." He growled. "I don't want to see that."

"I am sorry." I mumbled as he blew out the candles and pushed me onto the bed. His lips found mine in the dark, and I wrapped my arms around him. He liked it when I did that.

"Willic," I whispered. "The kids are right next to us. They will hear us."

"Then you better be quiet." He chuckled and shoved his boxers into my mouth. I gagged on the fabric, and whimpered. I wondered if this hurt him as much as it hurt me.

Probably not.

"Stop squirming." He whispered. Tears pricked my eyes. I hoped he did not see them.

Why did people think this was fun?

"Do it now, Baby."

Tears fell from my eyes as I obeyed. I was a good wife. I was an obedient wife.

"Willic Đèмаçrèχ. Open the door."

We froze at the voice downstairs. Willic cursed under his breath.

"How did he get here so fast?" When he noticed the fear in my eyes he tried to smile. "Don't worry, Babe. We're prepared for this. Do what we practiced."

I nodded and hastily threw my dress back on and tiptoed into Cerynn's room. My arms shook as I scooped her up, and crossed the hall to wake her siblings. She clung to me as I grabbed Ginny and Jaycobe from their beds, and shoved them into the hidden room. It was only big enough for two, so I kept Cerynn in my arms.

"Stay quiet. No matter what you hear." I set Cerynn in the hall closet, and closed that door, too. We should have made her a hiding place. I hoped The General would not look here.

Willic ran back up the stairs and pushed me into our room, slamming the door behind us. Briefly, he pulled me into his arms.

"I love you. Don't ever forget that, okay?" He let go and pressed his ear to the door. Heavy footsteps scuffled in the hall. Three sets of feet; maybe four.

"I know you're here. Come out." The General crashed into Jaycobe and Ginny's room, and I heard him knock their beds over. But he did not find them. Jaycobe and Ginny were safe. Then he went over to Cerynn's room and ransacked that, too.

Silence.

Frustrated breathing.

The closet door opened.

"Oh. Hello, Dear. What's your name?"

My hand flew to my mouth.

He found her.

He had my daughter.

He mumbled something to her, but Willic pushed me away from the door before I heard what he said. The door splintered, and black tendrils ripped through my husband. He stumbled back and clutched his chest. Blood stained his shirt, and he stared at the stains, confused. His hands reached out to me as he collapsed to the ground. I stumbled as I tried to catch him. Blood poured from his mouth as he tried to speak.

"If you survive... hide. Your calling isn't worth this." He gasped. I pressed my hands against his wounds, and nodded absently. The word danced on my tongue, but he put a hand up to stop me. "If you heal me, he'll know you're Àraid. Right now he thinks it's just me."

"What will I do without you?"

"You'll do fine. I believe in you."

The General broke the door down, but I did not look away from my husband.

"Show her the rod. We need no witnesses."

I glanced up at his order, and froze. He held Cerynn in his arms; a machete braced against her body. A guard held my mother in handcuffs. Tears danced in her eyes and blood stained her dress.

She told them where I was, why bother arresting her?

One guard stepped over the splintered door, and pulled out two long metal rods. Another guard pinned me down as he drove the rods into my ears. I screamed as he scraped the rods across my eardrums, and then my screams vanished. There was no sound anymore. The General whispered something to my daughter, and black veins snaked across her face.

What was he doing to her?

Her legs shook as she crossed over to us. I held Willic in my arms, and frowned at my daughter. Willic still gasped for air, but he was getting weaker.

Cerynn raised her hands towards me. Her lips moved in

an incantation I could not hear. Willic sat up between us, and pushed me out of the way as more tendrils sprouted from from my daughter's fingers. They wrapped around his heart, ripping it from his chest. He slumped against me, and the weight of his body pinned me to the wall.

I watched over his shoulder as Cerynn turned towards my mother. The tendrils drove into my mother's stomach and she, too, collapsed. The General released my daughter from his spell, and she fell to the ground, sobbing. I shoved Willic away, and crawled to her. Her arms wrapped around me, and I tried to soothe her. The General raised his sword, and I closed my eyes.

The blade bit into my shoulder, and dragged down towards my hip. It cut through my hand, and my daughter, and I shuddered as my mind painted pictures of her injuries. I swayed, and fell to the ground, feigning death. His sword prodded my wounds, and I fought not to move.

And then the sword was gone. I cracked my eyes open just enough to see The General retreating down the hall. His guards followed him.

I was alone.

I sat up, and looked down at Cerynn. The sword bit deep into my chest, and I lost two fingers, but I got off easy. His sword cut through her body. Her arm and leg lay on the ground next to me. Reluctantly, I looked down on my daughter.

She was crying.

She was alive!

Hastily, I wrapped my hands over her injuries, and whispered the very word Willic begged me not to say just moments ago.

"Læxlïeẓè."

Her cuts fused closed. She smiled as her pain eased, and then turned tearful eyes back at her father. She killed him, and now she feared him. She feared the body no longer inhabited. I pressed my hand to her head, and removed her

memories of his death. She did not need that guilt. I
stumbled to my feet with her in my arms, and, as I looked
out the window, my heart sank.
A dragon stood in my yard, mouth open, ready to bathe
my house in dragon fire.

I jolted awake, gasping for air, and looked around. Stone
walls. Piles of warm quilts. The glow of torches right
outside my window.

I was safe.

Why was I still haunted?

I reached under my pillow, and traced the cool metal of
one of my knives. The urge to pull it out and press it against
my arm nearly overwhelmed me.

I would not.

Not with my husband right beside me.

Peter's arms wrapped around me as a shiver coursed
down my spine.

"What's wrong?" He mumbled in his sleep. One of his
hands traced the scar down my throat, and his other hand
brushed the hair out of my face.

"It happened so fast. I did not know what to do. I did not
have time to think." I burrowed my head into his neck, and
allowed his arms to tighten around me. He mumbled into
my hair, but I could not hear him without my plate on. I
invented my plate four cycles ago, and Peter adjusted to it
almost too much, but I was still deaf when I turned it off.
My fingers kneaded the smooth scar behind my ear.

"Stop blaming yourself." Peter slid my plate over the
scar, and whispered to me in the dark. With my plate on, I
heard horses, and laughter. The house must have shuffled
again. Last night we were in a secluded wing away from the
sounds of the city, but the noise outside told me we were
close to Mainstreet.

Peter tapped the jar of lacelights next to the bed, and a
soft glow filled the room as the bugs woke up. They buzzed

around their jar, irritated that we woke them, and Peter tapped the jar harder. More glowing liquid dripped from their feet, and soon bathed the whole room in dim light. Peter climbed out of bed, grabbed his cane, and limped out the door.

I pulled out my knife, and stared at the blade. I loved the way it glinted in the light. So tempting. I pressed the tip into my arm.

Barely.

Not enough.

The door creaked opened, and I shoved the knife back under my pillow. Peter leaned against the door-frame; a goofy grin plastered to his face.

"What are you doing?" I covered a smile.

"I'm awake. So are you. I thought I could take your mind off your nightmares." His cane thumped on the floor. Sparks danced across the stone as he crossed back to the bed, and climbed under the covers. He kissed me, and pulled me into his arms. I slept in one of his old shirts, and did not feel very sexy, but the light in his eyes told me he did not care. I wrapped my arms around him, and winced as sore muscles protested the movement. Peter's fingers grazed the tiny stitches right below my belly button, and his eyes changed. He propped himself above me, and forced me to look at him.

"Do you feel ready? I won't do anything if you're not ready."

I touched the stitches.

"Clear her mouth, Peter!" I screamed. The Healer was busy stitching me up, and paid no attention to the tiny baby he just delivered. "Clear her mouth!"

Peter held her in his arms, but his face betrayed his horror. He slowly looked back at me.

"I don't need to, Dear."

Paperwork. Condolences. Repacking unused baby things. It happened again.

I lost another one.

I blinked and pulled myself away from the memory.

"I am okay, Peter. I can handle it."

He smiled cautiously as he traced his lips across my scar and down my side. With him, I enjoyed it. I never enjoyed myself with Willic.

His hands worked up under my shirt, and I tried not to cringe. I was so sore. It was too soon. His head disappeared under the sheets, and I hid a giggle as his stubble tickled my thigh. I groped around under the sheets, and wove my fingers through his hair.

His hands slid up my stomach, and his fingers worked the buttons on my shirt, but he did not take it off, just splayed it open, and sat back to look at me. He smiled as he studied me. Goosebumps pricked my exposed skin.

Embarrassed, I crossed my arms over myself, but Peter eased my arms back down and blatantly studied my body. The sheets once again covered me as Peter leaned down to trail kisses across my chest. I wrapped my legs around him, and gritted my teeth. I tried to smile, and ride out the pain, but he saw my grimace and stopped.

"You're not okay. Did I hurt you?" His hands ran over me, and then he threw back the covers and studied my stitches. "One ripped."

Only a tiny bead of blood appeared on the gash. I healed fast, generally. But Peter still worried. I brushed it off, and tried to pull him back into the moment, but it was lost. After some fuss over my broken stitch, he simply wrapped me in his arms, and drifted back to sleep. His happiness was waning.

I was losing him.

The suns shone through my bedroom window. Peter placed a protective invisible shield over the city many cycles ago, when he first moved here. His protection allowed our hidden Àraid family to walk outside without fear of the Raks burning sun. Somehow his shield enhanced the blue of the sky.

I stared out the window from my perch in the windowsill. My ear plate sat next to my empty coffee mug, and a nearly finished book sat on my lap, but, with the sunshine, I could not focus on the pages.

My house looked down on the city. I loved my perch. From here, I could see straight onto Mainstreet. I could watch people not plagued by nightmares and visions.

I could imagine what that life would be like.

People scuttled around the city, preparing to head out to one of our eight coal mines. A sea of black clothes, with our city's identifying color, purple, tied around their arms. I noticed some blue and green bands roaming around the supply stores. The storm yesterday must have trapped them away from their cities.

I got up and tip-toed over to the dresser. Peter was down in the washrooms, so I still had time.

I opened a drawer and counted the shirts.

Six.

All still there.

I opened the next drawer.

Eight more neatly folded shirts greeted me.

Just the right number.

The next drawer was missing two pairs of pants, though, and I worked myself into a panic before I remembered to count the pair Peter wore yesterday, and the pair he planned to wear today.

I checked the closet, too. Both of our trunks sat, untouched, in the very back, behind unwanted shoes, and stacks of books.

I could breath again.

Index, middle, ring, pinkie.

Breath. Breath.

Everything was where it should be.

Peter gave me those trunks for our fifth anniversary.

"One day I will take you to see the regions. We can visit all the trade sites."

He believed one day it would be safe to leave the city. I returned to the window and stared out into my forest. I hated this region. It was dry, and plain. Any "mountains" here were just tiny hills. I could not stand the emptiness. I planted the forest when I moved here, and breathed life into my trees. They grew around the city overnight, but the humans were too focused on their boring lives to notice my trees.

Life was boring here, but it was safe.

The Raks monitored the mines, and made sure everyone met their quota, but they never entered my city.

Not yet.

I heard recently that the Raks considered my forest haunted, and feared it.

That pleased me.

If this city stayed Rak-free, maybe Peter and I could live here forever. Our secrets, and powers, could die out without The General ever finding out who I was.

A pillow hit me, and I whirled towards Peter, frowning. His mismatched blue and green eyes sparkled as I smoothed my hair back into place. He wiggled his eyebrows at me, and stuck out his tongue. I suppressed a laugh, and tried to look sternly at my husband.

"Very mature." I bit back a smile. He grabbed a sword off the wall, and slashed the air as he hobbled towards me.

"You want meture, medem?" He smiled as he mocked my accent.

"I think you forget, old man, that you, too, have an accent."

"Yes, but I have a regional accent. It's not hard for people to place mine. They know where I come from. Your accent doesn't match the regions, Dear. Yours stands out like a forest in a desert." He pointed to my trees outside the window. He worried the trees would attract attention from The General, but I did not believe The General paid enough attention to this one tiny coal city.

Peter still pointed the sword at me as he drew near, and the metal blade poked into my shoulder. I grabbed the edge, and pushed it away from me as I pulled Peter towards me. His arms circled me, and he trapped my arms at my side. His hand raked through my crazy blonde curls, but as he pulled his fingers through them, the curls faded to black and straightened out. I tried to stay away from my natural auburn hair. The General knew me by that color. Though he believed he killed me, I did not want to risk him recognizing me. I usually tried to stay blonde, but with influx of emotion came influx of powers. Peter rubbed my now black hair between his fingers, and clicked his tongue.

"You're going to kill us all." He said it as a joke, and wanted me to laugh, so I did, but a knot of dread filled my stomach. He spun me around in a pirouette.

"That willworth is playing our song. Do you see him in that tree?" He pointed out the window. A small black bird danced on a branch. I could not hear him. Not without my plate, which still sat beside my coffee cup. I did not need to hear the song. Willworths copied what they heard. If Peter hummed the song the bird would sing it.

I smiled up at him, and we continued our dance. Books piled on any free surface in my room, and we picked our way through some piles on the floor. We fell onto the bed in a heap of giggles as our legs tangled together.

He could hear the song.

I could not.

Steps were missed and feet got stepped on.

We rolled on the bed, and I clutched my sides as we tried to smother our laughter in the pillows. I loved his face when he laughed. I spent hours studying his face so I would not forget it. His eyes softened and everything seemed normal.

The promises the darkness whispered were only nightmares.

Monsters that plagued me when Peter was not there.

Peter pulled off my shirt, and bent to kiss my stomach. He inched lower, trailing his lips down my waist, savoring the goosebumps he coaxed. His fingers unlaced the skirt I just put on, and he pulled it down before I could stop him. His lips stopped, and his smile froze on his face as he stared at my hip. Pain filled his eyes as he touched the cuts he found there.

Just five cuts.

I stopped myself after five.

Five made the pain livable.

When Peter looked up at me his eyes were filled with tears.

"I thought you were past this."

"I was. But sometimes I need to. Only sometimes." I could not look at him. I knew it upset him. He would say it hurt him, too. "I went eleven cycles without cutting, Peter. That should count for something."

Eleven cycles ago I had Jess. Jess kept me happy.

"It does count. I just assumed after eleven cycles you would be done. This wouldn't be an issue anymore."

"I can only handle so much. I needed an outlet." Eleven cycles ago I had Jess. And in the last eleven cycles I suffered countless miscarriages after Jess. One right after another, stacking up more and more pain.

"Let's stop trying for children." Tears shimmered in his eyes as he spoke, and his voice choked off.

"What about your dreams of a big family?"

He wanted double-digit children bursting a happy house at the seams. In eleven cycles I only managed to give him two children. I hated watching him give up.

"We can keep trying, Peter. Maybe we will get lucky." My latest miscarriage caused the cuts on my hips, but I felt better now.

"I can't keep watching you go through that. I can't keep watching you pretend it doesn't hurt you every time we lose one."

"It does not hurt." I lied. "Those babies never had a chance to become part of my life. Why should their loss affect me?"

Why did their loss affect me?

Why did I miss someone I never knew?

"I do not want to stop trying, Peter."

"We'll adopt, Christa. Big family, less loss. We adopted Quartnee."

"And you love her, but you never look at her the way you look at Jess, or Aurora." I whispered.

Just pretend you do not see my cuts. Pretend I am okay.

He stayed quiet while he studied the cuts. As I watched his grief, so plainly portrayed across his face, I wished he could be enough. But I let him down, like I let everyone down. I tried to distance myself from him. I tried to give him room to leave, to be happy. But when he left my side the nightmares taunted me, and the Raks mocked me. They were getting closer. They were planning something.

"Another child went missing a few days ago. A Locki." He said to the window, changing the subject. My heart sank. So many people disappearing.

Screams and children crying.

"Don't kill him, please! Let me keep this one."

"If you keep him alive on what we feed you, he can stay."

A whimper and a sniff, and a horrible payment for such a small favor.

"Christa."

I blinked the vision away.

"What are we going to do? We can't live a quiet life anymore."

"I cannot rise against him again." Peter crossed his arms, but I continued. "My husband and mother were slaughtered because we tried to go to war before. Cerynn was cut in half! Willic asked me to stay hidden. He said it was not worth it."

We had the same discussion several times a season. It always ended the same.

We will not go to war.

We are safe here.

"What are you going to do about the Locki child?" He went back to his original topic.

"What can we do? Iceloch is not our region."

"The Raks taking kids from Iceloch says something, Christa. They never cross into that region."

"Send them eight shipments of coal as a condolence, and hope they do not shut off trade."

Iceloch threatened to pull out before, but they controlled drinkable water. Cutting off trade would condemn the other ten regions to Dusting.

"Christa, this city is down to one meal a day, and we have no food shipments scheduled. How can we ask our people to work harder when they're barely getting by on the rations they have?"

"I will take care of it, Peter."

The breakfast bell rang as we spoke, but nobody moved towards the Ovens. Peter was right. Our food was running out.

"I will send some extra cornmeal down with our breakfast shipment. Cornmeal muffins should be a nice treat in the mines this afternoon, right?" I expected Peter to smile at my solution, but he winced as he looked up at me.

"I checked our rations before I came to bed last night. The barrels are empty. We have no food."

"None at all?"

"None."

Everyone came to me when they ran out of food. I always gave them some. I never considered eventually I would run out, too.

"Do we have any money? Would we be able to send

someone to Nalaise to buy food?"

"I have a handful of celets. Not enough for a loaf of bread."

A small knock interrupted us and I glanced toward the door. Jess eased the door open and peeked into the room.

"Mom, that was the breakfast bell. Do you want me to send down some food?"

Peter and I glanced at each other, and Peter sighed.

"How about, today, we go without breakfast? How would that make you feel?"

Jess's face fell, but then he laughed.

"That would be ridiculous. We didn't have lunch, or dinner yesterday. I'm pretty hungry now. This isn't a fun game."

"But I challenged you to skip five meals. If you eat now you forfeit the reward."

"I'm hungry. I'd rather eat."

I held my hand up and pulled Jess's attention back to me.

"I'll go check our rations and send something down to the Ovens soon. Go play." I turned back to Peter as my son scampered out the door. "You challenged our son not to eat?"

"Would you rather I tell him he can't eat because you gave our food away?"

"These people rely on me, Peter! What am I supposed to do?" I slid off the bed, and shrugged into a black blouse. I tied a purple band around my arm and headed for the door.

"Where are you going?" Peter still lay on the bed.

"I know you already checked our rations, but I need to see for myself."

He lunged from the bed as I raced down the hall. He knew my plans, but he could not run on his bad leg, so I beat him to the storeroom easily. I yanked the lid off the barrel, and stared down into the depths of what once was cornmeal. My hands hovered over the empty barrel, and I focused on the word I once knew well.

"Vÿððʒïx̣."

Slowly, the barrel refilled with fresh cornmeal. And then overflowed onto the ground, and kept spilling over. I squealed, and frantically searched for a word to stop the flow.

"Pæx̣a." Peter whispered as he entered the room. I could not hold back a giggle as I tried to scoop the overflow into other empty barrels.

"Sorry. I remembered how to start, but forgot how to stop."

Peter did not laugh.

"We're not supposed to use our powers. We're supposed to stay hidden."

"My job is to protect my people. I will not let them starve."

"Then why don't you summon a feast, and throw a party?" His anger startled me.

"Peter, I like helping in secret." I shrugged and scooped up a handful of cornmeal.

"Someday, that will backfire. Either stay out of their lives, or let them know just how much you do for them."

"Why?"

"Because loyalty goes to the highest bidder. The humans will think nothing of turning you over to save their skin."

"There is not one adult in this city that I have not helped in the healira. Almost all of them have some sort of prosthetic that I made them." I wiggled my two prosthetic fingers in Peter's face to make my point. "That must count for something."

"Just because you've reassembled these people, doesn't mean they're loyal to you. Stop risking so much to help them." He shook his head, and stepped out of the storeroom before I could form a response.

Inhibited

Cerynn

"Eight shipments." I confirmed as I handed a cornmeal muffin to the miner.

"We don't have enough coal for eight shipments. Where am I supposed to come up with eight shipments?" He twisted his black hat in his hands.

"I don't know anything about mining. I'm just telling you what my mother ordered."

"The Locki girl isn't even part of our region. Why must we drain our resources for another region?" Frustration weighed his shoulders down. "Havenden didn't send me fish when my boys went missing; Silverglass didn't send me jewels."

"Iceloch controls water. We can't afford to lose them."

He was the third miner today demanding I explain the orders. Everyone was missing someone. Everyone felt slighted.

"Why can't a different region send them extra trade?" The miner protested. "Have Wellwald send them meat. Everyone needs meat."

"If they don't have coal, they can't cook meat." I rolled my eyes. "Apart from water, which they have an abundance of, their highest need is coal."

"And tell me, *Princess*, how does eight shipments of coal ease the pain of a lost child?" All the miners called me princess. It wasn't a compliment. They said I was spoiled, and naive, because Mother ran the City of Purple Coal. Her children didn't have to work in the mines. We were the only ones without callouses on our hands.

"I don't know how, or if, it will help. Just make sure you send out eight shipments tonight."

He turned reluctantly, and disappeared into the depths of the mine.

"Wow. You're a tough sell. I'm screwed." A young man spoke behind me and I jumped. I spun towards his voice and studied him. Unlike our Coaltree black, the young man wore white, with a light blue cloak wrapped around his shoulders.

"Sorry. Didn't mean to scare you." His deep brown eyes twinkled under a white headband.

"Who are you? You're not from Coaltree."

"But I have registration, see?" He held out his purple band. "I'm from Icecrest. We're on our way to Silverglass but the Raks traded my life for my horse. My wife and I are stuck here until we can get another. They said I should talk to you."

"Well, actually my mother normally does that, but she's down with a headache today. I guess I could help." I shrugged. "Why are you going to Silverglass? That's very far from Icecrest."

"It's the last free region. My wife can bare our child without fear of it being recruited." He pointed at a young woman, also in white with a light blue cloak, sitting a few yards off. "The General's not up there, but he has his hands in all the other regions."

I glanced at the Raks guarding the mine, but they didn't react to his blasphemy.

"If The General recruits your child you should be honored. He only raises the best for his army." I frowned.

"The General just wants to limit and control us. I'm sick

of it."

"Are you crazy?" I lunged forward and covered his mouth. "How dare you question The General?"

"People are disappearing left and right. He's greedy. He's nervous. And something set him off. He's getting worse."

"He's the same as always."

"Okay, fine. Don't believe me. You will soon." He shrugged, and smiled. "Now how about that horse? I would like to leave before the gates close for the night."

I squinted into the dark horse barn, searching for Josh. The herder, Josh, lost his hearing after a swift kick to the head from a wild stallion we brought in a few cycles back. He kept the barn dark now so if anyone visited they'd have to light a lamp. Since he couldn't hear if someone tried to steal the horses, he set traps throughout the barn. With lamplight they were visible, but if anyone snuck around without light they'd be caught in his traps. The General ordered him to leave anyone caught in the traps. He said we should let them starve.

On the rare occasions when The General passed through our town he always stopped by to see who fell into the traps. His laughter would ring out through the barn as he prodded the dying thieves.

Out of habit, I laughed at one of the thieves while their body twitched in the last phases of death. The young man following me looked on in horror, but I assured him the thieves didn't deserve our sympathy.

I lit a lamp, and ducked into the barn. Seventeen horse stalls lined the walls, and terrariums lined the back of the barn. Hundreds of snakes twisted and coiled in their cages, and a few slithered through a small hatch in the wall. Unopened letters wrapped around the new snakes, and they dropped into a holding cage. Quite a few snakes piled in the holding cage with their letters wrapped around them, unread. Our mailer didn't show up this morning, and Josh hadn't had a chance to deliver the mail. Josh turned away from his favorite Paint when he noticed the light.

'Hello, Cerynn.' He signed. Unlike my mother, Josh chose not to wear an ear-plate; choosing instead to read lips and sign.

"This young man needs a horse that will make it to Silverglass." I faced him as I spoke so he could understand. The man's wife smiled, and placed a hand on her stomach.

"This is our first child." Excitement danced in her eyes, but behind that simmered poorly concealed fear. The General loved snatching babies to train for his army. He found it easier to raise them among Raks, than to try to train them as adults. The man wrapped her in his arms, and they both laughed nervously.

"We can't lose her." The man chuckled. "Or him. I don't know."

They both turned pleading eyes at Josh. He sighed and pointed to a pack horse. The young man examined it quietly.

"How much?" He asked.

Josh signed me the amount, and I translated.

"Four deshin."

The man whistled.

"That's too much. Do you have anything cheaper?"

Josh pointed to a small pony in the last stall. The man nodded, and patted the pony.

"How much is this one?"

"One deshin."

He winced, and watched his wife ease herself into a chair.

"That's still a lot. Do you have anything for six celets?"

Josh and I snickered.

"Six celets won't even buy you a grape. How much are horses in Icecrest?" I cocked my head, and tried to hide my amusement. His face fell, and his wife twisted her skirt nervously.

"We don't have horses in Icecrest. They all die." He pulled out six tiny silver celets and a cube of ice from his pocket. "Can you help me out here? This is all I have."

"What are we going to do with an ice cube, and not even enough money for a grape?"

The man smiled, and held out the ice cube.

"You'll help me out.

I can tell. You've always wanted to get your hands on some Crest ice. It won't melt for another half season. We don't trade much with Coaltree, so you've never seen ice."

I sighed, and grabbed the ice. He was right. I'd only ever heard of ice, and once saw a brick passing through. I'd never touched it. I was fascinated. It was so cold. Colder than the water we got from Iceloch.

"Fine. Take the pony." I pointed absently at the horse, and watched the ice in my hand.

"Thank you!" He exclaimed. He led the horse to his wife, and helped her on. Josh poked the ice in my hand, and his eyes widened, too.

"Have fun, you two. Do you want my celets?" The man asked as he led the horse outside. I shook my head. The ice was worth the pony. He tilted his head in thanks.

"Wait." I ran after him. "What's your name?"

"Ryker. Ryker Knack. But don't bother remembering me. If we meet again, I won't wear this face." He winked, and spurred his horse on, jogging beside as he and his wife made their break for freedom.

Inhibited

Jaycobe

"Tap it." Roland let out a stream of cigarette smoke and pointed at the pretty girl walking by. Almost everyone worked in the mines today, so Mainstreet wasn't very busy. We managed to find enough entertainment from the few wandering between their shops. Roland ran the trade route, which only went out six times a season, so our free time was abundant. Day after day. Always the same. Drinking and smoking.

As the oldest, Mother never looked at me twice. Her other children took up so much of her time. Like Mother, Ginny's talents lay in her mind. She invented crazy things that helped the city. I couldn't do that. My mind didn't work that way. Cerynn had her prosthetic arm and leg. I couldn't hold a candle to that. Jess and Aurora were miracles, and both Mother and Peter pampered them. And Quartnee was adopted. Obviously, she needed more love to prove she belonged. They forgot about me most days. I could probably kill this whole town and Mother would still focus on her other children more than she would be with me.

We sneered as another girl with a pimply face and ill-fitting clothes nervously stepped over us to get into the store.

"Paper-bag it." Roland sat forward and held out his hand for a fist-bump.

"Aw, man. What is "paper-bagging?""

"Tapping, but with a bag over her face so I don't have to look at it." He laughed his sick laugh. "I don't want to get that on me."

I shook my head in disapproval.

"It's not contagious, Roland. Girls are more than just pretty faces you know."

"Oh yeah?" Another puff. "Then why do I always have a pretty one, and you always have your baby sister? Pretty girls are status, Cobe. Power. Prestige. Headaches and nagging." He shook his head. "But totally worth it if you know what I mean." A sneer and a laugh. Typical Roland. "Wake up, man! You gotta live now, 'cuz you won't get another shot at today. Trade is slowing down. Prices are going up. People are disappearing left and right. They're not going to the prisons."

"How do you know?"

"With all the reports the prisons should be full, but they're not. I just did a coal run up there. The prisons are nearly empty. So where are all the missing people? They're Inhibited is what I say."

"That's a myth, Roland." I rolled my eyes. Mother should never have told him her Inhibited theory.

"It makes sense, Man. The General wouldn't get where he is today without controlling people. The Raks are just as powerful as the Àraid once were. More so. They killed the Àraid. Surely they're strong enough, and sneaky enough, to figure out how to possess someone." He put out his cigarette and lit another one. "We ain't safe, and we ain't gonna make it out alive. You can't die a virgin." The alcohol loosened his lips, and he took another long pull on his cigarette. "It ain't natural."

I rolled my eyes.

"Hey, check it out." Roland leaned forward and pointed

to his ear. A small earring nestled into his swollen ear lobe. "I'm an Àraid. I got the marks." He smirked. He thought he was so smart.

I leaned forward and pulled on the stud. The back of the earring popped off and the two pieces fell from his ear.

"Dude! Why did you do that?" He rubbed his bleeding ear.

"Àraid earrings are a part of them." I yanked on my own, but they didn't budge. "They never come off."

That information was hidden deep in Àraid folklore. No one knew that anymore. I only accidentally discovered it, and figured out then who I was. I tried to cut them off once, and that night a figure appeared in my room. I pretended to be asleep while he clicked his tongue in disgust, and fused more WhiteStars into my ears.

"The earrings don't come off, and every Àraid knows it. We can tell when you humans are faking."

Roland frowned.

"That ain't right."

"The human tradition of piercing actually began to help the Àraid blend in when they first went into hiding. But now it's more a fashion statement."

"Yeah yeah, Professor." He rolled his eyes. "Have you told your mom you figured it out yet?"

"No. I want it to be a surprise." I wanted my powers to be strong, so I could give my mother something to be proud of. Or I wanted to be strong enough to take over and destroy the Raks, since Mom refused to defend our heritage from the man desperate to snuff it out. I only told Roland about my powers because I wanted help learning how to use them.

"Com'on." He staggered to his feet. "I want to blow something up."

Boom!

The tree stump blew to pieces. Not surprising with all the explosives Roland shoved under it.

"Beat that!" He yelled. I rolled my eyes and snapped my fingers.

Three trees, all in a row, exploded and we ducked shards of wood flying past our heads. That ability I'd managed to master.

Roland laughed, and slumped on the debris. He took another long swig from his flask. It should be almost empty by now. The alcohol abuse already aged his pock-marked face, but even still he wasn't a bad looking guy. With him by my side, no girl would ever look at me twice.

"Come to my party tonight. Stay the night. Have a little drink. Find a pretty girl. Make magic." Roland gazed out of blurry eyes. "You're good at magic. It's like... your thing." He held both hands in front of him in fists, and then made an explosion motion, stopping to stare at this ability he just discovered.

"Dude... Did you know fingers can do that?" He repeated the motion, flexing and extending, over and over, awed.

"Come to my party tonight, bro."

I nodded noncommittally.

"I have to go. I have Aurora this afternoon. See ya later."

I took off into the woods as Roland muttered behind me.

"Man, you is always taking care of that baby sister." His gaze never left his still moving fingers.

"I don't know where she is, Sir. She isn't here."

"She came this way. I saw her."

"Sir, you put me in charge of these borders, and I promise you, she has not crossed them."

"If she finds that gateway without me you'll be the first I feed to the monster she creates."

Inhibited

Cerynn

"**M**other?" I knocked on the morgue door. I wanted to discuss the Icecrest boy, but she hadn't come out all day.

"Now is not a good time."

"It's never a good time. Can I come in? I don't like talking through doors."

Her sigh made its way through the door.

"Fine. Come in."

I pushed the door open, and stopped. Two women, and a man, wept over a body on Mother's examining table. One woman threw herself over the mangled body, weeping uncontrollably. Mother stood in the corner, arms crossed, eyes locked on the woman. Her lips moved as she silently counted the ticks from the clock, and then she sighed.

"It has been ten minutes, Ma'am. That is what we agreed."

"Just a little more time! Please." The woman clung tighter to the body, covering herself with blood.

"I know. It is so hard to let go." Mother crooned and

stepped over to the woman. As my mother hugged the woman gently my mouth dropped open in shock.

My mother? Touch someone?

But then I saw the gloves pulled up past my mother's elbows, and nodded. It didn't count as touch with gloves on. The woman relaxed into my mother's embrace, but didn't release the body. My mother didn't try to untangle the woman's arms from the gory mess, she just pressed her fingers into the woman's temple. I noticed she'd slit a finger on her gloves so she could poke her finger through and make skin to skin contact.

Mother's grey eyes shut tight, and the distraught woman stilled. Her eyes glazed over, and she blinked. Her arms relaxed and the body fell back onto the table.

Mother turned her towards the door, and pushed her out into the hall, memories erased. Josh told me about some people called Seers who could remove memories, but had no idea my mother was one.

The two other people hurried from the room, ready to help their friend home.

"Remember. You cannot tell anyone what you saw." Mother grabbed one and held them back. "We agreed to make her forget this tragedy, and *never* speak of it again."

"Of course, Ma'am. Thank you." Nervousness eked into the person's voice, and they ran from the room as soon as my mother released them.

Mother shut the door behind them, and returned to her table, ignoring me.

"I didn't know you could do that." I broke the silence.

"It was nothing." She waved a hand. "And it does not leave this room, understand?" Her condescending tone made me bristle.

She thought I'd let something like this slip?

No way. The General would arrest her for practicing powers instead of medicine. Only his closest most broken slaves were allowed to do that.

"Josh told me Seers carry Àraid blood." I sank into a chair across from her. "Which of your parents is Àraid?"

"Does it matter, Cerynn?" She sighed. "They are both dead now. The Àraid are dead now. Do not dwell on the past." She bent over the man. Her nose nearly touched his remains as she examined him. She'd tried to tie her hair up out of the way, but it sprang from its clips and fell in crazy curls around her face.

"What happened to him?" I switched subjects. Josh said Seers were rare, and not necessarily passed directly from a parent. She could have gotten her powers from a great-great-great-grandparent for all I knew. And her powers weren't strong. She could only view and adjust memories already there. A parlor trick compared to what the Àraid could do back in the day. I didn't blame my mom for wanting to keep that side hidden.

"He tripped and fell into a geyser. He boiled in there for days before it spouted and expelled him."

"But geysers are in Wellwald not Coal-" I froze. "They came all the way from *Wellwald?* How did they know to come to you?"

Her instruments clattered onto the table and she glanced my way.

"No. He got caught in a cave-in in the mines." Her words spewed past her lips rapidly. "It is my fault for pushing them so hard. I just did not want to lose Iceloch."

I'd never seen her so anxious, or form such a poor lie. I almost confronted her about it, but thought better of it. She wouldn't lie without good reason, no matter how terribly she concealed it.

"Iceloch wouldn't pull out."

"They might. They have before, and only the Àraid could talk them into coming back. I worry that if they pull out again, no one will be able to talk them back in."

"Then we should call the Àraid back."

"From the dead?" She frowned.

"Some of their powers stuck around. You just proved that."

Her eyes widened, and walls flew up.

"How?"

"You're a Seer."

She seemed to sag with relief.

"Oh. Right. But a Seer's powers are not strong. They are not impressive." She waved me away. As I stood a coldness in my pocket reminded me why I came.

"Look! I have ice." I pulled the cube from my pocket, and held it out to my mother. She barely looked at it.

"Where did you find ice?"

"A Crest came to buy a horse. He wanted to get his wife to the free region before she had her baby."

"You traded a horse for a piece of ice? I think the Crest got the better end of that deal." She looked up, and studied the cube. "He ripped you off. That ice only has about half a season left before it melts."

I frowned, and put the ice back in my pocket.

"What did you want?" Mother never looked up from her tools.

"He said The General is getting greedy. He said that we need to start preparing."

"We'll be fine."

"But he's not the only one that's said that. The General doesn't just stay in Nalaise anymore. Something happened. Have you heard anything?"

A small smile played around her eyes, but didn't make it to her mouth.

"You always try to take on more than you need. Do I run this city? Or do you?"

"Sometimes it feels like I do." I grumbled. "Your headaches are getting worse. I cover when you sleep all day."

She hit me with a stern glare.

"I had no idea you resented covering for me on bad

days." She whispered, hurt.

"I... I don't resent it." I blushed. "I'm just saying I wish you didn't brush off my input so quickly. What if the rumors are true?"

"It is my job to care for this city. It is my job to worry. I try not to look at what happens outside the city. Peter used to be a soldier. If it comes to war, He will know what to do. That is all you need to know." Her voice never rose in pitch. Her lips barely parted over teeth that only unclenched when she spoke. She never allowed her mouth to open wide enough for a knife to slip passed her teeth. She was convinced that someone was going to kill her that way, and she was determined not to give anyone a chance. When she spoke, her voice hissed out and wrapped around whoever she talked to, and yet she always kept her voice just above a whisper.

"Mom, Peter can't even walk without a cane. How much help could he possibly be?"

Her eyes flashed.

"Peter can prepare the city. Do not doubt him."

"And just *what* are you preparing for, Mother?"

"Your Crest friend is right. Something has happened. I do not know what, but something changed."

"Will you go to war against The General?"

"I have not decided yet."

"Let me decide for you." I slammed my hand into the table. "Look at the Wellwald Region. Look at Lightmont. Look at Icecrest. They all rose against him. The General's dragons devastated them. Three regions tried to fight, and three regions were nearly wiped out. If they couldn't do it united, why would you think this small city could alone? Those regions are just markings on a map now, Mother."

She let out a frustrated sigh and collapsed into her chair.

"I cannot figure out what he looked like."

"Did you even hear what I said?"

"Tales told around campfires. All well known. Do not

focus on those who lost. Find a way to win." She made eye-contact with me for two seconds; the longest eye-contact I'd had with her in a long time. "Tell me, Cerynn, what did he look like?"

I looked at the man on the table, confused.

"I am trying to restore his features, but I cannot figure out what he looked like."

His face was distorted, melted, and his haunted expression fascinated me.

What pain consumed him before death claimed him? Had he screamed?

I was about to offer some suggestions, but she wasn't paying attention to me anymore.

Mother turned back, again, to her work, and dismissed me with a small wave.

Christa

"**P**eter!" I moaned as I turned towards the hand pushing my shoulder. The sheets slipped down over the new outfit I modeled for him last night. A patient paid me with that because they had no money. Peter said it was a worthwhile trade.

More pushing on my shoulder.

The bed bounced.

"Let me sleep!" I cracked my eyes to glare at him, and found myself staring into Jess's eyes. I jolted awake and clutched the sheets to my chest. "Have you never heard of knocking?" My words slurred in my throat. He shrugged and grinned at me.

"You're deaf." His mouth formed the words carefully as he held out my plate. My head pounded as I squinted up at him.

Why was my son waking me up so early?

"It's a sunny, sunny day!" He bounced. "Papa wants us all to go on a picnic!"

I shoved a hand through my hair, but it snagged in the curls and I struggled to disentangle my fingers from the knots.

"Today?" I groaned, but he ran out the door without answering. I blew the stray curls out of my eyes and climbed out of bed. Under the lace, fading stretch marks zigzagged across my hips, but I glossed over them quickly.

Peter liked them. Peter said they were sexy.

My first husband did not think so. He loved me, he just disliked my imperfections. That was reasonable. It should not bother me.

But it did.

Why did Peter say he liked something that Willic hated so much?

Scars marred the insides of my thighs and arms. They mocked me for letting Peter down; for caving in to the bite of a blade. I also glazed over the scar covering half of my chest. It reminded me of that night. It never allowed me to forget.

A tear slipped down my face, and I did not catch it. I could cry alone. No one would judge me. I placed my hands on the sides of my face and gently lifted the skin, easing the slight lines around my eyes. Slowly my hands fell away and the lines reappeared.

Each one told their own story.

Each one appeared after some traumatic event.

I knew that was not true, but it helped thinking of them like that. As my fingers brushed the tender muscles on my stomach I winced. Peter said I should mourn.

I lost a child.

Again.

I mourned enough in my life.

Mourning got me nowhere.

Four scoops of coal added to the fire.

The pot above the flames refilled.

Buckets dumped into the tub.

I sank into the bathwater and ignored our diminished water supplies. I could not afford to waste it, but it soothed my aches. My fingers grazed over my stitches.

Pain seized my body, wrapped its fingers around me, and squeezed too tight.

I would not scream.

Peter laid beside me, smoothing my hair, soothing my soul. I curled into a ball as another contraction washed over me.

"I'm getting help, Christa. You need help."

"I do not need help." I moaned. "I can do it."

"You've been trying for three days. Christa, you're bleeding."

Exhaustion would not let me check his facts.

"I am sorry."

"For what, Babe?" The kindness in his eyes brought tears to my eyes.

"I wanted this one to make it. What am I doing wrong?"

"You're not doing anything wrong." His tears dropped onto my neck as he kissed my shoulder. "I'm calling a Healer down from the blue city."

The stitches itched.

"Clear her mouth, Peter!"

They were getting worse. Each one I lost was worse.

I crawled out of the scalding water, and wrapped a towel around my body. Numbly, I dabbed make-up over my visible scars, and wrestled my curls into pins. I draped a black dress over the demons that played across my body; hiding them beneath the fabric so I would forget about them for a little while. The purple registration band tied around my arm finished my look, and my eyes focused on the tiny tattoos on the inside of my wrist. A small teardrop for Willic. A tiny falcon from Peter.

More tears streaked my face. That tattoo was a promise. A promise to myself. A promise to Peter.

Next to the tattoo, a bleeding cut mocked me. Physical proof of the promise I broke.

The make-up I coated on my arms did nothing to hide the

scars.

I frowned. I did not have time to change.
This would have to do.

"Happy birthday, My Love." Peter raised his glass in a mock salute.

Was it my birthday?

I flipped through the dates in my head. The Season Of Death must have started a while ago. I could never tell here. Back home, when The Season Of Death started it never stopped snowing, but here it never snowed, regardless of the season. Unless I made it snow.

"Is it my birthday?" I frowned.

"The Thirty-Second Day, The Season Of Death, Cycle Seven-Four-Nine Post-War. That's your birthday."

It was.

How could I forget?

My mother warned me this would happen. She said it happened to all of them. I just thought I had more time.

Peter set a small box in my lap, and Jess and Quartnee straightened, eyes glowing with excitement.

"Open it, Mommy."

"Mother." I quietly corrected as I lifted the lid off the box. A dainty ring nestled in some tissue-paper. Silver band. BlackStar as the focal stone. Surrounded by WhiteStars. It was beautiful, but I frowned at simple gold band I already wore.

Was it not good enough?

"Do you like it, Dear?"

"Yes." I answered too fast, and Peter groaned.

"You hate it. I should have gone with my first idea."

"No, Peter. I love it. Really I do." I grabbed the ring and jammed it against my gold band. They clashed, but I tried not to notice. "See? It is very pretty, Peter. Thank you."

He chuckled and took the ring off, and then removed my gold band, too.

"This is to *replace* that old one. You're not supposed to wear them together."

"But you gave me the old one when we got married."

"Because I couldn't afford anything else." He slipped the new ring on my finger. "It took me all these cycles to be able to get you the ring I wanted to get for our wedding. But it's worth it. You're thirty today, you deserved something nice."

I studied the new ring. I did like it. Now that I knew why he gave it to me, it was very pretty.

"When I bought it The General charmed it. Whenever you take it off, I'll know exactly when and where, and I'll come for you."

My heart sank.

"The General knows you have this?"

"Yeah, I needed him to charm it."

"When did you go to Nalaise?" I spun the ring nervously on my finger.

"I put in an order the last time The General visited."

I did not like the thought of The General having that information. He could use it against us.

"Mom? Why don't you like The General?" Jess spoke up.

"What do you mean?" I glanced at my children. Peter could only talk Jess, Quartnee, and Aurora into a picnic. My other children did not see Peter as their father, and did not feel a need to spend time with him.

He was temporary.

Everyone was temporary.

"He's a nice guy. He takes care of us. But you're scared of him."

"He is not what he seems, Jess." I stared into my forest. Aurora crawled onto Peter's lap, and stuck her fingers up her nose. And people wondered why I did not hold my children. Sticky, grimy children. She reached her arms toward me, so I patted her head. I could not afford to get too attached. It would only cause pain.

"But do you really have proof, Mommy? Or is it another hunch?"

"They are not hunches if they are correct."

"So, no proof then. He's a nice guy." Jess poked his fork into a pile of grits.

"No. He's not a nice guy, Jess." Peter spoke up. "Just wait. He will do something soon."

Fear filled my son's face.

"I don't want war though, Mother. I don't' want to die."

My stomach turned.

"Do not worry, Jess. A war will not happen until the Rèx̱taÿлǎ is crowned." I tried to ease the fear in my son's eyes, but Peter cleared his throat, and caught my eye.

"Maybe your conspiracy theories aren't proper picnic etiquette."

A lump rose in my throat.

"You do not believe the Rèx̱taÿлǎ is coming?" I whispered. Peter looked down at his plate.

"You're the only one who still holds onto the King's promise. Nearly seven-hundred-and-fifty cycles have passed. Nobody is coming."

I nodded and bit my lip. The Rèx̱taÿлǎ would come. They were promised. The King never broke his promises.

"But you have been helping me plan." I struggled to speak past the lump in my throat. "You have been helping me prepare for the Rèx̱taÿлǎ."

"I didn't want to let you down." He reached for me, but I pulled away. "The King speaks in metaphors, Dear. He wasn't talking of a specific person."

"He said someone was coming." I whispered. He did not believe in me. I always thought he, at least, did. One tear slipped out, and he caught it with the back of his hand.

"Shh. No. Baby, I believe you. If you say the Rèx̱taÿлǎ is coming, they're coming. Okay? I believe you. I'm sorry."

He pulled my head down onto his chest. I stayed in his arms, but the comfort they once offered was fading.

The picnic fell silent after our argument. I never cried in front of my children, and I was embarrassed to allow such a show of emotion.

Once they cleaned their plates, they begged Peter to take them on a walk through my forest.

Without me.

They never wanted me to join. So I packed up the sparse picnic and retreated to the house. My bed called my name. My knife called my name. I would not give in to it. Not today. I just needed to lie down.

I did not wake the lacelights as I walked into my room. Dark rooms comforted me. I crossed over to my vanity, and opened my jewelry box. Though I did not have many pieces I treasured each one. I set Peter's gold ring next to the wedding band Willic gave me, and my eyes landed on the other gems and jewelry inside the box. They reminded me of better times. Safer times.

"You have a lovely collection." A voice behind me made me jump. An old man with fiery hair sat in my window seat. He smiled at me, and tilted his head.

"Ancient traditions are stirring. Your people are waking, Řèлїǎ."

"Do not call me that." I spat at the man as I shut my box. His eyes smoldered in the firelight as he smiled at me.

"I'll call you by your title, Řèлїǎ."

"That is not my title. It never has been."

"But it will be."

Panic rose in my throat. I just wanted a quiet life away from prying eyes. I knew this Àraid. He showed up every couple seasons and told me to go to war, but I could not do that. I could not risk the safety I built around my family. The screams in my head grew louder as I turned towards him.

"Find her, Scum!"

The snap of whips, and wailing trees.

A sinister grin.

Flaming hair and strong arms and the earth swallowing them.

"I couldn't let another one die so close to your gates." The Àraid whispered as he pointed to my bed. "I couldn't let him kill her."

Screaming and chains and blood.

The sickening, overpowering scent of blood.

Tears and pleas for mercy.

Laughter.

The woman on my bed had black hair, and misty blue eyes that screamed in pain. I could not look at her. Every time I looked at her the screaming overwhelmed me. The earth swallowed the Àraid man, leaving me alone with the woman.

"Cerynn!" I yelled over the screams in my head.

As I collapsed the darkness wrapped its arms around me. It sang me to sleep as the woman whimpered on my bed.

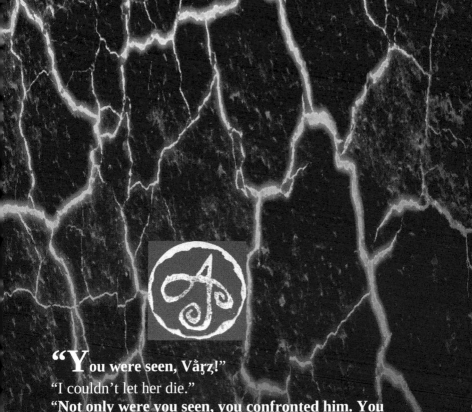

"**Y**ou were seen, Vǎṟẓ!"

"I couldn't let her die."

"Not only were you seen, you confronted him. You *challenged* him."

"I couldn't let her die! And I certainly couldn't let him take her back."

"*And you thought it would be best to save her in front of him? By doing so, you proved to him we are still alive, and still active.*"

"How long did you think we could stay hidden? We are Elders. Our job is to protect everyone, not just ourselves. Now the only time we see each other is to argue."

"**The Çvïl don't play well with Ɉǒṟđïл or Алṭvaṟ. We cannot handle the stupidity of the other Àraid races.**"

"We were meant to combine our abilities. We were meant to use your powers to see what's coming. Use the Алṭvaṟ to blend in. And it is mine and Elder Đæл's job to keep the terrain habitable, and the weather livable."

"**You are all useless.**"

"*Elder Çæлèṟ, The King chose all of us to guide the*

Rèлïă. *You are not better than Elder Vǎɼʐ, and Elder Vǎɼʐ is not better than me."*

"It is-s s-s-stupid to come out of hiding. We are s-s-s-safe where we are, why ris-s-s-k that?"

"Elder Pïlṻл believes The King's prophesy is coming to light even now. Even as we speak."

"Is that true? He never said anything to me. We rule the Çvïl together, why would he not tell me?"

"Maybe if you hadn't insisted on shutting out the visions, you wouldn't be surprised. I thought that's what you did best."

"The screaming got too loud. I needed to shut it out. That does not mean I cannot do my job. If it is truly an important vision, it pushes its way through."

"Then why didn't you get a vision the day she was taken? Why didn't you get a vision the day The General attacked Christa? Or when he wiped out the Jðɼđïл camp? We lost half of our members, and that could have been avoided."

"Oh, *that* I saw, but we are not united anymore. Your problems are not mine."

"You'll be sorry once a Rèлïă is crowned again."

"I will not follow the mad Rèлïă in the purple city. I do not care if her piercing gives her claim. She has been raised human. She cannot rule the Àraid."

Cerynn

Mother's screams echoed through the stone hallways. I glanced up from a cut on Peter's leg as a scream ripped through the healira.

"Was that?" I frowned, but Peter already launched off my exam bed. I waved a hand over the housemap on the wall, frantically trying to figure out where the house placed Mother's room in its latest shuffle. We searched the map a moment, and then Peter limped from the room; pulling me behind him.

Her first scream was just that.

A scream.

But the second scream that washed over us was my name, and I sped up. Mother sometimes screamed on her worst days. Scream weren't unusual. But she never screamed names.

Her door was ajar when we finally found it, and the room was dark.

"Make it stop. Take it back. Make it stop." She mumbled in the darkness. Peter plunged in ahead of me, and his cane clattered to the ground as he fell beside my mother. Her hands pressed against her head, and her eyes squeezed tight. I tapped the jar of lacelights, and they buzzed to life, lighting the room.

"Make it stop." She pointed at her bed. "Make the screaming stop." She pushed Peter towards the bed, and screamed again, then she curled into a ball with her arms over her head.

"Who are you?" Peter whispered to a woman laying on the bed. Her dress was dirty, and torn, and much to big for her scrawny body. Behind grimy strands of salt-and-pepper hair, her nearly white eyes filled with fear as she looked up at Peter. She pressed pale lips together, and shook her head.

"What's your name?" Peter tried again, and was met again with a vigorous head shake, but this time she also clamped a hand over her mouth. Her other hand scratched at her throat. I moved to one side of the bed, and Peter went to the other, slowly inching closer to the woman.

She clawed at her throat as we got closer to her, and her already pale skin lost its remaining color. Peter reached out a hand, but she lunged away from his touch. She went too far, and lost her balance. As she tumbled over the side of the bed, I jumped forward to catch her, but she hit my left arm and ripped the prosthetic out of place.

The arm, and woman, crashed to the ground, and the woman retreated to the corner. I picked up my arm, and latched it back into the framework that made up the better part of the left side of my body.

In the fall and scramble away from us, the woman still did not make a sound. I motioned for Peter not to move, and approached her. She pressed herself into the corner, but didn't fight as hard.

"Let me help you. You're hurt." I pointed to some blood seeping onto her dress. She pressed her hand into the stain and exposed the tip of a knife poking through from her back. She winced, but still wouldn't let me touch her.

I went to Mother's nightstand. She always kept parchment in the drawer. I pushed the parchment into the woman's lap, and handed her a quill.

"Who are you? Why are you here?"

She swallowed, and frowned at the quill, but she took it, and poised it over the parchment.

Alice. Safety.
"Safety from who?"

Prisoner. Escape.
I took the parchment and showed it to Peter. He paled.
"We'll give you safety." He whispered to her. Her hands found her neck again, and she didn't pull away from Peter. He took her arm, and helped her to her feet. She swayed and collapsed back to the floor, pulling Peter down with her.

"We can't guarantee safety, Peter. If she got out of the prisons, he'll be searching for her. She doesn't even have registration." I pointed to her arm, but Peter cut off my protest as she slumped in his arms.

"Nobody escapes the prisons. Cerynn. *She* is what changed."

Peter carried the woman to the healira for me, and laid her on the bed.

"You really should let your mother handle this. You haven't finished your training yet." He cautioned as I tied my apron around me.

"Mother is an incoherent mess on the floor. I'm this woman's better option right now." I shoved him out the door, and faced the woman. She drifted in and out of consciousness as I approached. Blood beaded between her lips where she'd bit through to cut off a moan. One hand still clawed desperately at her neck.

She struggled weakly as I tried to remove her dress. The filthy fabric clung to her as if she'd worn it for cycles, and I finally gave up slipping it off in one piece. As I ripped in to pieces to get to her injury a corset mocked me. I couldn't rip the boning like I'd ripped the fabric. I sighed and set in on the lacing. My breath caught in my throat when I finally freed her from the corset.

Bruises, of all shapes and colors, splattered across her body from the neck down. I rolled her onto her side, and studied her back. Deep scars from what looked like whips covered her back, and made their way around to just below her ribs. A small box nestled, embedded, in the small of her back with a switch on it. I flicked it on and off a few times, but couldn't figure out what it did.

A knife stuck out of her side right beneath her ribs. I'd never worked on this type of injury, but I pried the knife out of her back, and patched her up the best I could. The knife bore The General's insignia. She wasn't lying about needing safety. The General was protective of his weapons. He wouldn't like losing one.

As I eased her onto her back, my eyes landed on a small tattoo, a brand, right above her hip. 25423. An auction number.

How did she escape?

Her stomach bulged in the middle, contrasting the way her hips and ribs stuck out, and her arms wrapped around her middle; protecting the child that had been perfectly concealed beneath the corset.

"How is she?" Mother was pale, and her face was blotchy from crying. She leaned against the door, and peeked in.

"I think she'll be okay, but I can't get her to stop scratching her throat."

Mother tiptoed into the room, and stood beside the bed, taking care not to touch her.

"She is looking for a necklace."

"How do you know?"

"When you are afraid, what do you do?"

I thought for a second, and shrugged.

"I don't know, I've never been afraid."

My mother cringed.

"You cannot think of a single time you felt nervous, or afraid?"

"No. We're safe within the city. I have nothing to fear."

Again, she made a weird face. I thought she would be pleased to provide us with a safe home, but she only looked worried. Then she shrugged.

"When I get nervous, I squeeze my left hand with my right." She indicated as she spoke. "Alice came for safety. She is afraid. She is searching for a necklace."

"Then I can't help her."

"No. You cannot help, but maybe I can." Her voice cracked, and her shoulders slumped as she disappeared into the hall. She always carried herself proudly, but now she looked defeated. Her nightmares were getting worse.

She returned a few minutes later, and held out a necklace to the woman on the bed. Alice's eyes focused on the charm, and she finally stilled. Mother shoved a necklace into my hands. I latched it around the woman's neck, and she wrapped her hands around the charm.

"How did you know that was the necklace she wanted?" I glanced back at my mother.

"It is not. But for now, in her pain induced delirium, she will not know the difference."

"What happens when she figures it out?"

"She will go back to scratching her throat out. Hopefully we figure out what necklace she wants before that happens."

Inhibited

Jaycobe

"**A**nd they walked off into the sunset. Hand in hand. Better friends than ever before." I shut the book, and looked down at Aurora. Her flaming red curls spread across my chest, and she sucked her thumb furiously; eyes fixed on the closed book.

"Aw, man that was beautiful." Roland mumbled from the other side of the room. "Now come. Happy hour starts soon. I *need* to be first in line." He stood and stretched.

"I have to get her to bed first. You go on. I'll be there." I stood from my chair, cradling Aurora in my arms. She pulled her finger from her mouth, but didn't protest when I laid her in her bed.

"One story about the war of Àraid and Raks, Cobe?" She mumbled, eyes already fighting sleep. I sighed and knelt by her bed. Her eyes drooped as I started in on the familiar story.

"Once, the Àraid lived in beautiful castles, and looked over the humans. But they never mingled with humans. They were here to protect, and only look over the human cities. When trouble arose, the Àraid stomped it out before it affected life. Six Elders sat united under their Rèлïǎ. together

But a horrible massacre made The Collector come from his world, and steal Àraid souls back to his collection. One Elder was determined to get his family back. He deified the King, and passed, alone, through a gateway to The Collector's world; Šïχðɼ. He succeeded. He brought his family back from the world of passed life. But he brought them back cursed.

Because he was driven to bring back the dead, rather than join them, he caused them to no longer belong in this world. The curse they brought on themselves dictated that they would never again be satisfied. They would crave blood and flesh and power. The icy sun that once strengthened them now burned them, and they were covered in black scales.

The Rak who defied the King was more powerful than the others. He discovered powers even the King didn't know. He grew bitter at his punishment, and sought revenge on the King who inflicted it. And so, beside the icy sun that once powered him, he placed a burning sun. The burning sun strengthened the Raks, and pulled strength from the Àraid. The suns began an endless battle for the sky, and both races were sent scrambling to shelters. For a few cycles, the Àraid were able keep the Rak problem hidden from the humans. But the Raks reproduced quickly, and soon there were too many for the Àraid to stop.

Because the Àraid worked in secret for all those cycles, the humans' hearts were not loyal. Cities fell and people turned against the Àraid, believing the Raks were the truest power. When the war, and the Hybrids, came, The Àraid were not ready, and were wiped out."

Aurora drifted to sleep, dreaming of a heritage she didn't know was her own.

Christa

I was in the morgue.

I liked the dead. They made good conversation. They were not as frustrating as the living.

The screaming quieted here, and I could focus on the bodies, instead of the woman in my healira. Nobody escaped the prisons. She had The General's knife embedded in her body. He never bothered with prisoners.

She was a trap. She would tear my city apart.

But if I kept her locked away in the healira, she could not do much harm. I could focus on keeping the city safe.

But I could not quiet the screams.

Make it stop.

I laid my baby daughter out on my table. Peter said I should not use her. I should lay her to rest and experiment on adults.

I did not know why.

She was not in there anymore.

She would not feel anything.

Wires snaked from her to a Wilting Life bloom I contained in a jar. The bloom allowed me to bring a body artificially to life. They breathed and moved and functioned, but their brain was still dead. All the commands came from me. I pulled out a scalpel and pressed the blade against my arm.

Not hard.

Not hard enough.

I wanted to let out the anguish building inside me. I shook my head, and placed the scalpel against her tiny neck. Her hand reached up and curled around my fingers, purely reflex.

She could not feel anything.

Three quick strikes laid her neck open to the bone. I started counting in my head.

Four.

Five.

Six.

I pulled my kit out and stitched her up. Her eyes focused on me.

Deep, beautiful, miss-matched eyes.

Peter's eyes.

My eyes blurred, and blotted out what I could see of her. I was losing time.

Ten.

Eleven.

Twelve.

I pulled the thread through, tied it, and cut it.

Two seconds to spare.

A hand on my shoulder made me jump and I hastily brushed the tears from my cheeks. Peter turned me to him and pulled me into a tight embrace. I put one arm around him quickly, and then pushed him away. I could not afford to be interrupted right now.

His arms shook with anger, and he held me tighter than usual. Normally, he loved my experiments. He would sit for hours just watching me, serenading me while I played with my cadavers. He said what I did was noble; helpful. He thought differently now that his own child lay beneath my blade. He released me and looked down on his daughter.

I amputated her legs yesterday, and attempted to reattach them with the nerves still working. It did not work.

The day before, however, I snapped her neck and fully repaired it, reversing the paralysis. The bloom was the only thing that kept her alive, but I could work on that.

Peter covered the body with a blanket and scooped it into his arms, detangling it from the jar. As the artificial life drained from the body, Peter's face crumpled in pain and rage.

"How could you do this to me?" He hissed. "Everyday I'm forced to lose her. I see her alive. I watch her die. Everyday."

I was shocked, and as I looked up into his face, and read so much anger there, a pang of anxiety shot through me.

This was it.

He would leave me now.

He hated me for what I did to his daughter, so why would he stay with me?

The screaming was louder.

I could not focus.

I could not think.

I grabbed my head, and rocked in my chair.

Peter glared at me, then stormed out the door and down the hall, still cradling his daughter.

"Please do not leave me." I could barely speak past the lump in my throat. Peter did not slow down. "Where are you going?" I chased him down the hall. He was much taller than me. His long strides easily outpaced my short ones, even with one arm swinging his cane, and his right side leaning heavily on it.

"I'm going to bury our daughter. I'm going to give her a proper send off, proper closure, and I'm going hire someone to stand by my side and mourn with me because you won't!" The veins on his forehead bulged as he seethed. I had never seen him so angry.

"But I have not finished with her yet." I protested. "I

have a few more things I want to check."

He swung around and I cringed at the blow I expected. I knew Peter would never harm me, but I still expected it. The blow never came. He was calmer now.

"I know, to you, this is normal. You cope with loss by making it count for something. That's not how I cope." He shook his head. "I want to say goodbye to my daughter and not ever see her "alive" again. I held her for six hours after they cut her from you. I cried alone. I cleaned her. I dressed her. I readied her for burial. Alone. And then you stepped in and said "wait, I need to snap her neck first.""

"I did not say that." Tears pressed against my eyelids, but I did not allow them to fall. Not in front of Peter.

"You may as well have. I love you. I signed up for all your baggage and weird traditions. I signed up for the mini heart attacks I get every time you light yourself on fire. Really wakes me up, but also ruins a lot of our beds."

I blushed.

"But I did not sign up to seeing our dead child every day. Having to lose her *everyday*. Let me bury her."

I looked at the body, so tiny, so fresh. I thought of the advancements I could make with her untainted body. But then I nodded. Peter needed this. If I let him bury her, maybe he would stay. The research would have to wait.

Rain turned the tiny hole muddy.

Why did it always rain at funerals?

We were well into The Season Of Death. It should not rain. It should snow. I glared at the sky and whispered under my breath.

"Злав." The clouds parted and snow drifted down to cover the ground; perfectly clear skies. Cerynn was out checking the mines. She did not like funerals. She would have noticed the sudden change in weather, but nobody else noticed.

They asked me to speak today. I did not know where to begin.

"I do not understand most traditions." I started "I never have. They baffle me. We laugh and play and enjoy life, and then one of us dies and we act like the world ended. Death should not be that life altering." I surveyed the crowd "Your husband dies? Learn his trade. Your child dies? You have an empty room to rent out for income."

Peter raised a hand to stop me but I plunged ahead.

"Humans cry for their dead. They are the only species that does. Yes, other species mourn, but not in this all-consuming way." I continued. "The Àraid never grieved like this." I ignored the gasps, and tried to find a point.

"What does crying achieve? A headache and burning eyes." I tried to clear the tears from my eyes. "My dear husband, however, has gotten caught up in these traditions. He told me he *needed* this to say goodbye." I bore my eyes into Peter's. I could tell he wanted to look away, but he would not. Not from me.

"She is not here, Peter. You are saying goodbye to the ground, not your daughter."

Peter straightened and watched me.

"My child is dead. Gone before she had a fair shot at this world. But she is in a world without war, or pain, or death. Yes. I wanted this baby girl. Sure. It felt as if my heart had been ripped out when they told me she died, and I sometimes wake up with pain is so great I cannot breath." The crowd chuckled. "Breathe." I corrected, but silently chanted in my head. Index, middle, ring, pinkie. Breath. Breath. I touched my thumb to my fingers and focused on my next breath. Tight fingers of grief choked off my sermon.

I gripped the podium, and my fingertips turned as white as the snow on the grave. They frosted over. I was losing control on my powers. I pulled in as much air as my lungs would take, and tried to focus on where I was, not how I felt.

"I did not plan on speaking today. I did not know until this morning." I said to my fingers. "I planned on sitting by my husband, but I guess I am here now." I glanced back at the crowd. "Just one question, and then I will leave. How many heartbeats do you have left? People tell me all the time that they 'have time,' they can 'figure things out later.' I love to speak at a child's funeral because this is the best place to respond to that statement. Do you really have time? Do you really want to risk it? It only takes a few seconds to change everything. It took ten seconds for me."

Thunder cracked over the city, and I shivered.

"Ten seconds before I knew my child was dead, ten seconds before I had to learn to cope. That is not a lot of time. It is not enough."

As I looked around the somber gathering, and then down at the little box in the hole in the ground, I only knew one thing for sure. The smaller the coffin, the more weight it carried. When an adult died, the people around them shrugged it off.

"*They lived a full life. They were prepared.*"

No one knew what to say when a child lay in that hole. No words could express the emotions swirling in the crowd. Because the truth everyone knew, and no one said, was that they did *not* live enough. They were not prepared.

How could they be?

A scream pierced my mind and a vision crashed into my collected thoughts, scattering them.

A little girl clung to her mother as a Rak crashed into the room and pried them apart. He dug his fingers into the girl's shoulder and tasted her blood.

"What's her name?" The Rak asked the mother, and of course she answered.

"Anna. Her name is Anna."

The Rak smiled and knelt in front of the girl.

"Well then, Anna, what's your full name?"

The girl repeated her name, as she had so recently learned, probably. She was that age when parents ground a child's name into their head. Just like I did when my children were small. And, just like in my case, it was a deadly mistake. I could not prove they were using names, but they were. I knew they were.

The Rak rolled the girl's name around in his mouth, and as he repeated it, tested it, the little girl stopped fighting him. She stood straight, like a soldier, and waited for the Rak's order. He knew her true name. He controlled her now.

The mother's eyes filled with horror as her daughter turned back towards her, looking at her but not really seeing her. The child smiled and showed off her tiny baby teeth, now replace with jagged ones. With a small nod from one of the Raks, the girl raised her hands in front of her, and long vines shot from her fingers and wrapped around her mother, ripping away skin as they wrapped tighter around her arms. The woman bit her lip, refusing to make any noise, but the little girl was not finished.

It was too familiar. The same way he controlled my daughter.

Nobody believed my Inhibited theory. Nobody saw him control my daughter that day in our cabin. Cerynn did not remember killing her father. I wiped that memory from her mind. This child in my vision would not live long enough to remember. The Raks would kill her once she did what they needed her to.

I shook my head and tried to focus on Peter, on his beautiful green and blue eyes. I swallowed hard, and opened my mouth to continue, but stopped as my eyes focused on the edge of the city.

A man covered in blood limped up to the gate.

"There's a Hybrid in the mine."

Inhibited

Cerynn

Six cave-ins through the night ran my supplies dry.
Two mines were within a days trip from our city, but
neither had ever been this unstable. I worked all night
on the wounded, and, luckily, no injuries were bad
enough to send them back to the healira. Mother and I
were the only Healers in the city, and I agreed to work
today so she could be available for the funeral, but I was
tired after working through the night.

Josh and I were almost back to the house when an
alarm went off. I hadn't heard that alarm before. One
alarm, in the morning, and one in the evening, signaled
the start of shifts in the mines. But this wasn't a short
blast. This one never ceased. I covered my ears, and
looked around.

"Is that alarm for another cave-in?" I shouted over
the noise.

'Cave-ins send messengers. They don't sound alarms.'
Josh signed, unfazed by the alarm. 'I read in a book that
a constant alarm was a Hybrid signal back when the
Àraid were in control.'

A smoke signal rose above one of the mines. I was
tired. I didn't want to deal with another cave-in.

"It's not a Hybrid, Josh. The Hybrids never leave

Nalaise. It's just another cave-in."

Maybe Mother would hear the alarm up at the house, and take pity on the daughter who'd worked through the night. Maybe she would take over this one.

The mine seemed normal as we approached the opening. Usually if there was a cave-in the entrance would be filled with dust. I was so focused on the lack of dust that I didn't notice the bodies littering the ground until I almost stepped on one. Fourteen bodies, torn to shreds, stained the ground outside the mine. Sixteen miners worked this mine.

What happened?

I stared into the darkness of the mine. Something glimmered in the depths.

"I know she's near. I smell her fear. Bring me the prisoner escaped from her sentence."

Something wrapped around me, and pulled me into the darkness. There wasn't time to think as I flew through the musty air, crashing deeper into the mine. It was too dark to see the creature who held me. Bright yellow scales lit up beside me, and something crashed into my side and knocked me off course.

The yellow wrapped itself around me, and we crashed and rolled down a side tunnel. Then the creature unwrapped me and set me gently on the ground, unharmed. It turned and screeched at the glimmering eyes that followed us down tunnel, and fire cascaded out of its mouth and illuminated a Hybrid. I shielded my eyes, and tried to see what saved me.

A long tail swished on the ground next to me, and wings crammed into the small tunnel. It's claws were longer than my legs.

Dragon.

I reached out and touched the scales on its tail, but it shook me off, and disappeared down an access shaft. The Hybrid placed his hands against the wooden beams supporting the tunnel, and they began to smolder. He scraped a handful of embers into his hands and threw them at me.

Instinctively, I raised an arm to shield myself from the fire, and cold water splattered my arms. The Hybrid's eyes widened in surprise as the fire he threw at me turned into a tidal wave of ice cold water. Beneath the water stood a figure, partially concealed in the dark of the mine, with their hands raised in the air.

Smoke filled the small space, and burned my eyes and lungs. I coughed and scooted away from the Hybrid. He was distracted by the figure who drowned him in fire, but then he deflected it in my direction. I hid behind a carts, and held my breath against the smoke.

The Hybrid's skin faltered between skin, and scales, as he measured up his attacker. The figure brought down a cave-in on top of the Hybrid, and, beneath the rock, his blood pooled on the floor. But then his blood poured back into his body and the rocks scattered. He roared as he stood, and in his anger he seemed to grow.

The Hybrid grunted, and shifted his shoulder back into its socket. Our eyes met. He hissed and raised his arms. The rocks from the cave-in began to dance in the mine. I braced myself against the mine cart and closed my eyes.

I heard the figure mutter foreign words I almost recognized, and wind raced through the tunnels. Water poured from the ceiling, but didn't drown the flames. The Hybrid and the figure were matched in power, and together they painted a fantastic landscape of fierce, raw anger.

But the figure was weakening; pushing the Hybrid too hard, forcing his focus to stay on them. The wind died down, and the flames burned down to embers. He laughed at her.

"You are weak still. You think you're good at your game, but I am always better. You'll not beat me." His voice echoed through the mine. The rocks danced again, and one rolled over my left leg, warping the metal structure of my calf.

The skin peeled back on my leg, revealing the framework underneath it. Some of the braces snapped on impact. The Hybrid threw back his head and laughed in victory. He poised his sword over me. Somehow that felt familiar; like I'd been in that position before.

The figure ran up behind him and thrust a flaming sword through his open mouth. Another sword came around and separated head from body, splattering me with thick black blood. I hastily scrubbed the poisoned blood off of me as it started to sizzle and burn.

His head, still attached to the sword, engulfed in flames. His eyes closed and the body and head turned to dust. And the mine plunged into darkness.

"Do not be dead. Please do not be dead. Tell me I got here in time." The figure muttered. Fingers prodded my neck, and she sighed at my heartbeat. She helped me up, and we hobbled back out of the mine. In the sunlight, I could see the figure fully. She trembled before me, her eyes full of tears, and she shrunk away from my hand.

"Mother?"

"I did not have a choice. He was going to kill you. I did what I needed to do." She whispered. Her eyes filled with a fear I had never seen before.

"You're not a Seer. You're Àraid."

How did I not see it?

How did I never figure it out?

"No. This is a fluke." She lied.

"You're Àraid! Why are you hiding it?"

She covered my mouth, and hissed in my ear.

"The General killed the Àraid. What would happen if this news got out? He would swarm the city. He would kill my people for keeping me hidden."

I clamped my mouth shut. She was right. Despite my questions, it was a very dangerous thing to talk about. I needed to let it go until we were alone.

"How did you know to come?"

"A miner made it back to the gate. He told me." Her gaze locked on the woods, and her eyes filled with horror.

A man emerged from the woods. He slumped somewhat, but still loomed over us in a body built for battle. Agitation gave his eyes a crazed light as he rushed over to my mother. He pointed into the woods.

"You have to come back out with me. I have to find her."

"Unhand me, Sir, or you will join these people." Mother pushed him away from her, and pointed to the bodies on the ground. He raked his fingers through his hair.

"She's out there! I need to find her. Please." He held a tattered journal in his hands, and shook it in my mother's face.

"Who are you, and who are you looking for?" I stepped between them.

"I'm The Captain." He said impatiently. "And I'm looking for Alice. I was supposed to protect her. I promised her."

"She is in the healira." I blurted out, and my mother glared at me. Relief flooded his face, but he didn't relax.

"Then take me to her. Now."

† † † † †

I made him wait outside while I checked on Alice. If she was in bad shape when he saw her I feared what he would do. He stayed quiet while we walked back to the healira, and put up quite a fight when I suggested he wait. He wore a beat up grey suit. Suits worked for The General. They practically owned the regions. This man wasn't used to being told what to do.

Alice moaned, hands scratching her throat; face contorted in pain. She still twisted the necklace my mother gave her, but it no longer offered comfort. I hated bringing him in with her so restless, but maybe he knew how to calm her. I placed a cloth on her forehead, and tried once more to calm her, before I went to go find the man. He sat in the courtyard, and, as I approached, he put his head in his hands, expecting the worst.

"I need you to comfort her." I stated as I noticed blood staining my apron. His eyes widened, and he touched his chest, right over his heart.

"She's alive?" He rubbed his chest as he walked towards the door. I followed him back into the healira. She was thrashing now, eyes wide and unseeing. Tears coursed down her face, and her nails brought up blood on her neck. She'd torn off Mother's necklace and it lay on the floor next to the bed. The Captain sat on the edge of the bed and took one small hand in his.

Instantly, she stilled, eyes focused on him, and then she grabbed his shirt and pulled herself into his arms, burying her face in his chest. He hugged her, and rocked her slowly, careful not to hurt her.

"Here, Love." He pulled a necklace out of his pocket, and she managed a smile as he latched it around her neck. The one she searched for. I ducked out of the room to give them some privacy.

I heard the woman weeping behind the door, but she wasn't quite awake. She would drift back into a fitful sleep, and she wouldn't remember this when she woke up again. I peeked back through the door. She was already drifting off again. She felt safe in his arms. But as I watched him stroke her arms, and her back, I frowned. Hand-print bruises covered her arms and neck. Hand-print bruises from big hands.

His hands were the same size as the bruises.

Christa

I barely made it back to the house before my legs gave out. Tears pressed against my eyelids.

My secret was out.

I had no choice.

I had to protect my daughter. There was no other way. That man in the woods was bad news. I knew he was.

I felt it.

He brought chaos into my city.

I pulled myself along the stone entryway onto the carpeted stairs. When I built this house, I matched my childhood home as much as I could; except this house was bigger. The entryway was an exact replica. Usually it comforted me, but now it filled me with dread.

I looked back at the stairs, and then closed my eyes and saw her retreating up the stairs. She turned and smiled at me, and her laugh bounced off the walls. A gash through her abdomen bled down her legs and pooled at her feet. Too much blood. She would never survive. Her white eyes held no warmth, only pain. I covered my head and sank to my knees.

You are dead, Mother. Stop haunting me.

I blinked, but there was still a figure standing on my

stairs. The old man with flaming hair.

"You've denied yourself too long, Rèлïǎ."

"I did not deny myself. I resigned." I spat at him.

"It's not something you can resign. We need you."

"Nobody needs me. I am a broken mind trapped in a life I never wanted."

The old man smiled, sadly.

"Maybe you aren't ready yet. I will come back when you are." His robes whipped around his legs, and vanished.

Visions crowded my head as he left.

Screaming and whips.

Laughter and music, and critical eyes.

A terrified boy, shaking in an arena.

A raised hand.

White smoke.

The drums ceased.

Blood.

"Stop!"

Alice

40th Day, The Season of Life, 726-PW

A snake brought me a letter a few days ago. I don't know who sent
it. I think it's a threat. Micheal is out looking for a better job, so I
can't ask him what he thinks. The letter had very specific
instructions in it. It said if I didn't follow the instructions whoever
sent it would hunt me down, and kill me. Should I believe it? Should
I be worried?

"**I**s this all you have?" I frowned at the girl who stood
alone on the border of Icecrest, shivering in the snow. She
wore a ragged coat, more hole than coat, and clutched a
beat up book in her hands.

The letter said she would wait at the border, but I didn't
know she would be alone. She didn't say a word as we
walked back to my house. I held back a gasp when I
noticed bloody footsteps following her.

Did she go through Icecrest barefoot?

"What else would I have?" She spoke slowly, drawing out each word carefully. Her simple deerskin dress pinched her arms and middle, several sizes too small.

Havenden clothing.

How did she make it to the Mainland?

How did she survive Icecrest?

"I'm Alice." I tried to break her silence, but she still didn't say a word as we hurried up the path to my home. Her guarded eyes peered into my house, filled with curiosity. They scanned the walls, the floor, and finally rested back on me. She was seven. I was twenty. How different my life looked compared to hers. A warm bed every night. Loving parents. Clothing. I never needed anything, and here she stood, book in hand, asking what else she would possibly need.

"Thank you again for taking me in." She squared her shoulders and sniffed. I smiled at the terrified girl. I already felt like her mother. Already I worried about her. I was in way over my head. I hoped I could handle it. It couldn't be too hard.

"Come in, Child. You don't have to stand in the doorway all day."

She glanced from her grimy feet to the white tiles in the entryway.

"I do not think that good, Ma'am. You maybe have some water? I just wipe my feet off a little bit?" Her speech flowed from her mouth, like a song, carrying with it a heavy accent.

I ran upstairs to draw a bath, and then thought better of it, and simply grabbed a bowl and filled that with water.

"Do you...maybe have somethin' not so fancy?" She ducked her head, ashamed that she even dare ask. I shook my head and moved her into my living area, pushing her gently onto the couch. I sat down, cross-legged, in front of her a took a foot in my hand, wiping the grime away from the open sores. Her eyes focused on a picture frame sitting

on my piano.

Micheal worked long hours with a portraitist in the Trade Markets trying to capture our likeness on parchment. He managed to give me two realistic drawings of us together. One that we displayed proudly. One we kept private. He only bought two portraits, and just those drained our savings.

"Who's that?" Her curiosity got the better of her, and she crossed the room to grab the frame. I bit back a protest and tried to sop up her wet footprints with a towel.

"That's Micheal. He built this house."

She touched his face through the glass.

"He did well. He is your lover?" Her accent faded, replaced with a sophisticated speech a child shouldn't know. But her knowledgeable speech didn't disturb me as much as her title for Micheal.

"He's my fiance, not lover." I blushed.

"What is the difference?" She shrugged, and her eyes drifted down to the keys on the piano. "What is this?"

She restored the portrait to its spot on the top of the piano, and trailed her fingers across the ivory.

"It's a piano." I walked over to her. I assumed that once I named the instrument, she would remember and understanding would dawn in her eyes, but they still held the wonder of the unknown.

"What is piano?" Her fingers trailed down the keys, hesitating every now and then, as if she shouldn't touch.

"An instrument." I prodded, waiting for recognition to light her face.

"What is its purpose?"

"It plays music."

"Which is?"

She'd never heard of music?

I was dumbfounded.

How could a child not know what music was?

I played a few notes on the piano to demonstrate, and

*then sat down and played a song. When I finished I patted
the bench next to me, and smiled up at the girl.*

"Go ahead. Press the keys."

*Her fingers started at the bottom, pressing every key all
the way up the piano, and then she slowly went back down,
mesmerized. I picked up the bowl I'd washed her feet in.
The dirty water made me grimace, and I hurried to the
kitchen to clean it out. While I was in the kitchen the song
started again.*

*I slowly crossed back into the room and stared at the
girl. Her fingers flew over the keys, never missing a beat.
This child sat at my piano, copying the song she'd just heard
perfectly. Impossible. When she finished she looked up at
me.*

*"How did you do that?" I stared at the tiny girl before
me, but she only shrugged.*

"I felt it. I did what the piano told me to."

"Alice. Alice, Love, wake up." A hand shook my
shoulder gently. "Alice, they need to run some more tests."

My eyes focused on his face. The Captain. His hand
wrapped around mine and his eyes softened. He handed me
a parchment and quill.

"How much do you remember?" He asked. I smiled at
him and sighed.

<u>I remember you, and I remember him. But only vaguely.</u>

He frowned and rubbed my wrist.

"You were stabbed. I wasn't there. I should have been
there." His eyes clouded. "If you died..." He trailed off, and
kissed my fingers as tears slipped down his face. My hand
wandered along my stomach, and I winced when I indeed
found a wound.

"Do you remember what you were dreaming about?" His
hand stroked my forehead. I thought for a moment, but my
dream slipped just outside my grasp.

"It was a memory." He prodded, hopeful. "A dream about your daughter."

I honestly didn't remember anything.

How do you know it was a memory? Not just a dream?

"You don't talk when you're awake, but you talk in your sleep, and it matches what your journal says." He stopped. Our eyes met at the new revelation. "I'm sorry. I know I swore I wouldn't read it. I needed information I knew you wrote down, so one night I went looking for it." His eyes flared with panic as he grasped for an excuse, trying to justify himself to avoid a fight. A girl with purple hair interrupted us.

"I'm Cerynn." She announced. "We've met, but I doubt you remember. I have some questions." She sat and scooted closer to the bed. "I need to know your full name, please."

"Alice Bryell A-."

Cerynn cut The Captain's answer short, and the corners of her mouth jerked up in a smile that didn't ease any nerves.

"I'd like her to answer."

"Alice doesn't speak to anyone but me."

Cerynn's eyes never left mine.

"What about writing? She wrote her answers before you got here."

Anger wavered in his eyes when he turned back to me.

"That's not safe. I protect her, and I can't do that if she doesn't solely trust me."

"Why doesn't she speak?"

"She's been conditioned not to. Just because she left the prisons doesn't mean they left her."

Cerynn shifted uncomfortably.

"Could you prop her up, Sir?" She suggested. He climbed up on the bed behind me. His arms twisted under my back and gently pulled me up, moving my head to rest in the crook of his neck. My legs twitched beneath the covers. I hadn't even noticed. The Captain watched my face, and stroked my hair while Cerynn filled a syringe with a clear liquid.

"What's that?" The Captain's hand stilled.

"Don't worry, it's just something to stop the thrashing."

"She's pregnant! You can't give her medications." He grabbed her arm.

"Captain, I need to stop her thrashing or I won't be able to run any tests."

"You don't need to sedate."

"Then how can I-"

The Captain stopped her with a hand, and his other hand trailed down my back. It stopped on the box in the small of my back. I jerked my head ever so slightly.

No.

"I'm sorry, My Love." His fingers found the switch on the little box, and my legs stilled. Cerynn stopped with the syringe poised above my arm.

"The General." The Captain explained to her unasked question. "After an accident left her paralyzed The General got one of his Healers to make this for her."

"What sort of accident?"

"She gave birth to a Hybrid." The Captain muttered. I raised a hand to try to stop the conversation, but they ignored me. "The Raks experimented on her for cycles, and finally created a Hybrid with her. Up until then, they needed Àraids to have Hybrids, so this was a break-through. The Hybrid dug its way out of her back, through her spine."

I couldn't look at Cerynn; couldn't face her.

"She survived, amazingly. They couldn't afford to lose her, so The General spared no expense." He tapped it again. "He kept his options open with the box. He could turn her legs on and off at will. It's harder to fight if you can't move your legs."

My face burned, ashamed of the past I didn't remember.

"The General experiments on the prisoners?" Cerynn asked.

"Of course. The prisoners aren't good for anything else."

"What sort of experiments?"

"Classified." His sharp tone cut Cerynn off and she finished the exam in silence. She kept her eyes on her work, and pressed her lips in a tight line. The Captain held my hand tightly, continuously stroking the back of my hand with his thumb.

"I'm sorry." He said when we were alone again. "She needed to know." He arched an eyebrow. He still lay behind me, legs hanging off the side of the bed, arms wrapped around me. He ducked down and kissed my neck.

"Are you mad?" He whispered into my hair. I reached up and cupped his face. My thumb pressed his lips closed and I searched his eyes, looking for any sign of deception. My free hand felt around my neck.

"No." I whispered as I wrapped my necklace in my fingers, and rubbed the charm.

"Do you trust me, Baby?"

I hesitated.

What's your name? I wrote without thinking. That question filled my journal. Pages and pages of the same question, but he never answered.

"Do you trust me?" He asked again, more insistent. I pressed my lips together, and nodded. He pulled me closer and kissed me. He broke away and glanced towards the door.

"You think anyone will come in?" His smile was mischievous as he moved his legs up onto the bed. "Probably not." He leaned down and kissed me again.

His hands held mine level with my head as he braced himself above me, looking down. Another kiss. I couldn't help the giggle that slipped past my lips as he growled a joking growl. His legs shifted and heavy boots dropped to the ground. He kissed my neck, moving down to my shoulder and then back up. My mouth opened as he kissed me again, and my back arched without my command, pressing into him. Doing what it was trained to do after all those cycles as The General's slave.

An instinct I hated.

He nibbled on my ear as his hands wandered over my body. He wasn't The General. He was nicer. He didn't hurt me. But as he eased his larger frame down onto mine, memories flooded in and my blood ran cold.

I remembered who he was.

I remembered what he did.

He sighed, and pressed the smooth scar on my wrist. I shut my eyes. This had to be a dream. A dream that never ended. His thumb dug into my scar and lights flashed behind my eyes. I wanted to trust him, but I didn't know if I could.

† † † † †

A relayven's cry pulled me from my sleep. I reached for The Captain's hand, but found only empty air. The sneaky bird landed on the open windowsill. The General's relayven. It bore his markings. I fought my panic, and glanced toward the door. The Captain would be back soon. He would send the bird away. The relayven leaned forward, opened its beak, and the room filled with *his* voice.

"You shouldn't run from me. You were safe with me. You're not safe behind Christa's walls. I miss you. Will you come home to me?" The bird's eyes glowed to match the hate-filled eyes of The General, and it flew over to the bed. It clutched a sunstinger in its talons. The bird dropped the bug onto my chest, and it quickly scuttled under the sheets. I frantically tried to brush the bug off of me, but it was too fast.

It jabbed its stinger right next to my wound. My skin boiled from its poison. I whimpered and shut my eyes. The Captain would come soon. He would smash the sunstinger, and send the bird away. He would save me.

He always saved me.

Another sting, above my bellybutton. The baby flipped as my skin boiled. I bit my lip against the pain. I couldn't scream. I should not make a sound.

"You were better off with me." The General continued through the relayven. "The Captain was better before you. He was loyal."

Another sting; on my neck.

"I'm going to play a game. I'll give you three warnings, and then you will come home to me with open arms. I'll see you soon, Dear."

The relayven grabbed the sunstinger, and flew off into the night. Tears pressed against my eyelids. I would never escape him. I would never be free. The General needed me for his war.

He would not stop until I was back in his cage.

Inhibited

Christa

Three carts wheeled into the city. Everyone scrambled to see what they carried. One bore the Wellwald symbol on the side; a geyser with a pig bouncing on the spray. They carried meat, and salt. My mouth watered at the thought of meat. We ran out over a season ago.

The second cart had a tower covered in grapevines. They came from Witchcastle. Fresh fruit, and soap, and perfumes. The third carried a very familiar symbol, and I smiled. Seven fish swimming in a circle.

Havenden.

Home.

They brought us fish.

Today would be a good shipment day.

The carts stopped in the middle of the courtyard, and my people turned towards me. The drivers uncovered the back, and I stepped up to the cart from Wellwald. I gauged how much meat was in the wagon, and counted the people waiting for food.

"Okay," I addressed the crowd, "There is enough meat for each of you to take two pounds."

They groaned.

"You will step up to the wagon, one at a time, and

indicate what type you want. If, by the time you get up here, the meat you want is gone, you will have to make another selection. There will be no trading, and no grumbling. Proceed oldest to youngest, just like always. If an elderly is unable to get up to the line, you may step up for them, but remain fair. Cheaters will be handed over to The General." I checked the other two wagons, and directed how much each person got, and, too soon, the wagons were empty. On their way out of the city the drivers stopped by the mines for coal to take back to their regions.

I pulled the one from Havenden aside, and gave him a small barrel of water. He had a long journey home, and I did not want him to run out. He smiled gratefully, but did not recognize me.

Last time I was home I did not wear this face.

"You should go check on Cerynn's patient." Peter broke the silence, and I looked over my spectacles at him. "Go see how she's doing. She was in the Rak prisons. She survived. You could learn about The General's plans from her." He sat next to me, and took my sewing project out of my hand.

The sewing distracted me from my hunger, but it did not work well. I sent Cerynn down to the Ovens an hour ago, but with the new shipment the cooks would be busy. Our meal would take a while tonight.

Peter fiddled with the top of his cane.

"She's covered with sunstinger stings." He looked at his lap. "Those are from Icecrest. How did it get all the way up here?"

"The Captain." I blurted out his name. I did not know why, but his name screamed at me.

It is him. He did it. Do not trust him.

Peter turned towards me.

"How could it be him? He's a Suit. He's been in Nalaise

with The General. Farther from Icecrest than we are."

"He must have made a detour."

"Why?"

I shrugged.

"He is Inhibited. That is probably how they made it out of the prisons. The General sent them to trap me."

"Okay." Peter nodded slowly. "Okay, I believe you."

My heart jumped.

He believed me.

Finally.

But then I remembered what he said at the picnic and my blood ran cold. He was humoring me. I crossed my arms, and glared at him.

"I believe I told you something was coming, Peter."

"You told me a *war* was coming. You did not say a tortured prisoner was coming."

"Think about it, Peter. How did she get out? No one gets out. No one. It is a trap. The Captain is leading it." I did not want to talk. It gave me a headache talking about the war. I stood, but Peter caught my arm, and rolled up my sleeve.

There was only one cut. I only did one. I needed to.

Peter's jaw twitched and his hand tightened on my arm, but he did not say anything. Slowly, he raised my arm to his lips and kissed the cut. Tears dropped onto my arm, and I pulled away.

I was trying to stop.

I really was.

I just could not.

Peter sighed, kissed my hair, and limped out of the room. I stared at the cut on my arm, willing it to leave. Willing myself to go back and undo it.

It was just one. I had been so good.

Now the angry red scratch mocked me for not keeping my promises.

I tore my eyes away from the cut, before I could be tempted to add more to my arm, and went to go check on

Cerynn's patient.

I *was* curious.

Peter was right.

I wanted to see if she was real. I did not get a good look at her when she was in my room, and I still hated going into her space. She looked so much like my mother, and it hurt to see what she had gone through. I did not like seeing her. Seeing her made me picture my mother going through the same horrible things.

She was such a pure spirit.

She was so kind.

She deserved happiness, not the whips and chains and tears I heard in my visions.

I could not breath. Index, middle, ring, pinkie. Breath. Breath.

No one should go through that.

I leaned against the door-frame, and composed myself, before I made my presence known. Index, middle, ring, pinkie. Breath.

The brooding man, The Captain, sat by the woman's side, clutching her bony, bruised hand. His hands swallowed her tiny one, but he cradled it with a tenderness I did not expect. They told me he had not left her side since he arrived. He was very dedicated to his charge. But Cerynn was right, his hands matched her bruises.

"Tell me about her, Captain." I cleared my throat. He straightened in his chair, eyes never leaving her face. The flickering torch light made her face look sunken and haunted. Cerynn applied a foul smelling poultice to the sunstinger's stings, and the welts faded somewhat, but she still looked horrid.

"When I first saw her, she was unaffected by the war. That was a long time ago."

"You believe there is a war, then?" I interrupted.

His eyes met mine, and then he looked back at the woman.

"Oh, yes. There's a war. Maybe not one with cities burning and bloodshed, but there's a war. I did what I could to stop it, but I don't think I did enough." His hand rose to her face, and he traced her jaw. "I had to get her out of there. She wouldn't have survived much longer. She hasn't spoken much since escaping. When she went into the camps, she was a naive young woman. They stole both from her." His fingers traced the fine lines around her eyes.

"Why does she not talk?"

He stayed quiet a moment, stroking her hair away from her face.

"She was The General's prize. His trophy. He wanted to make sure that she cooperated with him so one day he sat her down in front of him and grabbed the edge of her fingernail with pliers. 'Don't' make a sound' he whispered to her as he started to lift the nail. Of course she made a sound. Of course it hurt. And the more she screamed, the more he pulled. Once he ran out of nails, he started in on the skin on her arms, and her neck. Still, that didn't work, so he resorted to poison. Now, when she speaks, it turns to fire in her blood. But it's psychologically linked, and only works as long as she believes it. She doesn't believe speaking to me will hurt, so it doesn't hurt. It preys on fear, just like the Raks."

Her hand twitched on the bed, and he covered it with his, curling his fingers between hers.

"You want to know what she's like, Ms. McCain?"

I only nodded as I tried to erase the images my mind painted of her torture.

"I begged her nearly everyday to run away with me. And everyday, she refused."

I started to speak, but he stopped me.

"Not because she like being there, but because she feared what The General would do to anyone he blamed for her escape. The guards tortured and raped her, yet she feared what would happen to them if she escaped. She said no matter what anyone did, they didn't deserve his wrath. She would rather remain as his prisoner, than allow him to hurt anyone else. That's who she is."

"A glutton for punishment?" I rolled the tears from my eyes.

"No!" He glared at me. "She's selfless. She pretends to be stronger than she really is. I'm sure you've noticed that." He pointed to an obserling perched in the corner. He knew we were watching him. "She's terrified of her own shadow, though. Your obserling won't show that. She's afraid he's going to find her again. Afraid they're going to capture her. She's afraid of who he's going to kill before he finds her." He paused, and looked at her, swallowing hard.

"Out there, three of her children died. Her fears came true, and The General killed the children to try convince her to come back. When she woke up a few hours ago, she didn't remember their deaths. I didn't tell her. I couldn't. It's not something you just blurt out. I would appreciate it if you, and the others working here, would allow me to be the one to tell her when she's well enough to take it."

The coppery scent of blood almost overpowered me, and I coughed in spite of myself. A faint trickle of blood ran down her chin. Cerynn told me she couldn't find the source. The blood appeared without reason, and any procedure to stop the bleeding would be dangerous. We agreed to leave it for the time being.

"Why does The General want her back so bad?"

"She was his prize. He owned her for cycles."

A lump rose in my throat as I focused on the purple bruises around her neck. Perfect hand-print bruises.

"He was killing her. I couldn't let him. Will you keep her safe?"

"Nobody is ever safe." I said without thinking and his face fell. The woman's labored breathing rattled in her chest, and The Captain kept patting her nervously, making sure she was still alive. I touched his shoulder, and he looked up at me. "I will do what I can."

"Dinner's done." Cerynn carried a tray into the dining room, and lit the torches around the room. "I got a plate for The Captain like you asked, though I think you should make him buy it. We don't have much food, we can't afford more mouths, too." She disappeared down the hall to fetch The Captain as we sat at our long table.

I always invited those who did not have much food to dine with us, and we always had extra people at our table. If we combined our rations, and sent a load down to the cooks, each person got a decent helping, rather than some getting enough, and others starving.

Tonight, though, we did not have many extras. The new shipment allowed everyone to eat without worry for one night. Tonight, only Josh and Roland were our extras. Josh did not have a family, and Roland's father made poor choices. Roland did not go home if he did not have to.

Cerynn and The Captain were just sitting down when an alarm sounded in the courtyard.

"Attention residents of The Purple City of Coal, please join me for a Demonstration." The General's voice range out.

Peter grabbed my hand, and pulled me close to him as we walked into the courtyard. The Captain paled behind us, glancing nervously across the courtyard to the healira.

"Christa. She's in there. He can't find her. Please."

"Go through the back of the healira. Do not wake the lacelights, and keep your head low."

He nodded.

"Thank you."

"Captain." I called. He turned back towards me. "You work for The General. I am not protecting you. I am protecting her."

He nodded. He knew.

"Have you gotten any fliers of new laws?" Peter whispered as we stepped into the courtyard. Demonstrations illustrated punishments inflicted on those who broke laws, but we had not had new laws in cycles. I shook my head, and focused on The General.

He would not recognize me. When we last met, I was young, with red hair and green eyes. That was the Àraid he killed. He would not look twice at my blonde hair and grey eyes.

He stood in the middle of the courtyard. Someone knelt in front of him with a bag over their head. Rak guards raided the buildings, and threw my people into the street. They did not go into the healira.

Not yet.

One of the guards held a board with two wanted posters on it.

One of Alice.

One of The Captain.

Both had high prices on their heads. More than anyone in my tiny city would ever see.

"Ladies and gentleman." The General clapped his hands, and the crowd went silent. Some of the guards reemerged from the houses, eating my people's food. Their *only* food. The General pointed to the poster of The Captain. "This is my dear friend. He's highly paid, and highly trained. I have reason to believe that he has been brainwashed by this woman." He paused to point to Alice's picture.

"She is very ill, and unstable. She escaped an esteemed healira in Nalaise, and needs to be returned as soon as possible. They were medicating her insanity, and without our Healers help, she will revert. In that place, she is very dangerous." He pulled the bag off the figure kneeling in front of him. One of the women that went missing half a season ago. I knew he was taking them. The Dragon perched on The General's shoulder hissed at the woman.

"If you see either of these people, please report it. Anyone found hiding them will be executed."

His dragon flew down to the woman, and bit into her throat.

The demonstration.

The visual aid of his punishment.

Peter's arm tightened around me as the woman fell to the cobblestone. A child screamed and ran to her, and the dragon killed him, too. I motioned for my people to stay still, and The General smiled.

"Have you seen either person?" He crossed over to me, and pointed, again, to the posters. Over his shoulder, I saw The Captain peeking out of the healira. His eyes filled with fear, and his lips moved in a silent plea. "If you hand them over now, I won't hurt anyone."

"You already hurt people, General." I hissed. The Rak guards allowed a man through their barricade, and he wept over his dead wife and son.

"Have you seen either of them?" The General asked again. The Captain ducked out of view as he surveyed the courtyard.

"No. I have not seen them." My eyes never left the dead woman as I lied to The General.

"Storm the buildings. Make sure she's not here."

The guards nodded, and dispersed into the town, but they never looked in the healira. It was too obvious a hiding place. It never occurred to them to look there.

"To the women of the town: you will no longer work in the mines, you will work in the bar. My guards will require entertainment on their breaks, and you will provide it. Or you will join your friends." He kicked the dead boy, and sneered. "My guards will be stationed at the gates, monitoring everyone coming in, and leaving the city. All the men will double their work in the mines to make up for the women. The children will spend their days with the Rak guards. They will be trained our way, and when they are of age, they will be sent to Nalaise for job assignment."

He met my eyes, and his eyes sparkled in triumph.

"People of the Purple City, you are no longer Rak-free."

Cerynn

"**W**ill I be sent away?" Jess broke the silence. I poked the food on my plate.

"Not yet, Jess. You're not old enough yet."

"How old do I need to be?"

My mother dropped her fork, and slammed a hand into the table.

"Can we just eat our food? Must we talk about what happened?" Her hands shook, and she twisted her left hand in her right hand. Her tell. Her fear.

"But I want to know!"

"You want to know what will happen, Jess?" Mother pinned him in her glare. "The Raks will come collect you. They will take you up to Nalaise for job assignment. They will strip you down so they can fit you for a uniform, and they will see your earrings, like mine, will not come out. Then, they will kill. Is that what you want to know, Jess?" Her body trembled, and Peter quickly stood and hurried around the table. He pulled her into his arms, and smoothed her hair, which faded to a deep maroon. Josh nudged my arm, and pointed to her hair. We were not used to being Àraid. I still had not learned about our powers.

Jess set his fork down, and looked at his lap.

"I don't want to die."

"We need to get out." Peter whispered.

"Out where?" Mother's frustration made us all tense. "His hands are in all the regions. We have nowhere to go."

"I'm sorry." The Captain whispered to his half empty plate. "I'm sorry I brought him here. He wouldn't have bothered you if I hadn't come."

"True. You should have stayed with The General." Mother's tone was sharp.

"I couldn't let her stay with him. I couldn't watch that anymore."

Mother pursed her lips. She looked like she was fighting herself. Jaycobe and Ginny sat across from me, but kept their eyes on their plates.

Wooden utensils scraped wooden plates as the dining room fell into silence. Outside, we heard the Rak guards kicking open doors; raiding homes. They wouldn't bother us. Healers were respected, and they wouldn't risk The General's wrath messing with the only two Healers in Coaltree. Not after they killed the one up in the Blue City. Mother took a few more bites, then sighed and pushed her plate away.

"He said she was in a healira in Nalaise. He said she brainwashed you."

The General's claims echoed in everyone's head, but nobody thought she would confront The Captain directly.

"He lied. She was his. She belonged to him."

"And you?"

"I was Alice's Suit. I cared for her when he was done with her." He got up from the table; picking up his plate.

"Captain, the cooks will make rounds to get the plates." I pointed out, but he merely shrugged.

"I'll take care of it." As he walked down the hall, my mother and I followed him. There was nowhere to "take care" of the plate. The cooks did that later. He ducked into the healira, and Mother and I stood just outside the door, craning our necks to see what he was doing.

Alice watched him cautiously as he pulled a chair closer to her bed. He balanced the plate on his lap, and helped her sit up enough to eat.

"You haven't had fruit in fourteen cycles. I brought you some fresh witchberries. You once said those were your favorite." He broke the witchberry pod in half and scooped the tiny berries into his spoon. Alice's eyes widened as he spooned it into her mouth. She looked as if she'd never tasted them before. She smiled as he helped her finish the fruit. But after that she was worn out, and drifted back into a fitful sleep. The Captain finished the plate while he watched her.

Her hand wrapped tightly around her necklace, and the necklace mother gave her sat on the table. Mother reached in and grabbed it, but The Captain stopped her.

"Thank you for trying to calm her. Usually necklaces don't help."

"I had to try." She shoved the necklace into her pocket.

"Where did you get it? Those gems are expensive."

My mother's eyes darted over to Alice, and she grabbed her left hand again.

"My mother gave it to me at my first wedding."

"Your first?"

"She did not make it to my second wedding." As she turned away from the bed, tears dropped from her eyes. I'd never seen my mother cry before. She pulled the necklace from her pocket, and studied it as we walked the corridor back to the main part of the house. We both paused as we passed the windows looking into the courtyard. Goosebumps rose on my arms. The grandmother of the boy murdered in the Demonstration sat in the courtyard. She held her dead grandson in her arms, and sang to him as she waited for dawn. We never buried bodies in the night.

She sang the song of the coal mines. The song of bloodied hands and tired bones. The song of cave-ins, and despair.

   The lullaby of orphans who outlived their parents, and children.

Alice

"*Run. I want to see you fight for your freedom.*" His whip slashed the backs of my legs, and I jumped. The gates were open; my chains undone. "*I want to watch you run.*" He shoved me forward, and I stumbled out into the desert.

On the horizon, I saw the ice lakes of the Iceloch Region. The General would not cross the border. I would be safe if I made it there. His whip bit into my back again, and I didn't wait for a third lash. He limited my food, and I was so weak now. I ran as fast as I could, but hardly made any progress. His laughter echoed behind me, and his whip wrapped around my ankle. I fell into the scalding sand, but as I spit it out, the sand around me turned to water.

Freezing, deep water.

I gasped as ice cooled the burns on my feet and back. I coughed, trying to rid myself of the liquid invading my lungs so rudely. He was getting closer now and water poured from him, washing over me as he laughed. My eyes could barely focus on the Iceloch Region. I didn't make it. He smiled and laughed again.

"*You'll never escape. I waited too long, and fought too hard to get you. No way will I just let you go.*" The

General snapped his whip again, and I cringed. "I'm coming for you. Your only shelter is me."

I panicked, flailing in the ice water. More liquid filled my lungs and I coughed again. He reached me and grabbed my arm, screaming my name; shaking me.

My eyes flew open.

"Alice?" The Captain's concern was almost touching. I coughed, and he covered my mouth with a cloth. When he pulled it away, the white stained red with blood. I gasped at the stain, and ended up coughing more. The Captain tried to calm me, but the harder I tried to control my breathing, the harder it got.

More metallic liquid bubbled up my throat. I couldn't inhale. I was choking, drowning in blood. The Captain put a cool hand on my head and quieted me with a sound. His hand moved down my arm and stopped on the deep scar in my wrist.

His fingers rubbed the smooth white gouge. I wanted to stop him. I didn't want to forget. He looked at me apologetically, and drove his thumb deep into the scar. Lights flashed in my eyes, and then there was nothing.

† † † † †

61st Day, The Season Of Death, 729-PW

I finally convinced the child to tell me her name. She's opening up to me. Her name is Chrissy. Her mother passed away. She wouldn't tell me how. Her father sent a snake to a random home. He didn't pick me specifically. She said he couldn't afford her, and sent the letter as a last ditch effort to keep her alive. I liked that I was the one to get *the letter. I hated to think what would have happened to her had she ended up in Nalaise. She might have been sold. Or murdered like Micheal was.*

Today she sent me out for a few hours so she could prepare my birthday dinner. My birthday is tomorrow, but I don't want to celebrate it. Micheal and I used to always have a quiet dinner, and retreat to our room. We would make a tent out of the sheets, and giggle and share secrets until dawn. Well... between other things of course. But Micheal is gone now. My first birthday without him. I can't think about it without crying. It might be nice to start a new tradition with this child. But when she asked me to go away for a while, she didn't say she needed to decorate. She said she needed 'to learn for the birthday'. Odd phrasing. One of the guys in town said wording like that sounded Àraid. But that isn't possible. The Àraid are dead. Right?

"*Èlđũhèʌ.*"
"*Fire*"
"*Ʒū̃ɾмèʌṯ.*"
"*Storm.*" Chrissy's voice filtered in from the backyard, but I didn't know who she was talking to.
"*Lèħđṯ'Çvï̈l.*"
"*Time*"

"Jꝺřïлèɽa."

"Life."

"No. No. No" He sounded frustrated; unusually angry at her mistake. "Jꝺřïлèɽa is earth. You get that one wrong every time! You have to think! Focus!"

I saw him through the window. A dirty, faded flannel shirt hung off his frame, though he must have once filled it out nicely. Stubble covered his chin and neck, and dirty hands twisted in a nervous tic. He paced anxiously, agitated by whatever they were going over. He kept glancing back at the house, eyes filled with paranoia and something I couldn't place.

My daughter sat at his feet. The sleeves of her too-loose sweater fell to her elbows, and cuts and bruises covered her arms. Her eyes never left her hands as he stooped and added another cut to the inside of her arm.

I covered my mouth, appalled, too shocked to run to her. His expression was like that of a parent forced to punished a child, but the knife he pressed through her skin wasn't discipline.

She never moved; didn't even look at him as the knife parted her tender skin. My shock wore off and I rushed towards the door, but my feet grew cold and froze to the floor. I glanced back out the window and watched blood run down my child's arm.

"Go over what you know about the races of The Àraid." The man barked. Chrissy sighed.

"We have done this already." She protested.

"Yes, and you got it wrong. Go back and don't mess up. This is important." He was gentle again, crouching in front of her and holding her arm encouragingly.

"The Àraid. A species created above the human race, with abilities meant to better the world.

The lowest rank of the Àraid is the Lèħ̱ꝺ̱'Çvïl Zₘèлçïa. They see the consequences of their actions, and those they touch. They are the only one of the three rankings that won't willingly reproduce with the Raks. The Lèħ∂ʇ'Çvïl Ƶʍèʌçïa would be too plagued by their actions if they tried to merge bloodlines. They also can move through time, and freeze time. When the Àraid were in control, they would slow time down. This allowed the humans to fulfill their quota for the day, and still have time to live. Mixing them with humans creates Freezers and Jumpers." Her hands wavered in the air and she heaved a tired sigh.

"Freezers can stop time for a few hours. Freezers make good Healers because they can pause the injuries of their patient. They also make good criminals because they are never caught. They are rarely seen, and prefer to live between time.

Jumpers teleport, but are limited to teleport in space, not time. They make good messengers. They do not handle conflict well, and, if they have not gotten control of their powers, they are likely to accidentally teleport when faced with stressful situations." She sounded like she was reciting a textbook.

The man stalked out of sight. My stomach tied in uncomfortable knots as I tried to figure out where he went. I twisted my necklace through my fingers, waiting. Chrissy's voice never faltered.

"Next up in the ranks are the Aʇvaɾ Ƶʍèʌçïa. The face-changers and mind-readers. They can turn into anyone and anything. They are glossed over and most likely to go to the Rak side because they want to be known. Mixing them with humans creates Seers and Shadows.

Seers read minds, and plant thoughts. They are sought out for advice, but they do not get any visions; they merely make predictions by reading thoughts.

Shadows mimic living faces, and are hired mostly for entertainment. They can do a play with only a few, and morph their face into their character. People do not consider that Shadows could also impersonate them, and steal from them easily." Her hands shook.

"*Last is the Ĵðṛïлѐṛa Ʒмѐлçïa. They control elements. Able to cause fire at a thought, or drown their enemies in rain. They also construct forests in an instant and can emit an electric charge so powerful it knocks out those around them. They were the first to breed with the Raks, and the most dangerous to do so. Their abilities don't directly correlate with responsibility toward the human race. They are least likely to have any guilt, and create the most ruthless Hybrids. Mixing them with humans creates Lights and Nights.*" She collapsed onto the ground, but the man didn't say anything. He still paced somewhere out of my view.

"*Light's powers are limited to fire, and are best suited in the coal mines. They carry a constant glow around them, and can never find darkness. Some people think the Lights are not gifted, but cursed.*

Nights remove all light, and use their abilities to get out of uncomfortable situations. Able to plunge any situation into blinding darkness. Their abilities only fail when put against Lights, and the two avoid each-other at all costs." She paused to breathe.

"*At the top of the ranks, encompassing all of the lower ranks are the Vèçлÿ Ètèṛлa; unending eternals. The royal race. They are very very rare. It is rumored that only the mix of Ètèṛлa and Hybrid blood will create the Ṛèxṭaÿлǎ, who is prophesied to signal the return of the King. I am a Vèçлÿ Ètèṛлa. You are a Ĵðṛïлѐṛa Ʒмѐлçïa.*"

"And what are the shortened nicknames of the rankings?" His voice was right behind me, and I stifled a scream. He smiled a wobbly smile and grabbed my arm, dragging me outside.

"*The Çvïl. The Aлṭvaṛ. The Ĵðṛďïл. And the Ètèṛлa-*" Her voice died away as he dragged me across the yard. Our eyes met, and something swirled in hers.

Anger?

"She was spying on us. She's heard too much." The man

shook me.

Chrissy's face changed to panic, and her eyes darted to the knife he left sitting on the stone next to him. When he released my arm and bent down for the knife I grabbed Chrissy, and pulled her back towards the house. Once we were through the door she slammed it shut and leaned against it. I reached for the sword Micheal left us, but as my hand stretched over the table the door burst open, sending Chrissy into the wall.

The man threw his knife and pinned my arm to the table. I screamed as my skin slowly stained red. He sauntered into the room, laughing a crazed laugh.

"We can't have humans knowing too much. Could be dangerous to the plan."

I grabbed the sword with my other hand, but I was weak and it was heavy. The man twisted it from my hands, and the metal melted over his arms.

"Elder Vaлṯij, why are you doing this?" Chrissy's voice was tiny, but did not waver.

"Elder Vaлṯij is dead, Child." He spat. "I killed him so I could get to you. You are very important." He turned back to me and held up his hand. Lightning shot from his fingers into the carpet at my feet. I screamed and jumped away, hand still pinned to the table. Chrissy let out a high pitched whistle, her face contorting in anger. Her hair, once a bright blonde, sank to blood red, and her eyes glowed violet.

"Stay away from my mother!" She pounced on him, clinging to him like a cat and scratching his eyes. He burst into flames and she dropped away, whimpering.

The floor lit and the flames soon found the rug I was standing on. I tried the pull the dagger out of my wrist, but it sank deep into the wood and wouldn't budge. He came towards me again, unaffected by the flames. He grabbed my arm and twisted it behind my back. My knee came up and caught him where his legs met his body, and he crumpled to the flaming carpet. My daughter stood over him. The flames danced in her eyes.

"Èlđúħèл." She mumbled. Violet flames engulfed his body, and his skin peeled back from his face, revealing black, shiny scales. Rak.

"Liar!" She screamed, kicking him over and over again. I grabbed my pinned hand and pulled with all my might. The dagger remained deep in the wood; blood glistening on the blade. My hand hung limp at the end of my arm, broken and bleeding, but free. The flames in the cabin grew higher, covering the furniture.

"You lied to me! You killed my friend and he was not finished activating me. What do I do now?" She wailed over the crackling fire.

"It won't matter. You'll be dead soon." He croaked. He reached up and pulled her down, her face inches from his. "The Raks are much smarter than you think. And with all the knowledge they now have on you, you'll be an easy one to fool." He chuckled, his laugh growing into a hysterical wail as lava flowed from her hands onto his chest.

She ran to me and pulled me out of the burning building, and we watched the flames consume and die down from a hill not far away. My beautiful house. Micheal's house. I shouldn't care about such a worldly thing, but I choked back tears as the memories burned below me.

Chrissy stared at the flames, and her voice whispered beneath out-of-control curls that she didn't brush out of her face.

"I killed him, Mama. I got so mad I killed him and I didn't even know I was doing it." Her arms shook as I wrapped her in my cloak.

"How did you do all that stuff back there?"

Her hair still hadn't returned to its natural color, but her eyes were once again hazel.

"It was easy. It is who I am." She shrugged, and held my arm up for inspection. Then she smiled and held her hand

over the cut. "Læχlïezè."
The wound repaired itself.
"I am sorry. This is not the birthday party I wanted to give you."

My eyes fluttered open, and my heart clenched at the memories that I tried so hard to forget. And then they were gone. Once again lost to my broken mind.

The Captain slept in the chair next to the bed, his head resting on a fist. His other hand clutched mine, and as I blinked the blurriness from my eyes, his eyes opened and met mine. His pained expression begged me to forgive him. I patted the bed, searching for my parchment, and then I poised my quill over the parchment.

<u>What's wrong, Captain?</u>
He just shook his head and sighed.

"You know I don't keep my promises. Why do you keep expecting me to?"

I was confused, and started to write out my questions, but as he withdrew his hand, a wound on my side burned. My hand clutched at it, trying to ease the pain.

"What's wrong?" The Captain reached for the sheets, ready to pull them back and inspect the injury. I grabbed a handful of the covers and pulled them up under my chin. I would not let him see. I couldn't remember what I was hiding, but I knew he shouldn't see.

"Alice, now is not the time to be shy." He admonished, gently detangling my fingers from the fabric. He flung the covers back and bared my torso, naked apart from the bandages wrapped around my shattered ribs, and some fabric wrapped loosely over my chest. His hands fell to his side, face expressionless.

An assortment of bruises covered me from shoulders to hips. Some were small, the size of the tip of a finger; others were about the size one would get from being kicked. Most were an ugly dark purple, but the older ones had faded to a nasty green-yellow.

"Who did this to you?" His voice barely reigned in the anger I could see just below the surface. His hands clenched and unclenched, and a muscle in his jaw flexed. A trembling hand reached out and traced one of the bruises, mesmerized.

"Was it one of the men in the last city? Did they do this to you while we were hiding?" He was getting more worked up, his voice rising. "Who did this to you, Counselor?" He yelled; frantic.

I don't remember. The quill trembled in my hand. _Every time I wake up, I have new bruises. I don't know how I get them._

Fury washed across his face, barely controlled. A frustrated scream escaped his mouth as he lunged at the wall, punching the stone. When he pulled his hand back, the knuckles were bloody. One finger twisted awkwardly where he hadn't properly prepared for the punch.

"The General is doing this. He's messing with us." He swore under his breath, and hit the wall, flat-handed. "Why didn't you tell me sooner? I could have done more to protect you." His hands raked through his hair as he paced the room. Any response I gave him now would only make him angrier. The rawness of his fury frightened me. I didn't know what to expect from him. He stopped and sighed.

"Counselor." He started slow. "How long has this been going on?"

I can't remember.

He sat on the edge of the bed and placed a gentle hand on my swollen belly. The baby kicked, hard, and my stomach seized; spasming over and over again. My hand covered his, but I couldn't meet his level gaze. I tried not to cringe. My stomach relaxed and my hand released. I was old to be going down the parenthood road again. I wondered if that was why this one was harder.

"I think you need to start wearing the corset again. They cannot know you're pregnant."

My heart dropped. I did not want to be confined to that thing again, but he was right. I would be safer with it on. I only nodded to him. I couldn't speak. The Captain leaned over and placed his face next to the swell.

"Hello, this is your father. I need to let you know something, now, so you can prepare. Your mommy is a very frustrating woman. She keeps too much to herself and doesn't let anyone help her. One of these days she's going to get in way over her head. But don't worry, I'll be right there to save her. Just thought you should know, so you wouldn't be worried." He smiled up at me as I chuckled and ran a hand across his back.

Then he pulled a new corset out from under the bed. He must have stashed it there while I was asleep. This one was black, to match the Coaltree dress-code. I loved not wearing the clothing The General flaunted me in.

I was too weak to sit up, so he held me off of the bed, and situated the corset under me, so I could lay down, and lace it up. It was so tight. I could barely breathe. He tried to tie it tighter, and I grabbed my necklace.

I stroked the necklace so I wouldn't say anything to him about the corset, but as I gripped the charm in my hand, The Captain rubbed his chest and grimaced. His eyes locked on my necklace, and he put a hand out to stop my rubbing. But he did not take it away from me.

"I'm sorry. It needs to be tight enough not to show." Sadness filled his eyes as he pulled the laces tighter. "The Raks are searching for you, and if they find you, they will return you to him. You know what will happen if he finds out."

I didn't know what would happen, but I didn't want to find out.

Inhibited

"**Y**ou said this was the one. You said you had her."

"*I'm sorry. I thought it was her, I swear. She fit the description.*"

"**Did she? Then why is her arm still broken? If she fit the description her arm would not be broken.**"

"*I didn't think to test that. I'm sorry. I should have thought of that.*"

"**Yes. You really should have. You'll not screw up again. Look at the crows. My crows. Watch them as you die. They'll circle above and when you die they'll come and peck your brain. As you watch my birds circle above, you will wish you tested her before lying to me.**"

Inhibited

Cerynn

Paintings lined the hallway. Mother always surrounded herself with art she related to. She'd bought spelled frames from Nalaise, and the pictures changed every ten minutes.

Peter wanted to discuss our defenses, in case the guards decided to raid the healira. He wanted to meet me in his office, and I hoped it was down this hallway, but every step took me farther down an unfamiliar corridor.

A whirring started to my right, and was soon joined on the left. The doorways started shifting, and disappearing. The house began to shuffle, again. I stopped, sighed, and placed a palm on a painting.

"Don't forget I'm in here." I muttered. The doors across from me were moving and changing. One opened and a hallway unfolded behind it. A wall shot up on both sides of me, giving me only that hall as a path. In less than thirty seconds the house calmed down again, the rooms inside it now shuffled.

"Okay, where have you put the office?" I whispered to the house. The painting I touched changed to a map of the house. A yellow path traced its way through newly formed hallways, leading from my location to my destination. As I walked through the new hallway, the paintings on both sides changed to show the map. I spent twenty minutes twisting and retracing my way through the house, and eventually reached the office.

"What took so long?" Peter was on duty for the next two hours, but had been expecting me at the start of his shift.

"I was trying to get Mother to tell me about the Àraid."

"She still won't speak?" Peter's eyes never left the parchments on his desk. Josh was behind on the mail today, so Peter volunteered to go through some of it.

"No! She says it's 'unsafe to discuss such matters in the presence of prying ears' and that it's 'not an important use of my energies to dwell on fantasies'."

"That sounds like her. Don't push. You're more than an hour late."

"The house shuffled on my way here, again. Put us at opposite ends." I rolled my eyes, annoyed at the parental tone he used.

"It's been shuffling a lot lately. This house is as paranoid as your mother."

She designed it to shuffle when it detected a threat, but we hadn't yet discovered whatever threat the house thought we faced.

The office was small. If I stood in the middle of the room and stretched my arms to both sides, I could touch the walls. Peter liked the closed off space, but I felt claustrophobic just looking in. Javis O'Surry, the current law-checker, was supposed to be on duty too, filing the rest of the paperwork, but his chair stood empty.

"He didn't show." Peter said, jabbing a thumb behind him at the empty chair. "Seems to be slow today so I think I can handle it alone, but we're going to need to talk to him. Last time he showed, he was so drunk my senses slowed just from the fumes. It ain't professional. S'all I'm saying."

"Well, I'll see what I can do." I'd fix it. I fixed everything. "What did you want to talk about? And while you're at it can you tell me everything you know about the Àraid?" I hit him with my most convincing 'daddy-do-this-for-me-and-I'll-love-you' smile. I liked to play that card. So did Jaycobe and Ginny. We preyed on his need to be accepted as our father. He usually did whatever we wanted, but this time he just shuffled his parchment, and shook his head.

"Sorry, Cerynn. If your mom says no, she must have a reason. She's kept it from you this long, a little longer shouldn't matter. Right?"

"Right." I muttered and focused on a birdcage in the corner of the room. "What's that doing here?"

"Oh, he was in the healira the night Alice was stung. I wanted to review his memories to see if I could see who planted the sunstinger."

"And have you found anything?" I found that little obserling in the woods a few days ago. His wing was broken so I took him to the healira, and when his wing healed, he wanted to stay. Very territorial birds; obserlings.

"I tried, but I couldn't find it in the memories." He opened the cage, and held up a blank sheet of parchment. The little bird hopped onto the table, and opened his beak. His memories drifted out of his mouth, and played across the parchment.

We saw The Captain pacing by the bed, agitated. He left view of the bird. Minutes later he stalked back into view, and crossed to Alice's side. His broad shoulders nearly blocked her from view. He bent down and whispered something to her. They seemed to be deep in conversation.

"I think if he planted the bug, it would be now." Peter spoke up. "He could be holding it in tweezers, forcing it to sting her but not releasing the bug. That would explain why we couldn't find it."

"That would work, but what's his motive? Why would he want to sting her?" I leaned closer to the image playing on the parchment. Peter shrugged.

"We have the when and the how, but not why. He seems to love her. I don't know why he'd inflict that pain."

We turned back to the memories, and watched The Captain. He continued talking, or stinging, Alice a few moments more, and then he straightened and left again, coming back a few minutes later with some coffee and book.

Then the memories scrambled.

"What is that? What happened?" I frowned and stroked the bird, hoping to calm it to clear its memories.

"I've been over and over his memories." Peter shook his head. "Obserlings record whatever they see. This is what the room looked like at the time. I don't know what caused it, or how it's possible."

"Could somebody plant the sunstinger here?"

"Maybe, but the obserlings outside the healira show nobody entering during this time."

The bird shut its mouth, and Peter flicked a grape its direction. It pounced on the fruit, and rolled it into the cage. Peter and I stared at the blank parchment for a minute, and Peter cleared his throat.

"I sent some obserlings out to patrol the perimeter, but one of them didn't get a good view. The picture was dark. Could you go check that section of the woods?" Peter gestured to a portion on the map. I agreed and took my leave. I needed to go out and check the mines anyway. Josh didn't like the forest, but he needed to exercise his horse, and followed close behind me.

The Lullaby of Coal had been running through my head all day. Josh shivered as I sang the haunting tune, and the willworths joined in the song. Copy-cat birds without a call of their own. They copied anything they heard. But with my own little choir, the song seemed even eerier.

Sawbills flew along side the willworths, and snapped at anything that got too close to the song birds. Willworths had no choice but to translate sound, and sawbills took it upon themselves to protect the helpless birds. Nobody knew why, but they were always found together.

The tops of the trees jutted above the buildings as we passed through the town. Children stopped playing their games to watch us parade by. Women with red-ringed eyes peeked out of the bar, but the Rak guards pulled them roughly away from the windows. The children cringed at the cries coming from within the bar.

Most of the children now played in front of the healira. Usually they never dared get so close to my mother, but right now she seemed safer than the Raks. They looked up at me through tears, and pleaded with me to save them. When we first moved here, it wasn't a Rak-free city. My mother drove them out. But she could not do that now. Not now that she was protecting Alice, and The Captain.

Josh and I reached the edge of town, nothing before us but forest, and plunged into the sweet smelling pine. The suns were still high in the sky when we reached the crest of the hill and looked down at the forest below. We both stopped, stunned.

Before us, blanketing the scalding desert, was the forest. My forest. I expected to see the orange-brown of dead leaves the maple trees fell asleep for the Season Of Death, but before me the trees were a deep black, their trunks dark grey, oozing black sap. We moved slowly between the trees. It felt like we were entering a tomb. Nothing moved. The wind didn't even stir the blackened leaves. The entire forest was poisoned. The willworths and sawbills wouldn't fly past the edge of the poisoned trees, and their song stopped abruptly.

We came to a clearing. There was someone in the middle of the clearing, propped up by a sharp spike protruding from his chest. His arms were limp at his side, and his head lolled back unnaturally. I motioned to Josh to stay hidden and approached the body.

The clothing was torn, and the black of Coaltree was

crusted with blood. His fingers were twisted and purple, bruised where they'd broken. Something had reached inside his arm and pulled muscle and tendon out and snapped them in two. His legs sagged, putting the full weight of the body on the spike.

Strewn on the leaves at his feet were his organs, but his heart was ripped out and tied, hanging, from his left hand. Tied around the ring finger. The face was eaten away, skin hanging from the sides and jaw. The eyes were white, and, as I looked closer, I saw maggots crawling through the whiteness. His jaw hung, slack, and a tongue, black and forked, flicked out between rotting lips. I took a half step back before realizing it was just a snake, curled in his mouth, and not a Rak.

I turned, ready to flee, when I saw something posted to a nearby tree.

Resisted and abandoned our law, punishment shall be dealt.

Beneath the post was a name.

Javis O'Surry.

Our Law-checker who didn't show up for work. I knew him. He often ate meals with us. He played with my siblings.

I looked back at the deformed body and shivered.

Christa

Rumors buzzed through my town. Word spread quickly about Javis, and I had no idea how to handle the onslaught of questions thrown at me.

"Who killed him?"

"Was it personal?"

"Are we in any danger?"

The Rak guards only laughed when I asked them what they planned to do with the body.

"We put him there, why do you think we'll do anything else with him?"

"Is this another Demonstration?" I had not received any law updates, but I had not gotten one for the last Demonstration either. The guards looked at each-other and shrugged.

"Why not? Yeah, it's a Demonstration of what happens to you if you say you've seen her, and you haven't." One guard leaned close to me, and hissed in my ear. "Or it could be what happens to liars who claim she's not inside this city. We know she's here, and we will find her."

Chills rolled down my arms, and I was glad of the sleeves I wore. They would see the goosebumps otherwise. The guard's head ducked down close to my ear, and his tongue traced my earlobe.

"Those are lovely earrings you're wearing. You can take them off, though, right?"

I froze. His arms wrapped around me, and his teeth closed around my earring, but he did not pull on it; he simply went back to sucking on my ear.

Do not push him away.

His lips moved across my jaw, and my knife burned in my pocket. It would not be hard to slip it through his throat. Kill him right here. But with his friend watching so closely I would not get away with it.

"Maybe I'll just take you for myself. I hear Healers are wild behind closed doors. They know all the right moves."

"Oh, she does, Lieutenant Vos." The Captain stepped out of the healira, and shut the door tightly behind him. He winked at me, and made a crude gesture. "But her competence in the bedroom isn't why we're here. We're here to find the escaped prisoner."

Both guards stood at attention, and saluted The Captain. I frowned.

He should stay hidden.

They were not supposed to know he was here. He nodded to me, and then addressed the guards.

"I would like to speak to Ms. McCain alone in the house."

The guards nudged each-other, and laughed.

"Okay, Boss. You "speak" to her. We got your back."

I blushed, but The Captain silenced my protest and pulled me into the house.

"Why did you stop me? They think you are... that we are..." I trailed off and blushed.

"Let them. If they think you're mine, they'll leave you alone."

"Captain, I am married. I do not want that reputation, even if it is false."

The Captain grabbed my arms, and shook me.

"They don't care about marriage, Christa. Nothing, not marriage, not status, not gender, will stop them. It's better they think you're protected by me. Believe me." He shuddered.

"Why do they even know you are here? Is that not dangerous?"

"I convinced them that I was transporting Alice from The General's house to the healira. Which is true." He hastened before I could correct him. "I told them she slipped away from me. I convinced them I didn't "go rouge." I didn't abandon The General. I've been tracking her, and needed to stop here when my horse died."

"And what good could come from this?"

"I'm on the inside now." His eyes gleamed. "I can get first-hand information. That could be helpful."

"Did you kill Javis O'Surry?"

Why did I question him directly?

His eyes closed off, and he glanced at his hands.

"No. I didn't know Javis O'Surry."

"I did not ask if you knew him. You killed him. I will prove it." I crossed my arms.

"I'm not your enemy. You need to trust me."

I did not believe him.

I wanted to get him out of my city. I wanted to bring the body back to my city, and bury him properly. The Captain stood between me and the door, and would not let me pass.

"Give it twenty more minutes, and walk a little crooked when you leave."

"Why?"

He smirked.

"They'll be timing me. I have a reputation to maintain."

My dragon met me as soon as I stepped into the forest, glad I finally came to visit him. I stroked his scales gently, kicking myself for not coming out more often. He must get awfully lonely hiding from everyone out here.

"Have you been keeping busy, Χðaṯ?" I smiled up at him. He snorted steam from his nose and his yellow scales lit up.

"I know you are mad. Things got busy in town." I fumbled for an excuse. He turned his head away. "Oh come on. You know I would never forget about you. It is just with all this observation it is not safe to visit."

A groan rumbled in his throat, dragging out and pitching up.

"If you are so lonely you should go to The Uncharted. You would find a mate there." My heart clenched at the thought of losing him. Χðaṯ hatched for me when I was only four cycles old, and followed me ever since. But he could not stay hidden forever. He could not stay alone forever.

His head snapped up and he narrowed his gaze at me. I held up my hands in surrender.

"Fine. You say you are happy here, I will believe you." I started deeper into the forest, and he followed silently beside. "I just worry you will be found. Only The General can own dragons." I chuckled as he grunted back at me. "I know I do not *own* you, but I fear The General will not allow such logic."

The leaves scattered over the forest floor swirled around us as we walked, and Χðaṯ batted a few in the air. He bounced around happily as we walked, excited I finally joined him again, but his joy faded when we reached the edge of the poisoned forest. As I stepped into the blackened forest he hissed desperately, but would not reach over the line to pull me back.

"Come on." I beckoned him, but he refused to cross the line. I wished he would come with me, but I plunged on alone.

It felt heavy here.

Oppressed.

The trees were dead.

Gone was the constant chatter between birch and elm. They stood tall and dark against the sky.

I wanted to scream, to run, to hide in my mother's arms and let her make it all better again. But that would not happen. I knew, I just would not accept it. I gingerly stepped through the dead forest, chilled.

I should not be here.

I was trespassing.

I could already smell the body, my heightened senses picking up the worst of the stench.

I always sought comfort in my forest. It offered me the solace I needed.

They invaded my sanctuary. This forest was dead, desolate and alone.

I was an intruder now.

Some dark evil chose this wood as its domain, and I was not welcome. Pain seared through my eyes and my hands flew to my head. Screaming echoed through my mind. I fought not to collapse as I pushed the vision out.

"Don't look at Ashal. Make your sacrifice and leave. Don't anger him."

I did not want to see.

I did not want to know.

I took three deep breaths, and counted to five. Index, middle, ring, pinkie.

The screaming lessened, but did not end. I pried my eyes open against the migraine. I had a body to examine. I could not do this now.

Something moved in the corner of my eye.

I dropped down and withdrew the knife from my boot in an instant. It flew out of my hand and hit him in the right shoulder.

"Peter!"

He stumbled.

"Oh, I am sorry. I am so sorry." I ran to him, pulling the blade from his shoulder and cleaning it on my shirt.

"You could have killed me!" He gasped. I ran a hand over the gash and tried to comfort him. "You stabbed me!"

"I am sorry! I did not mean to, I thought you were a Rak."

"You never miss. What's wrong? Why did you miss?"

"I guess I was preoccupied. Lucky for you." I punched him lightly, embarrassed at being caught so jumpy. He massaged his arm, wincing, but eventually agreed that I really had not done too much damage. I covered the cut with my hand. "Læxlïezè."

Power danced from my fingers, and his wound melted back together. He smiled and rubbed his shoulder, and our focus turned back to the body. The mess and gore was starting to smell, and I recoiled. I did not deal with rotting bodies much. Most of my bodies were fresh.

I pulled long rubber gloves up over my slim fingers and started picking up the organs scattered around the body. I tried to lift the stake out of the ground without touching the body, but I lost my balance and went down.

The body landed on top of me, and the dead smear of blood and liquefied flesh coated my hair, skin, and clothes. I spat out some of the stray mixture that found its way into my mouth, then vomited at the taste. Peter heaved the body off of me and helped me up, eyebrows knit together in concern. I straightened, and tried to put back on my cool exterior, but this shook me.

Had my mother experienced a similar torture?

I did not know.

I sat up nights trying block out the visions of what they did to her, but I was not always successful. I stared at the body, and my mind forced me to see her there instead. I could not breath, and my eyes blurred. Peter squatted on the ground next to me.

Silently, he placed an arm around me and wiped the grime from my face.

This was too big a task.

I could not handle it.

The Raks were inside the gates. They were watching me. I defended The Captain from The General, and now he was right back working for him.

How long before he spilled my secret?

How long before The General knew we were Àraid?

I placed a hand on the dead man's leg and, unwittingly, I lived his last moments. Saw him screaming and pleading.

"No, please. I'm sorry. I'll do what you ask."

The General's hand came down and twisted his fingers into ugly shapes. Bone ground against bone.

I recoiled, wondering how anyone could do such a thing for sport.

"I need to start training. We need to be ready to defend ourselves if it comes to that." I stood. My head was back on straight, and my emotions were again concealed.

The walls were back up.

"I need to start training my kids. They need to know how to use their powers."

Inhibited

Alice

8th Day, The Season Of Living, 742-PW

The General never allows me to be alone. There is always someone guarding me. Usually it's The General's Suit. Usually, but not today. Today it's a Rak guarding me. He keeps staring at me. The guards aren't supposed to touch me, but they don't obey that rule. The General would kill him if he knew this guard already raped me. Four times today, which I think is a record. It's not so bad. If I stay quiet, and don't resist, they stick to me. They leave Collin alone. That's all I want. It doesn't matter what they do to me anymore. I just need them to leave him alone.

I died a long time ago.

"If we let you go, do you think you'll ever recover

from this?" The Rak guard poked my bleeding shoulder. "Could you ever move past the good times I've had?"

I shut my journal, and stared at the guard, but I didn't answer him.

"The world outside is on our side. The regions are ours. If we let you go, would you support us?" He hissed as he dug his fingernails into my arm. I wouldn't flinch. That's what he wanted. I wouldn't give him that.

The suns were nearly set behind the giant prison in the middle of the camp. The hot sun won today. It won a lot more lately. The King's power was slipping away. The General was getting stronger. I turned my face away from the guard, and reluctantly focused on the prison. The General wanted to make sure I always saw the prison.

"Mommy. Watch!" Collin called from the yard. I tried to focus on my son, but my mind kept wandering. I could hear the Raks in the Telia. The music was loud, but their laughter was louder. There were six sacrifices today, so it would take them a while to finish their party. The General was sending more people into the Telia lately. He needed to make sure he stayed in power. And he enjoyed watching them play for their life.

He used to make me watch, but not anymore. He got tired of me trying to stop them.

The General's chime rang over the camp. He granted whoever was in the arena their life. The Raks didn't like that. A fight broke out again. They sounded like they were jumping into the arena. That was the joke. The General made the Telias seem fair. If you won his favor, you'd be pardoned. But the Raks never let anyone leave. If they were pardoned, the Raks jumped into the arena and killed them anyway.

My child didn't notice the noise from the Telia. He was too used to this violence. The other day I told him a story, and he interrupted me with a laugh.

"Mommy? What is a dad?"

Until that point I assumed that he thought of The General as his father, and I said much. "I know I'm not his, Mom." Collin stated. "I'm more human, or maybe even Àraid, than Rak. The General would never have a misfit like me." As he said it, he knelt in front of me, whispering so the guard wouldn't hear. "And I know you don't know who I belong to, either. I am a Hybrid. You're just a breeder. You only have one purpose."

He was right. He was more their engineered Àraid than Rak, but his eyes were black like a Raks. And as my son explained all he knew, he dug his fingernails into my arm, just like his father, and all the rest of them did. We never had the chance to finish our conversation that day.

The General came in and interrupted us. Collin nodded at me knowingly as The General attacked me. The General stole my strength and my freedom and I hated him for what he did, but I also knew that I earned this.

This was my fault.

When The General finished with me, he put an arm around my son's shoulders, and the two of them walked off, laughing together as I tried to pick myself up of the ground.

The fight outside the yard grew louder, and pulled me back to my throbbing shoulder and the moody Rak guarding me. The guard was upset that he had been left in charge of me and the child forced on me, and he glanced longingly toward the fence. He would rather be at the Telia. His eyes darted back over to me. I shifted uncomfortably, and tried to place my focus on my son.

"Watch this!" Collin jumped from the tree, landed wrong, and snapped his leg. With a small shout and a whispered word, the leg healed and he was up again.

I'd begged The General to spare Collin's life. He didn't listen when I begged for any of my other children, but this time he granted my wish.

"If you can keep him alive on the food we ration you, you can keep your kid."

My stomach growled, and I thought about the crust of bread I ate yesterday; the only bit I spared from his meal.

Collin ran to a tree and banged his fist against it over and over. I heard the smaller bones snap, and soon the end of his arm was a bloody stump. He cried as his other hand wrapped around the offending limb as if trying to stop it. I rose to my feet as the guard chuckled, his eyes never leaving my son. He pressed a small coin coated in my son's blood between his fingers.

I opened my mouth, but then The General's warning, and all those torturous nights, ran through my mind, and I bit my lip. I couldn't talk. I couldn't make a sound. I ran to the guard, and slapped the coin out of his hand. The coin dropped into the dirt, and his spell on my son released. Collin fell to the ground, holding his arm.

The guard hissed, and his mouth twisted into a horrid snarl. Then something changed in his eyes, and he lunged and caught me by the neck, shoving me against the wall. Pain erupted behind my eyes, and I pulled at his hand, gasping for air. A hand reached back and switched off the box at the base of my spine. My legs went limp. The only thing keeping me up was his hand on my neck.

His sharp fingers reached up my dress, dug into my back. He ripped off long strips of flesh and brought them to his mouth.

One chew.

One swallow.

Warm blood trickled down my legs. I couldn't breathe. My vision darkened. I went for the guard's eyes, trying to hook my thumbs into the sockets. I got one eye out before he restrained my hands again.

He flung me to the ground and was on top of me in seconds. His dislodged eyeball swung from the optic nerve, and black blood oozed from the socket where it used to be. I reached for the dangling eye, trying to pull it free, but he grabbed my shoulders and pulled me off the floor, and then *slammed me back into the stonework. I hit the ground hard and knocked the air from my lungs. A nightmare. I was trapped, living in a nightmare. A single tear tracked down my face, and his finger pierced my cheek as he stopped its path.*

"Oh, so that's how it's going to be." He slapped my hands aside and ripped his belt from its loops, striking me across the face with it. My teeth cut into my lip as I cut off a scream.

Don't make a sound.

His sharp fingers dug into my hands as I tried to fight. He wrapped the belt around my neck, and latched it tightly. The General taught him that. I could breathe, but barely. I couldn't fight if I couldn't breathe.

My dress ripped, and cold air danced across my stomach. As he leaned down to lick the blood from my face, his pointed teeth scraped across my cheek. I yanked a hand free and slapped him, but he simply pinned my hands again. I wasn't strong enough to move them anymore. His fingers trailed down my sides, ripping and tearing. They stopped at my hips and dug into my lower back.

"Brace yourself."

The guard was still above me, pinning me down. He held my arms above my head, and dug his fingers into my wrist. Fire danced in my throat as I whimpered. I could hear The General's voice in my head as his guard attacked me.

"Don't make a sound. Don't let me down."

Tears coursed down my face as I squeezed my eyes shut. The Rak looked human now. He invaded my memories and took the form of one of the faces he found there. I wouldn't look. They all chose Micheal's face. They all tormented me with his face. Even The General's nice Suit chose Micheal's face. The only Rak who didn't was The General.

Pain washed over me in waves and I kept my eyes shut tightly, hiding from this world, from this life I was trapped in. And then the guard was gone, and my eyes snapped open. Sharp nails dug into my shoulders and pulled me to my feet, switching the box back on and helping me regain my balance. Claws scratched my throat as he struggled to unlatch the belt, and then he pulled me into an awkward hug.

The General.

He always showed up; always stopped the attacks when he could. His Suit was there, too. He was holding the Rak guard, and hatred smoldered in his eyes.

"What should I do with him, Sir?" He was always so professional. The General shrugged.

"Whatever you want to do, Captain. I'm sure it will be sufficient."

It was odd watching The Captain and the guard. They both wore the same face. Micheal's face. But as the Rak understood that his life was in The Captain's hands, his skin faded to black scales. He sniveled and pleaded for his life, but as the Captain studied me shaking before him, and the blood dripping down my legs, a twisted smile crossed his face.

"You seem to enjoy a bit of rough play, Guard. I like to play, too." He bent the Rak across the table, grabbed the General's flag off the wall, and shoved the pole up the Rak. The guard's eyes widened in pain, and shock, as he tried to squirm away from the flag pole.

I cringed and looked away as the Captain pushed the pole in farther, and the Rak screamed. The General turned my head back to watch as The Captain pumped the flagpole in and out and the Rak slowly stopped struggling. The Captain stepped away from the dead Rak, and brushed off his hands. He left The General's flagpole inside the Rak, so that only his symbol was visible.

"Sorry for defiling your flag, Sir." The Captain's anger

still emanated off him, but he tried to reign it in. The General laughed, and slapped his leg.

"Any other time I would have punished you, but I must say, I rather enjoyed that. Did you enjoy it, Trophy?"

I refused to look at the Rak. I was glad he was dead, but as The Captain killed him, I could only imagine him doing that to me.

Would they kill me like that when they got bored of me?

When I didn't answer they both turned their attention to me.

My dress hung loosely off me; merely tattered shards of fabric. I tried to cover myself with the shredded pieces to hide from their gaze.

"I told them not to touch you anymore. You're my trophy." He pulled me slowly into his arms. I fought the urge to shy away from his touch. He hated that. "Come back with me. The Captain will watch the kid." He put an arm around me and led me back into the house, and pushed me ahead of him up the stairs, fiddling with the key ring on his belt.

The door to his room swung open and I stumbled back into my prison. He quickly shut the door behind us and locked all six locks.

"I told them not to touch you. They just don't understand, Baby." He grabbed my arm and pulled me to him, kissing my fingertips roughly. "You're my prize. My trophy. I don't want anyone messing with my prize." He bent and kissed my neck, easing the tattered dress to the floor.

I tried to hide the tears in my eyes, but one escaped and fell onto his shoulder. His fingers drove into my back, but he never looked up. He backed me up and pushed me onto the bed. Although it was softer than the ground, I couldn't hold back a whimper of pain.

He turned to the table he kept right beside the bed, trying to pick his next experiment. I shuddered when he spun back to me. One hand held a whip, and the other held a small knife. I scooted up to the head of the bed as his whip ripped through my skin.

"I don't want to do this, Baby." He crawled onto the bed and pulled me into his arms and rocked me gently. "You just keep making things harder for yourself. They don't need to be this hard, if only you'd behave. Stop tempting my guards." He smoothed my hair as he hummed softly.

My fingers began glowing an ice blue, and the small welts faded back to normal, healthy skin as he ran his rough fingers over them. I didn't understand what was happening. I didn't know why my fingers glowed. The General knew, but he wouldn't tell me.

He brought the small knife up and drove it into my shoulder, slicing slowly down to my elbow. I yelped, and pulled away, but he only dug deeper, slowly slicing his way down my arm before pulling the knife out.

"Don't make a sound, Baby. Not one sound." He leaned down and lapped up the blood, smiling at me. His smile grew as my fingers once again glowed, and the gash on my arm closed. His eyes softened and he nodded.

"I can't believe I found you." He murmured as he moved up to my lips and pushed himself into me, digging his claws into my arm, ripping it open again. He flexed his fingers and I gasped in pain. His tongue darted into my open mouth, and he bit my lip.

Collin rattled the door, and I tried to get up to help him, but The General grabbed me and shoved me back down onto the blood-soaked bed. Then he flipped me over and pushed my face into the pillows. That way, when I screamed, it would be muffled. He clicked handcuffs onto both wrists, and locked them to the bed, and then glared at the door.

"No." He growled, "My prize stays with me."

My child quietly slipped back down the stairs.

† † † † †

Hours later, a loud banging on the door finally distracted his attentions. I could barely open my eyes as he glared at the door. My head pounded, and my body screamed in pain. He unlocked the handcuffs and pulled me into his arms, rocking me, soothing me. The knocking continued and he shoved me off of his lap, kicking me and tossing a new dress at me as he stalked to the door. Skimpy maroon. Nalaise clothing. He unlocked all six locks and cracked the door.

"You've been here a while, Sir. I thought you might be hungry." The Captain's voice drifted through the door, and he peeked into the room. I couldn't move to cover myself with blankets, and all of me was on display for him. The General nodded, and left the room, and The Captain came to my side.

My face burned in shame and I curled into a ball on my side, trying to hide the more obvious wounds. He pulled some of the sheets up and patted the blood from my face, slowly moving down to clean the cuts on my neck and back.

"You'll get out of here. You will survive." He whispered. I tried to smile at him. He wanted me to smile. All I could muster was a grimace. The General sighed and slammed the door.

"Not so fast, Captain. You guard her. You don't touch her." The General grabbed my arm and threw me into the cage. "I'll be back tonight my little trophy. Don't wait up. I'll wake you." He winked and clicked another lock on the cage. He set his dragon, which was currently small, but I knew it could be bigger, right outside my cage. As he retreated into the hall, his keys jingled and the locks clicked into place one by one. The question the guard asked me came back.

Would I ever recover if I were to escape?

As I prodded the new bruises, and tried not to think about what he did to me, I knew I would never recover.

There was no way I could get over this.

I wrapped my body in a worn crocheted blanket and tried to imagine myself anywhere but here.

I woke to The Captain wiping my forehead with a damp cloth.

"Your memories are getting more frequent." He frowned at my wrist, rubbing it briskly, and he shoved a parchment into my hand. "How much do you remember, Dear?"

A strange question.

That day with the Rak guard. My eyes flew open and I shrank from his hand. *You killed him.*

He winced and pulled his hand back.

"Which one?"

There's more than one?

His eyes widened.

"No." He pulled out a tattered book and opened it to a page marked with a crinkled piece of parchment. "Okay, since then we," He looked back up at me, "Got married. Escaped. Sought sanctuary in a healira in Coaltree."

He glanced back over the page and then handed me the book. Bullet points and dates scrawled down the page, accompanied by a small explanation. The list went up to a season ago, but The Captain jotted the current date on the bottom. I couldn't understand. I cleared my throat, and whispered against the pain.

"How many times have I read this?" Fire smoldered in my veins, but I knew The Captain liked when I spoke. His eyes widened, and he gently traced my chin. I shifted the book on my lap. The book pages crinkled and ripped easily, and was stains discolored the white. The Captain carefully took it and put it back into his pocket.

"About fifty times. You lose your memories randomly." His hands smoothed my hair. "It varies how much you forget. You write in your journal sometimes, to record your memories. Or you did. You haven't in a while. I keep it safe for you."

"Where's Collin?" My voice sounded stronger now, and there wasn't as much pain, but he still bent to hear what I said. "Sarah? Hailey? Where are they?"

The memories drifted back, slowly. I remembered them. My children. They should be here. The Captain wouldn't look at me. His fingers stroked the boning on my corset, but he didn't remove it. I wished he would. It was so hard to breathe. Fire coursed though my veins as punishment for daring to speak, and I clamped my mouth shut again.

I shifted my gaze to the window, and frowned as I studied the landscape outside. I couldn't really remember, but it didn't look right outside.

Were we looking out on a forest last night?

He seemed disappointed that I wasn't talking anymore, but he smiled a genuine smile; so rare for him.

"I didn't have a chance to explain yesterday. A brilliant system, really. Christa McCain invented it. This house literally rewrites itself." His voice filled with excitement. "It rearranges the rooms, deleting and creating and completely remodeling. If you don't know how to work the house, you can get lost forever. Or deleted. If danger is sensed, it goes crazy. It gets the household members out, and spins an impossible maze for any intruders." He was pacing, worked up and appreciating the skill it took to create the building. "We are facing North today. If we walked that way long enough we would reach the Silverglass Region. I'm from there."

I've never been there.

"I know." He chuckled. "In Silverglass color can't exist. I didn't even know what color was until I came to Nalaise. Then I learned I was wearing green pants, and a very bright pink shirt."

I covered my mouth to stop my giggle, but The Captain joined in my laughter.

What brought you to Coaltree?
His eyes turned sad at my question.
"Well, I met... my wife in the Trade Markets of Nalaise, and moved with her to the Snartec. That's where she died."

I lived there.
Again his smile was sad.
"I know, Love. You told me before." He came back over to the bed, and took my hand. Outside the window, I saw a courtyard with some children playing quietly.
"Where are my kids, Captain?" I whispered again.
"They're in the forest." Was the reply, but the lips that the words passed through were pressed into a grim, white line.

"**Y**ou've done well. She's convinced. We can play now. Teach The Private to disguise herself."

"You mean with the skin, Sir?"

"**Yes. Use the girl behind this door as a mold.**"

"Yes, Sir."

"**Keep the girl intact. The Private will step completely into her skin to play this part. She has to be human. She has to be convincing.**"

"I understand."

"**You better. You're my last insider. Christa is paranoid. Right now her attention is diverted, but she'll figure things out eventually. Don't let me down like Javis, or you'll end up like Javis.**"

"I won't let you down, Sir."

"**Fine. Send in the children. Let's make them play.**"

Inhibited

Christa

"This isn't working, Mom."

"Not yet, but you will learn." I tried to sound confident, but her skills did not strengthen like mine when I learned them.

She needs to be activated by a Mentor.

I knew nothing of activating my children, but maybe I could start the process, and fully activate her later.

I pressed the knife against my arm, and made a small cut. I bit back a sigh of relief as some of my pain flowed out of my arm. I was teaching Cerynn. I should not focus on myself. I nodded to my daughter, and she shut her eyes.

"Læχlïezè."

The cut itched, but did not heal. Cerynn's eyes filled with frustrated tears.

"Why doesn't it work?"

I thought I could teach her. I thought I knew how. But a Mentor taught me. Maybe I was forgetting something. Maybe my mind failed me.

"You have to sense it. Focus."

She nodded, and poised her hands over my arm again.

† † † † †

"I did it!"

I jerked out of sleep and blinked. Cerynn bounced around the room, waving her hands.

"I finally did it."

The clock on the wall told me we were practicing her powers for five hours. I fell asleep a while ago. I blinked the blurriness from my eyes, and looked down on my arm. The cuts were gone. Healed.

"Great. Now for a bigger injury." I poised a hammer over my hand, and hesitated a moment.

It would hurt.

I took a deep breath, but before I could break my hand, a relayven burst into the room and blared an alarm. I stiffened at the messages that played through his beak.

Breach at the south fence.

Breach at the outer layer.

Breach at the river.

We stood frozen for only a second, before I launched from my chair.

"Cerynn, get Jaycobe, and go check out the south and outer. I will take the river."

She squatted by the river, scooping cool water up to her mouth with her hands. Poisoned water. With every sip, her lips dried, and her skin turned brittle.

"Stop drinking that." I grabbed the small vial of Iceloch water tied around my neck and held it out to the girl. It was not much, but it would stop the dusting process.

She did not even look up from the water.

She was a child, maybe four or five, covered in scratches. Toenails blackened with dirt cracked up to the root. Knobby knees scabbed over and wept pus down her legs. She looked up at me with watery light blue eyes. Snot dripped from her

nose, and vomit coated the front of her dress. She wore no
registration band.

How did she get so far into the region without being
spotted?

"Have you seen my mommy?" Her voice whispered out
of her tiny frame. She rose and pulled a wrinkled drawing,
very well rendered from what I could see. "We were
running to safety, but I think we got split up." She shuffled
over to me, holding out the picture. In it I saw three smiling
children, with parents embracing behind them. I looked
closer. Alice and The Captain. Excitement mounted at the
good news I would bring Alice, and then my heart sank.

"*Three of her kids died out there.*" The Captain told me.
I studied the photograph, unbelieving.

"You know my mommy." She watched me intently. My
plate barely picked up her voice. "She's hurt. You should
just let her go back to him. He'll let you live if he gets her
back." Her steps matched mine as I backed away from her.

Her hands flew up, and I barely managed to block the
onslaught of ice she shot through her hands. Shattered ice
cut my face, but the bigger chunks melted under the blaze I
ignited.

"Bring me my mommy!" Her scream was no longer
human, and rage flew through her eyes.

I poised my hands in front of me, and hoped my powers
would not fail me. I dreaded this confrontation. She
continued to walk towards me, growling under her breath. I
summoned some pebbles into my hands, and shot them into
her tiny body. She never slowed, just blinked at me as the
holes healed themselves.

I raised my arms and the trees swirled in obedience. They
scooped the girl into the air, tossing her high and allowing
her to land too hard on the ground. Black veins flashed
across her fragile skin and she shuddered and stilled. She
was not trying to heal herself. In fact, if my Inhibited theory
was correct about the black veins, she was *resisting* her

impulse to heal. I waited, watching her.

Nothing.

She convulsed on the ground as blood trickled down her chin, mingling with the tears on her face. I turned to go.

"Wait." The little girl reached out towards me, blood dripping from her tiny fingers. "You're going to leave me?"

"You tried to kill me."

She was crying now.

"No. That wasn't me." Her head shook firmly against the browned leaves under her snagged curls.

A step closer.

I saw my baby daughter; laid out on the table. This little girl was not much different. She was only a child.

Another step.

I knelt beside her, easing her tiny body onto my lap.

"It was not you?"

Blood ran onto my skirt, staining it.

"No. The Raks." She coughed. "I'm poisoned, but rejected. I have no control. You call it inhibited."

Inhibited.

I fought the impulse to push her from me.

"How would you know what I call it?"

"You're being watched. Just like me." She gasped for air. "They control me. I have no control. I just sit and watch." Just like Cerynn, that day she killed her father. Another cough, weaker. "I was trapped. It didn't matter what I did on my insides, my outsides would do what it wanted." Her words slurred.

"My mommy," she shoved the now stained picture into my hands, "have to tell her."

"Tell her what?"

"Tell her. Warn her." The fight drained from her. Her tiny body went slack. "Tell her. Danger. Don't let her forget."

With one last sigh, her eyes closed and the wheezing stopped.

Cerynn

"**I** want my mom!" The girl screamed on the ground. "Take me to her. Now!" Her pudgy cheeks stained red from the effort. Her arms thrashed against the ground, and the rocks cut into her arms. Her shoes lay where they fell, flung from her feet as they pumped the air. Her screams escalated. It amazed me that something so little could hurt my ears so much.

Then, suddenly, her screaming stopped. She crouched, hands poised in front of her like claws. Her eyes glowed amber as she studied me. I pulled out my knife, and steadied it. The glowing eyes belonged to a Rak, and all Raks should die. But I'd never killed before. Especially not a child. Even a Rak child. I swallowed and backed up a half step.

Then she lunged. Her teeth sunk deep into my left arm, and black poison ran over the fake skin covering my prosthetic. My knife shot up and over on instinct, and only when she crumpled to the ground did I realized what I'd done.

"I'm sorry." I whispered to her.

She only grimaced, and mumbled.

"Don't let her forget." A single tear streaked down her cherub face, and she went limp.

Inhibited

Jaycobe

The boy pinned her against a tree. She was crying. Oh, she was beautiful, even through her terror. He pressed a knife to her throat, but judging from the bodies littering the ground, he didn't need it. The bodies sprawled on their backs, arms splayed and legs spread. But on their necks, each neck, a small burned hand-print. The tops of their heads were gone. Blown off or something. The boy glared at me through glazed eyes.

"I promised her." He hissed. "I'll keep them safe. They couldn't get much safer than this." A maniac laugh. "Need to warn her." He faced the girl again.

His child's body only came up to her shoulder, but he proved he was much stronger than her. She pleaded with him, shaking her head as her lips moved in noiseless prayers.

"Do you know where I can find her? Warn her?" His hand moved to her neck; the exact spot as on the other bodies.

"No, I don't know where she is! No, please. Please. Please." Her breath caught in sobs in her throat. His fingers glowed, fingertips hot red, fingers easing into a light yellow.

"No!" The girl screamed, and pushed against the tree;

trying to free herself. My hands flew up on instinct, and a blue glowing orb flew from between them and drove into his side, knocking him off his feet. He rose, measuring me, ready to fight. Another orb hit him and he crashed into the trees.

"Don't let her forget." He spat at me, and then he disappeared into the woods. The girl fell to her hands and knees on the ground sobbing and laughing. I went to her side, a hand on her back. Man, she was beautiful. She looked up at me with glowing amber eyes. I'd never seen eyes so beautiful.

"Thank you. I owe you my life. What's your name?" She touched a cut on my cheek I didn't know was there, and rubbed my blood between her fingers.

I made a show of bowing to her.

"Jaycobe Francis McCain, Ma'am. Call me Cobe."

She giggled and wove her slender arms around me; fingers twining in my hair. Her head landed on my shoulder and she sighed. Then she pulled my face down and kissed me. Gratitude did crazy things. I melted into her kiss. She pulled my head down. My blood glistened on her lips as she whispered in my ear.

"Jaycobe Francis McCain." At her words my arms stiffened, and my body saluted her against my command. She smirked and tapped my nose. "You shouldn't trust anyone, Boy. You were too easy to fool."

Alice

65th Day, The Season Of Death, 729-PW

Her father showed up yesterday. He was loud, and drunk, and he hit me. I wasn't expecting that. He wore foreign clothes; maybe from the Havenden Region. I heard they wore sandals, and clothing made from deer-skin there. They made much better use of their hand-made clothes than anyone in Snartec. Everyone here was too poor to afford anything new. I just got back from the Trade Markets in Nalaise yesterday. What money I made yesterday was supposed to get me through the whole cycle, but the drunk man stole all of it. He pushed past me and made himself at home in my living room. Another much bigger man followed him into the living room. Chrissy was so excited that her daddy came to visit. But he came to take her away from me. She is my whole life.

What will I do if I lose her?

*T*hunder rumbled over the mountain ranges above our house, rebuilt from ashes after Chrissy burned it down. The one good thing about the Snartec Region. When the people pulled together, they could rebuild houses in a day or two.

I inhaled the fresh pine as I lay in my bed, waiting. Chrissy always found her way into my room during thunderstorms. I secretly loved storms because she was getting too big to want to cuddle with me anymore. During the storms she would cling to me.

I loved that. I didn't want to lose that.

The minutes ticked by, but my door stayed shut. I frowned. The thunder woke me up about an hour ago, Chrissy would have heard it by now.

Where was she?

The cold air coaxed goosebumps on my arms as I climbed from my bed to go look for her. I found her bed empty; sheets pushed all the way to the bottom of the bed. Her pillow was missing, too.

"Chrissy?" I stepped into the room. She wasn't at her desk, or her reading nook. Then I noticed a small, bare foot poking out from under the bed. I stuck my head under the bed. She stared back at me, eyes wide, frightened.

"What are you doing down here?"

"The monsters are coming for me," she whispered, "but they cannot get me here. I can keep them out when I am here. See?" A tiny flame burst from the tips of her fingers and lit the carpet on fire. She quickly patted it out and smiled up at me. "The monsters fear the light. They do not like my fire. I can summon the flames at will now."

Her smile vanished as more thunder cracked over the

mountains. I slipped under her bed, lying side by side with her. Her nearly-ten-cycle-old body fit much better than my twenty-three-cycle-old one, but somehow I managed.

"Why didn't you come to my room?" I smoothed her hair out of her face. She pointed to the white dress hanging from her wardrobe. I didn't want to look at it. I didn't want to remember the angry knocking on my door. The bruise throbbing on my cheek reminded me enough of the drunk man who stood on my door step and announced he was Chrissy's father. And I really didn't want to think about the bigger man standing behind him, waiting to be introduced.

"I am getting married in the morning. I cannot go running to you during thunderstorms anymore." She was the traditional age in the Havenden Region. As soon as they were physically old enough to get pregnant they married. But here, in my house, nine was too young. I fought her father fiercely when he told me why he was there.

"Ma'am," the man drawled. "I set up this marriage before you ever saw her. She's a woman now. Early bloomer, but not unheard of."

When I pointed out that he wasn't part of her life anymore, he laughed.

"Promise is promise."

I lost.

"Aren't you afraid?" I knew loud noises made her uneasy.

"Yeah," she gnawed on her lip, "but the man in my closet is afraid too, so I am not alone."

I froze.

"What did you say?"

"I said the man is afraid too, so I am not alone."

"You have a man in your closet?" I pushed myself out from under the bed and was ready to pull the closet door open, but she stopped me.

"Please, do not make him go. He makes me feel safe!" Tears shimmered in her eyes, and she positioned herself protectively between the closet and myself. I stumbled back into the bed, easing onto the patched-up quilt.

"Let me talk to him." She cracked the closet door and stuck her head inside. I could hear her whispering to someone inside. She looked back towards me and nodded slowly. "I think she will be okay." She whispered into the closet. She skipped over to me and threw her arms around my neck. "Be nice to him please."

A middle-aged man stepped into her small room. He had short brown hair, and one ice blue eye; the other was bright green. I pulled my attention away from his piercing eyes, and slowly took in the rest of him. There were tiny cuts, and scars on his angular cheeks. His suit was well tailored, all black, but torn and stained, and he leaned heavily on an intricately carved cane with a dragon head snarling from the top. His eyes widened when he saw me, and he dropped to his knees.

"Mom, this is Peter." Chrissy grinned. "He is like me. Sort of."

He nodded respectfully at me, but said nothing.

"Peter. How old are you?" I questioned. Chrissy squeezed my arm and groaned. The man cleared his throat.

"I'm thirty-five, Ma'am." The wrinkles around his eyes, and the way his eyes darted away from mine told me he was lying.

"Why are you hiding in a ten-cycle-old girl's room?"

His head jerked up and those mismatched eyes shot ice through me.

"It's not like that, Ma'am. I swear." He stumbled to his feet, leaning heavily on his cane. "I'm out a house right now and your daughter offered up this space. I was not aware that you were ignorant of my presence, and wanted to leave when I learned I would be staying in her room. But I honestly have nowhere to go."

I reluctantly met his mismatched eyes.

"Well, I think you should find somewhere else, soon. I

want you out."

"Mom!" Chrissy protested, "You just heard him.
Nowhere to go! Why can he not stay?" She ran to his side,
and nearly knocked him over.

"No, your mom is right. I'll leave." He nodded at me.
"Your daughter is going to spark greatness. Do not be too
hard on her."

I frowned at him, but he cupped my chin and held my
mouth shut, not allowing me to question him.

"I know who you are. I know what you will be. And I am
sorry about what you have to go through." He bowed and
strode out of the room. I rubbed my forehead and tried to
make sense of what he said. Chrissy sobbed on the ground,
and I slipped down next to her.

"He was my friend! He believed in me like you never
have!" She wailed. "He is going to mean something to me
someday."

"What do you mean?"

"I mean he knows me. He knows me when I am thirty."

"You're not making sense." I wanted to understand her,
but I couldn't.

"He is from the future. He is running away. Why would
you throw him out?"

"Chrissy," I sighed. "There's no such thing as time
travel."

"Yes there is!" She was adamant. "The Çvïl time travel!
Do you never listen when I talk?" Her eyes revealed the
wounds buried inside her. I nodded along to the nonsense
that man drilled into her head.

"Of course they do."

"You do not believe. You never have. You never will."
Her body remained stiff, aloof, as I pulled her into my arms.
She was getting married in the morning and I just tore a
void between us. It would take me many days to patch the
wounds I accidentally inflicted. I didn't have days.

Tears stung my eyes, and I tried to figure out why I was

crying. I cried for her. I cried because life was not fair. I cried because I was terrified of what would happen to her behind her husbands closed doors. I prayed that morning wouldn't come, or that that man would change his mind.

I sang her to sleep, believing that all would be okay. But, in the morning, the suns rose high over the pine trees, and I dutifully readied my daughter for her wedding day. Her face remained expressionless, and I knew why I cried. I cried because I lost her, and I wasn't sure I would be able to get her back.

† † † † †

67th Day, The Season Of Life, 730-PW

I haven't seen Chrissy since her wedding. I miss her. I'm lonely here.

I haven't spoken to anyone for half a season. I can't work in the mills

anymore, and I haven't *seen* anyone in days.

Except for him. I catch him sometimes, staring in through my

window. Sometimes he looks normal, but in certain light I swear his

face looks like a patchwork quilt. He doesn't look like the people of

Snartec. He wears a suit. Nobody here can afford suits. People here

rely on what money they raise in Nalaise. We rarely make enough. I

didn't. I'm out of money now. I've been selling my things to try to

buy food, but I don't have anything left to sell. I own one chair, one

bowl, one cup, and one spoon. And my piano of course. I would

never sell my piano.

I sleep on the floor. I don't have blankets. I don't have a change of clothes. I sneak down to the river and shiver, naked, while I wash my clothes. I think he spied on me at the river. I don't think I care. I don't like living so isolated. I don't know anyone here. I only knew Micheal and Chrissy. Micheal is dead. Chrissy is married. I'm forgotten.

I wasn't really worried about being out here alone, until yesterday. I went out for a walk, and when I came back he was in my house. He was sitting in my chair. I didn't say anything. I was too surprised. Food and clothes and blankets piled in the corner, and he pointed at them, and then at me, and I blushed. He knew how tight things were for me. He still scared me, but a the same time it was a relief to know that someone was trying to help. He didn't really scare me until I saw what he was holding. He tapped a knife against his leg. I turned to flee, but the door slammed shut, and wouldn't open no matter how hard I pulled. When I turned back around he was right behind me. He pinned me against the wall, and yanked my skirt up past my hips. His breath stank as he leaned down and shoved his mouth into mine. I pushed against the door, but I couldn't get away from him. His knife hooked into my panties, and they tore and fell away. I tried to push my skirt back down, but he shoved a hand between my legs and held it there. He wiggled his fingers slowly, and I hated my body for responding. He touched my necklace, briefly, and laughed. And then he pressed the tip of his knife against my jaw, just hard enough to bring a little blood to the surface. He bent and licked the cut, and closed his eyes as he savored it. Then he sighed, pulled his hand away, and sneered at me.

"You're nearly ready now."

He licked his fingers, and left. I keep my doors and windows locked now. I wasn't scared of him.

I am now.

Someone pounded on my door. I didn't open it right away. I glanced through the peephole first. Chrissy. I hadn't seen her since the wedding, two seasons ago, and flung the heavy door open; my arms already pulling her close before I saw her tears. I held her at arms length, taking stock. I didn't see any abrasions, and she looked well fed. I could breathe again.

Without a word, she crossed to the piano and began playing a sorrowful chilling melody that cut to the core. I doubt she noticed my missing furniture. Her eyes never left the piano. She played for hours, not allowing me to interrupt. Small flames danced over the ivory keys as tears silently tracked down her face. I placed my one cup, full of tea, on the top of the piano, but she didn't touch it. Finally, she put her fingers into her lap and looked at me.

"I am pregnant."

My heart dropped.

No.

She's too young, and small for her age. A girl her size trying to bring a child into the world would likely die. The death-rate was high for a full grown woman, but my child? My child would never survive it.

Her expression never changed. She stated a fact, simply news, nothing more. She didn't want congratulations. She didn't want sympathy. She just wanted me to know.

I held back tears as we sat, facing each other, in silence. Eventually, she turned back to the piano and resumed her song. Then, wordlessly, she got up and left.

I didn't see her again until the day her child ripped her apart.

A frantic knocking on the door jarred me awake. The Captain's arms tightened around me, and he raised his head away from mine to glare at the door. One of his hands absently stroked my stomach where, if I wasn't wearing a corset, it would bulge with growing life. He barely fit on the small healira bed, but he insisted on being near me. He knew it lessened my nightmares when he was close.

"We're asleep. Go away."

The knob turned anyway. A beautiful woman timidly ducked into the healira, avoiding the medicinal herbs hanging from the ceiling. She would not look at me. Her eyes darted all around the room, but never once stopped on me.

"Oh. Christa." The Captain's lips didn't move when he said her name; just kind of dropped it into the room. Her hands were motionless at her side, but her fingers flayed out stiffly. She was struggling to keep her hands down.

"I need to speak to you. In the hall please." Her voice snaked out from barely parted lips, and held a hint of an accent that I couldn't place. She spun and left, but I could see her hovering right outside the door. I sat up carefully, and The Captain slipped off the bed and strode out into the hall.

"Follow me." She whispered loudly. The Captain mumbled something I couldn't hear, which was met with more frantic whispers. My legs ached from disuse, and I wondered briefly if The Captain would let me walk around a bit when he got back. I shook my head. He was too protective. He wouldn't allow me out of bed until I healed completely.

Their voices faded down the hallway, and I smiled and took my chance. I swung my legs off the side of the bed, and gingerly tested my weight. My feet never recovered from The General breaking them, but that pain I was used to. The Captain insisted on keeping the curtains shut, and I missed the suns.

I took one step towards the window, and my legs gave out. I grabbed for anything to catch my fall, and snagged the curtains. They tore off the window, and covered me in a heap on the ground. I clutched my side, and bit my lip. The scab broke open. Pained seared through my side, and I was right back at his house again.

"You've been getting into trouble, Dear." His breath was hot in my ear as he pinned me to the wall. The wood panel scrapped against my face as I tilted my head so my nose wouldn't be broken against the wall. He wrapped my long hair around his hand, and jerked my head around so I could see him out of the corner of my eye.

My arms burned as I pushed against the wall, trying to save myself from being crushed. He pulled a pillow case over my head, and tied it around my neck. I blocked out what he was doing to me, and barely noticed when he grunted and shoved away from me. I slid to my knees, and turned to face him.

He hadn't finished. He had more planned for me. I sat in silence, and darkness, and strained to hear anything he might be doing.

"You've been wandering around. You're supposed to stay inside my house." He sounded like he was standing on the other side of the room. I tried not to sag with relief that he wasn't right beside me. *"Put your elbows together and hold out your arms."*

I knew they shook visibly as I obeyed him. Thick, prickly rope tightened around my arms, and pulled me to my feet. The edge of a table jabbed my hips as I bent in half over it. His hands ran across my back, down my legs, and stopped at my ankles. More rope wrapped around my ankles, and he tied them to the table legs.

He was gone again, somewhere in the room, lost to the darkness.

More silence.

Fear seeped through my pores. He could smell it. I knew he could. And then fire zinged across my back, and his whip snapped. I barely stopped the scream in my throat.

Another snap of his whip.

Another lash to my back.

I expected more lashes, but I heard the door open and shut, and knew I was alone. My body ached, bent awkwardly over the table. Blood dripped onto the table, and I wondered how deep these lashes were. Last time The General whipped me, he left me tied to the table until I passed out. I hoped he didn't do that this time.

The door opened again, and I heard a sniff. A child.

"Mommy?"

I froze.

Sarah.

Another snap of his whip, and a shrill scream.

"Mommy, have I been bad?"

"Yes. You've been awful." The General answered her cries. *"But I'll stop punishing you as soon as your mommy unties herself, gets that pillowcase off her head, and wraps her pretty mouth around my needs."* His laughter was set off by another snap, and another scream.

I pulled frantically against the ropes, but they wouldn't loosen.

"Shh, you're safe now."

Arms wrapped around the curtains, and me. I needed to get free. I needed to save my daughter.

"Stop thrashing, Baby. It's just me. It's okay." The Captain whispered through the thick material. His hands worked in the curtains, and finally freed my head. In my struggle to get out of the curtains, I knocked over a few herb carts. The Captain would need to pay to replace them.

"I'm sorry." I knelt on the ground, and started scooping up the herbs, but The Captain stopped me.

"Stay out of sight of the window. Don't draw attention." He hastily tacked the curtains back over the window, and the room was plunged back into dreary candlelight. "What are you doing out of bed?"

I hesitated before I answered him. I didn't have anything to write with, but he wouldn't be satisfied without an answer.

"I wanted to see outside. I wanted to see if the flowers are blooming."

The memory of The General still sat at the back of my mind, but I tried to focus on The Captain.

"You can't look outside. The Raks are swarming the city. If they see you, it's all over."

"I thought you said it was a Rak-free city." Fear fought to strangle me. I pictured them handing me back to The General. Pictured his anger. I couldn't swallow past the lump in my throat, and tears welled in my eyes.

"It was, Baby." He pressed a finger against my tears. "Don't worry, I'll keep you safe."

But as he said it, a relayven tapped on the healira door, and I heard *his* voice drift out of the bird.

"The games have begun. Your first warning was the man in the woods. You get two more warnings."

Christa

"Captain, I forgot to give you..." My voice trailed off as I stepped into the healira. Herbs scattered across the floor. Two carts lay broken on the floor. My beautiful curtains hung crookedly over the windows. The Captain knelt on the ground with Alice in his arms. Unconscious. Healira patients wore white, regardless of region dress code, but blood stained her white gown.

Why was she bleeding?

Cerynn was taking very good care of her. She should not be bleeding.

"What have you done?"

The Captain had her blood on his hands. I pictured him grabbing her from the bed, throwing her across the room. She must have reached frantically for the curtains, hoping they would catch her fall.

"What did you do, Captain?" My voice rose a notch. The Captain never looked away from her.

"I didn't do anything. I swear."

I knelt next to Alice. She shifted her head, and blinked her eyes open slowly. Tangled waves of salt-and-pepper hair, clotted with blood, bounced over her shoulders, and her eyes were such a light blue they were almost white. My mother's eyes had been dark green. That was the only way I could tell the difference between the two and I struggled not to hate her for surviving when my mother did not. But, at the same time I felt some relief at another chance to save her. Or at least someone like her.

We were low on water when she arrived, so Cerynn was not able to clean her up much.

I glanced up at The Captain. She was so little, so fragile. He was so rough. He worked for The General. He was an assassin before becoming her guard. He would always be rough. He would always be dangerous.

How did she end up with him?

Did she want to stay with him?

Or was she afraid of him?

She was afraid of him. She had to be afraid of him. That was the only thing that made sense.

He was bad news.

He would betray us all. I knew it, but could not prove it.

He still waited for my response.

"I am not ignorant to the rumors surrounding me." I frowned at him. "People say I am going mad. People say I cannot be trusted. But I protect them anyway. I protected you. I put my life, my family's lives, and the whole town, at risk for your wife. I will not stand by and watch you kill her." I attempted to yank her out of his arms. "You do not touch her anymore. You do not get anymore "alone time" with her. If I catch you hurting her again, you will be outside the gates before you can speak."

I struggled moving her back into the bed, and spun back toward him. I barely came up to his shoulders, but somehow I felt bigger than him at that moment.

"I'm a Suit." He chuckled. "Outside your tiny city I have a free pass. Kicking me out would do nothing."

"It would separate you from her."

He blanched, mouth forming a protest, but it died on his lips and he nodded resignedly.

"I didn't do it." He said to her, reaching a gentle hand to move some stray curls from her face. I slapped his hand away from her. During our argument she drifted back to sleep, and, asleep, she looked almost peaceful. Almost. I crossed my arms, and remembered why I came into this room. I nudged The Captain, and handed him the drawing from the little girl. I did not know where she got it, but it was of The Captain, and Alice, so I thought they should have it.

"What does "second warning" mean?" I flipped the drawing over, and pointed to the back. There, written in blood, were three names. Collin. Sarah. Hailey. Beneath their names was "second warning". The Captain blanched.

"I'm sure it doesn't mean anything." He shoved the picture into his pocket. He reached again for her, and as I pushed him away I brushed her arm.

Screaming and bones breaking and the heavy smell of death.

"The world outside is on my side, Trophy." The General's voice echoed through my mind. Alice lay at his feet, arms above her head. *"The regions swear their allegiance to me. Why do you still try to run?"*

"I will never be allied to you." As her hoarse voice whispered out of her, he kicked her. She screamed, and I cringed.

I shut out these visions for cycles, why were they tormenting me now?

"Not one sound, trophy. Don't make a sound. With you by my side, Dear, the Àraid will be crushed."

I blinked and shook my head. I was Àraid. He wanted to crush *me*. And he was so much stronger than I. Attacking him would get me nowhere.

Chin up. Lips closed. Fingers pointed only at yourself.

I chanted to myself, and tried to shove thoughts of war out of my head.

I predicted the war, but I would not be part of it.

Inhibited

Jaycobe

I followed the girl out of Mother's forest. I wanted to stop. I wanted to go home. But every time I tried to turn around, black veins flashed across my arms. She laughed and turned to watch me struggle.

"Don't try to fight your name, Dear. You'll never win that battle."

The little boy joined us on our trek across the region. He laughed when he saw me.

"He said it would work, but I never thought it would."

The girl nodded.

Who was "he"?

"Welcome home, Boy." The girl's skin faded to black scales, and she pointed to some buildings.

The prison.

Just outside of Coaltree, right on the border of Nalaise. The fences around the prisons were like the ones around our city, but they vaulted high into the sky, and curved inward. They were meant to keep everything *inside* their gates. I marched side by side with the girl through the spiked gates that opened on The General's command.

He stood just inside the gates, with his arms open in a welcoming gesture. The Hybrids and Raks stopped and watched us parade past. Humans were chained to the porches of houses laid out between more fencing.

Some of them looked frightened; ready to fight if anyone tried to hurt them. Others looked lost, like they had no reason to go on anymore. Their eyes were dead, and they didn't flinch as The General ripped off strips of flesh from their arms as he passed.

"Those ones have already been broken." The girl whispered as we followed The General through the streets. The General called her Private. "We push them. We push them and torture them and break them. You can see it in their eyes. Those fighters over there," she pointed, "they just came. You'll be training this new group, and then you'll win your name." She smiled, smug, and placed a key in my hand.

I walked over to one of the 'new ones', unlocked her shackles, and dragged her through the dirty street.

What was I doing?

She screamed and clawed at my arm, but I ignored her.

Why?

I don't do this.

What was happening?

I followed the Private and The General into an iron clad building, weaving through a labyrinth of rooms. All the doors were windowed. Behind every door was another person; men, women, I even saw some children; all were either dead or dying. I threw the screaming woman into an empty room and followed her in, kicking her hard and sending her sprawling across the floor. The door clicked behind me and I faced The General, at attention.

What was I doing?

"Okay. This is now your life." He smiled at me. "You won't have a name until you break this woman. Find a way to get her to tell you her name. Then your name will be Private, just like hers. We go in rankings here. There are ten ranks. The highest," He paused, "is General. Each rank has a breaking number. You'll stay at Private until you break a thousand, then your name will change to the next rank. You may break her anyway you want. Physical. Mental. Emotional. Doesn't matter." He shrugged and stepped out of the room. "We will let you know when you're done, but eventually you will learn to recognize it. Begin." The door shut and he peered at me through the window.

I turned back to the woman cowering in the corner, her eyes wide with horror. I measured her carefully, forming my tactic.

What was I doing?

I lunged at her and caught her around the throat, thrusting a fist into her stomach at the same time. She gasped, gripping at my hand at her throat.

My mother was going to kill me.

This was wrong.

I hit her again, and she keeled over, stumbling. There was a table in the middle of the room, and I threw her against it. The sharp corners tore the skin on her sides. As she lay, sprawled across the table, something animal reared inside me and I knew how I was going to break her. I advanced towards her again and slammed my wrist into her arm. Bones crunched under my blow, and a sneer spread across my face. I grabbed her chains and tied her to the table, preparing my prey.

What was I doing?

Inhibited

Cerynn

"**W**ould you stop hovering?" The Captain glared at me.

"Sorry. I don't know any other way to observe you."

"Maybe you could just go do your Healer thing, and leave us alone." He grumbled.

"My mother ordered us to never leave you alone with her." I crossed my arms. I argued with grumpy miners all day, I could argue with a Suit as well.

"I didn't hurt her!" He squeezed Alice's hand a little too hard, and she gasped. The Captain released her hand, and patted her arm gently. "You can trust me. I won't hurt her."

"Do you trust him?" I directed to Alice. She didn't answer. I didn't think she would. But her eyes darted away from both of us, and I wasn't sure if she really did trust him.

She ran her fingers through her hair, and made a face. It was tangled and greasy, and clotted with blood. Her gown, and the sheets, were stained with sweat from her nightmares, too.

The Captain got up, and left the healira. Alice patted the bed next to her, and I sat slowly beside her. She winced at the subtle movement, and then placed her hand on my cheek.

"I trust you. And I trust your mother." Her small voice cracked, but she smiled.

"*She doesn't speak. Not ever. Not without me right beside her.*" The Captain insisted when they first came in. As she spoke to me, she watched the door carefully, as if she feared him catching her.

"Why do you trust us?"

"The Raks have taken over the city, and still they haven't found me." She twisted her necklace in her hands, and rubbed her throat. She glanced toward the covered window. "They won't stop until they find me." Tears choked off her voice, and she strangled the necklace in her hands. The Captain crashed back into the room, and ran to her side.

"What's wrong, Baby? What happened?"

Her tears stopped as soon as she saw him. He pulled her into his arms, and wrinkled his nose.

"Cerynn?"

"What?"

"Do you have enough water for a bath?" He looked almost shy as he asked.

"Yeah. We just got a water shipment yesterday."

"May I clean her up?"

"Um, sure."

He scooped her off the bed, and followed me out of the room. I made sure the path was clear, led him to one of the washrooms, and grabbed a black dress from the closet. She would wear Coaltree dress-code now, and hopefully the black would help her blend in. I locked the door so no one would walk in. The washrooms were supposed to be public. The Captain stripped Alice down to her undergarments, and set her in the tub. After that he looked confused.

"Have you never drawn a bath, Captain?" I chuckled.

"I have," he frowned, "but usually bathtubs have a faucet."

"A what?" I frowned.

"To draw water. Plumbing."

"Yeah, our tubs have always been "faucetless"." I grabbed a bucket, and dunked it into the barrel of water. "Here we just pour water into the tub." I put the bucket over the fire, and filled another.

The bathtub took seven buckets of water, but Mother charmed the fire to be extra hot, and the water was warm enough in only a few minutes. I grabbed some bath salts from Witchcastle, and sprinkled them into the tub.

"What's this part?" The Captain pointed to the head of the tub, where there was a slight dip, and another, smaller basin.

"That's for hair. You rest your head in the dip, and pour water on the hair. It flows down into that other basin, and that way your bathwater doesn't get dirty."

"From hair?"

"Almost everyone here works in the mines. Their hair picks up a lot of dust." I gently scooped up Alice's hair, and draped it over the tub. If she stood, and let her hair fall straight down, it would brush against her knees. The hair basin wasn't made to hold that much hair, but we made it fit. The Captain continued to fill the tub, and I set in on her hair. I rinsed it six times before the water ran almost clear.

"Can I ask you something?" The Captain broke our silence.

"Go for it."

"What's your natural hair color?"

I paused and thought for a moment.

"Why do you want to know?"

"Because purple and blue are not natural colors."

"I like to experiment with different colors."

"Does it ever stain your clothes?"

"I wear black all day every day." I shrugged. "Why do you care?"

He pursed his lips.

"I had a daughter before..." He cleared his throat. "She

liked to change her hair color, too. She said it was her way of escaping her monsters. If she could control her appearance, maybe she could control her nightmares."

"Why did she have nightmares?"

The Captain twisted his hands as he squatted next to the tub.

"Your mother has kept this city safe, but it's the only one. In most regions, nobody sleeps without nightmares. Nobody escapes unscathed."

Alice's scars said that those fears weren't unreasonable.

"I color my hair for fun, not to escape anything. I'm naturally light blonde. It makes coloring easy. I order dyes from Witchcastle when I can."

The Captain nodded, and smiled as he studied my hair. Then he noticed my hands still scrubbing the blood out of Alice's hair.

"I can take over, Cerynn. I want to do this." The Captain took the hair soap out of my hand, and pointed to a chair against the wall. He was so gentle with her. He washed her hair, and her, and then very carefully scrubbed under her fingernails. He drained the tub, and poured another one. Then he sat next to the tub, and read her a book until she fell asleep.

"Why are you good at that?" I eventually broke the silence.

"It was one of my jobs when I worked for him. I kept her clean and presentable." His shoulders slumped.

"Why did you draw her a second bath?"

"He never touched her in the washroom. It was her only safe place. If she falls asleep in the tub, she has less nightmares. It sounds weird, but the washroom was our place. It's where we could be alone." He twisted her hair up out of the way as he spoke. Then he drained the tub, and dried her off. I handed him clean undergarments, and looked away again as he switched them out. I helped him put on the fresh dress, and then I led him into our house. Alice didn't need to stay in the healira anymore. I already prepared a private room for her.

As we snuck into the house, we heard the Rak guards trashing the healira.

Inhibited

Christa

"**M**s. McCain?"

I glanced up from yet another body on my table, and glared at The Captain.

"*Missus.*" I growled. "*Missus* McCain. I am married, Sir."

He rolled his eyes, and entered the morgue. I did not give him permission to enter my palace. This was my sanctuary. It was supposed to be quiet here, but when he walked in the screaming grew louder. I shot him a pointed look, and turned back to my body.

"Why did you move Alice out of the healira?"

"Call it a birthday present." I shrugged without looking up. "A room in a home is more comforting than a bed in a sterile healira."

"How did you know it's her birthday?"

I paused over the body.

"Um, I... she told me."

He shook his head.

"She wouldn't do that. She doesn't even know it's her birthday."

"She talks a lot when you are not around, Captain." I lied. The blood drained from his face, and he leaned against the table.

"What has she told you?"

"Enough." I peered at him.

What was he hiding?

Why was he so worried?

"She hasn't told you anything. She might be stupid, but she's not *that* stupid."

I fingered the knife in my pocket, and imagined what it would feel like to drive it into his skull.

Twist it through his ribs.

Gut him with it.

Adrenaline coursed through my veins, and my mouth watered. I should kill him here. No one would hear us. He thought his wife was stupid. She was not stupid. She was brilliant, and broken, and she needed safety. I could give her safety if I killed him.

He was not safe.

He would hurt her.

"What did this poor sap do?" He waved his hand over the body, and I withdrew my hand from my knife.

"Your people were 'just having some fun'." I spat at him. The body was mangled beyond recognition, but the whole town heard the screams of the boy they tortured before they relieved him of life.

"Yeah, they do have their fun don't they?" The Captain chuckled and headed back out the door. "Thanks for the room *Ms.* McCain. I'll enjoy sleeping under the same roof as you."

As the door shut behind him, I threw my knife. It stuck in the door, directly where The Captain's head should have been.

"Where is Jaycobe?" I had not seen him since the children in the woods. One short message. That was all he bothered to send me.

"Dear Mother,"

Who starts a note like that?

"Dear Mother, I am going to spend a few days with a girl and her father. She is too shook up to be alone right now. I'll check in later."

He still had not "checked in."

"Peter, where is he?" At my question he stopped mid-stride.

"Your son is perfectly responsible. He will be just fine out there." He crossed the room and put his arms around me. Peter eased us both back onto a chair, I on his lap, and looked up at me. "All of your kids are very responsible. They can go...days without needing you." He smiled coyly. "We could probably stay in here for days without being interrupted." He unbuttoned my dress, and pulled it open.

He pressed his face into my hair as his hands slowly traced the cuts on my hips. The cuts were healing, but still had scabs on them. I stood, and he bent and kissed each scab, and then worked his way up my side, back to my mouth. My eyes landed on a chest in the corner, and I pulled away from him.

"What is that?"

"What?" He mumbled into my hair, and kissed my neck. I pushed him away. "Oh, that. That's nothing. Don't open it."

But I already pulled the lid open.

"Peter, what is this?"

Neatly folded baby clothes filled the chest. Baby shoes. Baby coats. Baby jumpers. My eyes filled with tears.

"Why do you have these, Peter?" My legs gave out, and I fell to my knees. Peter knelt behind me. I dumped the box onto the floor, and sorted through it.

Twenty baby jumpers.

Twenty baby coats.

Twenty pairs of shoes.

Twenty.

I turned back to Peter. His eyes, too, were filled with tears as he stared at the baby things. He cleared his throat.

"I...um...I bought those things. Whenever you tell me you're pregnant, I buy another outfit. And then when you lose them, I put the outfit in this box so you never see it, and you never have think about it again."

Each little outfit had a tag with a date on it. And there were eight sets with the same dates. The twins I should have had. I could not find the one for the baby we lost a season ago.

"Where is the latest one?"

"I didn't buy one this time."

My throat closed up, and more tears rushed to my eyes.

"Why not?" I did not want to know, but I asked anyway.

"I just didn't want to get my hopes up this time."

I gasped, and sagged against him. He gave up. He did not believe I could give him another child. I could not breath. Peter rocked me slowly as I crushed one of the tiny coats to my chest.

Sobs wracked my body.

I could not stop them. I never cried in front of Peter. I needed to be stronger than that. Peter's arms shook around me, and I looked up at him. Tears streaked his face, too.

I caused him pain.

That was all I ever did.

The pain built inside me. I had to let it out. I needed to release it. I grabbed my knife from its holster, and slashed my arm before Peter could stop me. It let out some of my pain, but not enough. Peter twisted my knife out of my hand, and pinned me in his arms.

"We're going to get through this, but you can't pull away now. You can't give up, Christa."

"I never counted them." I sobbed into his shoulder. "I never knew how many I lost." I never went to their graves. I never counted them.

I did not want to know.

"How could I lose so many? I never had a problem with Jaycobe, or Ginny, or Cerynn. Why are you different?"

Willic never even wanted children. Peter wanted children.

Why could I not give him any?

Peter sat in the chair, and pulled me back onto his lap. He kissed me slowly, and then cradled me in his arms, and let me drift off to sleep.

We stayed that way for hours, just the two of us, surrounded by twenty unused baby sets.

Inhibited

Alice

"**H**appy birthday, Love." The Captain held two plates of food in his hands as he waltzed into my room.

It's my birthday? I scribbled. *How old am I?*
His shoulders sagged.
"You don't know?"

Of course I know. It was a joke. I lied, but he perked up.
"Sorry, jokes don't get through writing. You know, it's just me right now. You could talk." He pried the parchment from my fingers, and tore it up. "What would you like to do for your birthday?"

I pressed my lips together, and stared at the torn up parchment. I was afraid to talk.

Couldn't he see that?

The Captain sat on the bed, and pulled my journal out of his coat.

"Let's see." He flipped through the pages. He promised he'd never read it. I reached for the journal, but he held it just out of reach. "Ah. Right here. 'Micheal and I would always have a quiet dinner, and retreat to our room. We'd make a tent out of the sheets, and giggle and share secrets until dawn. Well... between other things of course.'"

I blushed.

"I wrote that a long time ago." I whispered.

"So what were these other things this lucky man got on your birthday?"

"We would...um..."

"Break the law? You know it's against the law to fornicate outside of marriage, and you never married Micheal. Answer the question, or suffer the consequences." He chuckled, but I cringed.

"Answer me, or suffer the consequences." The General's hand around my throat made it hard to answer him. "Answer me!"

"Alice?"

I dropped the necklace I was strangling in my hands, and stared up at The Captain. He grabbed my hand.

"You loved Micheal, didn't you? More than you wanted to."

"He left me."

"And you still love him all these cycles later. He abandoned you, and you still love him."

"Is that why you wear his face?" I grabbed the necklace again. "To remind me of what I had before the prisons?"

He shot me a smile and lunged towards me; pressing his lips against mine.

"Let's just do those other things you talked about. They sounded interesting."

I forced a smile, and pulled at his shirt. That I could do. I was trained well. He carefully avoided my bruises as he eased my dress up over my head.

"You love me. I know you do." He worked his trousers off, and I splayed my fingers through the hair on his chest. It tickled as it brushed against my skin. The General didn't have hair on his chest. I liked that The Captain did. I liked that he was different. It almost helped me forget what The General did to me.

He was slow, and gentle, and he wrapped me in his arms as we rocked slowly beneath the sheets. I kept my eyes locked on him. If I shut my eyes I would be right back with The General, and I wanted this moment to be nice. I wanted to be here with The Captain, not back in the camps.

"Your only shelter is me. Only I can keep you safe."

I gasped, and broke away from his kiss. I hadn't noticed my eyes shutting until The General's amber eyes flashed through my mind.

"What's wrong?" He paused and studied me closely. "Did I trigger something? What should I do? How can I help you?" He was so nice. So caring.

"Just keep talking. If I hear your voice, I stay here with you." Frustrated tears dripped down my face. He frowned, and sighed.

"Okay. What am I supposed to say?"

"I don't know." I scrambled. "Just...narrate?"

He rolled off of me, and groaned.

"I can't do that. This is supposed to be a loving moment between man and wife. This shouldn't be that hard!" He punched a pillow.

"I'm sorry!" I trembled. "I want to be okay for you. I want to be normal."

He pulled me into his arms, and situated me on top of him.

"Let's try this way. He never had you on top, right?"

I nodded and blinked the tears from my eyes.

"But I'm not trained this way, I don't know what to do."

"You don't need to. I'll teach you."

† † † † †

5th Day, The Season Of Death, 735-PW

I've been in hiding for a season. The Raks are getting closer. More

than half of my city is missing now, and the mills are suffering the losses. Graffitied around the town are phrases like "the darkness is coming." And "The General means harm." Chrissy's husband has been stirring up the town, trying to talk them into fighting back. So many cities are rebelling. So many are falling. People are screaming outside my hiding place, and windows are breaking. I caused this. I betrayed them.

Maybe if I just turn myself over he'll stop killing them.

I screamed as the dragon bathe her home in fire. My family was in there. They were all dead already. I saw their mangled bodies. But now they burned in front of me, and the Raks dragged me away from the fire. I couldn't think. I couldn't move. I couldn't scream.

They lifted me from the ground, and tossed me over one broad shoulder. I tried to fight them, but I could barely lift my arms. The world was a swirling mess of trees and shadows. Sounds faded. I didn't understand what was happening. I floated somewhere between fiction and reality. My struggle to understand lapsed to a struggle simply to stay alive. They called a halt.

"I can't wait until we get home." The General laid me on the ground and a knife sliced through my clothing.

His grin grew as he watched me struggle. I could scream now, and I did. Loudly. A new burst of adrenaline coursed through me, and I tried to fight him. I fought hard and tore three nails scratching at his rough scales. As he beat me, and tried to quiet me, I knew this was only the beginning.

† † † † †

Beginning Of The Season Of Life, 736-PW, I Think.

The General has been keeping an eye on me. After arresting me he

left me at the prison to be broken, but now he visits all the time.

He whispers to me when we're alone. He says he wants to buy me.

That he'll make me pay for running away. That I owe him.

The nights he buys me are bad enough, I don't think I can handle

being owned by him.

He tossed me into a cement room. A man stood right inside the door, hands crossed in front of him. He was tall and lean and his very presence was threatening. He wore the same face they all did. They mocked me with that face, and I did my best not to look.

"This is your chance to move up in the ranks." The Rak guard that threw me now kicked me in the stomach. The threatening man watched the guard.

"She has obviously been here for a few seasons. She's very pregnant. I don't want to hurt her."

"It's not my kid. Do what you want." The guard shrugged and kicked me again. "The General wants her broken before he buys her. He doesn't want to deal with her fighting. And he won't want to deal with someone else's child, so you'd be doing him a favor."

The man cracked his knuckles and chuckled.

"He needs a Suit to do a Raks job? I accept."

The General slammed the door open, and yanked me to

my feet. I clawed at his hands, trying to free my hair from his fingers. He slapped me, and threw me at the man's feet.

"I'm hoping to make her mine, but she's killed every Rak I've put up to breaking her. I couldn't afford to lose another one when you're right here."

The man laughed, looking me up and down.

"You? You killed every Trainer put to you? Impressive." His hand closed around mine, tightening. The bones snapped. I wouldn't scream. I hadn't screamed since that day in the woods, and I wouldn't give them that satisfaction. Another hand settled on my stomach, right over the baby, and he thrust a fist in roughly.

I bent over, gasping, as my stomach seized at the trauma. He shoved me to the ground. Then he caught my hair and yanked me back to my feet. His face contorted in fury, but he quietly whispered, "I'm sorry," before throwing me against the wall. He knelt down and yelled into my ear.

"Why do you hold out? You have no hope. Don't you know that? This is all you have to look forward to."

I reached up and slashed his face with my nails. He pulled some pliers out of his back pocket and ripped out each nail, tearing skin away with them. My fingers shook as I tried to pull back. I knew tears streamed down my face.

Don't scream. Don't cry.

Another contraction. Too fast. I swung up and clipped his jaw. He reeled and I jumped to my feet. I would fight. I would fight for my baby. I could hardly stand. My legs trembled beneath me, and I heaved air into my lungs. The man towered over me and pushed me against the table, I leaned back until my back wouldn't go any further. He looked at me, his eyes sad, and tried to force a laugh.

"I'm so, so sorry." Tears danced in his eyes, and his grip loosened for a moment, then he forced my back flat on the table. Bone ground against bone as he pushed me down. My legs went limp and numb. This was it. I was done. A scream ripped from my throat and the man's green eyes sparkled.

They won.

The General laughed, and clapped his hands as he came back into the room. The man let me go, and turned back to The General. I couldn't move. I tried to get off the table, but my body wouldn't listen.

"Good job." The General smiled. "You're the only one to make it this far up the ranks. You've earned your new name, Captain."

I screamed again as a contraction ripped through me. My back lifted up off the bed and my arms circled my middle. Cool hands smoothed over my forehead and I struggled to open my eyes. I slapped the hands away. I wouldn't let him hurt my child. I need to get out of this prison.

As my eyes opened and took in the stone, not cement, walls, my mind struggled to make the connection. I was in a prison camp. I was being tortured. The Captain leaned over me.

"I got you. You're safe." He smoothed the side of my face. I grabbed his hand, and my fingers inadvertently brushed my face. My skin felt cool, but I was sweating. My heart still beat too fast. My stomach clenched and I moaned, curling over my child. The corset wouldn't let me breathe. I was suffocating. I clawed at the lacing, and The Captain hastily untied it and spread it open. I inhaled deeply and calmed a little. Pain seized me and I curled off the bed.

"Alice? How much do you remember?" His tone changed now to one of concern. He placed a hand gently on the bulge in my stomach and cupped my head in his other hand. I couldn't speak, only gasp at the pain. I slapped him away, and tried not to cry. The contraction eased and I relaxed back into the pillows. This was false labor, it couldn't be the real thing. He paced around the room.

"How much, Counselor?"

"Everything." I spat at him. His eyes widened.

"Everything? Are you sure?"

Was that fear in his eyes?

I nodded as another contraction washed over me. He rubbed a hand across his face, debating whether to call for help.

"This is only three contractions. Don't worry." I tried to calm him but he shook his head.

"You've been regular for three hours. Don't the false contractions stay irregular?"

I tried not to show my panic. It would pass. It had to pass.

"Every thirty minutes they move five minutes closer together, right on the dot. That's how all your labors were. Very punctual."

It was too soon. The baby was too little. He sent a little relayven to get Christa, and while we waited for her The Captain shifted me onto my side, then stopped.

"You're bleeding." He placed a finger in the small of my back, right by the little box. It didn't hurt. It usually was very tender around the box, but I didn't even notice his fingers.

The door banged open and Christa crossed the room. Her hands frantically tried to pull her curls back into a ponytail, but the curls sprung out in crazy angles. Her eyes roamed over me carefully as another contraction hit.

"Premature labor?" She wanted to get the problem solved so she could go back to bed, but he shook his head.

"Not important. She's bleeding."

She frowned as she swiped a hand across my back. It came back covered in blood. Another contraction seized me, and I bit my lip. They were coming too fast. As it passed I opened my mouth, and gasped for air. The white pillow case turned red. Christa gently cupped my chin and pulled my mouth open.

"She is bleeding. What happened?" She eyed The Captain suspiciously.

"I didn't do anything. I swear."

Doubt wavered in her eyes.

"Get a cloth and wipe the blood off her back." Her hands rested on my stomach, and her lips moved slowly as another contraction seized me. She checked my pulse, and sighed. The Captain blotted my forehead as Christa left. He looked so worn down. I tried to comfort him, but another contraction hit. My back lifted off the bed and The Captain glanced out the door.

"Christa!"

She reappeared holding a jar, and a briefcase. A shimmering ball sparkled in the jar.

"This is a Wilting Life bloom. One of the only ones I have ever seen." She cradled the jar carefully in her arms. "The Wilting Life plant is only found in the Witchcastle Region. They bloom once every three-hundred cycles, and then the plant withers away. The bloom can diagnose any medical problem." Her fingers lovingly stroked the glass. The Captain rolled his eyes.

"I don't care how it works, how old it is, or even where it's found. Just make her better."

Christa frowned, but obeyed. She pressed my hand over the top of the jar, and the glowing bloom shot one long tentacle up into my hand. She bent over the jar, and whispered words into the glass. The bloom turned black, and then lit up and cycled through too many colors to count. I couldn't watch. It made me dizzy.

Another contraction.

I cut off a moan, and tried to relax.

That's what you're supposed to do right?

Ride it out and wait for it to pass.

It would pass.

She tapped the jar.

Another contraction seized me.

She stared, fascinated, waiting for it to pass.

She tapped the jar again.

Again my stomach seized as they built on top of each other. Exhaustion weighed me down.

Please stop.

She wouldn't relent. She whispered more words into the jar, and tapped it again.

Tap.

Contraction.

I was too tired to fight it. My body curled with it, and then I collapsed back onto the pillow.

Another whisper.

Tap.

Contraction.

I couldn't cut off the moan this time. I wanted to ask her to stop. I couldn't take this. But I couldn't form the words.

Whisper.

Tap.

Contraction.

I screamed.

I didn't know I could still scream, and her expression told me she wasn't expecting it. She set the jar on the night stand, and ran her ice cold hands over my forehead. She bent over me and whispered.

"What are they planning? What did they do to you? Will you let me see?"

My mind already flashed through the horrors of their camps. I slumped into the pillows and steeled myself to the terror that came with the memories. But her hands were gone. My memories cleared, and my eyes focused on the room.

The Captain hurled her body towards the floor. She put her hands back to catch herself, but they buckled and snapped. Her head smashed into the floor and she stilled. But only for a second.

She launched herself at The Captain and twisted her broken arm around his neck. Her feet were now well off the ground, and she had no leverage, but she didn't stop. He backed up quickly and smashed her against the wall. She braced her feet against the wall, but allowed the rest of her body to go slack.

His eyes told me he thought he won. But as he leaned away from the wall, she put all her strength into pushing away from the wall. He stumbled, unprepared, and fell to his knees. I heard the ligaments under his kneecaps crunching at the jarring solidity of the ground. He lurched forward and tried to catch himself, and the splint on his arm shattered. Christa caught the ground with her feet and stood, bent, over him, arm still around his neck.

"I don't want her to be part of your theories and battle plans. I want her past to stay there." He hissed at her, but her arm tightened; hand hanging uselessly at a broken angle. His eyes bulged, and his face turned red.

"One person's wishes are not going to stop me from doing what needs to be done." She said to his body as he lost consciousness and fell. Her face never changed expression. As she straightened she swiped her hand across the her stomach, and a smear of blood stain her fingers, but she ignored it. She crossed back over to me and tapped the jar again, absently brushing away hair that. During the fight it turned black, but now it faded back to blonde. Minutes passed in total silence, apart from the hissing from the jar.

"Who is the father?" She asked suddenly, pointedly, and handed me a sheet of parchment.

<u>The Captain.</u>

"It is okay if you do not know." She shot me a condescending smile. "No need to lie."

I was insulted.

"It's The Captain's baby." I spoke without thinking, and fire in my veins punished me.

"Well, then The Captain is a Rak." She sang. "You are pregnant with a Hybrid and it is killing you."

<u>I've had Hybrids before and never had a problem.</u>

She was wrong. She had to be wrong. He wasn't a Rak.

"You are older now. You are not on a Rak diet. Hybrids need different things than human babies." She glared at The Captain, who was awake again, but stayed quiet, watching Christa. "Your body is focused more on keeping your child alive, and in return, it is killing you."

"But why is she bleeding?" He spoke from the floor.

"I do not know." She blushed as she said it. The Captain scoffed.

"I thought your little plant bloom could diagnose anything."

"It can!" She defended. "But they are so rare, and people cannot study them well. It is saying that the baby is mostly responsible, but I do not know what the other colors mean."

"When she first touched it it turned black. What does that mean?"

"Death. And then the color after that was violet. That means reproduction. Put the two together, and it could mean the baby is dying, or the baby is killing her."

"Wow. I see you have that down to an exact science."

Another contraction hit me, and Christa fled from the room. The Captain sat on the bed, and placed his hands on my stomach.

"So what are we going to do, Alice?"

"Maybe I'll finally die."

The Captain frowned.

"Finally?" His voice broke, and my heart clenched.

"I've wanted to die since the day they arrested me, Captain. They never let me die."

"But you're free now. You don't need to beg for death anymore." He didn't understand. He thought he saved me. I tried to smile.

"You're right. I'm free now." I whispered, and hoped he believed me.

"Here, drink this." Christa ran back into the room, holding out a small vial. The Captain grabbed it out of her hand, and sniffed it.

"Is this poison?"

"No." She frowned. "Why would I poison her?"

"Well you seem pretty sure we are the source of all your problems, so why wouldn't you try to take us out." He said it as a joke, but the look she sent him was serious.

"Believe me, Captain, *when* I kill you, it will not be with poison." She grabbed it back, and pressed it to my lips. "Hopefully, if I overwhelm her system with everything it could possibly need, maybe I can nurse them along long enough for her to deliver the baby."

"By putting Alice's life at risk. I won't have it. Just terminate the pregnancy."

My eyes widened, and I grabbed my necklace. I couldn't lose this one. This one was his and I wanted it. Christa dropped the vial, and it shattered on the ground.

"Terminate?"

"Yes. Save Alice's life."

"By ending another." Her eyes glazed over, and her hands started shaking.

"It's not a life yet."

A lump rose in my throat, and I couldn't look at The Captain. Christa reached over the bed, and slapped him.

"I am a Healer. It is my job to save lives. *Any* life."

"Even mine? The General's Suit?" He taunted her.

"Why do you think you are still alive?"

The Captain shrugged.

"Whatever. Just end this thing so Alice can get better."

"My job is to save lives, and I can list, off the top of my head, twenty lives I could not save." As she spoke, tears clouded her eyes, but she didn't let them fall. "Please, let me save this one. If things start to unravel, then we can try your idea, but please let me save this life."

The Captain sighed, and looked down at me. I nodded my head, and hoped he would concede. His jaw twitched as he thought, and then, finally, he looked back at Christa.

"Fine. Do what you can. But if she gets any worse, you

will end it."

The tears finally fell from her eyes as she agreed. She brushed my hair out of my face, and smiled.

"Do not worry, Alice. I will save your baby." Her eyes filled with sorrow as she spoke, and her free hand rested on her own stomach. The Captain grunted, and left the room. Christa turned towards the window, and her mouth fell open.

"How long have you been standing there?"

"How long are you going to put off the inevitable?" An old man, with fire for hair, stood just inside the window.

"I am not putting anything off, Elder. Things are different now."

"So you will do what the visions are telling you?" He walked over to me, and held out a hand, but stopped when I shied away from him.

"Stay away from her." Christa spat out of her teeth.

"She's got your answer in her memories. Before she came you didn't know they experimented on prisoners. Before she came, nobody returned from him. If you look at what they've done to her, you will know he's not the ruler the regions think he is. He's dangerous. He's planning terrible things. You can't just stand by anymore. This isn't what you were created for."

"How do you know what I was created for?"

"That piercing in your cartilage. You might want to brush up of your Àraid history if you've forgotten what it means."

She pursed her lips, but didn't argue. The old man pressed two fingers to his chin, and smiled at me again.

"Look into her memories. Either you'll prove me wrong, and decide war is not the option. Or you'll see I'm right. I'll await your signal."

Smoke gathered at his feet, and consumed him. When it cleared, he was gone.

"**S**top interfering, Vǎɼẓ. Stop encouraging her."

"That's my job. To council the Ɍèʌïǎ."

"**She is not our Ɍèʌïǎ!**"

"*Maybe we should try encouraging her. So far she's only had bad experiences with the Elders. Of course she's hesitant.*"

"**What do you plan to do about that?**"

"I plan on answering when she calls. And you will, too."

"**I will?**"

"Regardless of how you feel about her, you cannot deny yourself. When she calls for us, we will be there for her."

Inhibited

Christa

The first time I met the fiery Àraid was the day Jaycobe turned six. He replaced the Àraid that pierced me. All Àraid got their piercings when they turn six. That day he saw mine, and since then he showed up ever season and pressured me into going to war.

I thought I told him off.

I thought I discouraged him enough to make him retreat back to his hole in the ground.

Hiding was safer. I did not want to be responsible for his death.

Element Àraids could not hide as well as the others. They always had some sort of element incorporated into their look. Fiery hair would not go unnoticed. I told him to return to the Wellwald Region, and keep a low profile. Wellwald was untamed and dangerous and The General would not venture there unless he was positive there were Àraid living there.

I thought he listened. I thought he finally gave up.

I wished he confronted me privately, instead of in front of Alice. After he left, she begged me to look into her memories.

I did not want to know.

I knew I would not like what I found there.

But the Elder was right.

This was what I was created for.

I gathered Alice, and my two eldest daughters, in one of the darkest rooms in my house. Reviewing memories was tricky. I personally never attempted it, but I knew how. Alice sat in one of the chairs to the side of the room with a blinded obserling in the palm of her hand.

I would join the bird and the woman using my abilities, which I did not have full control of yet. Alice said she trusted me. She was so pale, so tired, but some residual strength shone through the fatigue. She was a fighter.

She would be the end of me.

Cerynn and Ginny sat facing the blank wall with notepads on their laps. Jaycobe was not there. Stupid irresponsible child.

Did he not know we needed him?

Did he not know that *I* needed him?

He was my oldest child. I put more pressure on him. I knew that was wrong, but I could not help it. He was my oldest. He was my son. He should be here helping me.

The plan, I guess, would work with just us, but it would have been nice to have my son here. We were in Ginny's experiment room, and she did not bother to clean up before we started. Her schematics were strewn throughout the room, most incomplete. She worked long hours in her lab. She, too, was pale. I knew it was not from illness, simply a lack of light, that caused the lack of pigment to her skin. She stayed in her room whenever she could. It dawned on me that I had not spoken to her in a quarter season; this being the first time I had seen her.

The Captain was distracted by Peter, who was giving him a tour of the house. We had a little over an hour.

"Alright, Alice. Are you sure you want to do this?"

Her smile was watery, but she nodded through her obvious fear. I was trying to talk her out of this. I did not want to see what she went through in there. I spent my residual powers blocking out visions of what went on in there, and now here I was, opening those floodgates. I took a deep breath, and pressed one hand against Alice's head, and one against the obserling.

"Χúša."

The bird curled up in Alice's hands, and opened its mouth towards the blank wall. The wall lit up with a swirl of images, and I averted my eyes. Without my direction, it would show whatever it wanted, and I did not want to see the majority of memories I knew I would find.

"I am going to direct what memories you show us. Do not fight them. It will seem like you are going through it for the first time. If I think it is getting too hard for you, I will edit your memory. Do not try to change anything, just wait until I tell you to change it." Altering memories was frowned upon, but sometimes it was the only way.

Alice nodded, ready, but nervous. I kept my hand on the bird, and turned back to the wall. The memories flipped across the wall, and I finally settled on one.

She was up in the Nalaise castle, roaming the halls alone. The castle, not the prison. She was in his *home*.

"There you are. The General's been looking everywhere for you." A Rak guard jogged up the hall towards her. "How did you get out of your room?"

Her *room*. Not cell. Room.

She did not answer as she watched him approach. Two more guards approached from the other direction, looping ropes into lassos as if they were trying to catch a wild horse, but a broken woman who could barely stand.

The first guard stepped close and reached out to rake sharp fingers down her arm; pulling away flesh and eating it, savoring it. She cringed, and stared only at her reflection in a wall-hanging. Her terrified deep green eyes stared back. Deep green. Not white blue like they were now.

Deep green.

My heart sank.

Her vision blurred behind tears as the guard pushed her against the wall. Her hands started to shake as he pushed himself against her, and, in a flash, her hand shot up and caught his throat hard, crushing his windpipe.

No noise came out as his eyes widened and he collapsed on the ground. Everything stood still, and then the place erupted. The other guards rushed towards her, yelling for backup as she ran from their ropes. She turned down a hall, but was surrounded by angry guards. In the chaos they lashed out on each other as well as her.

She sank to the ground, and curled into a ball. Her ribs shattered as feet drove into her. And then someone covered her mouth and pulled her into a quieter room. Four sets of shackles graced the walls, two occupied. There was a couch in the middle of the room, but it dripped blood and poison. She looked up to see who pulled her inside, and froze. The General, his mouth dripping black poison, hovered above her. He ducked his head and bit deep into her shoulder.

"*I* punish them for touching you. Not you. That's not your job. Your job is to let them do whatever they want. You are *nothing*, Pet." He waited a few seconds for the poison to take effect, then handed her a knife. "Punish yourself for what you've done."

She took the knife. Her hands pulsed black veins as she dug the knife into the skin at the base of her index finger, sliding it out as if peeling a carrot. The skin rolled off, and she reached the nail-bed, digging in and peeling the nail off as well.

"Please, please stop."

He laughed at her pleas. She turned the blade towards herself, pressing it right above her collarbone. Black veins flashed across her face and chest. She applied slow pressure and blood pooled and ran down into the v of her chest.

"Please." She cried as he laughed and watched her.

"Alice." I could not keep watching that. And she could not relive it. Her face contorted in pain, and sweat beaded on her clammy skin. I needed to intervene. I touched her shoulder gently, trying to pull her back. "Come back. This is too much for you. Get out."

She sobbed; clutching her chest where the dagger in the memory pressed. I looked back at the wall, hand still resting on her shoulder.

The General watched intently as the blade cut a trail down her chest and rip the front of her shirt. The General smiled and crossed his arms.

Alice in the memory swayed, and collapsed, blood pooling around her. The General snapped his fingers, the bite on her shoulder pooled up and ran black poison down her arm. He took her hand and her fingers began to glow as the wound on her chest slowly closed.

Her eyes fluttered open, and she sat up slowly, leaning against him weakly.

"Your only shelter is me. Only I can protect you from them. You need to belong to me." He whispered, helping her to her feet.

"Now run." I whispered to her. He was grabbing the shackles, readying them for her. The version of her portrayed on the wall stood and bolted. Ginny furiously scribbled notes as Alice took us on a tour of the castle, running through the hallways, hurrying up stairs faster than her weakened body should be able to take her. She burst into the courtyard and ran to the front gates, but they would not open for her.

The screen went blank and she opened her eyes, terror still evident on her face.

"Was that too much?" I asked her.

She gasped for air, eyes panicked. Maybe this was crazy. Maybe I should not have done this. I reached up and checked her pulse.

Too fast.

She pulled away from my touch, eyes wide with terror and uncertainty. She did not see me. She saw the Raks. I was a Rak in her mangled mind. I paused, unsure, theorizing the next step, then slowly pulled a knife from my sheath.

"Cerynn, stand by." I only managed to teach her one ability between the chaos, but I taught her healing.

This would be her test.

My daughter stood and held her hands in preparation.

"Alice." I had never done this. I hoped it would work. I hoped it was not crazy. "Kill me. Save yourself, get out of here. If you kill me you can escape without trouble. I will not fight."

She stared at the knife in her hand, tested the blade with the tip of her finger, then lunged at me, driving it deep under my ribs.

I gasped.

It hurt more than I thought it would.

As she drew the blade back Cerynn's hands pressed into my back. The wound healed under my shirt. She stabbed again, this time right below my bellybutton and pulling up, shredding my skin with the serrated edge. I closed my eyes and feigned death. I dropped to the ground and the blade pressed against my throat. The woman stood over me, poised to slit my neck.

Cerynn, you better be quick.

Alice pulled and my skin parted. I could not draw breath. In my panic I forgot to keep my mouth shut, and as my jaw relaxed Alice pushed the knife deep into my mouth. I knew I would die that way. She found the best way to kill me.

She had taken me too seriously.

Cerynn could not fix this.

I thought of the memory of my mother throwing herself between me and my drunken father. Sacrificing herself for me. She was not doing that this time. Now she stood over

me, stabbing me over and over.
   Where was Peter?
   Would he be okay?
   Would he be mad at me?
   My eyes would not open.
   Dying was not as painful as I imagined.

Inhibited

Alice

62nd Day, The Season Of Death, 749-PW

The Captain doesn't like Christa. He doesn't trust her. And she doesn't trust him. I thought escaping would give me my life back, but it hasn't. I'm still there, in the prisons. Maybe not physically, but mentally I never escaped. The Captain tried too hard to keep me safe. I can't let him see how afraid I still am. I'm failing him. He wants me to be OK. He wants me to be free. Sometimes I get so lost in the memories it takes me a while to get back to reality. The only way I will be free is if Christa succeeds in killing The General. I need to help her. Christa is going to let me help her later this afternoon. Until then I'm just stuck here, in this room. Stuck with what little memories I have.

I stood in the quiet room; memories flashing through my head.

Everything.

Terror flooded me as I remembered The Captain. I remembered how we met.

I knew who he was.

I knew what he became.

I knew I should fear him.

I looked around the room. My mind struggled to put the pieces together.

I was standing.

I was sitting when we started. I gripped something in my hand, and held it up to the meager light of the candles.

A knife.

Blood dripped from the tip. I dropped the knife and reached for my necklace, remembering too late I'd left it with The Captain. My nails scratched at my neck, searching for the charm that wasn't there.

I heard a scuffle behind me, and reluctantly turned. Cerynn straddled a body on the floor. Ginny knelt beside her, but reached behind her and lit a lamp. Christa. She was sprawled on the ground, eyes shut. Blood pooled around her on the tile floor, and her hair shifted to a deep red. And then I recognized her. I *remembered* her. Chrissy.

"Give up, Cerynn." Ginny said as I sank to my knees at my daughter's head; placing trembling fingers on her neck, tracing the scar down to her shoulder. Blood washed away the make-up covering the scar. More blood ran from a wound on her neck, but her body was running out.

"She's gone, Cerynn."

No.

Cerynn leaned back on her heels, and buried her head in her hands.

You can't stop. You have to save her.

She was dead.

They told me she died.

Her skin was ashen, cold. I bent over her and pulled her into my arms. She was limp. I couldn't find a heartbeat. Cerynn put a comforting hand on my arm, and electricity flooded me. Her body jolted as it surged into her.

Again.

Once more.

I checked for a pulse. She had one. Very faint, but growing stronger. The cuts in her neck, and through her mouth, closed. Christa's eyes fluttered open and I was staring into beautiful smoke-grey once again. I never thought I would see those eyes again. She smiled up at me and touched her hair, stroking the curly tresses.

"Hello, Mother."

✝   ✝   ✝   ✝   ✝

<u>Are you sure you want to do this again?</u> I once again sat in the chair with the bird on my lap. Christa sat across from me, contemplating. <u>Last time I killed you.</u>

"Yeah and brought her back." Cerynn interrupted. "I would love to know how you did that because even the Èṭèᵣла can't bring someone back like that." Cerynn prodded, but I honestly didn't know how I did it. It was impulse. "Two things an Èṭèᵣла cannot do. We cannot heal ourselves, and we cannot bring someone back from the brink of death. The *only* things we cannot to. We burn up and die if we do that."

Christa nodded in agreement. Finally she spoke.

"We only have a few minutes left before your *husband* gets back. If we are going to learn anything else from your memories, it needs to be now." She touched her bird again, and the wall lit up. "I want to know what he is planning."

But I was already there, crouched in a little corner of a

room, pressing my back against the cold stone.

The door opened and The General came in, followed by The Captain. I wasn't supposed to be here. The General never allowed me into his office.

I glanced at my wrist, and thought of the tracker The General embedded under my skin. The tiny device told him exactly where I was, and accessed my memories to use my thoughts against me. I rubbed the spot, and hoped The General wasn't paying attention to the reading.

"The Elders are well hidden, Sir." The Captain sounded desperate. "Your guards haven't found them."

"Then they're not looking hard enough!" The General slammed his fist into the table. I shrank farther into the corner, behind the bookshelf. He couldn't see me. He couldn't know I was in here. "I need to find the Àraid, Captain. I need them gone completely. I'm running out of time."

"Why, Sir?"

"My trophy got her spirit back. She's not obeying." His voice drew closer as he spoke, and I held my breath. "She won't work if I don't have total control." He reached down and grabbed my ankle. I screamed, and kicked him.

"See what I mean, Captain? No respect. No control." He tapped my wrist. "I always know, Dear. You'll never outsmart me." He poked tongs into the fire, and pulled out a small, burning coal.

"Open up, Princess." He pried my mouth open and shoved the coal past my teeth. "Don't make a sound." He held my mouth shut, and I cried as it burned.

The Captain shifted as he watched me wilt.

"Sir, if you scald her too much she won't be any fun."

The General thought for a moment, and then nodded and let go of my mouth. I spat out the coal, and The General shoved me into The Captain's arms.

"Try it out. See if it's still fun." He laughed, but The

Captain frowned.

"That's not what I meant, Sir." He steadied me. "She's yours. I'm not allowed to touch her."

"Fine. As of today, you may touch her in any way, except that which leads to children. I promise there are other ways that are just as fun." He winked. "You're my best man. I share with those I trust." He tied my hands together, and lifted them up to a hook hanging in the middle of the room. My toes barely touched the ground now. I cut off a whimper and stared at my feet.

"Make her yours, Captain. I'll share her with you."

"How, Sir?"

A knife cut through my dress, and The General's hands ran down my back. He flicked off the box in my spine, and my legs went limp. The weight jarred my arms as I sagged against them. The General laughed as I swung against the ropes.

"Just like that, Captain."

"Sir, I don't understand why you're doing this."

"You need to break her. You did before, you can again. If I keep you by her side, breaking her over and over, I'll have control. Then I can use her to sniff out the Àraid Ρèлïǎ and their silly pieces."

"Pieces?" The Captain lifted me slightly, easing the pressure on my arms.

"When The King created the Àraid, he gave them objects to protect. United, the objects make the ruler unlimited. Their abilities don't drain their energy, and anything they can imagine is possible. Created to help the Ρèлïǎ, The King didn't foresee the Raks. He didn't foresee me. Àraids can't use their powers on themselves. If I have control of another person, they can kill the Àraid with my powers, and steal the objects for me. I only need three of the six pieces. My pet will unite them, and make me the most powerful."

He pressed The Captain up against me, and sneered.

"Take her name. Take her to my house outside the gates

and guard her closely until I am ready. I'm tired of keeping track of her, and making sure nobody else touches her."

"I thought you said she wouldn't work, because you can't control her." The Captain smoothed my hair as he spoke, and pressed my head against his chest.

"I think that problem will work itself out." He smiled, and left the room. I heard a lock click into place on the other side. The Captain lifted me off the hook, and laid me on the ground.

"Why do you still fight?" He was quiet. My mouth burned as I answered his question.

"Because when The King returns, I want to make sure I stand on the right side." I looked up into his menacing eyes and waited. I trusted those eyes once. "But I'm so tired of fighting."

He leaned over me, and I shut my eyes to block out the room around me. Pressure at my wrist made me crack my eyes to see what he was doing. He pulled off his belt and strapped it tightly just below my elbow, and then pinched the skin on the inside of my wrist with pliers. He pulled a chunk of skin free from my wrist. I cried out, surprised, and watch the blood flow onto the floor. His pliers probed deeper and pulled off more tissue.

"Stop." My arm shook as I tried to pull away from him, but he ignored me, going back a third time.

I squirmed and tasted blood where I bit through my lip. My arm was numb with pain. Then the pliers clamped around something and pulled hard. It was stuck, and as he yanked and pulled whatever it was out of my wrist I screamed and cried and begged him to stop. The device in my wrist shattered, but at last he pulled most of it free, and held it up for me to inspect.

"I hated him tracking you. Now he can't."

"He'll be angry that you broke it."

"I'll just apologize and tell him I got carried away torturing you." He smiled at me. "You belong to me now.

Just like The General wanted."

*I shuddered, and glanced, panicked, towards the door.
His voice hardened.*

*"He wants me to keep you isolated just for him. But once
you're outside the fence, you'll be free. Now that I took out
your tracker, we could hide right under The General's nose.
I will get you out of here. I'm going to save. You'll be mine.
Sound like a deal?"*

Again I shuddered, but he chose not to see.

*"I'm not a Rak. I won't abuse you like they do. You'll be
safe with me. It's me or The General. Come on Alice. After
all we've been through, why would you choose him?" He
pleaded. "He doesn't love you. He'll never care for you. To
him you're nothing but a prize, an item to enjoy, and lock
away somewhere under constant guard. He knows who you
are, Counselor. You need to be afraid of him."*

"What did you call me?"

He watched me for a second.

"You mean they haven't told you yet?"

"Told me what?"

He chuckled.

*"I'm not going to tell you. That'll give me leverage." He
held out a parchment. "Sign it."*

I read it.

"This is a marriage license."

*"Yes, very observant. They won't let you out of here if
you don't exist. You need to take my name. Sign it."*

*The pliers jabbed into my arm again, and I cried out,
shakily taking the pen and signing the parchment. He sent
the license through the snake tunnels, down to the registrar,
and carried me from the room.*

Christa shook me back to the real world.

"I knew he was a Rak! He is a spy. Why did you not tell
me? Why did I have to pry it out of your head. That is why
we are having all these problems. We are harboring a Rak!"

She was furious.

"No, Christa. He works for himself. They don't know his name." I couldn't keep quiet anymore. She would arrest him if I didn't speak up.

"What did you say?" She stopped and faced me.

"His name. If they know it, they can use it. You become a robot. You do what they tell you to. You don't get a say in the matter." My hand traced the deep scar on her neck. "They never knew his name. He was there for the money, so he did what they asked, but he's out now. He's trying, for me, to change."

Christa rolled her eyes and pushed my hand away.

"How did he hire The Captain without knowing his name?"

"He didn't need to. As soon as you're hired by the Raks, you become part of their naming system. Starting at Private, moving up the ranks to General."

"How many people did The Captain break to get his name?"

I pressed my lips together, and twisted my necklace in my fingers.

"I thought so." Christa taunted. "Captain is the ninth rank. He needed to break over twenty-five-thousand people to get his name, and you still ask me to trust him?"

Jaycobe

"**H**ow do you like living here, young man?" The General sat behind a desk, hands folded in front of him.

"I love it." I grinned. "Why? Have I done something dissatisfying?" After the initial shock of being here, I adjusted quickly. I enjoyed the camaraderie of my fellow recruits. All of us had been living in the dark but now we were enlightened.

Every recruit came in kicking and screaming, only to find how wrong we were. Although the humans thought the Àraid were gone, the Raks knew better. They knew the Àraid were the ones to watch out for. They were the ones screwing up the system. The General chuckled.

"Wrong? No. You have been nothing but enthusiastic of our work here. But, I want to know how strong your ties to your old life are. Have we broken you yet?"

Broken.

They called it that.

It was a painful process.

I didn't understand it at first, but like so many other things, it became clear. They don't break the person, they break the chains holding them. They wrenched and pulled at those chains and it hurt, but it was for the greater good.

"Yes, Sir, you have."

He toyed with a charm on a chain listlessly, contemplating.

"I need information. What is your mother's name?"

"Christa, Sir."

"No. It's not. I tried that."

"Tried, Sir?" I wasn't following.

"Your mother is tricky. I knew your father was Àraid, but I can't tell if your mother is or not. I need her name." He was talking to himself.

"Excuse me, Sir, but, why? Why does it matter if she's Àraid?"

He looked at me squarely.

"I need to gather the Objects of the Elders. Divided, the objects will be easy to get. But if the Elders unite behind a Rèлïǎ, it will be very difficult to divide them again. Your mother is skilled, and manipulative. She will stop me if she figures out what I'm doing."

My heart sank. My mother always got her way.

"She is Àraid, Sir. You need to stop her before she stops you."

"She hasn't proven she's Àraid. She may have told you to simply win you over."

"Let me talk to her, Sir, I'm sure I could show her how wrong she is." I rose from my seat.

"No. I can't risk you out there right now. But, we may need to take action. We need to take her out first. She's been meddling too long. And now, with the Rèx̠taÿла in their grasp, she's pretty dangerous. I need to get the Rèx̠taÿла back to safety, but I'm afraid your mother will figure out who it is. Then I'll never be able to save them." He put his head in his hands.

Why couldn't my mother realize how wrong she was?

"I'll let you go, Private." His voice was muddled through his hands. "It's almost time for Telia and you don't want to miss that."

I stood and retreated. I knew I was no longer needed.

"There you are!" The Private rushed towards me down the hall. "What did The General want?"

"Information for the war."

"Ah." She nodded her pretty head, and light bounced off the black scales. "I'm going out on the next mission. I've been cleared." Her eyes sparkled with excitement. Her arms wove around me and she put her hand on my chest. "I'm glad I picked you, I'm so sorry it hurt so bad. The auction started. You wanna check it out?" She was already leading me down the dark streets.

"Sold!" A loud voice rang through the crowd as a hammer slammed onto the table. The shaking girl in chains was led down off the stage and a man grabbed her chains and held out his change. The Private shivered next to me.

"They always look so sad when they're sold." She whispered.

They led another young girl up to the stage. She tried to move away from the Raks' advances, but the more she retreated the more they did. I was almost embarrassed for her having that done to her in front of all these people. But I knew it was for the best. One Rak moved fast and pulled her to him, covering her mouth with his. The crowed waited with baited breath for his answer. His lips moved down to her neck, then her shoulder, and he bit down, hard. Blood spurted down her arm as he pulled back, licking the red liquid from his lips. One jerk of his head.

No.

The auctioneer stepped up to the girl and drove a knife to its hilt beneath her ribs. The crowd went silent as she fell to the stage floor, her blood pooling and mixing with what was already there.

"Too bad." I wanted to buy her, she would have been nice, easy to break.

"She was useless. No control." The Private looked up at me, eyes wide, hoping I understood.

I glanced back at the stage. She still fought for life. A Rak jumped on top of her and several jeered at the pair. One spit on her, and black poison ran down her face, past her eyes as they closed for the last time.

More chains rattled as this time a boy limped across the stage. He brought the crowd back to their senses and soon they were laughing and jeering and groping again. Another bite, and this time a nod. The bidding began, but started way out of my budget.

"How about I pretend I bought you?" I whispered down to the Private. She smiled back up at me.

"Then take me home and break me, Solider."

Alice

62nd Day, The Season Of Death, 749-PW

Chrissy is alive. How can she be alive? I watched her die. She's alive, and she hates me. She thinks I am a spy. She thinks The Captain is a spy. She doesn't trust me. Why should she? I should be dead. I should have died cycles ago. You shouldn't trust a ghost.

"**M**other!" Chrissy slammed her hand onto the arm of my chair. "Stop writing in you little journal, and answer the question."

The Captain told me to write down any event that seemed monumental so I wouldn't forget. I promised I would write everything down. Chrissy was getting tired of waiting, though.

I shifted my weight, and switched to my conversation notebook. I poised my pen over the page and tried to remember what she'd asked. She asked something about The Captain, but I didn't remember what. I took a random guess.

I hated The Captain for a whole season after I met him. He was a Rak, in my eyes. He tortured me for money, that was it. I didn't understand how one person could embody so much hatred and for that I hated him. Ironic, I know, but it made sense at the time.

"*Don't make a sound. Don't say a word.*" The General whispered in my head.

Chrissy paced in front of me, a list of questions in her hand.

"Do you still hate him?" Her sharp eyes prodded me. She wasn't listening to my answer, but watching my reaction.

"*Actions speak louder than words, Mother.*" *She always told me after she recited exactly what I was thinking.*

My daughter. Not dead. I couldn't move past that. She wanted us to move on as if everything was fine, normal. The Raks killed her, I saw her fall in front of The General. His machete cut through her and her daughter.

How did she survive?

She wondered the same about me. Although she would never ask outright, her questions showed as much. She placed a hand on her hip and her uncontrollably curly hair sprang from the ribbon she'd tied it up in. I needed to break my ties with The General if I wanted her to trust me. I took a deep breath and cleared my throat.

"I'm sorry, what was the question?"

Her face betrayed her frustration, but she calmly repeated herself.

"Do you hate The Captain now?"

"He's a good man, Chrissy." I kept my voice low, and fought the fear it caused. I fought the images of what *he* would do to me when I spoke. She made a face, and rolled her eyes.

"That was not the question. Do you hate him?"

"No."

"Do you love him?" She dreaded my answer. I could see it in her eyes. I closed my eyes for a second, and remembered our moment earlier. He was so patient. He walked me through the whole thing, and made sure I was comfortable. He did his best to please me. Nobody had done that since Micheal died. Slowly, I nodded.

"I think so."

"How could you do that to Micheal? How would he feel if he knew you tossed him aside for some Rak? Some random Rak wearing *his* face."

I launched to my feet and slapped her before she finished the question.

"Don't ever say his name." The words tumbled out of my mouth. "He is dead. That's all there is to it. He would want me to be happy."

She rubbed her face and her eyes glowed violet.

"Happy with a Rak? Is that what he would want? Are you sure about that, Mother?"

I wanted to slap her again.

"The Captain isn't a Rak, Chrissy. I've already told you that."

"And I will never believe it. I am smarter than that, Mother. Micheal was smarter than that." She smirked to hide her tears. "But I guess it does not matter what he would have wanted since you killed him. Obviously you do not care about what he would have wanted. You just think about yourself."

I stumbled back into the chair and covered my mouth.

Was that what she thought of me?

Did she really believe what she said?

She collapsed on the ground and put her head in her hands, rocking. Three heel-to-toe rocks and then she let out an anguished scream.

"How can you not hate a Rak? They are everything you have ever spoken against. Everything you believe in? They are not."

"He's not a Rak, Chrissy."

"What are you talking about? Of course he is." Panic filled her eyes, and loose parchment on the desk fluttered into the air as her panic overflowed into the room. "He has to be a Rak." She was scared, so sure that she picked the right one to blame. She jumped up and ran over to me, gently touching one of the bruises on my face. The bruise was sensitive to touch, and I pulled away from her, aggravating the smaller bruises covering my back and arms. I remained quiet, hoping she would see for herself The Captain's innocence. I couldn't defend him. I wasn't sure how.

† † † † †

"Were you talking, Dear?" The Captain entered as Chrissy left the room. He kissed me gently. "You know you shouldn't talk."

I couldn't look at him as I showed him the words I'd already written.

I know who you are. I remember everything now.

He didn't speak as he sat on the bed next to me. He nodded sadly and took my hands in his, slowly wrapping his fingers around my wrists. His thumb stroked the scar on the inside of my wrist and I knew what he was doing. I tried to pull away, to stop him somehow, but he kept a firm grasp around my arm. His sad green eyes met mine and he mouthed the words 'I'm sorry', and then drove his thumb into the groove on my wrist.

Christa

"**K**nock knock." I already opened the door to peek into my daughter's room, I just wanted to let her know I was there. I allowed each of my children to design their rooms own rooms, and did not visit them often. I did not watch my children design their rooms. I allowed them that privacy.

While my other children went with the basic themes of princess, dragon, Gothic, sterile, and, even with my protest, posters of pretty women wearing less than they should, Quartnee chose a unique theme. She worked long hours with Peter to custom-make everything, and now her walls were dotted with paintings of crossed creatures. Above her bed was a painting of a horse, but instead of a horse's head, she changed it to a bear. Four pictures opposite that held images of birds with pieces of cats, and dogs, worked into the overall shape.

When Peter told me the theme my daughter chose, I thought it odd, but Peter calmed my concern by pointing out that her theme probably stemmed from her shape-shifting blood. Of course she would share a fascination with that subject. I hated to admit it, but he was right. Even when she was unaware of her powers, they showed through her taste.

Now she lay on her bed, playing with her favorite doll. On that particular doll, she removed the arms, and sewed on wings. She did so after a fight which ended with me forcing her to walk along with Cerynn on her rounds.

"This way my dolly will never have to walk. She can just fly everywhere, and won't be tired." She exclaimed spitefully when she showed me the doll.

"What are you doing in here, Mom?" Quartnee watched me suspiciously.

"I just wanted to spend some time with you. One-on-one time."

"We've never done that before."

Could that be right?

Had I really never spent time with my her?

My mind scrambled for a moment, any moment, to prove that I played with her, but it came up empty.

"Well, I am sorry about that. I want to start now. I want to spend time with you."

"To appease your guilt? To make you feel like a better parent to me than your mother was to you?" She sounded like she was quoting something she heard, and I wondered what my other children were saying behind my back. I pressed my lips together, biting back the retorts that sprang to my tongue, and sat next to her on the bed.

"What would you like to do with the time I have allotted you?" As I said it, I heard how cold it sounded, and the pain that clouded her eyes told me it hurt to hear.

"You don't need to spend time in here. I know you don't like your children."

My face burned in shame. I avoided time with my children so they would not know my secret. My secret was out now, but the damage was done. I gently touched her leg, trying to be comforting, but it just felt awkward.

She shoved my hand away, but stared at it for a moment. Then she lunged at me, and threw her arms around my neck.

"Are you really going to spend time with us now?"

"Yes."

"I want you to read me a story. You've never read me a story before."

Tears pressed against my eyelids, and I could only nod, but she did not seem to notice. She jumped off the bed, and ran to a bookcase in the corner. I smiled at the book she picked. My father gave me that book as a wedding present. She shoved the book into my lap, and I opened it. Sparks danced from my fingers as I traced the colorful illustrations and scrawling calligraphy that filled the brittle pages. My brother and I spent days translating the Àraid nursery rhyme to one that worked in the human tongue. He hoped one day the Àraid would not need to hide anymore, and I would be able to read the poem to my children. I guess he sort of got his wish.

"Okay, I will read this to you, but you need to pay attention. It might seem like a nursery rhyme, but it is true, and important, Quartnee. Do you understand?"

She nodded, and stretched out on the bed, nestling her head into my lap. It was then, looking down at my daughter snuggled against me, I realized the pain was less. Not gone, but less. I could focus. I smoothed her hair, and remembered Alice doing the same for me. I cleared my throat, and looked at the book.

> *"Straighten up, and pay attention.*
> *This tale is not one of invention.*
> *Memorize these words you hear.*
> *Lest our story disappear."*

My father wrote that bit. He was very proud of his rhyming human words.

> *"Once upon a time, a prince became King, and was sent to this world;*
> *forbidden to return until he calmed the violence of humans.*

Death does not exist in his world, and The King was not prepared for the death of this world." I interrupted myself. "The Àraid do not die unless they are killed. If nothing kills them, they just keep going. Legends say there are still a handful of the original Àraid hiding throughout the Regions. Àraid are not meant to lose people. The more they lose, the more their mind unravels."

The scars on my arms burned in acknowledgment.

"Left behind in Šïҳð̠ř, The Collector and The Mentor could only hope that the King would succeed where they could not.

The Collector could never unite the humans, because he cannot be seen by the humans. He simply collects, and delivers souls. That way they are not left subject to Ashal. The Mentor could not unite them because he never left Šïҳð̠ř." As I read the story to her, I realized how much we accidentally left out. I did not like interrupting myself, but she needed to know the full story.

"Uniting the humans was no small task, and our King did not understand how much of an undertaking it would be. The humans were used to conflict and violence, and did not see any reason to try to change. The King was not of this world, and could not understand them, so he created the Àraid. If he could not unite the humans, he would save them from themselves.

He began with three Àraid. Each one was given a small portion of his powers. They must work together to be strongest. He allowed these three new races to choose nine humans who would also be given powers, and converted to Àraid.

He named six of them Elders, to serve over the others. They painted the sky, and the trees, and the lake, and worked together to improve this world.

The King gave each race two objects, that together gave them control over the world. When the Àraid went into hiding, they split into their own groups. They failed to remain united, and lost their control.

But that is later.

The King gave each of the races a true name. True names hold power, and with that, control. The King granted them the power to learn the names of every object, and with that, control over the world around them.

Leħð̠t'çvil Zмèʌçïa was the name that he gave to the ones who controlled time. They were plagued with visions, and could alter time with little thought.

The Jðrілега Zмèлçіа controlled the Earth. They enjoyed their powers more than the first race did. For they were given the gift to manipulate water, and air, and land.

To the Face-changers he gave the name Алtvаг Zмèлçіа. They could change their appearance, but were unimpressed with their abilities when they compared themselves to the others. They hid their frustration from The King, though.

The Àraid swore to never tell their true name, for they knew the power a name wields over its owner. So two names they gave to their children. One name kept hidden, and one name answered to.

For a while this worked. But the humans wore off on them.

The King saw his people slowly falling apart, and created another race to help bind them. He picked someone new, to bestow the most powers, to embody the abilities of all of the others. She became Reлïð.

Her name was Rachel, and she was the first Veçлÿ Etèгла.

She managed to do what The King could not. The Àraid were united. The King was pleased, but he was now distanced from the Àraid. They had someone new, and only her they obeyed.

He went back to Siхðг, and returned for rare visits. He was ashamed for the pain he inflicted upon the world. The Àraid were united and fighting, but many were dying. He allowed the Àraid to go to his world to visit their dead. But The Àraid could not cross over without The King's power, or their souls would be severed by the gateway.

The humans began spending time with the Àraid, and some of them soon got laid.''

I paused and blushed.

Did the book really say that?

"Seers, and Lights, Shadows, Nights, Freezers, and Jumpers were now formed. Their powers were harder to pin down, and more limited than the Àraid.

Reл Rachel lived a long time before a stray human arrow stole her life. Her eldest daughter succeed her, and the people hoped she would be just like the first Reлïð. But she was not her mother, and the people

soon saw that this new ℛℯ𝓁ⅈä could be loved in her own way.
The new ℛℯ𝓁ⅈä was Ana. She trained her people for some kind of
conflict. The Àraid had been at peace for cycles, and could not
understand why an army was needed. But they trained anyway.
Before any conflict arose, the ℛℯ𝓁ⅈä took sick.
"A war is coming, but we will win." Were her last words and were
repeated for cycles in our darkest times.
The next ℛℯ𝓁ⅈä could not handle the damage done by such a prophesy,
or the betrayal that ended Mary's life. She was not prepared for such a
big challenge. The unity dissolved, and the people divided. The Elders
took control of their own races, and The King was asked to step aside.
A ceremony began for the Àraid children. The child would be ranked,
and given earrings to show what classification the child belonged in."

I stopped and pulled her attention back to me.

"Peter is high rank, which is symbolized by one piercing." I pointed to my ears. "I am second, and third rank." I had two earrings on my right ear, three on my left, and one cartilage piercing on my right ear.

"The King returned once more to his people. If they could dictate
ranks by piercings, he would dictate royalty the same way. He knew
ethics were more important than blood, and the way his people were
going, they needed a strong leader to keep them on track.
The regal piercing appears on the cartilage, always on the right, to
show our heritage."

I bore the regal earring, as did Cerynn. Jaycobe and Ginny did not, even though they were older than Cerynn.

"ℛℯ𝓁 Mary grew paranoid, and obsessively watched the ceremonies. She
never found out who would take her crown. The willows took her life,
but a daughter survived. Six cycles passed without a new piercing, and
then ℛℯ𝓁ⅈä Mary's daughter was given the regal earring. ℛℯ𝓁 Mary's
sister took up the crown until Mary's daughter was old enough to rule.
This young ℛℯ𝓁ⅈä was a natural-born leader. The training continued,
but the rumors of war ceased. The wonderful ℛℯ𝓁ⅈä gave birth to twin
daughters, and at their ceremony each got a regal piercing.
A tragedy stole the beloved ℛℯ𝓁ⅈä's life, and both daughters ruled after

her.

Side by side.

Once again the Àraid separated into their own races, and grew tired of defending the humans. An army divided is no army at all, and those sent into battle were doomed to fall.

The Àraid could not handle the loses they suffered, and they turned to their King to ease their pain. They begged for the souls of their dead to be returned, but The Collector took them back to his collection.

A soul without body is not meant for this world, but grief-turned-to-anger does not listen. Five Àraid snuck through the gateway. Returning without the help of The King placed a cursed upon them. A monster without love or soul, they would never again be whole. These monsters were named Raks by our outraged King.

He banished them from our castles. They still had the abilities of The Àraid, but used them for evil instead of for good. They started wars and caused the death toll to increase.

The twin Reʌiǎs rode out to try for a truce. They did not return. Not as themselves, for one of the Raks was father of the Reʌiǎs, and he knew their names. With the power of their names at his hand, he had control over them. The more they resisted this dark power, the stronger it got. The twin Reʌiǎs returned with their names stolen, and dark power danced in their veins.

They slaughtered their families, and filled the halls with blood. One child, a boy, the youngest, survived. But no one believed the tales of what he saw. He said he saw his mother the day she returned. He said her eyes were lifeless and black veins pulsed through her skin as she fought the poison.

The boy that survived earned the regal piercing, too. He was the first male to be crowned. People wondered if crowning a boy, to rule with the original King, was the right thing to do, but the piercing dictated who was the next to rule.

The next attack from the Raks sent the Àraid into hiding, and again they were on the verge of dividing. The young Reʌi was haunted by what the Raks did to his mother. Eventually he snapped, and went out, seeking ones blood for another. He killed off his army, believing

them Inhibited as well. The Àraid were appalled at the crimes of their Reʌï, and kicked him out of the castle. He never returned.
Five generations passed, without anymore conflict, but with another Reʌï on the throne, a new evil rose up. This Reʌï married a Rak, a prisoner of war, and a child was born. The child seemed normal, at first. Then one day he fell from a tree. He landed on his head, and his life should have ended, but he walked away from that tree as if nothing happened.
The Àraid could not heal themselves, and the Raks could not heal others, but this child could somehow do both. This Hybrid started the next war, and that's where we ended.
The Àraid were no match for this child, who would later be called General.
The King promised, before he was driven from our world, that one day he would return. The General took control of the regions, and has been fighting our King ever since.
The King predicted the Rèxĩaÿʌa, and promised to return once the product of Hybrid and Etèɼʌa is crowned. The Raks took over, and killed the Àraid they could find. But they failed their goal. Àraid are not gone."

And now I knew what The General was planning.
The long dead war was waking.

Alice

The woman who runs the city keeps coming into my room. She asks
me the strangest questions. Questions about The Captain. Questions
about the Rak camps. The Captain doesn't leave my side anymore.
And when the woman comes in, The Captain holds my hand a little
too tight. He rubs the scar on my wrist, and I silently beg him not to
press it. He promised he would never press it, but today my mind
was foggy, and I think that means he pressed it.

What does he want me to forget?

"These are our toys. This is where we play." The
little girl led me carefully into the cluttered room. She
found me this morning, bored and listless in my room.
Ever since they moved me into the main house I had too

much time to stare at walls. The Captain was being interrogated by the woman ambassador of the city, and left me alone, again.

The girl, Quartnee, asked me to play with her, and I jumped at something to do. She carefully helped me out of bed and we slowly moved through the house together, taking much longer than we should have because I needed to pause for breath every couple steps.

"You sit here," She pushed me into an elaborate arm chair. "I'll bring the games to you. That way you can rest and mom won't get mad at me for tiring you out." She punctuated her sentences with sharp, final nods, forcing her black curls to bounce against her cheeks.

"Now, what shall we do?" A finger tapped her lips as she thought. "Here," She pushed an unmarked box into my lap and pulled another chair over to me, struggling under the weight. I lifted the lid, but didn't understand what I was looking at. "Mother just taught us this game, now that she's teaching us about being Àraid and stuff. She spent actual time with me. Time with just me, not time at the dinner table where she leaves as soon as she can. Real time with me, all by myself." Her eyes switched back to the box.

"It's the Game of the Rulers." She stated matter-of-factly. I held up an intricately carved figure; dainty yet fierce. She wore a crown of ice on her head, and a scepter of fire extended from her hand.

"That's the Just Ŗèлïǎ. She knew all." Quartnee explained and reached into the box and pulled forth a young man, strong and stern, also crowned, but in silver branches weaving together above him. "This is the Unworthy King."

Eight more figures found their way out of the box, all dressed similar, and all accompanied with Quartnee's short explanation. Then she spread out a board, with a map of the Regions on it. On the map, the four original kingdoms were marked, too. The Kingdoms before the war. Before they fell. I didn't remember ever seeing a map that old before.

The box was empty at my feet, with ten royal figures, six
Àraid Elders, sixteen humans, eight Raks, and eight
Hybrids. She placed six objects inside six smaller boxes,
and placed randomly on the board along with five empty
boxes. One box for each region.

"In this game, you have to fight the Raks, to gain control
of the Regions. If you find all six pieces, you win. But if you
lose the Region to the Raks, and they get control of three of
the pieces, you automatically lose." She picked up one of
the Rèлïăs.

"This Rèлïă predicted, incorrectly, that the Àraid would
have mass casualties, but would eventually win the war. We
didn't win. No one knows why she gave us false information
but some think it's because she didn't want to cause a panic."
She picked up one of the Kings, and held him up, too.

"This King slaughtered five thousand Àraid because he
believed they were Raks in disguise. The people revolted
and dethroned him." She looked up at me expectantly, as if
waiting for praise for her facts.

"Quartnee, I'm sorry. I don't know who these people
are."

Don't Make A Sound!

Disbelief crossed her face as her jaw dropped.

"But you're old! This is history! Your daughter is Àraid.
You must know Àraid history." The figured she held in
demonstration of their wonder dropped from her grasp and
shattered on the floor. I stared at the beautiful fragments.
The crown off the Rèлïă's head sat, in one piece, next to
unrecognizable shards.

"How?" She climbed up into my lap and stuck her face in
mine, eyebrows raised. The stitches tore as her knee
rammed into my side, and I stifled a scream as my hands
flew to my side, already sticky with blood. She stared at the
growing red spot. "Did I do that?"

I gritted my teeth as an ache radiated from the torn
wound. I couldn't breathe through the pain, and I just

quickly nodded once.

"I'll get help!" She slid from my lap. I made a grab for her, but was too slow and her bare feet landed on the shattered glass of the Ṛèлïǎ. She crumpled to the ground and cried out as her hand landed on the crown. The points of the headpiece stuck all the way through her hand. I placed a hand on her back, waiting for her to cry. She glanced at my stained dress, and got up and ran. Bloody footprints followed her out the door.

"You need to stay *in* bed, Alice." The woman slowly sutured the torn wound, not bothering with anesthetic. "This will never heal correctly. Your chances of a discreet scar have flown right out the window." Her voice snaked throughout the room from between barely parted lips, and she glared at me as she shook her head.

"You are not strong enough. You should not be moving around." Her frustration oozed off her. "What, are you? A child? You need to be constantly entertained? I would have thought you would enjoy some down time after entertaining Raks for so many cycles." Her tone was sharp, condescending. I didn't understand what she meant, but she continued softly. "I did not tell my children. They do not know what happened behind those walls." Her lips pinched together in disapproval.

"Why would your children care what happened 'behind those walls'?" I could barely hear my voice as fire coursed through my veins.

"Because they are family. They deserve to know."

"Family?"

"Yes. You have grandchildren. I know that is a hard thing to comprehend but-"

I interrupted her.

"Your kids are my grand-kids?" I wasn't understanding

what she was trying to tell me. She stopped what she was doing and looked at me.

"That is usually how it works. Really what did they do to your mind in there? Physically, I know what they did. But not mentally." Her tone set me on edge. It was cruel.

"And just what, physically, did they do to me?" I challenged her.

"I know they used you. You were their slave. But The Captain told me he practically begged you to escape." She sniffed. "Makes me think you enjoyed the attention."

"*Enjoyed* it?" I gasped.

"Quartnee wants to see you, are you ready for visitors?" To her I would never be a victim. The seeds of doubt in her heart and surviving the prisons that no one survived only fueled her misgivings. She would never believe me. She didn't wait for an answer before opening the adjoining door. Quartnee rushed through and gently climbed into the chair behind me, revealing well bandaged feet.

"Quartnee! You are supposed to be in bed." The woman scolded.

"But I got bored."

"We will talk about this later." The woman ducked out of the room. Quartnee turned back to me.

"You really don't know The Righteous Ten?" She asked, hoping for a different answer. I shook my head. "But that's history! Everyone needs to know it! It's...it's...it's life or death or something!" She cut off my protest. "You need to know it. Good news for you 'cuz you're supposed to stay in bed, and I'm supposed to stay off my feet. And know what? When my feet aren't goin' my mouth is so I can tell you all 'bout them."

I smothered a chuckle, knowing she was serious.

"Mother is preparing to do something very crazy for the war. She's is on red alert. She won't let you hurt again, but don't let her meanness get to you. She's calloused, but she's right." She pulled a tiny bottle of nail lacquer out of her pocket.

"May I paint your nails?" She didn't wait for an answer. She moved onto the bed, and propped my hand on her leg. "Your nails are a mess. When was the last time they were done?" She sounded like she was parroting someone else as she studied my hand, but the practiced way she held the nail file told me this wasn't her first manicure.

"I've never had my nails done, Quartnee."

"Never ever? But they would look so nice all done up. Look at them."

I didn't like looking at my hands. They had been broken so many times that they were merely twisted monsters of what they once were. I didn't want to draw anymore attention to them. The little girl held my hand firmly so I couldn't pull away, and primed her brush. I looked away from my mangled hands, but she called my attention back to them when she finished polishing them.

Reluctantly, I glanced at my hand. The child chose a dark purple that, oddly, complemented the bruises on my hands.

"Let those dry for a while." She slid a book onto my lap. "This has pretty pictures if you get bored."

I was already falling asleep, but I gripped the book, and squeezed her hand as I slipped off to sleep.

Christa

"**Y**ou need to focus." I sighed. "Light the candle. This is easy, Cerynn."

"Easy for you!" She was not making any progress. The candle still sat, unlit, on the table. It did not even smoke. She mastered healing quickly. Fire should be easier than healing.

"You need to picture it. Just close your eyes, picture what you want, and say 'Zɾïèl'vÿzt'." I demonstrated and the candle burst into flames. "Лèÿçu." Flames consumed the candle, and in three seconds. "Simple. Try again."

Cerynn took a deep breath and placed another candle on the table. She closed her eyes."

"Picture what I want. I want the candle to be on fire. Light on fire! Zɾïèl'vÿzt!"

Nothing happened.

"Wait." I held up a hand. "You can not just picture it on fire!"

"What?"

"Our abilities are senses. You have to picture the sensation of lighting the candle. Picture the match. Striking the match. Holding the burning match to the candle." I snapped her attention back to me. "Do *not* picture the match burning your fingers. Very painful. It is like mentally walking through lighting a candle so you do not have to actually do it. Close your eyes and try again."

"Ʒṛïèl'vÿẓṭ." She sounded unsure now, but the candle flickered to life anyway. "I did it!" She gasped.

"Yes, finally. Now practice that until you do not have to think about it. Do it until it becomes second nature. Then I will teach you a new word."

She did not notice my departure.

"Ʒṛïèl'vÿẓṭ." The whispered word filled the room with a soft glow, without any real source. I no longer needed a candle. My desk was pushed against the far wall; littered with various sculpting tools. A cleared space right in front of my chair displayed the shattered porcelain Ṛèлïǎ. I managed to partially reconstruct the base and it sat separate from the pile.

No one would bother me here. This was my sanctuary. The morgue. I retreated here when I got overwhelmed.

I waited too long to teach my children, and I had no idea how to activate their powers. They could still use them, but not to their full potential. Only the Elders knew how to activate an Àraid.

I sank down into the cushioned chair and slipped some spectacles on, pulling my hair back into a messy bun. I studied the pieces through my glasses for a while, then gave up and propped a magnifying glass between me and the pieces.

"Knock-knock," Peter tapped the door as he nudged it open. "May I come in?"

I smiled at him and nodded, watching his cane thump across the floor towards me.

"What are you doing? Here I'll help you." He waved his free hand as I tried to stop him.

Too late.

The pile of pieces rose into the air and swirled together, picking up speed and the adhering to each other. Less than a minute passed and the Ṛèлïǎ slowly lowered back onto the table, restored, with no sign that she was ever broken.

"I wanted to try to repair it the human way." I glared at him.

"Sorry, I should have asked." He again waved his hand and his cane began to twist and grow, shaping into a chair that he eased himself into, keeping his bad leg straight out.

"Are you okay? I haven't seen you since you found the clothes."

"I am fine." I said too fast as I tried to shut out the memory of the baby clothes. Peter pursed his lips, but took the hint at my sharp tone.

"How are the lessons going?"

Idle chatter. I hated idle chatter.

"Fine."

"I don't think Quartnee will be able to stay off her feet for long. She's much too active." He studied the figurine, avoiding my gaze. He was waiting for me to vent, just like he always did when he knew I was upset.

"The woman is a moron." I finally blurted out.

"She was bored. You should put something other than a chair in her room," Peter ignored my outburst, although concern filled his eyes. "Maybe you could send Cerynn down to the library to pick out some books for her. Or paints and parchment, or yarn, or musical instruments. Give her something to do in her room and she won't be so inclined to leave it."

"Maybe I want her to leave the room." I snapped. "Maybe I want her to leave this house. Get caught by the Raks. Stop causing so many problems." I looked at him squarely, but he still would not meet my gaze.

"I don't think that's fair."

"She could have left the prisons cycles ago, Peter." I

slammed my hand into the table. "The Captain begged her to leave with him before she agreed."

"You're on his side now? I thought you didn't believe his innocence."

"I do not. And I never will." I crossed the room, and grabbed a sword from one of the drawers. Peter pulled a sword from his cane too, and I beckoned him from the room.

✝ ✝ ✝ ✝ ✝

In the courtyard, Peter and I sparred back and forth as the suns set. The hot sun won today, and, although the city was shielded from the hot suns harmful effects, some of the heat got through and soaked into the cobblestone. The heat still radiated from the cobblestone long after the suns set, and burned the bottoms of my bare feet. It was nice to finally feel something, but as I moved over the burning stones, the bottoms of my feet grew slick with blood.

"So what are you going to do about her?" Peter questioned. He moved much slower without the help from his cane, and it was all I could do not to take advantage of his weakness.

"Well, she is family, so I will let her stay." I jabbed and he dodged. "But that does not mean I have to ever see her. This house is big."

"I meant to keep her busy."

"Oh, I will leave that up to you. It was your idea." He paused, and I slashed his arm with the tip of my sword. "You are slowing down, old man."

"And you're a cheater." He was good for me.

He kept me sane.

He was the only one that knew the torment I hid from. Only he sat up with me all night when the visions consumed me. He sang to me even though I could not hear him, because he knew I enjoyed how his deep voice resonated in his chest as I lay my head against him.

I wished that could last forever.

"I love it when you smile." He pulled me into his arms. My head fit perfectly under his chin. "It takes a good twenty cycles off when I see you happy."

"So when I smile, I look like I am ten?" I smiled again, knowing it only deepened the wrinkles around my eyes; not eased them. My first husband did not like the wrinkles. I grew up too fast for him. But Peter liked the results. He liked the cycles of torment visible on my face. His hands caressed my face and he kissed my forehead.

"You are the most beautiful person." We laughed and twirled in our courtyard, but then he sobered. "How old is your mother?"

"Why?" I stopped twirling, out of breath. He caught me and disarmed me.

"Because I want to get her age-appropriate activities."

"Oh, she is in her early forties."

He hesitated, and returned his sword to its sheath, leaning on the cane once more.

"Really?"

"Yeah, why?"

"She looks closer to sixty than forty cycles old."

"Well, she *was* tortured for cycles, and that takes a toll." I pointed out.

"Exactly." He slammed his cane on the cobblestones.

"What?" I was confused.

"If she wanted to be there, if she enjoyed it, like you accuse her of, she wouldn't have aged like that. Torture takes its toll. Having a good time doesn't." He slowly traced the lines around my eyes, then turned and strode out of the court yard, satisfied. I sighed, and turned back to the house, but froze when I saw a Rak guard at the healira door.

"What are you doing?"

The Rak paused, and faced me.

"I burned myself. I'm going to get some herbs for it." He

held up his hand to showed off his burn.

"The healira is occupied right now. Can you wait?"

Cerynn was dressing Alice's wound. She would be caught.

If she enjoyed it, she would not have aged like that. She would not suffer from the nightmares and panic attacks.

I had to protect her.

The guard shrugged and shook his head.

"No. I can't wait." His hand closed around the knob, and started to push it open.

"You cannot go in there."

His head snapped back towards me.

"You dare order a Rak? Why would you be so brave? You're hiding something in there, aren't you?" His lips curled back over stained, jagged teeth. I stopped his hand as he tried again to open the door.

"Stop interfering!" His nails slashed across my face. "Let me into the healira right now, or your punishment will be swift." He licked his lips, and his eyes wandered over my body. One hand shot out and rubbed my breast over my blouse. "So firm. So in need."

I could not let him into the healira.

I had to protect her.

I grabbed his hand, and slammed it into the wall. Bones crunched, and he howled in pain.

"Oh, you'll regret that." His clawed fingers wrapped around my neck, and squeezed. I still had my sword, and I thrust it through his stomach on instinct.

He stumbled against me, and weighed me down as he fell. By the time I shoved him off me, and retrieved my sword, his blood covered me.

The other guards knew.

Their heads already swiveled my way as their tainted noses picked out the stench of a fallen brother. Black eyes locked on me, and nine guards surrounded me.

"Killing a Rak is a death sentence."

"We can't kill a Healer. Not after the last one."

"He's right. The boss won't stand for another dead Healer."

"What should we do, Captain?"

The Captain was just joining the group. He stank of beer and whores, and I wondered if Alice knew what he did without her. His eyes widened when he saw the dead Rak.

"What happened?"

He was going to find your wife. I was protecting her.

"He touched me." I gritted my teeth.

The guards laughed, and The Captain clicked his tongue.

"How should we punish her, Sir? A life for a life?" One grabbed my arm, while another slipped his knife from its holster. I struggled against them, and yanked my arm free. I pushed the guard closest to me, and he fell into his brother. One on top of the other. Both died quickly as I pinned them to the ground with my sword. There were still seven Raks left, and I only angered them.

"Death isn't a punishment. Surely you could find a different way to make her regret her actions." The Captain suggested.

It took three of them to restrain me, and lead me to the center of the courtyard. I screamed as they tore at my clothes, and sharp fingers ripped into my skin. One guard called out to my people to watch my punishment. The Captain crossed his arms, and settled in, chuckling.

He looked like he was going to enjoy the show.

I shut my eyes, and focused on containing my powers.

Let them do what they want. Do not show them your powers.

They were raping someone else.

Not me.

I was far away from here.

Safe.

That was all I wanted.

I just wanted to be safe.

But I was not far away. I really was receiving this assault. And they laughed the whole time.

I noticed that more than anything.

They enjoyed it.

Each one changed their face to look like Peter, and I was forced to stare into mismatched blue and green eyes narrowed in hatred. I had never seen that look in his eyes. I knew it was not him, but it was hard to watch him do this to me.

My screams only spurred them on.

I did not want to scream, but the sound escaped my throat anyway.

"We know you're hiding her. Tell us where she is, and we'll stop." One hissed.

I could not speak. I could only shake my head. I would never give her up.

Somehow I ended up on my knees before them, and my mouth was propped open. I was going to just let them do what they wanted. I was not going to make trouble.

But then I glanced around the Rak. My children stood in the doorway.

Eyes wide.

Mouths open.

Peter stood beside them, but he was not watching. He slumped against the wall; head in hands.

I could not succumb in front of them.

My head was yanked away from the Rak, and another took his place. Another one grabbed my hips, and braced himself behind me. I had to fight them.

"Look at her piercing. R̀℮лïǎ, according to tradition."

Tears joined the blood, but they did not relent.

"I'll be able to tell my wife I raped the R̀℮лïǎ." Another grating laugh. "It's everyone's dream to rape the R̀℮лïǎ."

I shut my eyes, and focused. I had never used the words before, but they presented themselves, and I could not just let the Raks do this.

"Z̧ũ̈ÿð z̧r̈ïèl'vÿz̧t̲ ǎ Бǎл." The words were muffled, but they still worked. Simultaneously, the guards stopped their attack, and clutched their chests.

Seven bodies fell to the ground, convulsing. Blood and vomit spurted out of slack jaws. Their skin bubbled, and burst, and ran like liquid off of their corpses. And all at once, they stilled, and my assault ended.

Peter and The Captain picked their way through the bodies.

"Why did you not step in? Why did you not stop them?" I cried. "I kept you safe! I thought you would try to do the same!" I could not control my shaking as I wept in the courtyard.

"I didn't want to blow my cover. I couldn't risk it."

"So you just let them..." I could not finish. I did not want to relive what they did to me. Peter touched my shoulder, and I flinched. He withdrew his hand, and sat beside me.

"I protected you!" I screamed at The Captain. "I kept your secret!"

He stopped in the doorway, turned back towards me, and shrugged.

"Thanks."

Inhibited

Jaycobe

"The Àraid *Rèлïǎ* launched a direct assault on us." The General spat the word out like it made him want to vomit. "She slaughtered the guards I sent to find Alice and bring her home to us. It's only a matter of time before she attacks us as well."

Panic spread like a wave through the Raks and Recruits.

"With an Àraid leading them, they'll be strong. We have to prepare." The General stood on his balcony, looking out over the city. Everyone was there. Everyone except those we hadn't freed yet. They were still in the lock-down facility so they didn't hurt anyone while they were brainwashed.

"I have some of my best people working on an escape route, and I still have a man inside her city, so we will know when they are about to strike. No surprises." He paused. "However, I need help from you as well."

The crowd stood a little taller. He *needed* us. We could help.

"I need you to set aside half of everything you bring in. Half the food you buy, half the income of your household. Those stores will go to the army I raise up to fight her."

The crowd murmured, concerned.

"I know things will be tight for a while, it will be hard to go back to rations since we've lived free so long, but can we do this for ourselves?"

A few halfhearted affirmatives.

"No. No. Can we do this?"

"Yes!" The response was stronger, but not great.

"Can we do this?"

"YES!" The people were excited again, busy figuring out how to live on half of their supplies.

As The General retreated back to his office, the workers dispersed. Everyone was anxious to begin helping.

"Private!" A voice barked behind me, and I turned to see two burly guards barreling towards me. "The General wants to see you."

They let me find my own way to his office. Eventually, I found it and knocked tentatively.

"Come in." The General's voice floated through the door. He was haggard, worried for his people. I could see that clearly.

"You wanted to see me, Sir?"

"I'm going to send The Private out to try to take out the Àraid ruler. She needs to be stopped before she finds the Rèχtaÿлă. While the Private is gone I'll need a new right hand man." He looked me over. "You seem to have taken a liking to her. And you study best with her. She leaves in two days, be ready to take over her job by then."

I ran from the room. I had to find her.

"Cobe!"

She called through the corridors as she ran to find me. She was the only one to use my name. To tell your true name gave them your heart. To tell someone you name was to give them complete control of your powers; to use or abuse. She hadn't told me her name yet, but thoroughly enjoyed using mine when we were alone.

"Cobe!" She flew into my arms, kissing me. "I'm going

in two days. I'm going out to the field! I get to take on an actual real-life Àraid." She was so excited, so happy to finally be trusted out there. She kissed me again. "Isn't that wonderful?"

I tried to be excited for her. I tried to muster a smile.

"Yeah." It didn't come out like I'd hoped.

"What's wrong?" She frowned.

"Nothing." I picked her up and swung her around, enjoying her laughter as she held tight to my shoulders.

"Cobe, stop." She giggled, but kept a serious look in her eyes. "Really. What's wrong?"

"I'm scared for you. I don't want to lose you." I pulled her close and tucked her head under my chin as her scales shifted to a patchy skin tone. Long hair sprouted down towards her shoulders.

"You won't lose me. I'm the fastest on the mission. I'm top of my class, and she doesn't know we're coming. What do you think of my disguise? Human enough?"

I stiffened and ignored her question. My mother would kill any Rak she caught.

"I don't want you to go." I couldn't tell her to stay. She was her own independent person, but I wanted to forbid her from leaving.

"I'll be gone for two days. That's all. Don't worry, everything will be fine. We're going to use the Captain's wife's memories, and take the form of people in them so the McCain's won't suspect a thing. We still have all of her memories stored. I could be anyone. I could be your mother, if I wanted." She chuckled. "But I won't. I think that would be a little too obvious." She squeezed her arms around me.

"Don't worry, Cobe, I'll be back before you know it. And when I get back, I'll tell you my name." She smiled up at me, and my heart jumped. She was so beautiful. I didn't want to stop touching her, but eventually she pulled back and straightened her shirt. I hadn't noticed that I had lifted it until she pulled it back down over her waist.

"We need to save her. She's not safe there and you know it. The McCain's will kill her when they find out who she is. Her only safety is here, behind these gates. We can't let The General down now, can we? He's done so much for us."

We shared one last kiss, and went back to our lives.

The Private and I spent the next couple of days together, we did nothing without the other. And on the morning she left I held her in my arms in our bed, stroking her back and silently begging her not to go.

"I don't know if I can make it two days without you. That's too long." I moaned.

She laughed, pushing her self up to look me straight in the eyes.

"Jaycobe Francis McCain." She paused. "Your mother must have hated you." She laughed again, and I joined her. "Jaycobe... McCain. I love you. More than I expected to when I recruited you. To me you were the enemy. But now you are my world. I will be back in two days and you will show me just how much you missed me. Until then, hold on to this." She held out a sealed envelope.

"I want to see how good you are at resisting temptation, so don't open that until I return. I have to go now, I leave in less than an hour." She jumped off the bed, taking the sheets with her. "I love you. I'll see you later. Do the laundry, and please clean the dishes."

"Private! Come join us." The General beckoned to me from his office. He, and a few of the high ranking officials were waiting for an update on the raid that she went out on. On his desk sat a blinded obserling. The blind ones could be paired with other obserlings, and relay what they saw. On the wall, several angles of my mother's house were portrayed from obserlings The General sent into the city.

There she was, back in the disguise she wore when I first met her. Two guys flanked her, and they carried between them an injured child. I recognized him as one of the Inhibited we'd been training.

The General held out a chair for me, and we sat facing the display, watching their slow progression through the house. They were admitted to the healira without incident. Cerynn doctored the boy. I hadn't noticed that I actually missed them. I was actually sad that they would get hurt, but this was my new family. I was home now. And happy with the Private. I watched as the Private broke off from the group and made her way into the main house.

Slowly, she opened one door after another, looking inside and then closing them and moving on. Quartnee was in the living room when she found her. They stared at each other.

"Who are you?" Quartnee asked, rising. Her feet were wrapped in bandages and it looked painful to stand. The Private crossed to my sister with her arms held out in a welcoming gesture. As she passed by an arm chair she grabbed a blanket and knelt in front of my sister. Slowly she wrapped the blanket around Quartnee's legs.

"What are you doing?" The small girl tried to push her away, but the blanket restricted her movement and she fell onto her back. The blanket burst into blue flames, and Quartnee's screams soon filled the room. The Private ducked out of the room and walked down another corridor. My hands balled into fists.

I'm sorry, dear sister. This is for the best.

Cerynn heard the screams and raced towards the living room. Quartnee was still screaming, but I couldn't see her through the fire. The Private was free in the corridors, but as she opened a door and ran inside my heart lodged in my stomach. She found what she was looking for.

The morgue.

Mother sat at her table, a body in front of her, but she jumped at the movement. Their eyes held for a moment, and under my mother's gaze The Private's skin darkened back to her beautiful black scales. Mother launched from her chair, knife already drawn and flying through the air. The Private ducked and ran back out into the hall. The house sensed danger, though, and shuffled.

She took the next available door, and ended up in Alice's room. She smiled in victory and whisked Alice into a headlock, knife to her throat. Alice was a good bargaining chip.

"So she is there! I knew it!" The General hissed at the screen. "Bring her home, Private."

The Private nodded towards the obserling, and led Alice from the room, using her as a shield against my mother. Rage smoldered in my mother's eyes, but she lowered her bow. The house placed them all back into the living room, and Quartnee whimpered on the floor, her legs bloody and burned. The Private inched towards my mother. A door opened and the two guys that came with her walked in. Mother threw a knife and it sliced cleanly through one of their heads, killing him instantly. The Private yelled and dug her knife into Alice's arm, dragging it down to her elbow.

A warning.

Alice was limp, she didn't even flinch. Her jaw clenched as she fought to remain stoic. Then, in a blur, she braced herself against the floor and flipped the Private over the her shoulder. The knife in her arm twisted and stuck and The Private was disarmed. An arrow pinned the other Rak guard to the wall, and Mother already drew another from her quiver.

Alice was on top of the Private and I was on my feet.

"I need to get there, now!" I yelled, but The General wrapped a hand around my arm, holding me back. "I need to help her!" I couldn't breathe. I was panicking. I couldn't watch this, but somehow I couldn't look away.

Alice covered her face in a blanket, wrapping it tightly. Already I could hear her terrified screams. The older woman bent over my girlfriend, made eye-contact with the obserling watching her, and whispered.

"Tell The General I'm free now."

The blanket erupted in dark red flames. Her screams lasted only a moment. Soon her body stopped flailing, and I fell to my knees.

This couldn't be happening.

Inhibited

Christa

"Who let it in?" I stood over the Rak body, and watched Alice pace nervously, obviously shaken. "The Captain let it in, did he not?"

I killed all the Rak guards.

Why were there more?

How did The General know I killed his guards?

The Captain was working with him again. That was the only explanation.

Alice could not answer; only stare at the burned body in horror. The girl burned easier than I thought she would, and died fairly quickly. Her buddies lay where they died, too.

I knelt by my daughter, assessing her legs. They were badly burned. I doubted I could save them, but she should recover fine after the operation. I lifted her into my arms and turned to leave.

"Cerynn, come with me, I will need help during the surgery." I noticed blood dripping freely down Alice's arm, but she waved me away when I tried to look at it. She crossed the room and rummaged through one of my cabinets. Quartnee was limp in my arms. Right now she was in greater danger than my mother.

"Alice."

She looked up, meeting my gaze. I could not say it. I did not know how to word it. But she held my gaze and slowly nodded. She knew.

"Mommy?" Quartnee finally woke. I had started to worry. She blinked a few times and then her hand drifted down to her legs, poking the casts. "I can't feel them." Her brow furrowed in confusion.

"I know. They are dead."

"But don't you take dead things off?"

"Normally. But I think, once you are strong enough, I can try to rebuild them. I have made progress in my lab, and I think I can do it."

"But don't dead things rot?" She pushed herself onto her elbows, but then decided that was too tiring and laid back down.

"Yes. But if I massage the right creams into them several times a day, I can preserve them."

She nodded, satisfied, and fell back into a fitful sleep. Our housekeeper entered the room and crossed over to me.

"You should be resting."

"Why?"

"We all watched what the guards did to you. That's not something you just recover from."

I swallowed and shoved the memories away.

Stop reminding me. I would be okay if people stopped bringing it up.

"I need to make sure my child is safe. It is my fault she was injured. They wanted me because I killed the guards."

The Captain must have sent for more guards. He told The General what I did. I needed to get him off my land.

I shut my eyes and saw Peter's mismatched one's staring back at me, narrowed in hatred while he forced himself on me.

No. It was not Peter. It was the Raks.

I flinched at Miss Lorraine's hand on my shoulder, and shoved the hate-filled eyes out of my mind.

"She could have died today." Her voice was low. "She could have died, and the last thing she would have heard was how unnecessary I think it is to learn defense."

"Well, on the plus side, she would not be thinking about it after she died." I tried to pulled myself out of my memories, but Miss Lorraine did not laugh. "Listen. I do not care about what you said. You understand now and that is all that matters." I rose and she took my seat.

"I want to go to check on Alice. Can you keep an eye on Quartnee for me?"

She merely nodded.

The kids laughed behind the door; obviously recovered from the trauma of earlier. I cracked the door. Jess and Cerynn sat on the floor, and they each had a musical instrument in their hands. Josh sat on the couch, and Alice perched next to him, feet up, arm sewn. She spotted me quickly and beckoned me in.

Her smile eased the tiredness in her eyes.

Jess glanced up quizzically.

"Mommy hates music. Always has."

Alice frowned, and beckoned me again.

"I cannot stay. I have some things I need to do. I just wanted to check on your arm."

"I've missed your music, Chrissy." She whispered.

"Mom can't play." Jess piped up.

"That is right." I nodded, with a significant look to my son. "I cannot play because I need to dispose of the dead Raks."

Before he could dig me into a deeper hole I turned and left.

† † † † †

"She killed the Rak?" Peter knelt next to the bodies, untouched since the fight.

"I watched her do it."

"Still think she's on their side?" He shifted the girl's head to the side with the end of his cane. The burns on her face oozed black Rak poison; deadly when touched.

"What better way to make us trust them?"

She was working with The Captain.

That had to be it. That was the only explanation.

Peter would not look at me as we examined the body. He would not touch me. Had not touched me since the attack. I could not think about the attack though. I needed to pretend it never happened. I needed to focus on our growing safety problems.

"Where is she?" The Captain slammed through the door, and froze in his tracks, staring at the bodies on the floor. "What happened?" His voice was quiet as he fell to his knees. One was in a brace from our scuffle, and he hastily straightened it out.

I did not answer; just watched him. Measured his reactions.

"Did you know them?" Peter asked. The Captain nodded.

"I filled their orders. I went on raids for them. I recruited her." He took her hand. "What happened?"

"Your wife killed her." I glared at him, remembering the way he crossed his arms and watched the guards hurt me. The way his eyes narrowed in concentration as he studied them. The shrug as he flippantly thanked me for saving his wife's life.

"No. Alice wouldn't hurt anyone." He shook his head firmly.

"Well, she torched your girlfriend, so you may want to rescind your statement." I crossed my arms, and shot a pointed look at their joined hands. He dropped her hand, and put his back in his pocket.

"I want to see her."

"I'm sorry I didn't defend you." He whispered as we walked to Alice's room. "I can't blow my cover."

"How did they find out so quickly that I killed the guards?"

The Captain shrugged. I hated his shrug. His shrug was disrespectful. I was about to say something, but we were at her room; now deserted except for her.

"You lost your admirers." I chirped. She blushed and looked down.

"Suddenly I'm a hero for something unpraiseworthy. I'll never understand the mindset of children."

I glared at The Captain as he rushed across the room and grabbed her shoulders, shaking her.

"What were you *thinking*?"

I moved close enough to stop him if he lost it.

"*Never* interfere with the Raks. That's *my* job. How could you be so *stupid*?"

"Captain." I spoke a quiet warning. "She did what needed to be done. If she had not stepped up like she did, people could have died."

He whirled on me.

"People *did* die. My people. My *friends*."

I pressed my lips together.

"I thought you said we were done with that life." Alice's voice was accusing.

"Never talk!" He gave her another shake. Her head snapped back, and her hand rushed to her neck. Whiplash. "I am done with that life." His eyes never left hers. "But just because you finish the book doesn't mean you forget the words."

Alice's eyes widened in surprise. I felt excluded, like what he said held more meaning than I could understand.

She rubbed her throat with one hand, but the other ran over the back of his head comfortingly. She carefully rose out of her chair, clinging to The Captain for support.

"I want to take a walk. Captain? Will you join me?"

He was already leading her from the room. I was being shut out. I wanted to protest, but they pushed past me and strode off into the night.

Alice

"**W**hy would you do that?" He fumed. "They sent obserlings into the house. The *General's o*bserlings." His voice lowered, not wanting to draw attention, but urgent. "Do you understand what that means?"

I shook my head.

"The General knows you're here. He's going to come after you. You blew our cover." He stopped and placed his hands on my shoulders, turning me to him. "He can stop looking, he found you. He can pull you back whenever he wants. He might pull you back as soon as tomorrow."

"Might?"

"He wanted you away from the other Raks. As long as he knows where you are, he can come to you. He doesn't need you behind his gates. But he's going to want to punish you for what you did, and he won't do that in a city run by an Àraid. He might send you back to the prisons to be broken again."

My hand flew to my mouth.

"He can do that?" I always thought that once he found me he would kill me. It would be painful, but it would end. I hadn't considered the idea that he would send me back.

He let out an exasperated sigh.

"He owned you for more than a decade. Most of his slaves don't make it even a quarter season. He won't let you die. He can't afford that."

"Why?"

"Because." Another sigh, "Because of who you are."

"What do you mean?"

"I can't tell you, Love. Not yet."

I whirled away from him, and reached for a tree, bracing myself as my head spun. He didn't move, just watched me as I regained my balance and proceeded into the forest. He called after me, following a few paces behind.

"Alice, you can't push me away. Not now. Not with everything."

I spun toward him.

"And just what *is* everything?" Tears burned hot tracks down my face. His shoulders slumped, and he swallowed hard. I could barely make out tears in his eyes in the gathering gloom.

"I just... I want to know." I whispered. "I need to know. What can you tell me?" My throat hurt, and I couldn't swallow. His eyes changed. A look of disappointment and surprise locked on his features.

"Don't you know?" He moved closer and took my hands in his. "I can tell you that I love you. That I'm one-hundred-percent crazy about you. That every time I look at you all I see is the fight you've been though, all your battle scars. Everything I couldn't save you from." He touched a groove on my jaw.

"And every detail of your battle makes you even more beautiful." He hooked a finger under my chin and tilted my head up towards his. His lips brushed the tip of my nose. "I love you, Counselor, and it kills me because no one can know." He pressed my back against a tree, and pinned me between his arms.

"I love you." His hands twisted in my hair, then

wandered down to my lower back, pressing me into him. "I love you."

I muffled his voice behind my lips. I kissed his neck where I knew he liked it, and ran my hands across his back. The dark made the forest eerie, and I wanted to go inside, but he wasn't ready yet.

Please, just get this over with quickly.

I pressed my back against the tree, and hooked my legs up around his waist. A twig snapped behind us, but The Captain didn't notice. I wrapped my arms around him, and held on. My hair snagged on the tree bark. The tree shook, and leaves fell around us as The Captain braced himself against it.

Someone started clapping as they emerged from the shadows.

"What a show. And you warmed her up for me. You're so considerate."

The Captain barely glanced at the Rak.

"Like I'm going to let you have a taste?"

"You will if you want me to keep your secret. Otherwise, The General will take her away from you, and give her to me for being such a good scout." The Rak stood beside us now. Tears pricked my eyes. This was supposed to be just The Captain and I.

Would I never be free to have my own life?

"Back off, Lieutenant Pay. She's not yours." The Captain growled.

I wanted to push the Rak away from me, but I couldn't. I wasn't allowed. Lieutenant Pay yanked The Captain's knife from his belt, and pressed it right beneath my ribs.

"You let me have a turn, or I'll send The General her heart."

The Captain paled and tears filled his eyes. Unarmed and so exposed he had no way to protect us. My legs shook as my feet found the ground.

"I'm sorry, Baby. I can't risk your life." The Captain

whispered as Lieutenant Pay wrapped his arms around me, and pushed me onto the leaves. He ripped my dress down the front, and laughed when he saw the corset.

"You're already too skinny, why are you wearing that thing?"

The Captain lunged for his knife, but it'd already cut through the lacing. He stopped when he saw the bulge in my stomach.

"Oh, Captain." Lieutenant Pay groaned. "What have you done?"

"It was an accident."

"You weren't allowed to touch her that way. Only he is allowed to give her children."

"I'll let you have her whenever you want if you swear you don't tell him about this."

Lieutenant Pay laughed at his proposal.

"She's hot. That's true. But I'll get a better reward from him." He pushed his knife through my shoulder, and pinned me to the ground. As The Captain knelt to help me, the guard escaped into the night.

My secret was out.

Jaycobe

"**W**ell, well, my Pet is going to have a baby." The General sounded glib, using a manic, singsong voice. I barely heard him. I hadn't moved since I watched her die, just stared at the blank wall where the obserlings visions once played. She was dead. Alice killed her. "Well, we can't have that, now can we, Private?"

I shook my head, trying to clear away the picture of her burning body.

"I'm sorry. What?" I met his gaze, but couldn't really focus.

"Alice. She's having a baby. That needs to be stopped." He prodded, waiting for me to make a connection, but I just wasn't understanding.

"We need to bring her back here. She can't have this child behind their gates. Can you imagine what that would do? We'll bring her back here and help her bring her child into my world, not that crazy demented one." He was pacing nervously again.

"Couldn't we just kill her?" I rasped. The General stopped pacing and faced me, surprised.

"Kill her? No. No, that would do no good. Well, maybe it would." He said thoughtfully, and then shook his head firmly. I turned back to the screen.

"She deserves it. She deserves to rot for what she did."
My head pounded, and blood dotted my hands from where
I'd pushed my nails through my palms. The General knelt
beside me.

"I know you're upset, but would killing her make you feel
any better?" His voice was gentle, comforting, but it didn't
touch the hatred burning inside.

"Yes. It would. It would make me feel better to kill all of
them. Every last member of that city needs to die."

He looked surprised, but then slowly nodded.

"Okay, then go. Go kill all of them." He waved a hand.
"I'll organize a party, maybe ten members, and you can take
them down and wipe out that city. Just make sure you bring
her back, alive. She doesn't need to be in one piece," He
winked. "Just alive. Would you like that, Son?"

I nodded.

† † † † †

The whole place felt like her. It was her house, but now, I
guess, it was mine. Her clothes were still scattered on the
bedroom floor where we'd hastily dropped them our last
night together. I crawled onto the bed, pulling the covers up
to my nose and breathing deeply. Just like her.

I couldn't cry anymore, and my head pounded, but I just
needed to do something. I couldn't think of anything, except
sleep, so I laid back, prepared to rest and plan my revenge.
Then I remembered the envelope she gave me. Her last
words. I pulled it out from under the pillow and carefully
broke the seal.

The piece of parchment had three words on it. Only three,
little words, but suddenly I couldn't hold back. Deep
wrenching sobs shook the bed as I clenched the parchment
in my hands. I couldn't breathe.

I wanted them dead and I wanted them dead now.

They ruined everything, and I would end them.

The parchment dropped to the ground as I jumped off the bed and piled every weapon I owned on it. I needed to avenge her, because she loved me. I knew she loved me. Completely and unconditionally. Because on that parchment were three little words. Her name. Her true name.

Sarah Louise Foster.

Inhibited

Alice

72nd Day, The Season Of Death, 749-PW

The Captain couldn't find the Rak from the woods. After he got me
back to the house, he went out to search for the Rak, but he never
found him. He must have gone back to The General to tell him
about the baby. The General will be very angry about that.
The Captain never leaves my side now. He barely lets go of my hand.
I don't think he sleeps anymore. He keeps saying The General is
going to come for me now. I never asked for any of this.

I just wanted to be free.

The door to my room slammed open.
"How did you do it? How did you kill her?" Chrissy
strode into the room, studying the jar in her arms. I
moved my shoulder around, trying to move past the pain,

and studied my daughter.

"How did you burn her? You are not Àraid. It has been bugging me for days. I have checked over and over again. You are nothing special." She held out a vial, and I took it and drank it.

I tried not to make a face as the liquid burned my throat.

"I cannot understand how it is even possible."

"You still believe I'm on their side, don't you?" My voice was rough. "You think I'm with them."

I saw it in her eyes, but she pressed her lips together and looked away.

"People go into those prisons. They never come out. Why should you be any different?"

"But-"

She stopped me before I could say anything.

"Anyway, I am having a small group over. I am going to teach them some things about the Àraid, since everyone now knows I am one. The meeting starts in ten minutes. Would you like to join us?" She was being courteous, trying to show that she still cared, but her heart was nothing more than ice and stone, and no warmth came from her invitation.

I nodded, fighting tears. We were together again, but it would never be the same.

There were only three people, other than Chrissy, her husband, and myself, at the meeting, but they were enthusiastic. They seemed awed that Chrissy would even look at them, much less invite them into her home. Or offer to teach them about the Àraid.

I couldn't stop staring at Peter, at his blue and green eyes. So unique, so familiar. I had seen them somewhere, but I couldn't remember where. Chrissy wouldn't look at me, and Peter's eyes merely grazed over me, before settling elsewhere. I fidgeted uncomfortably.

The hands on the clock tick slowly by. Two hours of being ignored. We were just wrapping up, and bringing out some snacks when we heard a loud crashing.

Shattering glass.

Chrissy shot out of her chair, and bounded up the stairs to the second floor. I was close behind, dreading what we would find. As I rounded the corner, a breeze ruffled my hair. The floor was littered with parchments, blueprints, and pages and pages of notes in meticulously neat handwriting. I couldn't see the carpet through the parchment.

"Chrissy?" I whispered.

She stood in front of three floor-to-ceiling windows. The middle one was shattered, and parchment fluttered in the breeze. She stared out into the courtyard, her expression stormy.

I moved to her side and put an arm around her, following her gaze. My breath caught in my throat. There was a girl in the courtyard. She lay on her back, arms and legs twisted under her. Eyes vacant. Mouth dripping black. Throat ripped out. I couldn't tell who it was; she was mangled too badly. I turned to Chrissy. She knew the girl.

"Who is that?"

She inhaled sharply, her breath catching.

"That's our research. All our progress on the Raks. She had it. She knew it." She sank to her knees, rocking slightly, and started gathering up the pieces.

Written in the glass around her body was the word "three". The third sign. The General told me, 'three signs and I'll come for you.'

I shivered.

"Chrissy. Who is she?"

My daughter held out a hand, and I took it, helping her back up to her feet.

"That's my daughter."

Inhibited

Christa

Ginny is dead.

That was all my mind would play. It repeated it over and over.

Ginny is dead.

Ginny is dead.

Twenty-one. The number was rising. I could not do this.

What do I do now?

My mind was numb.

Mother asked me a lot of questions that I did not understand.

Questions that did not matter because my daughter was dead.

It was bad enough that he stole me from myself, but now he was stealing my children from me, too.

Twenty-one.

Parchment fluttered. I needed to save the parchment. I needed to save the research. My books were ruined.

Who would want to harm my books?

My research fluttered in the breeze.

Why?

Mother was crying.

Why was she crying?

It hit me again.

She was crying because Ginny is dead.

My Ginny. My eldest girl.

My smart one that never socialized.

"I'm sorry. I should never have left the prisons. I'm sorry." She muttered again and again. But that did not matter because my daughter was dead.

When was the last time I saw her?

Maybe this morning in passing.

Did I say anything to her?

No.

What was the last thing I said to her?

I remembered we fought. I was proud of her accomplishments, but wanted her to be more involved with her siblings. I did not remember the last time I let her know I loved her.

Peter was there.

His arms were around me, but I did not feel them. I was not wearing my plate, so I could not hear what anyone was saying.

Peter's lips moved, and he pointed to my feet.

Who cares about my feet?

My daughter is dead.

Did no one understand that?

I looked down at my feet and saw blood soaking into my beautiful carpet.

How did that happen?

Those stains would never come out. I would need to re-carpet the whole hall. But then the carpet would not match the rest of the house, so I would need to redo that as well. That would take a while. That would get pricey. I did not have the money to re-carpet my house. Maybe I should just go with stone.

Sparkling glass shifted as I moved my feet and pieces of my broken window stuck out of my soles. I thought it would hurt more.

I looked back down into the courtyard. My beautiful daughter, laid out just like my real mother. Peter tried to restrain me as I walked toward the open window, but I shrugged him off, and jumped down to be with my daughter.

I landed hard, but it did not hurt.

Nothing hurt.

I stumbled forward. My leg bent at an odd angle. I crawled to her side and checked for a pulse.

I did not know why I checked.

It was just necessary to be absolutely sure she was dead. Her hand clutched a piece of torn cloth. I eased it out of her fingers, and held it up for inspection. It was not black. Coaltree dress-code was black. But I had seen this material recently.

It hit me. I knew what it was from.

Peter limped towards me in the courtyard, but I rose and ran the other direction.

I knew who this material belonged to.

I knew who killed my daughter.

My leg buckled and I fell. My face smacked into the cobbled stone.

I had to get up. I had to get him.

I could not open my eyes, but it did not matter.

I knew who killed her. And that was all I was thinking about as I faded out.

The Captain killed my daughter.

A cool hand pressed against my forehead. Some scratches on my cheeks stung, and I could not breath through my nose. My head was killing me.

Why was I so sore?

Glass pressed against my lips, and then water splashed into my mouth.

Where was my plate?

I could not tell if anyone was saying anything to me. I tried to open my eyes again. Success.

Alice stood above me. She looked older than her cycles again. Haggard and worn out. Her lips were moving, but my eyes were blurry and I could not read them. Her hand smoothed my hair.

"What happened?" I do not know why I asked, I just wanted to give her something to do, remembering too late that I would not hear her.

Peter entered my limited vision and held up my head. His hand slid up the back of my head, and clicked my plate into place. I winced, eyes watering as feedback pierced my ear, but soon it settled down, and I was part of the conversation again. Alice held my hand in a vice grip, her fingers worrying the back of my hand. Peter and Cerynn whispered in the corner.

"I healed your leg, Mom. But I couldn't heal your face for some reason. Sorry, but it's going to look ugly for a while."

I could not remember what happened, but as my free hand opened I saw the plaid material balled up inside it. Everything flooded back.

I was going to kill him.

"Chrissy," Alice leaned in towards me. "Do you need anything?"

"You caused this. She would not be dead if you were not here."

My mother's eyes were already filled with tears, and she cringed.

"I know. I am so sorry."

I turned my head sharply away from her, hoping she would get the message. She grabbed my face, and turned me back towards her. Her eyes filled with tears, but anger also swirled there.

"Why do you keep shutting the world out? Why do you refuse to feel?" Her tears overflowed and ran down her face, but she did not wipe them away. She was not ashamed.

"The world." I measured my words. "The world does not care one way or the other. We could all vanish to the world. The regions would keep on going. Trade would keep running. People would stop dying. We are not important. We do not matter. What is the use of feeling? Such a waste of emotion."

Cerynn and Peter watched me now, too.

"You can't mean that." Alice shook her head. "Don't bottle it up, or it will be worse later. I tried to shut it out, too. Look what it did to me."

I still saw fear in her eyes, but I cut her off.

"And then what? Then you recovered. Then you got out, and claimed your fame. The woman who escaped. Then you got better than us?" All my anger and frustration rose to the surface. "Then you grew up and realized that no matter what happened you would be better." I sat up and grabbed her arm tightly, ignoring how she squirmed in my grasp.

"You have the ability to bring people back from the dead." I hissed. She looked as if I just slapped her, and I wondered if I did. "I was dead, and you brought me back. Why did you not do that for my daughter?" I shoved her away from me and her face crumpled. She leaned down on her knees, bent in half.

"You think you are so great. You are so full of yourself. The woman who made it out. But you are nothing to me."

She barely met my gaze, but my words hurt her the way I hoped they would.

"Twenty-one, Mother. I cannot do it anymore. I cannot afford to care about anyone, they all end up hurting me. You pushed me away all my life, and I still clung to you. I am done. I do not want to see you again. Leave."

She could not rise. She tried, but her legs shook too much.

"Peter, help her."

He looked as though he wanted to argue, but he did not. He made his way over to the small woman, and lifted her easily to her feet. She did not struggle, but cast me one last pleading look before the door closed. I did not know why she would let me down now, but I knew that letting her back into my life was a mistake.

I lost my privacy. I lost my fidelity.

Now my daughter was dead.

Why was she dead?

The Captain.

He was why she was dead.

He was why everything happened.

And she brought him here.

I *needed* them out of my city right now.

Peter limped back into the room, and eased himself onto the bed next to me. We had not had intercourse in days. Peter had not even touched me since I was raped. I did not want to think about why. It hurt to think about why. I wanted to prove to him that I was still me, but as I gazed into his eyes panic overwhelmed me.

What if I saw the same hatred?

What if it really was him attacking me?

I shut my eyes, and pictured his eyes the way they were before the attack.

Filled with love. Filled with hope.

"Christa, look at me."

I shook my head and kept my eyes shut. His eyes in my memories would never change. I memorized his eyes.

But if I opened my eyes, what would I do if I saw disdain in his?

Peter's arms unwrapped, and he got off the bed.

"Where are you going?" I called after him.

"The couch. We have some things we need to work through before I can sleep next to you."

"My daughter just died and you are making me sleep alone?"

He tried to make eye contact, and I quickly shut my eyes before I saw them.

"Can you honestly say you want me in here right now?"
I did not.
Not really.
But I did not want to be alone either.
"I'll send Cerynn in here to be with you. Goodnight *Ms.* McCain."

Inhibited

Jaycobe

"It's time. We need to bring her home." The General patted my back. "Go get 'em. Our insider took out the girl, so all you need to do it take out your mother, and the other sister."

I'd been planning for this. Every night I imagined what I would do to them for killing her. The General wouldn't let me kill Alice. He said he had better plans for her.

I wanted to kill her.

Why wouldn't he let me?

But I was somewhat satisfied with the knowledge that she was going to get hers.

"Alright, let's move out." I had a few guys at my disposal, and lots of weapons. This shouldn't be too difficult. I couldn't teleport, so we had to walk, but we made good time and soon I stood on the steps of what I no longer called home.

It felt strange knowing that the next time I saw my family I would be ending their lives. I hesitated for only a moment, but then her face danced in front of me again, and my hatred flared. The gates opened, and the guards nodded at me. I signaled them to wait. I should go in first.

No one would suspect me alone. The town was quiet, everyone was inside. I heard one of Roland's parties in the bar on main street, but the lights were off everywhere else. It was past curfew, and the humans wouldn't risk being caught.

I snuck into the first house on the block. Everyone was asleep. I killed the three children quietly. They never saw it coming. But the husband I woke. I made him watch as I tortured his wife. He cried and begged for her life, and I smiled and broke her. I wrapped her hair around my hand and held her against me, and I made her tell me her name.

Just her name.

That's all I needed.

Once she gave it to me, I controlled her completely. I laughed as her husband struggled against the ropes that tied him down. She screamed and he cried and I laughed.

Life isn't fair.

She was losing too much blood; losing consciousness. My job was done.

With her name, I forced her to skin her legs, her arms, and then I made her slit her wrists. She convulsed on the floor as she fought for her life. The man cried out and the ropes released. He threw himself on her, and I killed him there. I moved on to the next house and did the same thing. In the next house, there was a baby sleeping in the cradle. She looked like Aurora. I loved Aurora. I spared the baby. I could take her back to the prisons and raise her right.

Soon I'd hit every house. I wiped out the entire town, except for Roland's party. I would leave them. He used to be my friend and he never did anything to hurt me. Him I would leave. And maybe when I was through here, I would recruit him, too.

Alice

Her daughter is dead. The General warned me. Chrissy wants me to get out of her house. She wouldn't let me comfort her. I started to pack, but The Captain stopped me. I didn't want to cause her any more pain. If she wanted me to leave, I would leave. But The Captain won't let me. She is heartbroken. I want to go comfort her, but she will just throw me out again. I thought escaping would be a good thing, but it's only cost others their lives. I never wanted anyone to die for me.

I'm not worth it.

"I need to go back. I need to stop all of this." I could barely control my shaking. "I'll go back to The General.

and he'll stop this."

"I won't let you do that."

"Why not?"

The Captain sat on the windowsill, and peeked out the window.

"It's not going to end just because you go back to him."

"Yes it will. He's punishing me."

"No, Alice. He's playing with you." The Captain's lips pressed together. "He's convincing you to come home. Once you're home he'll punish you. This is not punishment."

No. He wanted me back. If I went back, he would leave them alone.

Wouldn't he?

"You're going to help me wipe out all the Àraid." His breath smelled like blood as he leaned over me. He rarely asked me to come to the Telias. Not after the first time; when I interfered. Laying behind him was the latest victim. "Here, Baby, do the honors." He held out a knife, and pointed to the little girl laying in the blood.

"Why are you punishing me?"

"I'm not punishing you. Death isn't punishment, Dear."

"Promise me you'll keep one of these on you at all times." The Captain's urgent voice pulled me away from the memory as he glanced around the room nervously. I was still sobbing. I couldn't stop. I tried to bring the girl back. It didn't work.

"Alice." The Captain pulled my attention back to him. "Three warnings. They've all passed. He's going to come for you. You have to promise me." He held out an assortment of knives. Each had its own concealed holster. I picked up one and tested its weight in my hands. The Captain was panicked.

"Please?" He grabbed my hands.

"Okay. I promise I will keep one of these on my person at all times."

"And promise you will use it on anyone. *Anyone* that tries

to hurt you."

"What?"

"Just swear to me." He pleaded.

"Okay."

"*Anyone.*"

"What do you mean, Captain? What's wrong?"

"They will put on Micheal's face." He shrugged. "They always have."

"You're wearing Micheal's face. I eventually got used to it." I pointed out.

"Yes. I made you trust this face again. I'm worried you won't be able... I just... I need this face to not interfere. You need to defend yourself, no matter what." He sighed.

"But-"

"No. I've given you weapons before and when you went against this face, you hesitated. You can't do that this time."

"Okay, I won't."

"Do you promise, Alice?" His face filled with worry.

"I promise."

He nodded as the relayvens around the house chanted an alarm.

"What is that?" I covered my ears. The Captain shoved three knives into my lap and shouted over the blare.

"Strap these on. Go get Quartnee, and Jess, and go to the forest. I'll go find out what's happening." He was out of the room when I looked up from strapping on the knives.

I stepped out into the hall, ready to go down two doors to Quartnee's room. But it wasn't there. The house was shuffling. I was completely lost.

I turned to go back into my room, but the door was gone, I had no choice but to go forward. Chrissy taught me to keep my hand on the wall when the house was shuffling. Then it wouldn't delete me. I worked my way down the hallway, and ended up in a living room.

The staff were running, shouting to each other. No one noticed me, except Christa, who hesitated only long enough to narrow her eyes at me and dash out of the room. I was searching for Jess when a hand clamped around my arm.

A boy grabbed me and put a hand over my mouth. A well aimed elbow found its way into my ribs, and they cracked against the blow. I bit down on his arm, and he let go and shoved me to the ground. I crawled into the closest room and shut the door behind me.

The walls were all white stone. Floor to ceiling cupboards covered three walls, and a table stood against the forth wall. I ran to one of the cupboards and pulled it open. A body filled the space behind the door. I moved to the next one. Another body. I heard the doorknob clicking and the door started to open. I cast around anxiously for something to hide in. I ran to the table and hid under it.

Jaycobe threw the door open and locked his gaze on me. His manic eyes cried black tears.

"Don't try to hide from us. We'll always find you." He laughed, and his hands flew into the air and made fists. The room started shaking, and the doors of the cupboards fell open. Bodies fell all around us, landing hard on the table above me. They were mangled, every body in that room had something wrong; not one of them was whole. The boy's arms dropped as he surveyed the corpses. A slow smile spread across his face.

"My mother, the experimenter. She thought keeping these bodies around was a good idea." He cocked his head and knelt to grab my hand. "I guess she's going to learn different." His arms raised again, slowly, and the bodies around me started twitching. One locked a clammy hand around my wrist, and, although it was still pretty weak, it pulled me from under the table and dragged me to the boy.

"How are you doing this?"

They were too strong, I couldn't free myself from his grasp.

"Alice, Darling." His tone was condescending. "I'm not doing this." He touched my singed fingers. "You are."

Jaycobe

Her powers were easier to manipulate than I thought they would be.

She was so weak.

So unsure.

The power to raise the dead.

Anyone who's anyone has attempted it for centuries, and here this pathetic woman didn't even know what she was capable of.

That was good.

She would be much harder to control if she knew. She struggled against the Inhibited.

Didn't she know she was fighting her own strength?

No, her face only held confusion when I told her she was controlling them.

"Come on." I jerked my head towards the door, and two Inhibited dragged the stupid woman from the room. I let the others roam free through the house, they would cause panic if nothing else. I made Alice go in front of me, and two Inhibited covered my back. I was protected by an army of dead. Anybody we met in the hall I killed.

I spit on Alice's neck. She cringed as it sizzled and burned, but she didn't reach up to wipe it off. She just let it sit there, smoldering. She knew she deserved this.

Deep down, she always knew.

One of the Inhibited reached down her blouse and pulled out a small dagger.

"You must have been thinking about grabbing that." I took it from the cadaver, testing the blade with my fingertips. "Whatever you're thinking, they are too. They will always be one step ahead of you." I twisted her arm back, spread her palm across one cadaver's back, and held it there as she whimpered. And then I drove her dagger through her hand, pinning her to the dead.

She screamed, hand flying to her mouth to stifle the noise.

"Keep moving." I prodded them down the hallway.

People raced frantically ahead of us, but they stopped and watched us. Alice limped, bent awkwardly to accommodate her arm. The cadavers moved easily, eyes alert, ready to fight. The Captain leaned against one of the door frames, and I nodded to him. He frowned at his wife, but nodded at me and didn't move to save her.

And there she was.

My mother.

She stood tall in the middle of the room, facing us, angry.

"Hello. It's been too long." I bellowed. "Why don't we make this simple? Everyone drop your weapons," I put my knife to Alice's throat. "Or I kill her." I waited, knowing mother would never risk Alice's life, but she stared defiantly back.

"Go ahead." Her eyes dared me, challenged me to live up to my word. Alice gasped, and her eyes begged me not to.

I couldn't kill Alice.

The General said no.

I stopped, for only a moment, trying to decide what to do, and my powers drained from me. Alice's eyes deepened to black, and held my gaze as my vision flickered.

"Stop. What are you doing?"

Heat poured from her as the cadavers started dropping

around me.

"Stop." I dug my knife between her ribs, twisting and grinding it to the hilt.

Her eyes faded back to white-blue and the bodies righted themselves. Her blood dripped from my hands as she stumbled to the ground, holding her side. Mother simply watched her, motionless, expression neutral.

Her expression was always neutral.

Aurora skipped over to Alice, humming softly, and put a hand on her shoulder. Power danced from Aurora's fingers and healed Alice's side. Aurora was always more powerful than us. I wanted Alice to be in pain. I frowned and grabbed my baby sister. Her arms wrapped around my neck in a loving embrace. I looked back at Mother.

"Call them off."

Her face now held panic as she watched the two of us.

"Jaycobe. Look at me. I am your mother." She pleaded, but still hadn't done what I asked.

"Call them off!" I was losing patience.

"That is your sister. Your favorite sister. You love her. Do you not remember? You two would tell stories to each other for hours, just the two of you."

"Yeah, Man," Roland stepped through the crowd and stood by my mother. "You love her. You would do anything for her. What are you doing?"

"She betrayed me!" This had to be done. My whole family was a threat to the Raks. "I need to do this. You don't understand."

"I guess I don't." Roland shook his head. "My best friend would never put his family in danger. He wouldn't pull a knife on his baby sister. Look at her. She's defenseless."

But the crowd wasn't, still.

"Time's up, Mother." I braced my knife and slit Aurora's throat. Her eyes widened in surprise, and then closed as she slumped in my arms.

Mother gasped, covering her mouth with both hands. She

fell to her knees as Roland screamed at me. Her shoulders shook as she fought to hold back tears.

She wouldn't cry.

She never cried.

I couldn't hear anything anymore. Adrenaline pounded through my ears as my sister's blood soaked through my shirt. Slowly, it dawned on me what I was doing. This was my sister. My best sister. My favorite. I looked back at Mother, horrified.

"I'm sorry." My lips barely formed the words.

My sister's head rested on my shoulder; her red hair brushed against my cheek. I tried to put her down, but my arms wouldn't move. With a mounting dread, I realized The General was controlling me. He had to, to insure I actually did what I was supposed to. I fought the orders, knowing I wouldn't be able to hold off long. One foot haltingly moved forward, trying to catch my mother.

"Run." I could barely spit the word out, and an arm rose to point to the front door. Black veins rippled down my arms as another wave of poison flooded my system.

"Every time the person resists, another blast of Rak poison invades their system." The General told me during training a season ago. "Either they give in and do what they're asked. Or they die. Win-win."

Another step.

"Mom, kill me before I kill you." I pointed my blade toward her.

She shook her head.

"I cannot."

Alice

The little girl slumped in his arms, eyes closed, mouth open. Blood ran from her lips and covered his shirt. His arms shook as he pointed his blade directly at Chrissy. The boy begged for death, arms pulsing black.

"Run." He could barely talk. He was fighting the Raks, but it wouldn't last long. Black veins pulsed through his face and arms. I froze.

Rak poison.

Memories flooded in.

"Kill her. I need to know!" He yelled.

He hated yelling.

Yelling showed lack of control. Another wave of poison washed over me, and my skin pulsed black. I inched towards the girl laying in the arena. The General paralyzed her to make this easier for me.

"Kill her!"

I couldn't. But I couldn't stop.

The General shoved me to the ground beside the girl, but I couldn't drop the knife. I landed with the knife sticking out of her chest. And then the poison released and I frantically tried to stop the bleeding. It was too late. The General laughed. He had been working on making the poison stronger. Concentrating it. Injecting it to add to the *power of true names.*

It had never been strong enough to control me before.

It was now.

It was strong enough to force me to take a life.

Jaycobe still resisted, but his arms shook. He couldn't hold out; it had too powerful a hold on him. Christa simply stood and stared blankly at her son. Peter stopped in the doorway, holding Quartnee in his arms, and Jess followed close behind. Cerynn was right behind him, but ran to her brother once it registered what was going on.

"Stop me, Cerynn. I can't stop it." He was crying, fighting a war he could never win.

I felt a hand on my back, and The Captain lifted me to my feet.

"Let's go." He whispered, pointing to the door.

My granddaughter wrapped a hand around the knife, and it slowly turned to ash. The cadavers stood at attention, ready to fight, but waited for a command. I beckoned to Peter.

"Take them into the woods. I'll be there soon." I pushed The Captain towards Peter, urging them out the door. The Captain looked down at my hand, which still bled, but didn't hurt anymore.

"Come with us. You're not strong enough to fight this battle."

"That is my daughter." Chrissy stood frozen in place as her children wrestled on the floor at her feet. "I can't just leave her."

"She hates you. Genuinely despises you. Why would you stay?"

"Because hatred won't ever win wars."

He sighed, and shot me a half smile.

"I knew you were more than just a pretty face." His hands found the baby and he waited to be rewarded with a kick. "Don't do anything stupid, and bring both of you back." He gave me a significant look, one last side hug, and pulled Peter through the door into the night.

"I can help." The timid maid, Miss Lorraine, spoke up. She stood in the doorway, wringing her hands. "What can I do?"

I thought for a moment.

"You can get Chrissy out of here, no matter how much she fights you. Then go to Ginny's office and save the plans she made. We'll need those eventually."

She nodded.

"Okay, then what?"

"Then get out of here. Don't come back in for anything. Keep them safe."

Again, she nodded, and ran to my daughter.

"Mother." Jaycobe spit from between clenched teeth. "I'm sorry." His face was completely black now, and he struggled to stay upright as his sister attempted to disarm him.

"Mrs. McCain, we need to leave, now." Miss Lorraine tapped Chrissy's shoulder. Chrissy's eyes were glued to her children, and she shook her head. "Actually, yes." Miss Lorraine nodded her head firmly, looked back at me, and sort of shrugged.

She grabbed a vase off the table, and crashed it into Chrissy's head. As Chrissy slumped in her arms, she put her over her shoulder, like a sack of potatoes, and ducked out the door.

Now it was just me, Cerynn, Jaycobe, and the cadavers in the room. I hooked my arms through Jaycobe's, pulling him up off his sister. The baby gave an angry kick. The Captain still insisted I wear a corset to hide my growing stomach, but the baby was running out of room. My eyes watered as the burning pain spreading through my abdomen.

"Is the real Jaycobe still in there?" Cerynn whispered, her eyes locked on her brother. I shook my head. The real Jaycobe died the day The General took him in. His legs flew into the air, trying to kick her, and I stumbled backwards, landing hard against a wall. Cerynn reached out for me, but hesitated, calculating.

"When I tell you to, Alice, get out of here."

I nodded, and she took off into the maze, the cadavers following her. Jaycobe swung behind him and connected with my temple.

Lights flashed as I released him, stumbling into the middle of the room. He pushed me down, and flipped me over so I faced him. He wasn't fighting the Rak poison anymore. His skin stayed one color, but the hatred in his eyes smoldered and burned.

"You killed her. You took her from me."

Something wrapped around my arms; binding them to my sides. My body rose in the air, and smashed into the wall. He was back at my side as I fell to the ground.

"I want to kill you."

I believed him. A knife glinted in the corner of my eye, but I couldn't turn my head. His fingers pressed into my eyelid, and he held my eye open. The tip of his knife lowered toward the inside corner of my eye, dropping closer.

"I can't kill you. I'm not allowed. She had the most beautiful eyes. All sparkly and black. They were mischievous eyes that didn't have the chance to see enough. Your eyes, however, have seen too much."

Cold metal poked my eye, and I tried desperately to blink.

"Jaycobe." I could barely whisper.

"No! Don't talk. You don't deserve breath. But I can't kill you!"

Pain shot through my eye and I screamed. He left it there; let the knife sit in my eye for a while, and laughed as I screamed and struggled to get it out. Hot blood ran down my face and I attempted to cover my eye with my hand. His hand was on the handle again and he slowly dragged the knife through my eye, slicing it in half. I screamed and fought him and tasted blood in my mouth; dripping down from the eye socket.

"A present from me. Something to remember me by." He yanked me to my feet and pulled the blade from my eye. I quickly covered it with my hands and turned to flee. The pain was unbearable. I couldn't see. Blood stung my other eye, and I couldn't open it.

"Alice, get out of there." Cerynn's voice filtered through the window. I wanted to leave, but I couldn't move. Jaycobe grabbed my arm, and I stiffened, ready for another blow. Instead, he dragged me to a large window and threw me through it. Glass shattered around me, and cut my back as I landed hard on the ground and rolled.

The house exploded behind me.

Huge billowing flames rose into the night as the entire place was engulfed in fire. Jaycobe's body landed next to me with a thud, crackling from the fire. Chrissy screamed and ran to her son. She gathered him into his arms and rocked him back and forth, glaring at me.

"Bring him back! Bring him back!" Her face contorted in sorrow and hatred. "He is my son!"

I had never heard her voice raise louder than her normal monotone. I honestly didn't think it could. But as she screamed at me to help her son, I realized that I never understood her like I thought I did. I never could tell how she would react. I never could predict her. She crawled over her son and grabbed my shoulders, shaking me.

"Bring him back right now!" Her eyes were dry, no tears, but her hair turned into a flaming red.

She was losing control.

Inhibited

Christa

It was gone.

Everything.

Gone.

The Captain stole it all from me.

Myself. My house. My daughters. My son.

Twenty-three.

It would not stop.

I held him in my arms. He was still hot from the fire, but he was limp. *She* looked down on me with one hand covering her eye, which spurted blood down her face. Peter was with me now; hugging me.

"Bring him back!" I was yelling.

I knew it. I should not yell. My chest constricted. It hurt to breathe.

My eyes burned, stinging from anger and the fire dying down from my house.

My beautiful house.

I loved that house.

I put so much work into that house.

The Captain knelt beside that woman. My mother. I hated her. I never hated anything more. I wished she stayed dead. Instead she brought her Rak husband home with her.

"Hi, Christa, this is my husband. He is not a spy. I promise. By the way, I am going to get all of your children murdered. Because of me. Is that not great?"

I hated her.

I hated The Captain.

He looked so concerned; so worried about his stupid wife. And then he dared to reach down a hand to help me up.

How dare he?

I grabbed his arm and pulled him down next to me, squeezing his face in between my fingers.

"I know you killed Ginny. I know you killed everyone. I do not buy your story."

He was a good actor. He looked genuinely confused, but I knew better. Alice pulled me away from him, but I gripped his face harder. Heat flooded my hands and burned the stubble on his cheeks. He clamped his mouth shut.

He would not scream.

That would be too easy.

Alice pulled at me again and I whirled and slapped her. We stared at each other for a moment.

I could not believe I did that. But it felt good.

I raised my hand to strike her again, but she fell to the ground at my feet, sobbing. Instead, I kicked her injured ribs. She cried out in pain, and it soothed my nerves. My foot rose to kick her again, but she grabbed my leg and swept my feet out from under me. She pinned me to the ground and waited for me to stop struggling.

"I don't care about your grievances against me." She whispered, but my plate still picked it up. "Look around you, Chrissy. Cerynn got out. Quartnee and Jess too. You haven't lost *everyone*."

"*Christa*!" I screamed. "My name is Christa! I am not the daughter you once had. I am not Chrissy anymore!" I spit in her face. She blinked tears from her eyes.

"I know you want to lash out right now, but you can't.

Your people need you." She pointed to the small gathering of people that were left. The town, too, was burning, and bodies were heaped in the streets.

The whole town.

I quickly counted the survivors. Apart from the people from my house, there were only forty-six people left. Forty-six. Out of five-hundred-and-six, forty-six survived. Roland emerged from one of the burning buildings with a tiny baby in his arms. Only he and the people from his pathetic rave survived. They stood huddled together, staring at me.

The fight drained from me.

She was right.

I was being selfish.

"Fine. Let me up."

Her hands released and she helped me to my feet. Her fingers danced around her injured eye, and she cringed at the blood covering her fingers. I rolled my eyes, and prodded her eye.

"Læχlïeʒè." I did not want to heal her, but I knew Peter would never let me hear the end of it if I refused to do something so simple for such a petty reason.

I was still angry, I was just controlled now.

She blinked her restored eye a few times, and smiled at me. I slapped her to make sure she knew I had not forgiven her. My dragon circled above us, confused. He landed next to me, and I placed my hand on his shiny scales. I remembered the box I kept on the porch. It was full of things my children thought were rocks. It took me cycles to build up such a dangerous collection.

Did the fire burn it?

I sent my dragon to go find the chest, and turned back to the group. We should go to Iceloch, but for tonight we would go to the woods. Those trees were mine. They were loyal to me. It would protect us. Iceloch would be the best place to go, but I could not risk taking our troubles into another region. I could not endanger them.

My dragon scooped up some smoldering remains of my house and flew into the sky, dropping the ashes in the woods, spreading it out. Tiny fires sprang up where the pine needles caught, and soon the entire forest was illuminated with our impromptu candles. I took Quartnee from Peter and led our tiny group to our new home, waiting until they gathered in the middle, huddled, frightened.

I lifted my hands towards the trees towering above us. Slowly, they awoke. It had been so long since I used my powers, but they still understood my order. They bent and swayed and some branches knit together. Around us the trees were parallel to the ground, knitting together, forming a wall of wood and leaves. The trees inside the circle swirled and twisted their branches and raised their roots from the ground, constructing little houses and shelters around the perimeter. Some roots formed steps, so I could climb to the top of the wall and look out on the world. Branches formed a roof that could raise in good weather, and lower down to shield us during bad weather. A section of the wall also opened, to allow the dragon and wood creatures to enter at will, and for us to go out on scouting missions. With one final survey of my work, and a click of my fingers, the wood turned to ice. Wood could burn.

Ice did not burn.

Alice

73rd Day, The Season Of Death, 749-PW.

I couldn't bring the boy back to life. I tried. Just like I did with

Ginny.

It didn't work.

~~Chrissy~~ Christa hasn't even looked at me today. She sat on the wall

all night long. She never came down. Peter won't look at me either.

He sat below her, at the base of the wall, waiting for her to come

down, but she never did. He cried silently for their dead, since

Christa wouldn't join him. Aurora's body burned in the fire, but

Peter built a small shrine for her, and mourned without his wife.

The Captain keeps his head low. He doesn't want any more

attention. He hasn't left the cabin today, but last night he sat out

and watched Christa on the wall. There's a storm brewing between *them.*

<u>*I am afraid of what will happen when it boils over.*</u>

That terrible night was behind us. The suns both rose over our camp, but luckily today the cold sun won.

At least Christa was given that reprieve.

I didn't sleep. I tried, but every time I fell asleep I would be back in my prison; back in his possession. Then I would jolt awake and bury my head in The Captain's side. He would hold me, and rock me until I fell back asleep, only to wake up again a few moments later, and start all over. My hand would always be tightly wrapped around my necklace, and my fingers hurt as I eased them back open. He would stare at the charm, an odd look in his eyes, but never asked about it.

I still absentmindedly stroked the chain as I observed the little town from the porch. Christa was still out there. I wanted to go to her, to comfort her somehow, but every time I started to go to her, my face would sting where she slapped me, and I'd see the hatred in her eyes as she spit in my face. She wasn't the daughter I knew. This wasn't the same person.

A throat cleared behind me, and brought my attention back down to my level. Jess stood with his hands behind his back, shyly looking up at me. I smiled at him to ease his shyness. He studied the ground and rocked back and forth.

"Could you maybe play with us?" He looked at a group of three boys around his age, then back at me hopefully.

I nodded, smiling at him, and held out an arm so he could help me up. He ran to my side and pulled on my arm, pulling me up off the porch. He skipped by my side as we moved towards his friends.

"Did you really survive the Raks?" The littlest boy asked. I hesitated and then nodded slowly. They were in awe.

"How did you do it? What did they do to you?" Small fingers prodded the scars on my arm. "We want to know every detail."

I frowned at them, and pressed my lips together.

I couldn't tell them.

I needed to protect them.

Jess shook his head firmly.

"My brother just murdered my sister, and most of the town. Ginny was murdered, too. The whole town's been wiped out and we all lost someone. We need to know what they're capable of. Please?"

I took the boy's hand and we walked a few yards more; the other kids followed.

"The Raks are fast and ruthless. Don't let them catch you. That's all you need know." I kept my voice low, but fiery pain still flooded my body. The boys watched me. They tried not to stare at me as I limped ahead of them. They wanted to know all about my injuries, but I tried to change the subject. "How well do you boys know how to defend yourselves?"

Their voices clamored over each other, anxious to prove to me just how "cool" they were, and glad for an output of their energy. Soon they were brawling in the courtyard, yelling and fighting like little boys do. One of them pulled me down with them and we rolled in the dirt. We wrestled for awhile and then collapsed in a heap of giggles.

"I am glad you find our recent massacre so amusing." Christa stood above us, hands on her hips. She grabbed Jess's arm and yanked him to his feet, flinging him behind her. His arms flailed as he tried to remain balanced.

"Christa," I was on my feet again too, holding onto one of the boys as leverage. "Christa, leave him be. He's just a child."

Jess ran to my side and hid behind me. I put a hand on his

head as he buried his face in my side.

"I didn't mean any harm, Mom. I just wanted someone to pay attention to me." His hands gathered the front of my blouse, and tears soaked in where his face pressed against me.

"So you are stealing my children now?" Her voice held so much pain. "Am I not a good enough mother? I cannot show my kids enough love so they go to you?"

"No, Mom, that's not it." Jess spoke up.

"Then come here." She stood expectantly, waiting for her son, but he only clung harder to me. "Come on, Jess." She lunged and grabbed him, shoving me to the ground. She paused and stared at me. I gripped my side, wincing, and the boys huddled around me. She knelt and placed a hand on my broken ribs.

"I am sorry. I overreacted." She wouldn't let me get up. "Not yet, you landed pretty hard, I want to make sure you did not break anything." Her eyes softened.

Jess squatted down beside me and whispered in my ear.

"She's been having more mood swings lately. Papa says you can't get mad at her when she's mad because she doesn't even know that she's being mad."

I watched my daughter, confused. She didn't react to her sons accusation; just calmly examined my injuries.

"What do you mean, Jess?"

"Her mind is unraveling. The Àraid were never meant to lose people. The more they lose, the less they cope. Mom has lost lots. Plus, with her rape, and the fact that she's also letting the Àraid in, it's all happening too fast. So when she's yelling at you, just remember she's just yelling at her mind for failing her. That's what Papa tells me. Her mind is her prized feature and now it's shutting down. It makes her paranoid because she isn't sure what's real anymore."

Rape? She was raped? The guards aren't allowed to harm anyone outside the prisons. The General was very firm on that.

Christa's hand shot over and slapped his mouth, then clamped his mouth closed.

"Loose lips sink ships, Jess." She was angry again, trying to push her frustration down deep inside herself. She sighed and got up, reaching down to pull me up with her. "I lost my temper and I should not have. And I should not have yelled at you before either. It was not your fault Ginny died, but I blamed you anyway."

"When were you raped? You could report that. The General would punish them."

"And kill me. But it does not matter anymore anyway. Do not worry about it."

"Was it because of me?"

"I do not want to talk about it."

I shook my head, and grasped my necklace as I listened to her. She paused and pointed to it.

"You still have that old thing?" Tears sparkled in her eyes, but now so did a happiness I hadn't seen there since I came here.

"Yeah, I still have it." I blushed as she laughed.

"You held onto it, through torture and running and sleeping under the stars. Amazing."

"I made a promise, Christa."

"Promises are just empty words these days."

"What's going on here?" The Captain's voice boomed over the courtyard as he strode over to us. Gone was the laughter in Christa's eyes, replaced with burning hatred as she turned towards my husband.

"Why are you still here, *Captain*? Have you not done enough?" She met him halfway across the yard and they stood at odds, measuring each other up. He swung first. His fist clipped her jaw and sent her sprawling in the dirt. People came out of their houses and gathered around the two, whispering fervently.

"Why do you insist on blaming me? Can't you see I'm as innocent as you?" He was yelling at her. Something snapped. He no longer had the patience to defend his position.

"You were so chummy with the Rak guards. You should have seen this coming. If you were on our side you would have warned us. You are not on our side."

"Prove it."

"You spend your time away from her down at the bar. Sharing drinks with the Raks. Sharing *girls* with them."

My mouth dropped open.

Was that true?

The Captain glanced from me to Christa, and then back at me.

"The drinks I shared, but I've always stayed loyal to you, Alice."

"Why would she believe you? You are a Rak!"

His foot shot out and kicked her before she could finish her sentence. She scrambled backwards, still on the ground. She ran into my legs. I grabbed onto her so I wouldn't lose my balance, and was transported back in time.

I saw my daughter, ten cycles old again, cowering from her raging drunken father.

"I do not want to marry him! I want to stay with Alice!"

"You'll marry him, and you'll please him. You don't get a choice in this, Brat." His belt flew through the air and she blocked it with her arm, biting her lip as the leather tore her skin.

And then I saw her, pinned down by seven Raks; attacking her just like they'd attacked me. Behind her I saw The Captain, arms crossed, watching them rape my daughter. He was smiling. Chuckling.

I let go of Christa's arm and stepped back, horrified. She was in a ball on the ground, arms over her head.

"Captain, stop." I tried to grab onto him, but he dodged me.

"Not this time. I'm not letting her off easy this time." He grabbed her arm and pulled her to her feet. She didn't try to fight; she was overcome with terror. He threw her to the ground and stomped on her back. She whimpered and tried to get to her feet, but he shoved her back to the ground and dug a knee into her stomach. She gasped for air as he held her arm out to the side and broke her wrist with his elbow. It was too familiar. It was the same way he'd tortured me.

I ran to him and tried to pull him off of her, but when he turned to me he wasn't seeing me. His fury clouded his vision.

He was crazed.

He rose to his feet and caught me around me neck, squeezing off air. The baby somersaulted and kicked in protest, and I clawed at his hand as he held me off the ground. He threw me to the ground, but I managed to grab his arm and pull myself back up.

I grabbed his face and forced him to look me in the eye. Our foreheads pressed together and the tension in his face eased as we stared at each other. A muscle in his cheek twitched and he back away from me. He spit on the ground where Christa was on her hands and knees, gasping for air.

"I'm sick of you and your accusations. I'm on your side." He kicked her right beneath her ribs and she landed hard in the dirt. "How many of you want to follow this psycho? This woman who doesn't believe you. Who makes up her own story for you?" He spoke to the gathering around him. They watched their fallen leader quietly. The Captain sank to his knees and I dutifully went to his side, the proper wife, but I kept seeing his smug expression as his guards attacked my daughter. His lip was bleeding, but he seemed fine.

Christa tried to push herself off the ground and collapsed again in a heap, cuts and scratches covered her arms.

I was torn.

She was my daughter, he; my husband.

The people were slowly clapping, gathering around him and congratulating him. The men were shaking his hands, and the women fussed over his scratches.

Peter knelt at Christa's side; bent low while she whispered something in his ear. Blood ran down her face, and he tried to blot away the majority of it with his sleeve. Her fingers curled around his cane as he worked his arms under her body, struggling to lift her. His leg buckled beneath him and they both tumbled back to the dirt.

He tried again.

This time he braced his bad leg against a rock, and worked his way to his feet, but halfway up his leg collapsed again and he dropped her. She rolled away from him, and smashed her head into one of the half buried rocks in the dirt, wincing as she folded her arms over her head. He crawled to her and pulled her into his arms, rocking slowly, not attempting to rise again.

Nobody bothered to help.

Everyone was too busy talking to The Captain to even notice their struggle. I moved towards the two, but a hand caught my wrist. The Captain squeezed my hand in warning.

"I wouldn't do that if I were you." His voice was quiet, his face stern. I shook off his hand and challenged him.

"Is that a threat?"

He worked his jaw as he studied me, and then simply shrugged.

"It's whatever you take it to be."

I turned away from him and knelt beside my daughter.

Christa

Blood stings eyes.

People do not tell you that.

Soap stings eyes; it is a warning on the bottle.

Sometimes air stings eyes, but everyone knows that.

*People screamed and flames burned buildings and my
eyes. I shook my head and was in my living room.*

De ja vu.

I have done this before.

*Peter, explaining to me who The Captain was. A
sunstinger in her room.*

More screams.

Raks everywhere.

Alice.

Missing.

I had to find her, that was all I knew.

I cannot do this.

I shut my eyes tight and put my arms over my head.

I cannot do this.

This must not happen.

I opened my eyes again.

They stung.

Why did my eyes sting?

I licked my lips and tasted blood.

Blood stings eyes.

My mind was stuck on a loop. I felt myself jolting and rolling around as Peter tried to pick me up. I could not move.

My eyes shut again.

"Welcome back. Enjoy your stay." The General stood above me, hand clutching a metal spike.

"Look, Mom. I'm flying." Jaycobe sat on a dragon, barely lifted off the ground. He was five. Before I hid his abilities from him.

Stop it, please.

I dug my fingers into my temples and opened my eyes. Alice was above me, wiping my face with a handkerchief. She was muttering something, but my plate must have fallen off.

The Captain beat me.

I never lost before.

The memories and visions pelted my brain, begging audience. I focused all my energies on keeping them out. Peter removed his cane from my fingers and rose to his feet. My arm was slung around his shoulders, and Alice was on the other side.

Chains and blood and crying.

Alice crying.

Bleeding.

The General laughing as he smashed me into the concrete wall.

"Marry me. Join our bloodlines."

The Captain was there. I could not see very well.

Blood clouded my vision.

No stop.

I could not keep them out. I could not stop the visions. I wanted to. They were too horrible.

Peter's hand braced my head as they laid me on one of the beds in our cabin. Jess was there, too.

He looked worried.

Why was he worried?

Blood stings eyes.

I could not think.

I was on repeat.

Alice had a wet cloth and was cleaning some of my cuts.

Why was I bleeding?

I lost.

I never lost.

What was happening?

My head hurt. I could not see. I could not think.

Why could I not think?

"What do you think? Think she'll like it?" He held up a chain in front of me.

The necklace was beautiful. It sparkled and caught the light just right. The charm was a black tear-drop, inlaid with sparkling Firestones. Twining around the drop, and the silver chain, were three snakes. I nodded to him.

She would like it.

She liked fancy things like that. He turned the charm over in his hands and pointed to the snakes. On the belly of each snake was a pair of letters.

CM

MT

AA

I did not understand.

"Chrissy. Don't you know what these are?"

"No." I frowned.

"Our initials. CM is you, Christa McCain. AA is your mom. Alice Avens. And MT," he paused, "is me. Micheal Tallante." He dangled the charm in the air, swinging it slightly. "The friend I bought the necklace from put a spell on it. Now, whenever your mom grabs it, like if she's scared or something, I'll feel it in my heart. I will always know

when she needs me. I chose snakes because they're your favorite animal. And Firestone, because they're only found at the bottom of the black lakes of Silverglass; which is where I'm from. I put the initials on there so we'll all be a family. This way Alice will always have us."

"Firestone is an expensive stone, Mikie. Can we afford that?"

They were always trying to find new ways to save money. I knew we did not have money to spend on Firestones.

"My boss gave it to me. He said I could consider it a starting bonus."

Nothing in the world came free.

I wondered why his boss would give him such an expensive necklace.

Micheal was a nice guy. I never saw two adults so lovey. My real mom was never like that with my dad. These two were always nice, and whenever they fought they made sure I knew when they made up. It was not any of my business.

Why should I know?

It was nice being there and seeing it for myself, though.

He was on a trip when I first moved in with Alice. That was the biggest fight they ever had. Alice explained that he did not live with us yet, but that they were going to be married, and so he deserved to have a say on the house. He built the house, he should have a say.

I wanted him to like me. I did not want to be kicked out when they got married.

My hand closed around the necklace.

"When are you going to give it to her?"

"Tonight." He slumped in the chair. "I have some news I don't think she'll like. I got this to kind of soften the blow. I'll give her this, and make her promise to only take it off when she stops loving me." His eyes sparkled.

"Then when she's yelling at me, I can point out that she's still wearing the necklace, and she'll forgive me." He laughed, but still looked worried. "In a perfect world

perhaps."

We could hear her singing through the open window, and I knew soon she would ask me to come out and help her take down the laundry. We were in The Season Of Death right now, and the snow was deep, but we had to dry our clothes outside.

I did not like spending that much time in the cold, but Alice loved it.

We listened for only a moment, and then Micheal rose to his feet and joined in the song, striding out and placing an arm around her waist, holding her from behind. She laughed up at him, and they kissed.

Right in front of me.

They were always doing that.

They were always happy.

He swung her around in the air, accidentally knocking the clean clothes into the snow.

"Micheal, stop." She was out of breath, and looked at me significantly.

"Oh, she doesn't understand yet." His hand was not on her waist anymore, and she was pushed up against him tightly.

"Understand what?" I did not want to be left out. And the thought of them knowing something I did not was horrible.

They were kissing again.

They did not even notice me.

Micheal picked her up and set her on the table, still kissing her. Her dress rode up to her hips, but she did not attempt to fix it.

It was cold.

She should fix her dress.

He pressed tightly against her, but Alice's eyes met mine and she broke off the kiss.

"Micheal, we can't."

"We have before." He teased her, but she looked sad,

and shook her head slowly.

"I know, and it is very nice," she half-smiled at him, "but we shouldn't. We're not technically married yet. It's forbidden by law."

"That makes it so much better." He moaned, and pushed his face back into hers. His fingers worked to untie the corset Alice always kept laced so tightly, but she pushed his hands away.

"Leave it on. Please?"

"Oh, a little fantasy play? I can work with that. So what am I?"

"No, Micheal. We need to stop doing...this. We're not married."

"We're basically married." He argued.

"But if we're caught-"

"If we're caught, we lie. It's not that hard." He whispered. Indecision wavered in her eyes. Micheal glanced my way and told me to go back into the house, sit on the couch, and count to five-thousand.

He always did that.

That was our game.

I gladly went back into the house, but had to start over several times because their giggles and quiet,'shhh's made me lose count.

That night, I woke to them yelling.

Alice was crying and pleading. I could not make out what they were saying, but it was not nice. Their voices rose and fell and rose again. I wondered if they would wake me up to tell me they made up, or if they fought all the time in the night and never told me. I pushed the covers off the bed and slowly opened my door. If they were going to apologize later, I wanted to know what for.

"I don't want you to go!" Alice screamed. "It's

dangerous. Name one person who survived." She paced in the middle of the living room. Micheal sat on the couch.

"It doesn't matter. Money's tight and it's the only job offer I have."

"But Micheal, the Telias? Guards die at the Telias. Tempers get hot there. Ashal doesn't just kill prisoners."

"I'm not going to chop wood my whole life! At least this job is interesting."

"This job will kill you!" Her hands furiously worked the necklace he apparently already gave her. He chuckled, and Alice's eyes widened, furious.

"What are you laughing at?" Her voice was still loud, but she tried to control it.

"The necklace, Alice. Are you going to take it off?" It was almost a dare as Micheal crossed the room and pulled her into his arms. She stared at the charm in her hand and then back up at him.

"I promised." She whispered and he bent low and kissed her gently. She shook her head and tried to get out of his grip. *"You should go home. It's getting late."* He ignored her and eased himself to the ground, pulling her down with him. *"No, Micheal. We can't."*

"Sure we can."

"But I don't want to."

"You never want to anymore." He pouted. *"You used to be so much fun."*

"We could be executed, Micheal! Is that not getting through to you?"

"I could die at the Telias. You should be doing my every command to keep me happy." He chuckled.

"I can't risk this, Micheal. I can't risk my life for a few minutes of pleasure."

"I can do better than a few minutes. Let me show you."

"No, Micheal. I don't want to." She tried to get up again. He kissed her and pushed her against the legs of the couch, pinning her there. His hand worked under her dress and he

covered her face and neck with kisses, but she did not kiss him back.

I did not understand.

She loved kissing him. He kissed her mouth again, pressing her harder into the couch. I frowned as he took off his shirt, and then unbuckled his pants.

I gasped and covered my eyes.

What was he doing?

I cracked my eyes open. He struggled to take Alice's dress off, but she fought him.

Why did he want to do that?

That was weird.

He was breathing loudly between kisses, but Alice pushed him away.

Telling him to stop.

He pushed her onto her back and sat on her. Her dress was up, and his pants were down, and I shut my eyes. I tried to focus on drowning out his grunting by counting to five-thousand. I made it to one-thousand before Alice stopped protesting, and moaned.

Their moaning, and grunting grew louder, and it was hard to focus on counting. And then the grunting stopped, and I heard a scuffle. I cracked my eyes and saw Alice scrambling for the powder room. I heard her throwing up just out of my line of sight.

"Oh, come on." Micheal threw his hands in the air. "I wasn't that bad was I?"

She was crying as she reemerged from the powder room.

"Micheal." She sagged against the wall and worked to fix her dress. "Micheal, I'm pregnant." She wrung her hands and stared at the ground.

Micheal groaned and said a word I was not allowed to repeat. He sank back against the couch with his head in his hands. They stayed that way for a long time, and then Micheal looked up at Alice.

"So what are you going to do about it?"

She sagged. That was not the response she was hoping for.

"Well," she started slowly. "If we get married they won't execute us. They won't be able to prove we broke any laws. We'll just say we adopted the baby like we adopted Christa."

"What if I don't want a family while I'm working in the Telias?"

"Were you planning on just leaving us behind for this new job? Were you just going to abandon us?" She frowned.

"Maybe. There's plenty of available women around that area. That's where I found you."

"Those women are slaves! They don't want to be there."

"But they won't put up as much a fight as you. Not if I own them. They'll be more fun than you." He did not mean what he said, I could see it in his eyes.

Alice could not though. Her shoulders slumped and she stumbled to one of the chairs, hand over her mouth, eyes brimming with tears. His hands raked through his hair and he paced nervously.

"So you're just going to change all those promises of marriage, and toss me aside for some whore?"

He stopped and looked at her.

"I never asked you to marry me."

Her eyes widened as he continued.

"I asked you to come with me, but I never asked you to marry me. I don't want to get married. I'm too young. I don't want to be stuck in a rut."

"Stuck?" Her shoulders shook with sobs, but she tried to control the crying, glaring at him instead. "You told me you loved me. You told me you wanted to stay with me forever."

"Yeah, and I don't know, maybe I do. But at the time I said it to get you to open your legs." His cheek twitched.

That was his tick.

That was how I knew when he was lying. But Alice did

not see his cheek. Right now all he wanted to do was hurt her, even though he loved her. Right now they were more like my parents than ever, and I dreaded how this night would end.

"Then, maybe," She was choking on sobs. I could barely understand her. "Maybe I don't want to stay with you, either."

He slammed a fist into his leg and launched to his feet.

"Don't play that game. Don't do that to me."

I did not like this.

They were so angry.

I waited for him to point out the necklace again, and then they would go back to kissing and laughing.

"We are in this together. That's what vows are, Micheal. Through better and worse. This is worse!"

"We haven't said vows yet!" He spat on her.

Actually spat on her.

Her eyes widened, enraged. He was only hurting her more, and I wanted to go interfere.

"It's going to be okay, Micheal. We can have a real ceremony. We can wait until the baby is born. I'm about two seasons along now." She gave a half smile as he stared at her. She was struggling to calm down. She knew her emotions were getting out of hand. She always told me not to let my emotions lead. She said that was her weakness. Her emotions always spoke first.

"Two seasons! It took you this long to tell me? How did you hide it?"

"The corset. I was afraid of what you would say!"

He shook his head and mumbled.

"There goes our number one option."

She slapped him. Her eyes were filled with tears and her hands shook, but she slapped him so hard he stumbled before he regained his balance.

"Don't even think about making me give up this baby. My baby.*"*

"Oh it's all about you, isn't it?" He rubbed his face. "You, who got disowned from your parents. Who was there when that happened Alice? Who helped you out? Me. And when we moved here and couldn't afford to buy a house, who cut down the trees and built you one? Me. Then one day I go out of town to make us some money because we're flat broke, and when I come home I find out you've adopted a freak for a child."

I shoved my hand over my mouth.

Freak?

"I let her stay because that's what you wanted. I accepted her because I wanted to keep you happy. And now I find out that you have my whole life planned out to fit your needs perfectly. How convenient. Well, maybe I'm not done shopping yet. Maybe you were just a place holder until I found someone, anyone, better." He was crying now, too, and Alice reached out to him, hugging his waist, shaking her head.

"Please, please tell me you don't mean that." She pulled his face down and kissed his cheek, but his eyes were hard.

"No. I need to do some things for myself now. I need to live my own life before I live the life you've planned for me. I'm going to go get this job, I'm going to send you tri-season payments for your stupid little family plan, and if I'm still single in three cycles, I'll come back and make you my wife, but I want to see who else is out there first." His voice dripped with sarcasm and he held her close to him.

He did not mean it.

He wanted to stay.

I knew he did.

I saw it in his eyes.

Alice did not know that, though. She had never been good at sarcasm. She screamed and slammed her fists into him.

"Get out! Go! Leave! Go find someone better. We don't need you!" Tears soaked her face, and she tried to hold back her sobs.

"Alice," He was serious now. "Alice, no. I do love you. I always have. I'm sorry."

She did not say a word.

She just wrapped her hand around the necklace and yanked on it. The chain broke and she flung the charm to the ground. Everything in him collapsed as he stared at the shiny silver and black, but without another word he turned and left.

Days passed.

Mother never left her room.

Never unlocked the door.

Never let me in.

When I pressed an ear to the wood I could hear her crying on the other side, and sometimes at night I would hear her in the kitchen. I did not want to talk to her, though.

She threw him out.

I liked him.

I rescued the necklace and repaired the chain. The patch job was obvious, but at least it was fixed. I would give it back to her when she was better.

I did not see her for a quarter season. Then half a season passed and Micheal was still gone. A knock on the door startled me. It was a Law-checker from town. He had a letter tucked under his arm. We studied each other for a second, and he cleared his throat.

"This household got a snake in a few days ago, and nobody has picked up the letter. I wanted to make sure everything is going well here. Is Miss Alice Avens home?"

"Yes." I did not move.

"May I speak to her?"

I thought about the locked door.

The piled up dishes.

The untouched laundry.

"She is not seeing anyone right now." I read that in an old book. One with butlers and maids and lords and ladies.

"I really need to speak with her, please."

"She has not left her room in a few days, though."

He frowned and poked his head through the door. The room had not been cleaned in a season.

I wished I had cleaned it now.

It was embarrassing to watch the Law-checker take in our mess.

"So you've been alone for days?"

"Yes."

"Does that scare you?" He reached for my arm, but I jumped out of his grasp. He pulled out a note-pad and began scribbling on it. "May I come in?"

"I am not supposed to let anyone in when Mom is not home."

"But you just said she was here; in her room."

True.

She was here.

So I could let him in.

He kept writing in his note-pad as he came in. He asked me to show him around, and asked a lot of questions, and his frown just seemed to get bigger; especially when he saw the blanket I laid out on the hearth, and the ashes in the fireplace overflowing onto my blanket. We were in Snartec, so I could burn any wood I could find. I did not have to worry about trading for burnable wood. I kept the fire going all the time, but it would not fit inside the fireplace anymore. He made me put the fire out, and then noticed how cold the house really was.

"Chrissy," he knelt in front of me. "Do you like living here?"

"No. Not right now. It used to be nice, but mommy keeps to herself now. She just needs time. Soon it will be back to normal."

"How would you like to come stay, just for a while, at my

friend's house? They have a few kids your age, and their house is never cold. You would have people to talk to. To play with."

"Leave Mom? Alone?"

"Just for a little while. Just until she gets back on her feet."

"Would there be food, too?" I had not eaten in a while. Food sounded good.

The man's eyes turned very sad, and he took my hand.

"Yeah, let's go."

"Wait." A door creaked behind me, and we both turned towards Mother.

She looked terrible.

Her hair was a mess, her eyes were very red, and she clung to her door.

"She doesn't need to leave."

"Ma'am, this child is extremely malnourished. She's been left alone for days, and sleeps next to a fire hazard. I'm sorry but you have successfully lost your parental rights."

"She is not my parent! She just picked me up at the border!" I was trying to help, but I only seemed to make the man madder, and Alice sadder.

"I came by to give you this letter, Ma'am." He handed her an envelope. "And now I will be taking this child to a better home." He took my hand and pulled me out of the house.

I glanced back at the cabin from the road. My eyes were blurry, but I did not cry until I looked back at the house.

Until I saw Alice in the doorway crying, too.

The new family was not too bad.

They were just so boring.

I had been there for two days, and they never let me out of their sight. And they always talked like I was made of glass.

'Whatever you want, Dear.'

'Would you like to play, Dear?'

'I'm sure Alice is just fine by herself stop asking about her, Dear.'

I did not like how nice they were.

No one was that nice.

And they would not let me even go see my mom. They just made me sit in my room, with all the toys and books I could want. And three full meals a day.

It was too predictable.

There was nothing to worry about. It was scary. So the second night, after the man and woman both came in and read a bedtime story to me. After they both tucked me in, and after they both wished me a goodnight, tapped the lacelights awake, and both finally went to bed, I put my hands against the window. I closed my eyes, and tried to remember the words I once knew well.

They were fading now.

They were harder to remember.

But the word soon floated into my head, and I whispered it to the glass.

"Zèr̤t."

The glass disappeared and my dragon's head popped out of the bushes. He was waiting for me. I knew he would. I jumped on his back, and only briefly looked back at the house. I did not want to stay here. I would rather be cold with Alice, then warm without her.

The cabin was dark when we landed, and the front door was open.

"Mommy?" The door creaked as I pushed through it. My dragon was right beside me, but he barely fit through the door.

"Mom?" I saw a soft light under her door, but I did not hear anything. The house was picked up. Mr. Law-checker told her that if she got the house back on track, he might let

me come home.

It looked like she was trying.

The house was spotless. Except for a piece of parchment in the middle of the room. I went over and picked it up. She would not like to have a mess.

It was the letter Mr. Law-checker brought her. I knew it was private, but I read it anyway.

Micheal Tallante and Sarah Foster pronounced dead on the 10th Day of The Season Of Life, 727-PW, when Mr. Tallante's horse spooked and bolted. Their carriage broke free, and rolled off a cliff. Both were deceased when a Mailer found the bodies a few hours later.

I stared at the note, horrified.

She did this.

My mother sent him out.

He would not have been there if she had not sent him away. He would not have been with her if it was not for Alice.

I missed Micheal.

I liked him.

Slowly, I folded the letter and put it back in its envelope. I slid it under the door to her room, quietly speaking through it, hoping for a response. I hoped she was in there. But now I was mad at her. Because this was her fault. So now I hoped she blamed herself. I hoped she was happy with what she did. She did not say anything, but I could hear her moving around in her room.

I leaned against the door and waited. I wanted to be here when she came out. But when the suns came up, and she still had not come out, I began to lose hope. I dozed off and on throughout the day, and the night came and went without a sound from her. The next day, too, came and passed and I knew she must be hungry, but she did not come out. I gave up and went to bed that night, but a scream woke me.

"Christa!" She never called me that. I ran to her room but the door was still locked. "I need help!" I shook the door but it would not budge. "Go around, the window is open."

It was so cold outside.

There was snow on the ground.

Why was her window open?

All questions fled my mind when I crawled into her room. She was on the bed, every blanket in our house piled on top of her. Sweat beaded up and ran off her face and her eyes did not seem to be able to focus. I knew I should rinse her off with a cold cloth, and glanced around the room to find one.

A wash basin sat on the dresser, but the water was red. I settled for stroking her forehead with my hand instead, but she reached up and grabbed my arm, stopping me. She winced and shifted, her breathing labored. She mumbled under her breath, and her eyes would not focus on me. I bent over her to listen, but I did not understand what she was saying. She was talking, but she was not saying anything.

"Promise you won't do this, Christa. Don't deal with your pain this way. Promise." Her eyes were full of pain, and urgency, as she pleaded with me.

Do what?

What did she not want me to do?

I quickly nodded anyway. She looked so desperate.

"I promise, Mother. I promise."

"I should have never gone to the trade markets. But his smile... I am sorry, Mother. I did this. This is my fault. I should have never opened that letter." She shook her head and looked back at me. "I shouldn't have picked you up at the border that day. I should have just let you stand there alone. You ruined everything."

I looked away from her as my eyes stung with tears. She did not know what she was saying.

She was very sick.

She had a fever.

But even as I told myself she did not mean what she said, I remembered all the times I felt like an outsider. I was always just "there". I was not really part of her family. I did not want her to see me cry though.

I did not want her to know that she hurt me.

She did not know what she was saying. When my birth mother got sick a few cycles ago she ranted about how I was the worst thing that ever happened to her. She went on and on about how I ruined her life, too. My father comforted me and promised that she did not mean those things, and when she got better she did not remember saying any of it.

She swore I was wrong.

She swore she loved me.

But I knew the truth, and I never forgot. And now it was happening again.

What was wrong with me?

Why was it so hard for people to like me?

I glanced around the room as Alice moaned on the bed. She mumbled about snake people, and gold, and I did not want to listen. I was afraid she would tell me to leave, or tell me she hated me.

I knew that was next.

That always came next.

Her dress lay on the ground by the bed. All she had on was her tiny little nightgown. The one Micheal bought for her, and did not want me to know about. She gasped and grabbed the front of my dress as she pulled me down next to her.

"Get my bag." Her teeth clenched, face contorted in pain. I did not care if she did not love me.

I loved her and I did not like seeing her like this.

I was scared.

I could not lose her.

I did not want her to die.

I reached towards the dresser and my fingers closed on the cold leather. Alice was training to be a Healer. The pay was better than chopping wood. I placed the bag beside her on the bed. She pulled a long leather strap out and placed it between her teeth, gnawing on it. She threw back the covers and I gasped.

She was covered in blood.

Blood coated her legs and the sheets were stained. She was fatter than I remembered. I could not see any injuries on her body though, only her legs. I was very confused.

"Christa." She drew my attention back to her. "Do you remember that day when I broke my leg and you healed it?"

I nodded.

"Do you remember how to do that?"

Again I nodded, though her leg wasn't broken now.

"I'm going to need you to do that again. Okay?" She pulled out a tiny knife and a small bottle of iodine.

She poured the iodine onto some bandages and rubbed them all over her stomach, turning it an odd yellow color. She held the knife over her stomach, but her hands shook. Her eyes filled with tears, and she worked the leather between her teeth. With a deep breath she pressed the knife to her abdomen, slightly below her belly button. I shut my eyes as she whimpered against the leather.

I did not want to watch, but I was fascinated.

Her stomach was open, and her hand was inside. Tears coursed down her face and she carefully pulled and tugged at something inside her. And then both hands were in and her whimpering rose to a scream against the leather. Her hands reappeared holding a perfectly formed, tiny, baby. She pulled the baby free and then went back in and pull out a gelatinous blobby thing.

"Now, Christa." She hissed. She could barely open her eyes.

I placed my hands on both sides of the opening and

whispered.

"Lœɣlïezè."

It closed as if nothing ever happened. The baby on the bed was not moving. It was stiff and purple and messy. Alice closed her eyes and pursed her lips, chin quivering.

"It's my fault." She whispered over and over again. I sat there staring at the tiny baby.

I thought babies were born screaming, and I waited for this one to start to move and struggle, but it did not. The cord was still attached and I thought maybe if I cut it the baby would wake up, but as I poised the scissors over the cord Alice's hand stopped me. She was shaking, and could not speak, but a simple shake of her head told me all I needed to know.

This baby was not a normal baby.

This baby was not alive.

I crawled onto the bed next to Alice and she turned her face towards the wall and cried quietly. This baby was dead.

Micheal's baby.

He should have been here for her.

Why did he have to listen every time she told him to do something?

But Micheal was not here for us.

Micheal was dead, too.

Cerynn

They followed him now. The whole town rallied behind The Captain. I sat in the dirt in front of our cabin. Peter and Alice wouldn't let me in to see mother.

She was crying.

I could hear her through the walls.

Crying and thrashing.

I rolled my eyes. She was the ambassador or out city. She should be taking charge. But instead she cried in her cabin, and a stranger led our people. I should have stepped up. I could lead them better than he could.

Alice's voice rose above Mother's cries as she tried to calm her. The door creaked open and Peter limped out, leaning heavily on his cane. Josh stood, held out a hand, and helped Peter sit on the low step. A muffled cry from the cabin made Peter wince and put his head in his hands.

"Every vision she's blocked out for cycles are now flooding her. Everything she's pushed down. She opens her eyes and looks right at me, but I don't know if she sees me."

Josh patted his back as I threw some pebbles in the dust at our feet. Jess was off playing with his friends, and The Captain was holding a meeting with the rest of the town.

We weren't included.

He didn't want us. He told me if Mother promised to keep her head low, and not make trouble, he would allow her to stay.

"She's done so much for these people, it doesn't seem fair to kick her out." He laughed as he said it. The town laughed with him. We were alone now.

The outcasts.

The tolerated.

Loyalty was figurative during war. Just a lot of nice words that don't mean anything when a better offer comes along.

I remembered Mother was supposed to rub Quartnee's legs with something to keep them from rotting. When Mother created the houses, she made one for herself, and one for Peter.

Separate buildings.

I didn't like that.

I didn't like how they looked at each other after her "punishment". But I couldn't worry about that right now.

Numbly, I rose and went into our other cabin. Quartnee was asleep on the bed. The room stank of herbs and rot. There was only one bottle in the room, and I dumped its contents into my hands. We were almost out, so I used it sparingly. I tried not to gag as I rubbed the foul smelling concoction on her legs; they were shriveled and bony.

"Where's Mom?" Quartnee was groggy, rubbing sleep from her eyes as she watched me.

"She needed to lie down for a little while. So I'm here." I tried to smile, but she frowned at me.

"Mom makes it fun. Mom makes it into a game." She crossed her arms over her chest.

"Well, I can make it into a game."

She threw her arms up in exasperation and fell back onto the bed.

"Not *now*. It's not the same now. Tell Mom to take some drugs and get over it." Then she realized we weren't in the healira anymore. "What happened?"

"We had to move."

"Why?"

I hesitated.

"The Raks attacked us."

Her eyes widened.

"Was anyone hurt?"

I only nodded and kept rubbing her legs. She stayed quiet and fell asleep again within minutes. I kissed her head softly and stepped back out into the courtyard. The Captain's meeting dispersed, and everyone was just kind of milling about.

Josh was at my side in seconds, and together we made our way back over to where Peter had fallen asleep. The top of his cane slipped, and I saw the glint of a sword he kept hidden within.

Ever watchful.

I didn't wake him, but I clicked the cane back together. If The Captain knew we were still armed, he would find someway to remove our weapons, as he did with everyone else in town.

We couldn't afford that.

Inhibited

Alice

I sat up with her all night.

She never woke, but I think she knew I was there.

I hope that comforted her. I could hear The Captain out in the

courtyard talking to his new followers. He didn't come to fetch me,

but I am afraid that he will be very mad when he does come get me.

I wasn't scared of him. I think that I loved him. But he smiled in her

memory of the attack, and when he hit Christa he wouldn't stop.

He *couldn't* stop.

I am afraid now.

Christa would be fine. There were no permanent
injuries. But every time I touched her she pulled me into

her memories. She was thinking about Micheal; about when he left us. My heart clenched as I sat through the memory with her.

That terrible night. I couldn't even remember what we fought about. Well, I remembered why I sent him away, but I didn't remember what started it. And I remembered the baby.

Micheal and I had been so young.

So young and so in love and so unprepared. I was scared when I found out I was pregnant.

I wanted to go home.

I told Micheal that every day, but Micheal said that we would be fine, we would figure it out on our own. We didn't need them. We were "only" ten miles from town.

To him, we could do anything. But then he left. I kicked him out, but I hadn't considered that he would never come back. He was always there for me. When my parents kicked me out, he was there. When I moved to a new unknown region, he was right beside me. But I kicked him out, and he never came back. For days I just cried. I tried to eat, for the baby's sake, but I couldn't keep anything down.

The day we got the letter telling us Micheal was dead, I could barely get out of bed. My back hurt so bad I couldn't breathe, and my stomach kept cramping.

I knew.

From the moment I woke up I knew I lost the baby. I let it go longer than I should have because I hoped beyond hope I was wrong. I didn't remember telling Christa that I shouldn't have adopted her. I didn't remember telling her she ruined everything.

How could I have said such things?

I cringed now, knowing that she remembered it. I didn't mean it. I loved her more than if she were my own. I was ashamed that she lived with those words for so long. Such harsh words on such young ears. I dealt so much damage.

No wonder she hated me. No wonder she had been so

aloof after that night. I just figured she didn't know how to deal with what she'd seen. I had no idea she wrestled with being "unwanted".

My hand wound around my necklace as Christa continued the memories.

Why are you thinking about that?

Why are you dwelling on that night?

I felt every movement over again.

The incision.

Feeling around, trying to grasp my child.

I felt light headed and let go of Christa's hand. I couldn't go through this again. She looked peaceful now. From outside her head no one would know the torment she lived with.

I reached for her hand again, but the door of the cabin was thrown open and startled me. The Captain's frame filled the doorway as he stooped and entered the small cabin.

"Why are you in here, Alice?" He was angry.

"Because she's my daughter."

"And I am your husband. I needed you today, too." He put his hands on my shoulders and squeezed them. "It's time for bed now, Counselor. Come with me."

It was still early in the day, and a wave of nausea hit me when I finally understood his meaning. He took my hand and led me out of the cabin, across the courtyard, and into our cabin, pushing me roughly onto the bed.

He eased his shirt off his broad shoulders. It was only then, as I measured up his strong frame, compared to my small one, did I realize how outmatched I was. He could snap me in half without trying. I didn't even come up to his shoulder. Tattoos covered his arms and chest chains, fire.

"We need to remain united, Counselor. You can't choose her over me." He bent and kissed me, gently, lovingly. I was confused. He wasn't being mean. He wasn't yelling, or hitting me. He was being kind. I didn't know that I craved a tender touch until his hand traced my chin, and trailed down my neck.

I didn't know if I was afraid of him.

Here, in the moment, I didn't think I was.

I fought so hard to keep my feelings for him neutral. His lips moved to my neck and he shoved my hair out of the way. My arms went around him, and pulled him closer to me.

"It's her, or me, Counselor. Do you love me?"

I couldn't think clearly. I felt dizzy.

How did this happen?

I was so careful. Slowly, I kissed him back. This wasn't my robotic response from cycles of training.

This was different.

He was more nervous than usual. I was terrified. This was different. He wasn't directing me. I acted on impulse. His lips found mine, and, slowly, I kissed him again. My hands moved to his hair and I twisted it around my fingers. He pushed me back onto the mattress, propping himself up above me, never breaking contact.

"Do you love me?" He murmured between kisses. My mouth formed the word yes, but I couldn't say it.

"What is your name?"

"What?" He pulled away and stared at me.

"I want to know your name. The Rak way of proving love. I just need you to prove it. I just need to know you're not using me."

He shook his head.

"That's not how it works. You don't get to decide if you love me. Either you do or you don't."

"Tell me your name." I insisted, rising halfway off the bed.

His eyes weren't loving anymore. He pushed me to the bed and pinned me down, smirking as he looked down at me.

"No."

I cried and shut my eyes tight. I didn't want to see him. I

ruined it. Again. Everything had been going well, and then I ruined it. My eyes cracked open to stare at my husband. I clenched my eyes so hard that I could see the veins in my eyes. It was like looking through jail bars as I stared at his angry face. I shut my eyes again as unexpected tears fell from his eyes onto my neck.

Later, as I tested out which muscles would bruise, I knew it was my fault. I knew I could never love anyone again. And I knew The Captain wouldn't accept that.

Inhibited

Christa

My head was pounding.

It only pounded these days.

It had been a quarter season since The Captain overthrew me.

No one spoke to me, or Peter.

They left some food on our side of the line every morning, but no one crossed it. They had drawn a line in the middle of the courtyard, like some feuding town. Me and my family on one side, the rest of the town on the other. And *he* acted like he was doing me such a favor *allowing* me to stay.

I saw her over there every day. She would watch me carefully, but never came over. She never crossed the line. The Captain probably scared her back into his shadow. I noticed fresh bruises dotting her arms and neck yesterday.

The Captain was going to kill her.

I felt it.

They allowed Peter to sit in on the meetings every night, and he reported that some of the more brazen men in town were using her as a reward for jobs well done. Peter said The Captain claimed he tried to stop them, but of course I did not believe that.

She was a slave once again.

She escaped nothing.

She was so pale. She looked almost grey yesterday, and I had not seen her yet today. I heard the screaming again. A nearly constant hum now. Screaming and the snap of whips.

It was just in my head.

I knew that.

Vision or memory though I could not decide.

Jess and his friends threw a ball back and forth over the line. Never crossing it.

Smart kids.

Normally, Alice sat out there with them and told them stories, or played games with them. She was teaching them how to fight, and they were getting pretty good.

Where was she?

Why had I not seen her?

Peter told me he heard her scream last night. Just a short scream that sounded like it was muffled midway.

The Captain probably killed her in her sleep and was disposing of her body right now.

It would not surprise me at all.

He was crazy.

He was guilty.

Peter said I was obsessing.

False.

I was right.

It is not an obsession if it is right.

And I would continue being right even when the whole world thought I was wrong.

Even when all these people I *saved* and *protected* turned their backs on me.

They were afraid I would kill them like I did the Rak guards.

Why would I kill them?

Why did they not trust me?

Roland was The Captain's right-hand-man now. They

stalked around, owning the place, heads bowed low in conversation.

I could not trust anyone.

Roland was a Rak, too.

He looked shifty like a Rak.

Peter said I was wrong.

I was not.

I was never wrong.

Never have been, never will be.

I was not not crazy.

The suns moved across the sky and people came and went. Still I never saw Alice.

She was dead.

I knew she was dead. The Captain killed her last night. I was right.

I knew I was.

Peter did not agree.

Why did he not agree?

He always agreed with me.

My head hurt.

Visions flashed through too fast to study them.

I could not think.

I could not focus.

I needed something to do. I had never been idle in my life. But my people got uncomfortable when they could not see me. They thought I was plotting something. Silly people. Any good 'plotter' could do it right in front of you and you would never know. I thought about playing a prank on them just to prove it.

But I did not want to.

Where was Alice?

I was getting worried.

She did not look good yesterday.

Should I have said something?

Could I have helped?

I squinted against the bright sunlight. The Captain was

striding across our line. He came over to me and grabbed my arm, pulling me along with him. He never said anything. I struggled in his grip.

What was it about him?

Why could I not beat him?

He shoved me into their cabin and shut the door quickly, locking it.

"What are you doing?"

He shushed me and led me into their bedroom.

"Make her better."

Alice lay on the bed, eyes shut tight. The scene was too familiar. Blankets piled high on top of her. Sweat ran off her forehead as she thrashed and moaned. Her fingers clawed at her neck, but her necklace was not there. I frowned, and pulled her hand away from her throat.

"I didn't want her to break the chain." The Captain cleared his throat. "It would be very hard to get it repaired without drawing attention." He pushed a medical bag into my hands and pulled her blankets back.

Blood everywhere.

Too much.

I took the stethoscope and placed it on her abdomen.

A heartbeat.

The baby was still alive.

"When was the last time she took her medication?" The words tumbled out of my mouth. "For the baby?"

"What?"

"The medication! She needs the medication." I searched the tiny room trying to find the vial she needed. "When did she take it?"

The Captain shrugged.

"Before the house burned down I think." He was a tall man, built for battle, but he looked so small sitting next to her, holding her hand. His hand nervously raked through his hair and then drifted down to the stubble on his chin.

"Is that bad?" He knew the answer. He grabbed a wet

cloth and blotted her face, trying to cool her down. "She insisted she was fine. Just a headache. She could sleep it off." He was close to tears. "You can help her, right?"

I studied my available tools.

"We have two options." I calculated them as I spoke. "Option one. I send her into a coma and control all nutrients. I could probably carry them both to term, and then deliver the baby."

"But..." He prodded.

"But, there is a very tiny chance I formulate wrong and she goes into premature labor, which I would not be able to notice because she would be in a coma."

"Option two?"

"I take the baby now. It is too little to survive but Alice would be fine."

"I won't put any risk to her life. Take the baby now."

My mouth dropped in horror.

"Captain, most likely they would both be okay."

"But there is risk and I could not stand losing her. I will not risk it. What do you need?"

I shook my head.

"I will not do that to her. She already lost so much. Do not take this too."

"She'll have me. We'll have each other. My mind is made up. I'll do it myself if you won't."

It felt like my mind was being torn in half. I closed my eyes and saw a beautiful little girl laughing and playing. She held up a freshly bloomed flower, and Alice scooped it out of her hands excitedly. But even as I watched her, her happy laughter was replaced with screams, and she faded to a cold concrete room.

Chains and blood and screams.

I opened my eyes.

"Do not make me do this, Captain. You do not know what it will do."

He grabbed the scalpel out of my hand and posed it over

her stomach.

"I won't risk it."

"Alright. Alright," I lunged for the sharp little blade. "I will do it." Slowly, I cleaned her abdomen, stalling. I took a deep breath.

I could not believe I was about to do this. I made the incision, cringing, and reached in for the baby.

Tears filled my eyes.

All the children I failed to carry, and he was forcing me to end this one, too.

Why was he making me do this?

Alice moaned and shifted her head on the pillow, but did not wake.

I found a leg and pulled, supporting the body with my other hand. A squirmy little girl made her appearance to the world. I cut the cord and handed her to The Captain, going back for the placenta.

The baby was not crying.

"Clear her mouth, Captain." I tried to keep one eye on the baby as I closed the gash I made. He just stood there, holding her in his arms like he was afraid she was going to burst into flames. She squirmed, and her face screwed up in frustration. Her mouth was open, but no sound was coming out.

"Clear her mouth!"

She was turning blue.

I could not think; could not form the words to heal Alice.

"Clear her mouth, Peter! Clear her mouth."

"I don't need to."

I searched bag for a pre-threaded needle. Just one. She was losing too much blood.

"Captain, unblock her airway!"

Three stitches in the string broke.

I could not think.

What was I doing?

Tears filled my eyes.

I practiced this. I was ready for this.

What do I do?

I checked her pulse.

Weak.

"Mother. Do not give up on me now. Please."

I could not heal her.

I could not find the words.

Tears dropped from my eyes onto the blood running on her stomach, and I watched, transfixed, as tiny clean spots streaked the red. So unsanitary. So fascinating.

I healed her cycles ago, why could I not now?

My mind flashed through all the words I ever learned, but I could not find the right one.

Black fog filled the room, and, in the corner, I saw him.

I should not look at him.

I did not look at him.

But I would not allow him to collect her.

"Get out of here. There is nothing for you here." I spoke before I could think.

There were legends of the people who dared speak to The Collector.

Those people died.

They were collected instantly.

But I did not die, and the figure in the corner forced me to look at him, briefly. He pinched his ash-white chin between his pointer and middle finger.

The Àraid salute.

His hollow eyes never left mine as he bowed and vanished. The black fog faded. I still could not think of any healing words. I was still panicking.

Slowly, Alice's hand covered mine.

Even dying, she somehow found a way to try to comfort me. I squeezed her hand, and it heated up in my grasp, slowly turning an ice blue. My gaze shifted from our joined hands back to the incision I made. It closed while it glowed a matching blue as our hands.

I did not understand.

Her eyes fluttered open, for only a moment, and she winked.

Alice

The Last Day Of The Season Of Dying, 749-PW

I've lived out in this cabin almost a cycle now.

The General pays The Captain to guard me outside the gates so the other Raks leave me alone. I like it better here. I am still a prisoner, but it's not as bad as it was. It's almost normal. Out here, I almost forget how horrible it is. I almost think maybe I overreacted. But then The General comes to me, and reminds me that it is bad. I need to get away from him, but it's not worth it to run. He is my life now. I have to accept that. His visits are getting shorter, and he doesn't come as often. Usually it's just me, The Captain, and the kids. But I think that will change. Something happened, and The General is not going to be happy about it. It was an accident. It was just one moment.

I didn't want to think about what this meant. I couldn't. I vomited again, and leaned back against the wall, wiping sweat from my forehead. When I closed my eyes I saw his fury.

Yelling. Screaming.

He even threw down a chair before he swung a punch at me. My eyes flew open and I lurched forward again, dry heaving. I heard a knock on the door, and his voice filtered through the panels.

"Are you alright in there?" He shook the knob. He would be mad that I locked the door.

He made me promise never to lock it.

"Counselor, let me in."

My stomach convulsed again. The wood splintered and he elbowed pieces out of the way.

"Counselor?"

I scooted into the farthest corner; cowering from him. I waited for the yelling; for the sound of his belt flying through belt loops; the snap the belt made as it connected with skin. I waited, face covered, for him to start in, but he knelt beside me and wrapped me in his arms, rocking me. His arms tightened as I shied from the touch.

"What's wrong?" His hand smoothed through my hair and he tilted my head to look at him. "Our deal was no locked doors. No secrets."

I pushed him away and pulled myself up against the counter, catching a glimpse of how horrible I looked in the mirror. The faucet squeaked as I turned on the cold water; splashing it over my face, washing away the sweat. I still hadn't answered. I didn't plan on answering.

"Mom?" The front door slammed and I heard shoes thudding off feet. The children would be hungry.

They would come and find me soon.

I glanced back at the man on the floor. He studied me, calculating. I reached down to help him up, but ended up tumbling down into his arms. A laugh slipped past my lips, and his eyes widened as I slapped a hand over my mouth.

"You've never laughed before." He pried my hand off my mouth and slowly shifted so my back pressed against the wall.

I stiffened.

Not again.

Please, not again.

I tried to focus on his green eyes. Green, not black. The Raks had black eyes. He didn't.

"I held up our end of the deal, right?" He was still talking. I hadn't heard what he said. I jerked my head in a nod. "I'm not going to hurt you, but I need to establish boundaries to keep us safe. Do you trust me?"

"Tell me your name."

He chuckled and loosened his grip.

"Yeah. Can't do that Counselor." He stood and pulled me with him, steadying me. "Your kids want their dinner. Go." He pushed me ahead of him through the door, but whispered in my ear, "We'll talk about this later."

† † † † †

The children were asleep, and the man was in the parlor, drinking some wine The General provided. This was The General's house, outside the camps, away from his guards. Only he and The Captain were allowed inside the house, and I was never allowed outside. I wished I could go outside. I wanted to go see the flowers blooming in the fields. But Rak guards waited outside, ready to shoot me if it looked like I was trying to run. The Captain stayed and protected me from brave Raks who came inside, but he didn't protect me from The General.

No one stood up to him anymore.

The General hadn't visited almost a season. At least there was that. Maybe he was bored with me.

Finally.

Dishes clanked in the sink and I turned on the hot water, gasping as scalding water splashed against my mangled hands.

"What?" The Captain was by my side in seconds, gently easing my hands flat against his so he could get a good look at them. "What did you do?" His voice was soft.

My fingers were red from the water, and he dipped a cloth in cold water to dab on the burns. He pushed me into one of the dinning chairs.

"What happened?"

It was only now that I realized he was asking for the third time.

"I was distracted." I couldn't look at him. He was being nice now, but he couldn't stay nice.

No one that worked for The General stayed nice.

They all wanted something. I kept waiting for him to hurt me. He hadn't yet, and it was driving me crazy. Every move he made I expected him to hit me, but he never did.

I wished he would just get it over with.

I hated the stress of waiting.

I blinked back frustrated tears as he knelt in front of me and took my hand in his, gently bandaging it.

"Distracted with what, Darling?"

I stopped, taken aback, and looked away, afraid to tell him.

"I was just, um, just thinking." I stammered. He chuckled and silenced me with a finger. He leaned forward and pulled my head down to him, and kissed me. I pulled away from him before I realized what I was doing. My hand flew to my mouth, horrified. I was supposed to allow him to do anything he wanted. Those were the rules. His hand rose in the air and I flinched. He hesitated, and then pulled me down onto his lap, rocking me back and forth.

"I'm not like them, Alice. I'm not going to hurt you." He brushed tears from my cheeks and kissed my nose, moving down towards my mouth. I quickly covered my mouth and scrambled for the bathroom, barely making it.

His hand ran across my back while I lost my supper. His fingers brushed my neck as he pulled my hair out of the way. When I finally finished he handed me a glass of water.

"Come on, Alice. I'm not that bad am I?" He started to laugh, but stopped when he saw I wasn't smiling. *"Am I?"*

I shook my head.

"Well good. I do have a reputation to maintain."

I stifled a sob. This wasn't happening to me again. It couldn't be happening again. He was serious now, concerned.

"What's wrong?"

I twisted the necklace in my fingers and thought about the night I tore it off. The night I ripped it off and threw it to the ground. The night I lost Micheal.

What if something like that happened again?

What would I do out here alone?

"Captain." I sighed, *"I'm pregnant."* I squeezed my eyes shut and waited for the yelling, the punches, and breaking glass, but it didn't come. I flinched when he wrapped his arms around me.

"Really?" He didn't sound angry. I could only nod. His arms squeezed around me and he kissed the top of my head.

"You're not mad?" I tried to push away from him, but he wouldn't let go.

"Mad? Why would I be mad? This is wonderful. We'll finally be a family." His arms tightened around me, but then he stepped back and ran a hand through his hair. *"No. This is bad. This is really bad."*

My heart sank.

"Why?"

"The General cannot know about this. You can't tell anyone."

I shuddered at his name, and nodded quickly.

"If he finds out, he will take you back. He will kill me to get you back. I broke our contract. I'm not supposed to touch you that way..." He trailed off and pointed to my stomach, and then hugged me again. "He will kill me. And then he will kill our baby."

Our *baby*.

He thought of it as our baby. This wasn't a problem to get rid of, it was a slight hiccup we could work through. He pulled me into his arms again and kissed me.

"I'm excited about this, Alice. This is wonderful news. We just need to keep it quiet. We need to run away or something so we can live in peace away from him."

I wanted to cry.

He was happy.

He wasn't yelling.

He grabbed my hands and led me out of the bathroom. I stiffened when he opened the bedroom door. I knew what he wanted, and didn't want to give him any excuse to be angry with me. I needed him, or I would be stuck here forever.

I couldn't afford to make him angry now.

I sank onto the bed and, with shaking fingers, struggled with the laces on the front of my dress as The Captain disappeared into the closet.

"What are you doing?" He stood in front of me, a little box in his hands, but he dropped it and knelt in front of me. He shoved my hands aside and re-tied the laces, and then pulled a blanket up over my shoulders.

"That isn't your life anymore. You don't need to do that for me." The bed sagged under his weight as he moved to sit beside me, carefully placing the box in my lap. "Open it."

The hinges were rusted, and the wood was weathered, but the lock was brand new, and he placed the key in my hands. I slowly clicked it open and lifted the lid.

On top was a tiny pair of blue socks. I picked them up

and turned them over. My gaze shifted to The Captain, but my question died on my lips when I saw tears in his eyes.

"I bought those. When my wife told me she was pregnant, I went out and bought her those. I bought her all the clothing in that box." He shook his head sadly, *"But she never used them. She never had the chance."*

I put an arm around him and leaned my head against his chest. Tears dropped from my eyes, but he brushed them away and gave a sad chuckle.

"Don't worry Alice. This one will get that chance. I won't let anything happen to it."

I groaned and opened my eyes. My head hurt, and I squinted against the light seeping through the window. The Captain sat in a chair right beside the bed with a purple blanket rolled up in his lap. His gaze never shifted from his lap, and I tried to reach for his hand, but I was so tired.

"Captain?" I could barely speak. He winced and looked up at me. Tears coursed down his face.

"I had to. You understand why I had to?"

"What do you mean?"

He shifted the purple blanket on his lap. Wrapped beneath the fabric was a tiny baby girl, eyes closed, barely breathing.

"She's perfect. She really is. I didn't know she would be this perfect. I thought she would be a blob. I didn't know she would be so..." He stopped and searched for the words. "She's a tiny person." He whispered, awed.

My hand shifted to my now squishy stomach. The firm bump from my baby was gone.

"What have you done?" I gasped.

"I couldn't risk it. I wouldn't risk losing you."

I touched my baby girl's head, and she moved ever so slightly.

"I want to hold her."

He nodded and sat next to me on the bed, shifting the tiny

bundle into my arms, helping me hold her. She opened her eyes and squealed. A small hand wrapped around my finger. Tears flooded my eyes.

"She's going to be okay, right?" I looked up at The Captain. He shook his head.

"She's too little."

Her breath rattled in her chest, and her eyes fluttered.

"Then why is she here?"

"I told Christa to do it now."

My baby's cries rose, but were interrupted with coughs, and faded quickly down to rasps.

"Maybe she's hungry." I suggested, but she screwed up her face and pushed away from me.

"She's not hungry, Alice."

"Not again, Captain. Please don't let this happen again."

I propped up our daughter on my knees and clung to his shirt, begging him to make this all better.

"Don't let it happen! You have to stop this!" I couldn't lose this child. She was struggling for air. I stroked her chest and tried to sooth her, but nothing helped.

We sat like that for hours, just the three of us.

She stopped breathing in the early hours of the morning.

I didn't believe it at first, I thought maybe she would pull through. The Captain said she was special, so I thought maybe she would do something special, but she didn't. The Captain tried to take her from me, but I fought him.

"Why was she born, Captain? She was too little." I was hyperventilating. "Why, Captain? Tell me why this happened?" I hit him, over and over, until he caught my hands and pinned them down.

"I did it because Christa said that if she let the baby go farther you could die."

"*Could?*"

He shrugged.

"She said there was a chance, and I couldn't risk it." He was crying almost as hard as me, but I didn't believe his tears. I looked down on our dead daughter. She was so small, but so perfect. She'd had a chance, and he took it away from her.

"I won't forgive you for this. She would have been fine."

The pain in his eyes made me want to eat my words, but every time I looked at him all I could think about was how he killed my daughter.

"I want you to leave, Captain. I can't look at you right now."

He took my hand and rubbed a thumb against the scar on my wrist.

"It's okay, Alice. I won't ask you to forgive me. I won't need to."

I tried to pull away, horrified.

"You wouldn't. You promised." My eyes burned with anger and sorrow.

"I don't keep my promises, I never have. Why do you keep expecting me to?" His voice was harsh, and he jerked his head toward my daughter. "Say goodbye." His hand never left my wrist.

I stroked her feathery angel hair, wishing life back into her tiny body.

"I don't want to forget, Captain. I don't want to lose her."

"I don't care."

The pressure on my scar increased slightly, and I bent to kissed her head lightly. His thumb dug into my scar and light flashed behind my eyes.

I fought it.

I fought him. I grabbed his face and pulled him low over me.

"How many times have you done this to me?"

He didn't respond.

The more I fought the madder he got. His nail dug into my wrist; breaking through the skin and sinking deep into my wrist. I screamed and fought him, but I wasn't strong enough.

Inhibited

Christa

"Captain, let me in! I want to see her." I pounded on the back door. He insisted no one see me on this side of the line. The door cracked open and he shoved a small bundle into my arms.

"Get rid of this. Then we talk."

Her baby.

The tiny, stiff baby that would have had a chance.

Stupid Captain.

Stupid selfish lying traitor.

I would not cry for that child.

I could not.

I took the baby to my wall, and waved my hand over her tiny body.

Crystal and topaz swirled around her body, encasing it in a beautiful casket. Branches stretched out and circled around the casket, twisting and twining it into the wall, a monument to the child lost. I touched the crystal gently.

He killed her.

Why could no one see that?

Black fog swirled around my feet.

I closed my eyes on instinct, then cracked them open just a little. The Collector stood in front of the tiny casket. One long, bony finger traced the outline of her body.

I was not supposed to look at him, but I could not look away. I grew up on legends of him but I never believed. Belief in a creature that put souls in a jar and took them back to his collection sounded absurd. But that creature now stood here collecting Alice's baby.

"I thought you were supposed to collected Àraid souls." I blurted out. "The legends say you collect Àraid souls." I should not speak to him.

All the legends said not to say anything to him. The black cloaked figure turned towards me. He did not lash out, he just turned. I did not look at his face again. I would not go that far. Instead I studied the tattered cloak he must have worn for hundreds of cycles.

"I collect the souls of the King's friends. The protectors, the heroic, and the courageous. The legend has been changed over the cycles. It now implies that only Àraid are heroic."

"Are we not?"

"You were never meant to be a hero. Àraid means protector, not hero. And the Collecting is not only for Àraid. Humans can be courageous, and heroic, too."

"A baby that lived less than a day is no hero." My voice choked off.

"But she could have been. Do not question me, Ŗѐлïӑ, or I might collect you too."

"Did you collect my children?" I sniffed. "Were they heroes?"

"I did not collect your son, Jaycobe. He was no hero. I left his soul to Ashal." His hollow eyes bore into me. "But the others? Yes, I keep them all safe."

"All of them?" My eyes filled with tears.

"All twenty-two. The Mentor and your birth mother are looking after them until I collect you. Which won't be long if you keep questioning me."

I fled back to The Captain's cabin.

I did not want to watch the figure collect the child. I did not want to risk him collecting me. He was only a myth, but he was a dangerous one.

I knocked on the door, and tried not to look behind me.

"Okay, it is done. Let me in." I hissed through the door. It opened and he pulled me through quickly.

"She's in the bedroom." He looked terrible. He had not slept or combed his hair, and his eyes were swollen from tears. He did not move to go to his wife. He just sank into one of the kitchen chairs and stared at the empty table.

Fine.

At least I would not have to see him.

I opened the door and put on a smile for my mother. The same smile I gave her after that moment in her cabin as a child. The smile I created when I realized that I had no choice but to love people, even when they did not love me.

"How are you feeling?"

She was so pale, and she looked so much older than her cycles. Fresh bruises peppered her arms.

I knew he was beating her.

Those were not there yesterday. I touched one and she flinched, pulling away from me.

"Who are you?" Her voice was rough. She needed water, but I got stuck on her question.

"What do you mean? Mom, it is me. Chrissy." The bed sagged as I sat next to her. She shook her head and pulled a knife from under her pillow, poking it into my ribs.

"Chrissy died. Stop tormenting me with her and just do what you came to do." She jabbed my ribs and I jumped up.

"Alice. Mother. It is me. I am not dead."

She did not believe me.

"Captain! Help!"

The door opened behind me and he put a hand over my mouth, pulling me out into the kitchen and shutting the door behind him. He spun me around and pushed me into one of the chairs while he sank into the other and put his head in his hands.

"What have you done to her, Captain?" My voice held a warning.

I would kill him if he made any wrong moves. I should just kill him now, but I wanted to know what he did. He looked up at me, eyes bloodshot.

"It was not supposed to go like this. I never wanted to hurt her." He stood and pulled a hand-whittled cup from one of the cupboards. "Coffee? It'll be a long story." He poured without waiting for me to answer.

I nodded and took the steaming cup carefully, studying it and smelling it for any trace of poison.

It seemed clean.

He eased back into the chair and looked at me frankly.

"I saw her, from a distance, the first day they brought her in. A group of us always hung out right inside the gate, waiting for our next assignment. She drew everyone's attention. The camp stopped to watch her. The General brought her in, specifically. He never brought anyone back to the prisons, at least not alive." His eyes glazed at the memory.

"She was beautiful. She walked with dignity. She had just been captured by the Raks, but she walked through their gates with her head held high. There was blood on her shirt and she clutched her side tightly, but she *walked* through those gates.

I was fascinated by her. I felt sorry for her. I felt sorry for the pain she was going to live through at his hand. They took her into the breaking rooms, and I didn't see her again for many seasons. I figured she died. Most die. But then they brought me to her, and told me to break her. She was pregnant. I didn't want to harm her, I wanted to get her to a healira. No one ever survived Rak births. I didn't want her to die. But if I didn't torture her they would kill me. I was the one that broke her back, not the baby. She doesn't know that.

That baby didn't measure up to The General's standards, so he disposed of it. Alice lived. The General couldn't believe she lived. He took her as his prize, and put a tracker in her wrist that connected to her mind. It read her thoughts, and predicted when she was planning on fighting him. He was always one step ahead of her. He kept her locked away in his room. A treat for only him. He killed anyone who touched her, and rarely let her out. Every time she came out, she looked worse. She was broken, malnourished, and terrified.

Cycles passed, and every time I saw her I felt worse for her. Every day I waited for her to emerge, just to make sure she was still alive, and one day I decided to talk to her. She was chained in his backyard, and he'd asked me to guard her. She was so afraid. She was no longer the proud woman that walked through our gates. She was a tiny woman, who huddled at the end of her chain. She wouldn't look at me. She flinched whenever I came near. I wanted to help her, but I didn't know how.

The day came and went in silence, and The General was pleased that I did not touch his prize. He asked me to guard her again the next day, and the day after that, and she began to warm up to me. She started talking to me. It started with whispers. She was so afraid to talk. But as time passed, and I did not harm her, she regained some confidence. She told me about her past, every detail that could be told.

And then one day she smiled. She smiled at me and caressed my face gently. The General saw. He saw that she initiated it. He flew into a rage and attacked her right there in front of me. He never harmed her when people could see. He didn't want people to know what he did. But I wasn't people, I was only a Suit. He didn't mind if I saw, because I belonged to him, too.

She cried and reached out for me to save her, but I couldn't. If I saved her he would kill me. I tried to leave, but she caught my hand and held it tight. I wanted nothing more in that moment than to ease her pain. In a small way, I think I did.

When he finished, I held her in my arms and soothed away her tears. That became ritual. The General didn't mind that I comforted her. He trusted me. I would stand by and watch, and calm her when he'd finished. His beatings weren't as effective. It was torture for me to watch that every day, but she needed me.

She didn't know who I was, or what I did, until one day when he chained her in the front yard, not the back. I was bringing in a new shipment of people that day, and she watched me lead them in. I didn't see her. I didn't know she was watching.

One girl tried to escape and I chased after her. I caught her easily, and slapped her. She fell to the ground and I kicked her. She spat at me and I killed her, quickly and easily. Just like I had many girls and boys before her. Then I looked up and right in front of me was Alice. She was horrified.

Her eyes filled with tears and broke my heart. I moved towards her, to explain, but I'd just undone all of my work. She was the terrified shell of a woman once again. After watching the walls fly back up around her I knew I had to get her out. If The General knew I was going to steal his trophy, I would have been killed in a second. I started spreading rumors, tales that she regained her fighting spirit. I didn't expect her to help, but as they sent Rak after Rak to break her, she succeed in killing them.

The General threw me a curve-ball by asking me to take her out of the camp. He wanted her away from his Raks. He hated anyone else touching her, but he didn't mind me. He asked me to take her to a house outside the fence, and to stay and guard her when he wasn't there. That's how I got out to easily. Once outside the fence it wasn't as hard to slip away.

I hated that he was reading her thoughts all the time. I

needed to stop that. I just needed to pull out the tracker he implanted. I pretended to torture her, and passed the broken tracker off as simply getting carried away.

Something went wrong, and the tracker shattered in her wrist. Apparently I didn't get all the pieces. There is still some embedded in her wrist, and every now and then her memories reset. If the scar is pressed too hard, she forgets. Everything. Every morning I would wake up and she would have no idea who I was.

And then it started resetting at random, only forgetting pieces. She started remembering who I was, but not what I did, or vice versa. She told me last night she would never forgive me, so I made her forget. I pressed harder than I ever have before. She went too far back. She still knows me, but she knows nothing else."

"You deleted your wife's memory because she was mad at you?" I could not believe him.

How could he?

Who did he think he was?

"You decide when she is and is not insulted? How many times have you done this to her?" I grabbed him and shoved his chair over. It crashed into the floor, splintering under his weight. "How many times, Captain?" I screamed at him.

I could not focus.

I could not think.

Fire shot out of my hands, flashing around his small cabin, but I wouldn't allow the flames settle on anything.

"I was just trying to spare her pain." His arm protected his face.

"That is not your choice!" I lunged towards him, but a hand caught my arm and a sharp blade pressed against my neck. I froze.

"No, don't. She's just angry. She won't hurt me." The Captain spoke to whoever held me.

"You made me promise, Captain." The blade cut into my neck as Alice's hands shook. "You told me to use it no matter what. Didn't you?"

He held out his hands and walked slowly stood and walked towards us.

"This isn't what I meant, Baby."

Her knife wavered for a moment, and that was all he needed. His hand shot out and wrapped around her wrist. It was wrapped in thick bandages, but he took her knife and cut through them, nicking her arm. The scar on her wrist was bleeding, and he pushed a finger deep into her wrist.

"I'm sorry, Darling. This is for the best." He told her as she screamed and squirmed, and then went limp. He eased her to the ground and kissed her forehead.

"I'm sorry." He whispered to her, and then he turned back up to me. "I don't want to, but sometimes I have to." His touched the cut on my neck, but I slapped him away.

"You say you care for her." I whispered. He nodded, but did not say anything. "If you do care for her, why did you choose that face? Why Micheal's face?"

"What?"

"I know that guards pick a face and stick with it, but why did you choose that face?"

He went back to his wife, and pulled her into his arms.

"When we were in the prisons, almost all of the Raks chose this face when they tortured her. They ruined this face for her. I needed her to trust it again. This face meant something to her once, and I hated that they stole that from her. Trust me, Christa, I'm not trying to hurt her."

"I do not trust you, Captain. I will find your weak spot. I will kill you." I knew he was guilty.

He stole her trust, and her memories, and I knew he was somehow feeding information back to The General.

He had to be. It could not be anyone else.

I did not know how he was doing it, but I would find out.

Cerynn

Mother sat on top of the wall again. She rocked nervously, and hadn't spoken in days. Peter didn't even try to reach her anymore. He spent time training Jess and his little friends in sword fighting, and barely glanced at my mother.

"Josh, what are we going to do?"

He wouldn't answer. He never did. He just let me talk until I arrived at a conclusion.

So we sat, Josh and I, watching all Roland's little friends. The Captain had stepped into his old role as Suit, and whipped all the survivors into warrior shape in a matter of days.

I was baffled as I watched them spar across the line. Their skills were way beyond what they should be.

The only thing The Captain did to train them was take them, one by one, into his house. When they came back out he'd have them battle each other. Suddenly strung-out coal miners were able to hold their own in a fight.

I wanted to cross that line and wipe those smug looks off their stoned faces, but as I watched them, I knew I could not beat them. I glared at them from our deck, and then jumped into the dirt and tossed Josh one of my knives. I needed some practice.

† † † † †

"Mother, you need to look at these plans." I shoved my sketches toward her cowering form. "I've never led a revolution. You have."

She cringed.

"People died in that revolution. People died, and we made no progress. We ended up just like we always were. It was useless."

I stared at her.

"But we don't have a choice now. They wiped out the city, we have to strike back."

"It does not matter. They are not the problem." She rocked as she hugged her knees. "He is. He is the only problem." She wouldn't look away from The Captain's cabin. Her hair was uncombed, her eyes wild.

"Why do you think he's the problem?"

"You saw him at the attack. He smiled! He enjoyed it!"

Images rushed back and I tried to block them out. Mother on the ground. The Raks circling her. The Captain smiling as he watched.

"And I now know what he put her through. He told me what happened to her in there. I did not want to know." Her eyes were hollow, haunted. She screamed and put her head between her knees, rocking slightly.

"I will not be happy until he is dead. I cannot focus with him out there." Her hands clawed at her face, scratching deep grooves into her cheeks. Her hair deepened to black and her eyes glowed a bright gold. She collapsed onto the entwined branches and clutched at my legs.

"Make it stop, Cerynn. Please, make it stop." Red tears dripped from her eyes, and flames rippled out of her mouth. She grabbed the knife hidden in my boot, and drove it into her stomach.

"Mother!" I lunged to pry the knife from her, and covered the wound with my hand. "Læҳlïeҳè." It melted back together and she opened her eyes again.

"The King did not give you permission! Do not heal without permission!" Her fingers danced on the air, tracing invisible lines. "Make it stop. I want it to stop." She grabbed my hand and I suddenly felt what she felt. I was being ripped apart. Past and future were colliding. It was falling apart. My head filled with screams and nothing but pain.

She released me and the world righted itself.

"I cannot handle it. I cannot stop it." She whispered. "Please, make it stop."

Then she flew into the air, spinning wildly. She latched onto her dragon as he swooped low, and they flew off together.

† † † † †

Night fell. Mother didn't return. Peter checked the window every four minutes, and dinner sat untouched on the table. It wasn't a good dinner. Nobody in the family ever cooked before, but all our cooks were killed when the city fell.

I stabbed my fork into some potatoes, but I wasn't planning on eating.

Peter checked the window again.

Nothing.

He started clearing away the dishes, scraping our untouched food straight into the trash.

No one spoke.

No one moved.

We were all waiting for even a hint of her. I didn't tell Peter that she stabbed herself, haphazardly and unconcerned, wishing my knife would kill her. He would only worry. My mind wouldn't stop painting pictures of her body, killed a thousand different ways. Beautiful, peaceful ways. If she died she'd at least be at peace. Her pain made it hard for me to hope she'd come back. I almost hoped she did take her life. I almost hoped she ended everything. She'd be at peace, and I could take her place. I could be the Ambassador. I already knew the job well, and was braver than she was. I could confront The Captain. Kick him out. Take my city back.

Make it stop, Cerynn. Make it stop.

I never knew how tortured she was.

Nobody knew.

"Come out here, Captain!"

We all jumped at her voice.

"Come face us. Tell us what you do to her! Tell us how you beat your wife into submission!"

Peter limped out the door in seconds, cane forgotten.

Mother was playing with fire calling him out. She stood in the middle of the courtyard, right on the line. Fire consumed her legs, and her hair danced in the light.

"You cannot walk into my life and steal my people away from me. I am the *Rèлiǎ* and I will not allow you to dictate my life." The flames around her swirled and danced, shooting sparks in every direction. The Captain appeared on his porch, and Alice leaned weakly on his arm.

What had he done to her?

As he jumped from the porch, Alice tried to stop him, and tumbled off the wooden platform. He turned to help her, but flames covered her. They didn't burn her, but they also didn't allow him to touch her.

"Stay away from her." My mother hissed. "You are going to kill her. I have seen it."

The Captain turned back to my mother, eyes pained.

"I won't. I love her. Why would I harm the only thing I actually love? Does that make sense to you? You're wrong."

The flames grew with her anger.

"I am never wrong. How dare you assume that I am wrong!" Her dragon dropped down into the courtyard and swooped in and out of the glow of the flames.

"Look around you, Christa." The Captain pointed to our people, all ready to fight her if he said so. "You're outnumbered."

Her laughter rose into a crazed cackle.

"I am always outnumbered."

Ice swirled in the air and formed a beautiful casing around Alice, protecting her from whatever would happen. The Captain knelt beside the cage and put his hand up to the glass. Alice weakly raised her own hand and put it up against his.

I closed my eyes so I could focus, trying to remember what Mother taught me. Flames rose up around me as I walked unharmed through Mother's flaming sea.

"Don't you see that he cares for her?" I yelled over the crackling flames. "Let her go."

She couldn't see me as she faced me. She was too consumed in her own fury to see anyone.

"I am Rèлïǎ. No one tells me what to do."

"You're going to upset the status quo, Mother. Remember, you told us 'there is a delicate balance between peace and chaos'. Don't upset the status quo."

She wailed and rose into the air, flying around the courtyard before settling back onto the line.

"I am no longer interested in preserving the status quo. I am interested in overthrowing it." She hissed and her flames wrapped around The Captain and lifted him into the air, twisting around him, but not burning him.

"Okay," He panted. "Okay, we'll work this out. You want me to leave? Done. I'll leave as soon as you let me down. You want her? Done. Just don't harm her." He pleaded. She hissed again and his bonds tightened.

"Please, Christa. You're right. Isn't that what you want to hear? You're right. I'm here as a spy. I'm feeding the Raks information. I also want to kill Alice and ruin everything. That's what you want to hear right?"

The flames started to burn and he screamed. His people circled Mother, all holding ropes looped on the end like a lasso. They were trapping her. She was cornered.

"You just let me go, and we can talk about this like human beings." He spit out through the flames. Mother watched his followers; figuring out his plan.

"I am *not* human! Do not try to play games with me. You will not win." She raised her open hand, folding her fingers into her palm. The flames grew around The Captain and consumed him. His cries rose as the burns worked their way through his body.

But even as we watched the fight play out in front of us, another wail joined the sounds. This wail grew and rose and then a shattering sound drew our attention to the ice cage around Alice. It lay in tiny pieces at her feet. She was crying and shaking, walking into the flames surrounding my mother. They never harmed her. They parted at her feet, and as soon as Alice's outstretched hand touched my mother's arm, the flames extinguished.

I blinked against the sudden darkness and flinched at the thud of The Captain hitting the ground; no longer controlled by my mother's anger. His continuous groans told us he was still alive. I couldn't see a thing. I'd never experienced a darkness so complete. I felt my way towards The Captain's groans and covered his mouth, silencing him as I healed his burns. Mother would kill me if she knew I helped him.

Without his cries, the silence was as complete as the darkness. I blinked against the night and squinted to see anything. Nothing. I heard the tick of the Captain's watch, and impulsively counted the ticks. Four minutes passed, and then a thud in the middle of the courtyard caused my heart to constrict.

What happened?

The lamps in the courtyard re-lit, and the gathered crowd whispered their confusion. The middle of the courtyard was burned. Ashes swirled in the slight breeze, but it wasn't the scorched ground that confused us. The middle of the courtyard was deserted.

Alice and Mother were gone.

Inhibited

Alice

My face pressed into dry leaves. The smell of pine overwhelmed me. My wrist throbbed, and I lifted my head to look at it.

Bandages.

How did I get here?

A young woman sprawled in the leaves next to me, motionless. She was important. I just didn't know why. The suns were up now, I think I remember it being dark before.

Everything hurt. Every muscle screamed against movement. A groan passed my lips as I tried to get up, and in a flash the woman was on top of me, pinning me down.

"What have you done? Where are we? How did you do that?" As she studied me, her eyes flared violet, and then settled down to a smoke-grey. I'd seen those eyes before. I just couldn't place where.

"The King is returning." She shoved her hand over my mouth and chanted quietly. "The darkness is frightened. It knows it will soon be drowned in his fury." Her wild eyes wandered over the forest. "We should not be here." She jumped to her feet and took three very measured steps away from me. Then she sank to the ground and put her head between her knees, rocking slightly.

I sat up and brushed the hair out of my face. She hummed softly, and lowered her knees to the ground, crossing her ankles in front of her. She shoved the leaves in front of her out of the way, clearing a circle. Her hand hovered above the circle, and slowly the leaves started to organize themselves.

At first it looked like they were simply lining up, but as I studied them, I noticed they were arranging by color and size. They settled into their little arrangement, and the woman stood and took off her shoes. She placed them in the center of the pile, and raised her hands. Water dripped from her fingertips, dripping onto the pile of leaves. Once her shoes were thoroughly soaked she picked one up and held it to her ear.

"What are you doing?" I broke the silence. She spun towards me, eyes crazed. Then she winked and began twirling in circles.

"I am always outnumbered. That is what I told your husband. Always outnumbered." Her laughter filled the forest around us. She glanced back at me to see if I was watching. "Outnumbered no more." Her arms raised above her head as she spun into a blur.

She spun, and I got dizzy watching her, but just as suddenly as she started she stopped. She stood still in the quiet forest, glancing at the swaying trees. A quiet whistling built into a howl and as the wind picked up, people appeared. The forest around us filled with people. The woman smiled at me triumphantly.

"You see, Mother?" She waved her arm around the gathering. The people knelt in front of her; heads bowed. "I am Rèʌïǎ. I was always Rèʌïǎ. Your husband knew. He knows. He does not want me to be Rèʌïǎ. He told my people I am horrible. He turned them against me, so I built my own army." She knelt before me. "He killed two of my children, and one of yours. You cannot trust him. *We* cannot trust him." She grabbed my hands and looked back at her followers. They were waiting for her orders.

"Wait here for my signal. I need to get her back before The Captain comes looking for her." She helped me to my feet and pointed to one of the men.

There were six people who looked higher-ranked than the others. One wore an old suit and tattered cloak. The cloak was embroidered with foreign letters and clocks. He had straight long blonde hair, and very chiseled features. Around his neck was a charm that looked like an hourglass. Inside the top portion was a map that kept changing, and in the bottom portion; a map that stayed the same.

Next to him was a woman wearing a tattered dress, embroidered with the same design as the man, and also a cloak. Her bright purple-red hair was half up, but looked as if it had not been touched in cycles. Her tired eyes screamed in silent sorrow, but I could only focus on the color. One was ice blue, and one was bright green, like Peter's eyes. So rare. Around her neck was an ancient clock face, with seven hands all rotating independent from the others.

Another woman smiled as she teased a dog barking in the clearing. As she stood and turned towards me, I held back a gasp. Half of her was normal, human looking. But her other half was made up entirely of snakes and spiders. They coiled and crawled over each other to make up her leg and arm, and hung out of her mouth. Around her neck was a piece of what looked like a mirror, but it wasn't reflecting the forest around us. I couldn't tell what it was reflecting.

She turned back to the dog and whispered something to it. Its tail sagged, and then its legs turned to human arms and legs and it unfolded into most of a man. The dog head, and tail, stayed, but everything else was human. His belt buckle also looked like a mirror, but it, too, didn't show what was around us.

On the outskirts of the crowd stood another woman. Her

arms folded in front of her, and she frowned at the world. Her dress was made of ice, and her hair was a waterfall, dripping over the icy dress and creating a cloud of steam around her.

Next to her was a man in long robes, made of coals. Sometimes the wind hit him just right and send a shower of sparks onto the woman, and her dress would sizzle as she tried to put out the sparks. His hair danced on the air like fire, and smoke rolled off of him like a cape. He was the one the woman called over.

"You win. Keep an eye on them. I will call you later." She put my arm around her shoulders, supporting me as we hobbled into the forest. "I doubt you remember how you brought us here, so we have to walk back. Do you know who I am?" Her voice was cheery now.

I shook my head. She sounded like I should know her, but I honestly didn't.

"Well," She picked her way through the leaves barefoot. "I am your daughter. Do not worry if you do not remember me. That, apparently, happens." She nodded slowly. "I am going to kill your husband." She smiled at me, like she was telling me about a present she was going to give him. I couldn't comprehend what was going on.

"I called my people. They answered. But they are not fully loyal yet."

I cleared my throat.

"And what about the leaves and the shoes? Is that how you called them?"

She thought for a moment, then laughed.

"No." She didn't explain further. We walked a few more paces, and she collapsed to her knees, sobbing. "He hurt me. He killed my children. He took everything from me." She screamed and pushed her face into the leaves. "Make it stop, Mother. Make it stop." She rolled onto her back and stared into the sky. "I cannot think anymore. I just want to be normal."

I squatted next to her as she sobbed uncontrollably.

"I lost too many. I hate death. Death needs to go on a long vacation." Dirt stuck to her face as tears dripped onto the dirt. "And you," She gasped. "You lost so much. So many children. Just like me." She shook her head. "But somehow you stayed sane. For the most part." She crawled into my lap and put her arms around my neck. "I never cry, Mom. Not for anyone. Why am I crying?"

I held her as if she were a little girl, and memories filtered back. With the memories came tears. Tears of sorrow for the pain my daughter was going through, and tears of joy that I finally had this moment with her. She was finally opening up to me.

"You do not understand what it is like, Mother. Imagine your worst fears, your nightmares, picture all of them. Are you doing it?"

I nodded as her fingers fiddled with my necklace. Her eyes softened, and she stroked the charm.

"Imagine wanting nothing but a normal family. Imagine finally getting one. Mother. Father. Daughter. Happy and together. Imagine knowing that they did not love you. But you do not care because you loved them and that was enough. And then you get an unshakable feeling that it was all ending. Seeing it end in your head. Every time you talked to your family you knew every conversation took you closer to the last one." She gently traced the initials on the back on the necklace.

"Imagine watching the people you love most in the world die, over and over. Every time you close your eyes." Her body shuddered as she took a deep breath. "Every time something changes, your mind tears just a little bit. Imagine not being able to tell any of your friends, because they will turn you over to the Raks. Imagine keeping all that to yourself." Her eyes watered as she met my gaze.

"I had a thought." She rolled out of my arms and pulled her knees up to her chest. "The three of us," Her voice cracked. "We have all died inside. The Captain's love for life died. He loves you, no doubt, and he loves money. But he no longer values life. He is willing to end a life if it will make his way easier. I think he could have been a great man, but he cannot see past the price tag. That is a great loss." As her tears hit the ground, they splashed into crystals of glass, coating the ground with the shattered pieces.

"My love for knowledge died. I know too much. I cannot appreciate it anymore. I am a genius, and I hate it. That too, is a great loss." She crawled back towards me.

"But you," her fingers pressed into the bruises on my arms. "You lost the most. You lost life itself. You looked death in the eye and he refused you; yet you no longer fit in the world of the living. The Raks destroyed your spirit, but will not release it from your body. You are a hollow shell of who you used to be. You are not my mother."

I opened my mouth to protest, but she put her finger to my lips.

"Not my mother. Not yet. But you will be. I have seen it.

Christa

Make it stop.

Make it stop.

Make it stop.

I am Ŗèлïǎ.

Visions should not torment me like this. They should leave me alone.

I am Ŗèлïǎ.

But I had no power yet. My people followed me but they really were not loyal. I needed to wait. Right now they still wanted to hide, like they had been hiding since the war.

They questioned me.

Questioned whether I should rule.

Questioned whether I was right about The Captain.

They would not believe me until The Captain was behind bars, or dead, which would please me more.

Somehow Mother brought us both to my meeting place.

How did she know where I was building my army?

How much did she know?

She intrigued me. When I lived with her I was so wrapped up with my own powers, I never noticed hers. She said she did not, but I heard of many people that went most of their lives without finding their power. I wondered what type of Àraid Mother was.

I did not think she was Ètèгла.

I could not believe I never noticed powers.

How selfish could I be?

How did I never notice?

She was never anything but my mother.

My mind flipped through every memory of her, but she was normal in all of them. My birth mother showed her powers even when she tried to hide them.

Screams and whips and tears.

I curled into a ball.

Make it stop.

Make it stop.

My face was wet.

Why was it wet?

Was I crying?

I never cried.

Why was I crying?

The pain was too much. I needed it to end.

I had no one to turn to.

Not even Peter.

I was tainted for him now. He could not even touch me. He hated what they did to me, and he hated that I allowed it.

"I want to die, Mother. I want it to stop." I whispered. "Please, let me die. The army is here. You do not need me anymore." My eyes opened but I could not see. The pain was too much. It blinded me.

Twenty-three.

I could not sleep anymore. Every time I slept, the darkness whispered promises to me.

Promises that could not come true.

I could not let them happen. The darkness was my enemy

now. I hated the darkness. I used to love it, but it threatened me now.

"I cannot save you. Please do not make me watch. I cannot see your pain anymore." I whispered. She shook her head.

"I'm not in pain, Christa. There's no pain." She smiled at me through her tears.

"You are in agony. You do not need to hide it anymore, Mother."

She smoothed my hair, but would not look at me.

"There is no pain, Christa. Everything is fine."

My body was stolen.

My children; dead.

House; ashes.

My people turned against me.

I just killed a baby.

Everything was not fine. I fought him last night. I tried to win my people back.

I lost.

I hated that man.

That man was the darkness.

He was the promise.

I could sense it.

I was never wrong.

She said there was no pain.

Why did I feel her pain?

"I cannot win this war, Mother. I am outnumbered, and out-armed. The Raks own the trade systems. They are united against us. We are divided against ourselves. There is no way I can lead that, and your husband will not risk your life for anything."

"You'll be fine, Chrissy. You're the smartest person I know. You're cunning. You'll think of something."

The laugh passing my lips tasted bitter.

"Cunning is an illusion. Cunning is just hiding our faults and exposing theirs."

"Exactly. Sometimes that buys all the time you need."
Her smile was small, but she was brave. She knew the risks
I would need to take. She would stand behind me all the
way. I started thinking about what a great team we would
be, but then I remembered her guilty lying husband.

He would stop us.

I knew he would.

"If we want to be friends again, Mother, you are going to
need to get rid of your husband."

She winced.

"He's a good man, Christa. He won't hurt us."

"He already hurt us. Look at what he did to you!" I
screamed.

"What do you mean by that?"

I wished I could erase the fear from her eyes. I was sick
of seeing the terror I had not been able to prevent. My
shoulders slumped as I broke eye contact.

"Nothing. I did not mean anything by it. I am just saying
you should be careful with him. A monster lurks behind his
eyes."

My dragon landed beside us, and Alice reached up a hand
to stroke the tightly stacked scales. She used to be so afraid
of him, but somehow he won her trust. She turned back
towards me, and peace shone through her fear.

"I once was scared because I thought the monsters would
come for me. But maybe not all monsters are bad."

I bit my lip. She was quoting me. I said that exact thing
the day I brought a baby dragon home.

She remembered.

How could she remember that?

She pulled herself up and started walking back towards
our camp.

"I know you don't like him, you've made that clear, but
just because you don't like him doesn't mean he's bad. I need
you to trust me, Christa. It's going to be alright.

Alice

She lost it. She was talking, but she wasn't making sense.

"Tell me about it, Mother. Tell me about death. Does it hurt?" She staggered around as she tried to follow me.

"I'm not dead, Christa." I sighed. I was usually the one who didn't understand what was going on. I was usually unable to remember how I got there, but now Christa was the one lost to the world between reality.

Her dragon walked by my side, casting nervous glances back at Christa. Even the dragons knew something was wrong.

"Make it stop!" She screamed and fell to the ground, clawing at her arms and chest. I ran to her side and tried to restrain her, wrapping my arms around her thrashing body.

"Christa, calm down."

She screamed and thrashed on the ground.

"Make it stop, Mother! Make it stop!" She pounded her fists into my chest. "Make it stop." Her breath rattled in her chest, and she coughed and sobbed and finally collapsed in my arms again. She could barely breathe as she whispered to me.

"Make the screaming stop. Please." Her hands slowly

went around me, and her sobs lessened as she drifted off to sleep.

The forest was still. Too still. We shouldn't be out here.

My hand twisted in my necklace. I remembered why I wore it, and the vague hazy memory of Micheal crowded out the warm feeling I got when I thought about The Captain. I shivered as ice flooded my body. I promised Micheal I would only take the necklace off when I no longer loved him, but Micheal was dead.

Why did I still wear the necklace?

The Captain would ask me to get rid of it every so often. I always expected him to get a little angry when I refused, but he would only smile and nod.

"Well at least one of us is good at keeping promises." He would say, sadly. I didn't want to think about Micheal, or The Captain.

I stared down at my tormented daughter, and wondered if I could have done anything to save her from this. She shifted her head and her hand slipped from around my neck, settling on top of my knife holster. She blinked slowly and her hand closed around the handle. Our eyes met and instantly I understood.

"Make it stop!" She pulled out my knife and plunged it towards her neck. I reacted faster than her, and she stabbed my arm instead of herself. I bit my lip as she screamed in anguish. "The pain is too much!" She grabbed my arm and the knife sizzled as my arm tried to heal around it. She grunted and gripped the knife and pulled it roughly out of my arm. I slapped a hand over my mouth to keep from screaming.

"Why would you stop me? I want it to end! Please!" She was a danger to herself. "Please let me die, Mother!"

I grabbed her head and hissed in her ear.

"How selfish can you be?"

Her eyes widened as hot anger flooded my veins.

"You are so important. The pain doesn't matter now. I

told you it would be bad because you hid from it for so long, but that doesn't give you the right to kill yourself. You've been dealt a crumby hand in life. So what?"

She started to protest, but I cut her off.

"Every breath you take, someone else takes their last. Be grateful for what you get. Now get up and play the hand you've been dealt." I pushed her from me. I couldn't look at her right now.

When she was a girl, after our first fight, she told me she believed there was only anger. Everyone felt the same kind of anger. My hands shook as I studied my grown daughter, and I knew there wasn't just one kind of anger. There were two.

There was the anger that filled your body with a burning hate. The anger that filled your eyes with tears, and made you want to lash out and vomit at the same time. The anger that said you cared too much.

The other was anger that caused you to shut down. Cold, dying anger. You felt nothing. The anger that said you no longer cared.

As I sat there, trying to reign in the hot anger I had allowed to lash out on my daughter, I realized she was fighting cold anger. She was angry at me, and angry at the world, and she no longer cared. She wanted to die. She hadn't heard me.

"Alice?"

I turned at the new voice. Peter, The Captain, and Roland stood in the clearing. Christa screamed when she saw The Captain, and kicked towards him. Peter came to his wife's side and The Captain helped me to my feet.

"Make it stop." Christa sobbed on the ground, chanting it over and over again. I buried my face in The Captain's side and tried to drown out the noise. Christa punched Peter in the face, and Roland joined him trying to pin her down. She gnashed her teeth at them both, and struggled to get up.

I squeezed my eyes shut. She was dangerous. I knew of

one way to control her, but I promised never to use it. She told me how to stop her after a particularly bad vision that turned every object in her room to ash.

"It is for emergencies, Mommy. Please, do not use it. I just need you to know how to stop me. How to turn off the Àraid."

I stared at her, writhing on the ground, fighting her husband. Slowly I started humming. It was an unfamiliar tune at first, but I quickly remembered it. The song she brought with her. The one she always played when she needed to think.

I switched from humming to singing and she quieted, watching me cautiously. The Captain tried to hold onto me, but I motioned for him to let go, and, reluctantly, his hand released. I knelt beside my daughter and smoothed her crazy curls out of her tear soaked face. She smiled weakly and joined in our song. I pulled her into my arms and rocked her gently as we sang together.

"Christa," I whispered as she continued humming. "I love you. I hope you know that." I pressed two fingers to her temple, and focused on the word she taught me cycles ago.

I thought about The Captain pressing the broken groove on my arm, and knew what I was doing now wasn't unlike what he did to me. I didn't want to harm her. The longer I was around her, the more I remembered.

I was still groggy in the mornings, but the memories came flooding back every day; I didn't want that to stop. I almost changed my mind, but then the image of my knife floated across my vision. She would harm herself if I let her. I closed my eyes and whispered.

"Ʒɾалũla."

She glared at me as she slowly relaxed until her body went completely limp. Peter cried as he tied her up, and Roland took off with her in his arms, ready to put her in our makeshift jail. The Captain pulled me into his arms, and I could no longer hold back the tears. He held me, smoothing my hair, as I cried. He never rushed me, and almost concealed his grimace as I subconsciously blew my nose on his shirt.

"I shouldn't have done that. I didn't have a choice." I said to my hands. The Captain tilted my head to look at him.

"How did you know to do that?"

I just shrugged.

"I guess you're not the only one who doesn't keep their promises."

Inhibited

Cerynn

They locked her up in the prison she built for The Captain. Her screams pierced through the walls and echoed in the courtyard. With her powers turned off she couldn't escape the visions.

She had no choice but to watch them now.

She had nowhere to hide.

I sat outside the jail for two hours listening to her anguish. I should've let her die. I did her no favors healing her. She would be at peace if I let her die. She was a danger to everyone now.

Peter strode across the dusty yard and knocked on the door to the jail without glancing at me. He was greeted with moans. He sighed and set the plate of food he brought her on the ground.

"Come fence with me, Papa." Jess jumped at the chance to try it out the stick he'd been whittling to a point all morning.

Peter raised his cane and halfheartedly tapped Jess's stick. He would play, because his son wanted him to, but his heart wasn't in it.

I studied my left hand. The fake one. Without my supplies the fake skin was peeling and I could see metal. I knew it was coming off of my face too. I wished I could go get more supplies. If Mother taught me more about being Àraid, I would be able to hide my face with my abilities, but she went crazy before she could.

The door to Quartnee's cabin creaked open and caught my attention. Our housekeeper slumped against the frame. She'd been watching Quartnee since we got here. I almost forgot about her. Her shoulders slumped as she gestured to me.

I didn't want to go.

I wanted to go home, to the normal and the sibling rivalry. I wanted to go back to before we were Àraid. Before Alice showed up and ruined everything.

Reluctantly, I drug my feet through the dust towards Miss Lorraine. She wasn't crying, but she was close. She shift her eyes, trying to clear the tears.

"Quartnee has a fever. Alice did everything she could, but it doesn't look good." She led me into the darkened cabin. It reeked. Medicinal herbs were splayed haphazardly across the table, and more plants hung from their stems in an attempt to dry them.

Rot rose above the other smells.

Rot and decay and death. Alice bent low over my tiny sister, and didn't look up when I gently tapped her shoulder. Quartnee was awake, but her cheeks were flushed and her eyes shifted around the room, not focusing on anything.

"Hey, Sis." I whispered, sitting on her bed. "How's it going?"

She smiled. Her body was shutting down, but she smiled at me.

"I can't see no more, Cerynn. My eyes don't work." Even her voice was small. Alice sniffed and wiped her nose on her sleeve.

"Her fever rose too high. We couldn't lower it in time. I don't know if the damage is permanent." She wrung out another cloth and set in gently over my sister's eyes. "The fever is down for now, but it will come back unless we do something about this." She flung back the sheets and another wave of rotting decay washed over me.

Quartnee's legs were skin and bone, and even some of that was gone. The herb paste sat on her legs, but it wasn't helping. They were infected. They were rotting away right in front of us. Mother's solution hadn't worked. The porch creaked and I heard the front door open.

"I don't think there is much more we can do about her legs, Cerynn." Alice rubbed my arm. My mother's knife flashed through my mind. Maybe I should use it on Quartnee. Maybe I should just relieve her of the pain. It would be quick. She'd be free.

I shook myself.

What was I thinking?

I couldn't kill her.

Could I?

The door to Quartnee's bedroom opened and The Captain slowly walked over to his wife, studying my sister's legs. I didn't want him here, but I didn't have the energy to tell him to leave.

Mother was right.

He caused this.

I didn't know how, but he caused this somehow.

I would prove it.

I shook my head. I couldn't start thinking like that. We were a team. No matter what happened we were in this together.

"Is she dying? Are her legs going to kill her?" The Captain finally asked. Alice only nodded. He watched my sister for a moment, and then shook his head and left the room.

The minutes ticked by.

I was frozen.

I couldn't help her.

I didn't know what I could do. I was about to turn and leave when The Captain stormed back into the tiny room holding an ax.

"We aren't letting this child go without a fight." He pushed Alice onto the bed and shoved a belt into my sister's mouth. "Bite on that, Sweetheart." He whispered. "Alice, hold her hand. And hold Cerynn's as well."

He raised his ax, and Alice made an attempt to stop him, but the sharp blade crashed down onto the bed. Quartnee screamed as the ax bit into her leg, right below her hips. He lifted the ax and brought it back down onto her leg. It took three hits to free her from the rotting limb, and then he started in on the other leg. After the second blow Quartnee passed out, thankfully, so she didn't feel us wrestling her legs off. I dropped to my knees and buried my face in Alice's lap.

Make it stop.

Make it stop.

My mother screaming over and over in my head. One of Alice's hands still held my little sister's hand, but her other hand rested on my head. Her hand was warm.

Unnaturally warm.

I looked down at their joined hands. Alice's hands were glowing bright blue. Quartnee opened her eyes and looked up at Alice.

"I knew you would come through." She winked and looked down on her mangled stubs.

The Captain sat back and stared in awe as the bloody stubs started to glow a matching blue. The skin rippled over exposed tissue and began bubbling, slowly growing into two perfectly formed, brand new legs. Quartnee flung her arms around Alice neck, nearly toppling them both off the bed.

"I love them. Thank you."

Alice chuckled and rocked the girl in her arms, but cast a confused look to The Captain. He just shrugged and eased himself off of the bed.

"Okay, come on, Darling." He swung Quartnee up into his arms and walked out of the door.

"Captain, where are you going?" Alice struggled to her feet.

"Trust me." He called back through the house as I looped my arm through Alice's and supported her weight.

"I don't trust you!" I shouted back.

I wanted to run after him, but Alice wasn't strong enough to do that. He was halfway across the courtyard before we made it to the door. I wanted to stop him. I dreaded what was about to happen.

He was walking towards the jail.

Inhibited

Christa

My arms chaffed against the chains holding me up.

She betrayed me.

I finally trusted her and she betrayed me.

She stole my powers.

I could not escape the chains.

I screamed again as another vision crashed through my head.

This was not fair.

I had no powers, and yet the visions persisted. Peter hardly came to me anymore. He would not look at me. He sat outside the door and brought me food, but never talked to me.

He used to hold me during my nightmares.

He used to try to make things better.

I knew he could not handle it. I knew he would not stay.

I was alone now.

Alone with my visions.

I screamed and pulled at the chains holding me. They slid easily over my arms now.

Blood made them slick.

"Peter!" His name slipped past my lips before I knew I wanted to scream it. I could not help it.

I needed him.

I hated needing him.

I did not *need* him, but I really really wanted him to come soothe my pain again. He was so good at it.

He moved on the porch, but he did not come in.

"Peter, please." I could not stop the tears now. I was right about him, but I did not like being right this time.

The door creaked open. Peter stood in the doorway, hovering just outside.

"Peter. What happened to us? You used to stay with me when it got this bad."

He shook his head.

"I can't. You're not who I married." He slammed the door before I could answer.

Make it stop.

Make the pain stop.

She betrayed me.

It was not worth fighting anymore. I did not want to do this anymore.

My arms were numb, held above my head, and I relaxed, putting my full weight onto them. Blood dripped into my hair, and down my face. It was hot, running down my cold arms; warming them up.

Make it stop.

Please, make it stop.

Screaming and the crack of whips.

"You came back?"

Did I say that?

Who said that?

"No don't listen to him!" That was The Captain.

I could not bring the vision into clear focus. I could not see what was happening.

Future or past?

"Peter." I whimpered it this time. He could not hear it. But suddenly he threw the door open and glared at me.

"You tried to kill yourself. Twice. You went off for hours

without telling anyone. Alone. You don't listen to reason. The message you send is that you want to be alone." He sagged against the door-frame. "You don't want anyone. I want to help you, but I don't know how. I'm afraid if I try to comfort you before you're ready you'll push me away and I'll never get you back."

"Why would you want me? I cannot keep you safe. I cannot keep you happy. I cannot give you children. I cannot keep our surviving children alive. And I cannot even keep my body pure for you."

Screams.

Fire.

"Get out of here, Mother, I can't stop."

My son's body, burning in the remains of my city.

"I am sorry." I choked. "I am not what you wanted."

He leaned against the door, crying, and then he looked up at me and smiled.

"I should have come to you sooner. I wouldn't want you to be anyone else." He crossed over to me, gently touching my face. I flinched at his touch and avoided his eyes. "I knew when I married you that you were different. You pushed me away because you were afraid that I wouldn't be able to handle all your baggage. Remember, Christa? Remember how much you fought me?"

I nodded. As long as he talked, the pain was less.

"I remember." I whispered. Hesitantly, he touched my arm, and this time I did not flinch.

"You said I wouldn't be able to handle the real you."

I hung my head and shut my eyes. He sounded like himself again. I did not want to say anything to mess that up. He hugged me. I could not hug him back, but that did not stop him.

"Why won't you look at me?"

"Why did you not touch me since the attack?"

He cringed.

"You know why, Baby."

"Because I am damaged."

His arms tightened around me.

"No. No that's not why."

"Then why?"

"When I first met you, you were fire and ice. You wouldn't let anyone near you. I begged you to trust him, and he brought the Raks into the city. I begged you to protect her, and that got you..." He swallowed hard. "I was afraid you were mad at me for getting you into this. They used my face. They mocked you with it. I was afraid you would blame me."

A sob caught in my throat.

"They used your face! I saw hatred in your eyes and I am so scared I will see it again!" The words spilled out of my mouth too quickly. I wanted to stop them, but they were out there.

He tried to pull my face up to look at him, but I shut my eyes.

"That's why you won't look at me? Christa, you won't see hatred in my eyes. I swear you won't."

"I know that. In my head, I know that. But it was such a good copy of you. I cannot move past it."

"Do you want me to leave? Is that what you're suggesting?"

My heart sank.

"Do you want to leave?"

"Do I make thing worse for you?"

"No, Peter. You make everything better. You make the pain stop."

He kissed me, lifting my feet off the ground, easing the pressure on my arms.

"I'm sorry, Christa. How can I make you trust this face again?"

"I do not know." I was crying again. I never cry.

"We need a safe word. Between only us. Anytime you doubt me, you can ask for that word. A word that means 'I love you'. A word that tells you I'll never stop loving you no matter what we go through."

"I like that idea." I took a deep breath, and tried to control my tears.

"So... what word do you want to use?"

I shut my eyes and watched the words swirl in my head. "Đṛavǎṛ."

"Trust that day will come."

I nodded.

"Because the darkness does not consume me when you are near."

"Okay, đṛavǎṛ." His arms tightened again.

I liked the way he clung to me. Like he needed me. Like only together could we keep breathing.

"It's our song." Peter whispered into my hair. "Our song is playing."

It was not.

It could not be, but I did not care.

Peter danced for both of us, swaying to the nonexistent beat. His cane thumped as he twirled me in circles. It almost seemed like we were back to normal, but then the chains tightened around my wrists and I remembered where we were.

"Peter, make it stop. Make me forget, just for a moment." I could not handle it. "Đṛavǎṛ, Love, Focus on me, and nothing else." He pressed his forehead to mine, framing my head in his hands. His cane was abandoned on the floor. He stood without it.

For me.

"I must play the hand I was dealt." I knew that now. No matter how much I wanted to be free of these visions, I needed to live with them. No one could help me.

"Captain!" Someone screamed in the courtyard.

Peter dropped me and spun towards the door, but stopped when I screamed. I bounced on the end of the chains. Peter was by my side again.

"I'm sorry. I didn't mean to." He was trying to undo the chains, trying to ease the pressure.

"Captain!" It was Alice screaming.

"Peter, open the door, I want to see." I gritted my teeth as he gently set me on the ground, and turned towards the door. With the door open I could see most of the courtyard. The Captain was striding towards us. He held a small bundle in his arms. I could not tell what it was. Alice pushed herself away from Cerynn and chased after him, stumbling since she was barely strong enough to stand.

"What's going on?" Peter stepped out onto the porch.

"Unchain her." The Captain commanded. "Bring her out to me."

Peter shook his head.

"You'll kill her."

"Just bring her out. I'm in control here."

Peter crossed his arms and leaned against the wall.

"I won't."

"Roland then."

The boy pushed Peter aside. Jaycobe's friend.

I watched that boy grow up, and here he was, helping The Captain. The boy grabbed my chains and unlocked them, pulling me out of the cabin. He jerked the chains and I tumbled into the dirt. Peter stumbled after us.

"Stop."

The Captain stood above me now, still holding that bundle.

"Don't harm her." Alice threw her arms around me, shielding me from her husband. "Whatever you're planning, don't do it. She's been through enough, Captain."

He knelt in front of us and put one arm on his wife; still holding something in his arms.

"Look at you." He said to me. "You don't even fight. You're not even trying."

"Why should I? I have no powers anymore. There is no way I could win. Do what you want." I shuddered as I remembered what they did to me.

I could not protect myself now. I was weak without powers. He shrugged.

"Even if the serpent isn't venomous, it should pretend to be." I sagged at his words. I didn't want to fight anymore. "Christa, I offer you a peace offering."

I shoved the chains off my wrists and rubbed the raw spots.

"I do not want a peace offering. Why should I trust you?"

"Exactly. I've been under your roof for more than a season. You've always assumed, from the very beginning, that I was the bad guy. And I never gave you reason to believe otherwise. I've always told you I'm not a bad guy, but I've never done anything to prove it."

I refused to look at him. He stood by and watched.

He *laughed*.

He killed my children.

"Here." He pushed the bundle into my lap, and it giggled. Quartnee wrestled herself out of the blanket, giggling and smiling up at me.

"Look at my legs, Mommy. Look at them. They're better. They're whole. Look what he did."

I ran a hand over her legs. They were perfect.

"You did this?" I did not want to believe it.

"Yeah. This is my peace offering. I don't want to hurt you, or your family." He stuck out his hand. "Let's work together. When they came after Alice they lost my loyalty. I want them gone as much as you, and I know the inter-workings of their camps. We can raise an army. We can take them down. But you need to trust me."

I did not want to.

Trusting him would be like saying I was wrong.

I am never wrong.

But he had information on the Raks.

If I refused to trust him, and failed this war on my own, could I live with it?

Inhibited

Alice

37th Day, The Season Of Life, 750-PW

Almost a season has passed since Christa's house was attacked.
There hasn't been another attempt to capture me. Christa always
makes sure someone is at the watch-tower. She is determined not to
be caught off guard again. She and The Captain are working
together now. Somehow he convinced her to at least give him a shot.
I watch from a distance everyday. Christa hasn't spoken to me since
I disarmed her. As I sit now, watching a tiny ball of fire flick around
my hand, moving slowly up and down my arm, I understand why it
was so dangerous for her to tell me how to disarm her. I didn't turn
off her powers; I *stole* them. I now possess every ability Christa ever
mastered. I can summon them at will, and am constantly transfixed
with my creations. She still hasn't asked for them back. She

probably assumes I won't give them to her. I'm not sure I want to.

I have kept all of this hidden from The Captain, of course. He wouldn't understand. With her powers came the visions. The visions that tortured my daughter for so long now torment me. I understand why she wanted to end it all, just to make it stop. There are days when I don't think I can handle it either, and I just curl up in a ball and try to drown out the world.

The Captain worries about me. I constantly catch him watching me while he is supposed to be working on a plan with Christa. They are in my kitchen now. Christa never asks why I stay in bed so late in the day, or why I quickly walk past them into the courtyard without looking at them. She doesn't care. She doesn't visit me anymore. She comes to help him.

Together they have drawn up accurate blueprints of the Rak camps. The Captain caught a few errors where my memories led her wrong. I wish I could join them. The Raks harmed me more than them, I want to help. They change the subject whenever I try to get close. The Captain is protecting me, Christa is being spiteful, and I am completely cut off.

None of the towns-people talk to me. I am The Captain's wife, and they are all afraid of me. Christa's children side with her, and avoid *me at all costs. The Captain isn't really interested in talking anymore either. Other things, sure, but not talking. Christa is now his ally, and he spends most of his time making sure her attention stays on him. I am left to wander around uselessly.*

I shut the journal and sighed. The courtyard was only interesting the first three times you studied it, after that there was nothing to see. All the books burned in the fire. No music. The dragon brought us food, and baked it with his fiery breath, so there was no cooking to be done. The flowers were getting ready to bloom, and I was so excited for that, but they wouldn't bloom for at least half a season. I couldn't wait to sink my hands into the soil, and coax more flowers into the sun. But, until then, I devoted hours to testing the limits of Christa's powers. It was exhausting, but enjoyable.

My favorite ability was ice. I made ice sculptures that hung off the roof, and danced in the wind. The ice never melted until I told it to, and then it would sparkle with the passing light of the suns. I didn't like the idle time. During those moments, my mind would recreate what happened in the Rak camps. I was slowly remembering, and I didn't want to.

† † † † †

53rd Day, The Season of Life, 743-PW

His last beating was one of the worst ones. I don't know how long it

<u>will take for me to recover, but he told me he had something bigger</u>

<u>in store today. He told me this time he would break me. How much</u>

<u>worse can it get? Isn't he bored yet?</u>

<u>Can't he let me go?</u>

"Hello, Baby, I'm back."

I shut my journal, and shoved it under the mattress before The General saw it. He grabbed my throat, and pinned me in front of him. He kissed me, and I had no choice but to kiss him back. His tongue explored my mouth, and I gagged on the rot that came with it.

He ripped my dress off, and placed his hands at the small of my back. His fingers curled inward and dug deep into my back. I was forced to cling to him as he pulled his hands up to my neck, and then brought his fingers around to directly under my chin. I didn't cry anymore. I didn't really think it hurt anymore. Maybe my nerves were dead.

I was dead now; so why not my nerves?

He didn't heal my back. He just turned me around and watched the blood cascade down my legs. The gashes on my neck were deep. I was losing a lot of blood. He pulled me against him, and pushed my hair to the side; lapping up the blood from my neck as he walked me over to the table. He bashed my head into the table, and the darkness reached up to consume me, but I fought it.

He wrapped my hair around his hand, pulling me off the table. My head spun and my legs shook. He smiled as he watched the blood pool at my feet, and then he released my hair.

I fell to my knees before him, and he nodded in approval. This was the first time I'd been on my knees before him. He tried for seasons to have me kneel. He inserted a spider gag so I could not bite him, and shoved himself into my mouth.

"Finally!" He grabbed my hair, and held me in place as I fought against him. I tried to pull away, but he pinned me down. As he pushed farther I vomited against him, and he pulled away and slapped me.

"Beg for your life. Beg and I will grant you immortality." He hissed in my ear.

I didn't want to live if it meant living with him. Vomit and saliva dripped past the gag. I hung my head in shame. This wasn't the life I imagined.

"Or you can die and I'll just continue my experiments on your children."

My head shot up, almost hitting him since he leaned close to me to whisper in my ear. I couldn't do that to them, I couldn't leave them with him.

"Please don't kill me." I couldn't speak around the gag, and he unbuckled and removed it. I rubbed my jaw, and gritted my teeth, fighting the frustration and helplessness he rubbed in my face. He grabbed my hair and yanked it back, putting his face close enough to mine that I could smell his rotting breath.

"What? I can't hear you." His forked tongue flicked between his teeth as he waited. It was getting harder to think.

"Please, don't kill me. I want to stay with you." My mouth barely formed the words, but I knew I said the right thing.

"Kiss me and prove it, Darling." He sneered.

My hand pressed tightly against the gashes on my neck, but my arms were getting weaker. I took my hands away from my neck and blood ran freely down my chest. My arms wrapped around his neck and I pulled him down towards me, covering his mouth with mine.

He laid me down on the scratchy carpet and kissed me back. The grooves on my back hurt enough to keep me *awake, but I was so tired. I was tired of him; of this castle; of being manipulated so easily. Pain flared against the dirt in my wounds, and I gasped.*

"Not great, but we can work on it." *He whispered, and grabbed my hand. My fingers instantly glowed, and the wounds started to heal, but it hurt so much. My body convulsed, and The General pulled me into his arms.*

"It doesn't usually hurt." *I moaned into his shoulder.*

"You waited too long. You're too weak. These will definitely scar."

My body screamed. I wanted to sleep, to escape it all, but The General kept prodding the gashes on my neck.

"Don't sleep, Darling. As soon as you pass out you stop healing."

"Let me go. I'm done. I can't do it. I can't handle it." *My vision blurred as he set me on his bed.*

I thought I finally won as he left, and I sagged with relief against the pillows. Soon this would be over, and I would finally be free.

My relief was short lived.

There was a commotion in the hall, and then the stairs creaked. He struggled back up the attic, back to me. He shoved my daughter in front of him.

"Mommy?" *She was three. She didn't understand why I was covered in blood. She didn't know anything but this life. None of my kids did. To them it was normal for their mother to stay in bed because she bled too much the night before. But The General didn't let them up here. This was his sanctuary, he didn't like my kids in here.*

"What are you doing here?" *I wanted to sound firm, in control, but I couldn't speak above a whisper.*

"I'll let you go. I have her now." *He grabbed my daughter. I tried to stop him, but just tumbled off the bed.*

"General, leave her alone."

"You told me to let you go." *He sneered at me and dug his fingers into her back. She cried as he pulled his hands up to her neck.*

"Leave her alone, General. Please."

"Mommy, was I bad?"

"No, Honey. You weren't bad."

The General watched me carefully.

"What will you do for her?"

"Anything." His eyes sparkled at that. I would live to regret it. But how could I when I did it for my daughter? "I'll do anything for her."

He didn't hesitate to grab my hand. My fingers glowed and my daughter's back soon glowed a matching color as the wounds healed, and soon she scampered back down the stairs to the safety of the kitchen.

"You'll come with me to the Telia right?" The General was getting dressed as he asked, barely glancing at me.

I only nodded. I knew I could do nothing else. I knew it wasn't really a question. I would go with him, I would be his trophy, and I would pay for hesitating when he told me to do something. This was my life. I would never be free. He came and knelt before me again, placing a hand on my shoulder.

"I will find you. You can't run forever. You're only safe behind her ice castle so long. I know where you are. I'm coming for you."

I gasped and jerked away from him, shutting my eyes. He couldn't know where I was. The flames I'd allowed to dance around my arm now shot out in several directions. Hands were still on my shoulders. I squeezed my eyes shut and tried to pull away, but the harder I fought, the more the fingers drove into my arms. The fingers weren't sharp though, they weren't cutting into my arms, just holding onto them.

"Alice?"

That wasn't The General's voice. I cracked my eyes, staring into one blue eye, and one bright green one.

"Peter?" I relaxed and the flames settled back into my hand. I covered the ball with my other hand and the fire was gone.

Slowly, my surroundings started to register. I wasn't on the porch anymore. I was halfway out the gates. I was walking out of the camp, and I hadn't even been aware of it. I still wanted to walk out that gate. My feet slowly shuffled one in front of the other, heading into the forest. My feet were ahead of my body because Peter held me back, and I fell back against him.

"Alice!" He exclaimed and stumbled back. His cane hung from the crook in his arm, and did neither of us any good. I landed hard against him as a poof of dust clouded around us. He didn't move. His hands released my arms, and fell to his sides.

"I'm so sorry. I-" I scrambled off of him and started to help him up, but he was limp. "Peter?" I shoved my fingers into his neck.

He still had a pulse. He lay in a puddle of blood, though. I needed to wake him up, but I was standing now. I was walking into the woods, leaving him behind. The harder I tried to go back to him, the faster I walked into the forest. I couldn't even turn around to look at him. My eyes roamed over the trees. I hadn't seen the forest since Christa and I were out here.

The trees looked different now. They should have been dotted with new blooms, but they were black. The leaves were black, the bark was black, and black sap cascaded over the trunks like a waterfall. Staring into that blackened forest made me wonder if maybe I simply had become color blind, but then I caught a glimpse of blue. A blue suit leaned against one of the trees. I didn't want to see who stood in that suit, but my eyes searched for a face anyway.

The General crossed his arms, and smiled at me smugly.

"I told you I would come for you."

I stood still now. I wouldn't go back to him. He reached a hand out towards me, beckoning me. My hand reached back towards his. I tried to pull it back to me, but it hovered between us, pulsing black veins.

How did he learn my name?

"Peter!" Christa screamed behind me. She would see me. She would see how weak I was. I tried to turn around. I tried to fight against the poison. Our hands almost touched; mine trembled, but his was sure. His eyes were cold, and calm.

"You belong with me. We both know it."

Arms wrapped around my waist and spun me back towards the camp.

"Stay away from her." The Captain wouldn't let go of my waist. He only needed one arm to hold me securely against him, and with the other arm he pointed a knife at The General.

"You stay away from all of us. I don't want to ever see you again. If I do, it will be your last day." The Captain shook with fury, and The General easily pried the knife from his grip.

"I'll leave, Captain. I'll let you do your best to reinforce your camp. I'll watch you do everything you can to keep us apart. And I'll laugh as she walks back to me with open arms. I'll laugh as she chooses me over you because I know that will just eat you up. I'm content to bide my time, because it will make the dance more entertaining."

In a flash of light he vanished. I sagged against The Captain, but he pushed me away.

"What was that? Why were you going back to him? Am I not enough for you?" His eyes held confusion and hurt.

"I couldn't stop, Captain. I wanted to, but I couldn't." I kept waiting for my legs to start walking again, but they stayed where I told them to. Something rammed into my shoulders and I frantically grabbed at The Captain as I lurched forward.

"What have I ever done to you?" I started to turn towards Christa's voice, but something hit me and my head snapped back against The Captain's chest. "Why do you keep taking things from me? You are bad luck! You are death to everyone around you!" Christa pulled her arm back for another punch, but an intricately carved handle hooked around her fist and stopped the punch.

"I'm fine, Christa. She didn't mean to hurt me."

She swung around and punched Peter in the face as he spoke. He reeled back and jabbed his cane blindly behind him, trying to keep from falling again. I tried to reach out and grab her, but The Captain held me back.

"Let them fight this one out." He whispered.

"Do not defend her, Peter! You saw! You saw the black veins. She is a Rak! You are a Rak too! Is that it? Is that why you let her out? Why you let him get so close?"

Peter held out his hands as his eyes filled with tears.

"Đṛavǎṛ, Christa. Trust."

She dropped to the ground, limp. My hand covered the throbbing bruise on my face as I watched her. She didn't move as The Captain nudged her with his toe. Peter, too, stood with a hand on his face watching his wife. Nobody spoke, nobody dared, and then a piercing shriek filled the forest around us as she curled into a ball.

"Make it stop! Make it stop!" She reached up and grabbed the front of my shirt, pulling me down next to her. Her arms went around me and she buried her face in my shoulder. "Make it stop. Please. Just end this whole war. I cannot do this. It is too much."

I could barely hear her whispers as tears soaked through my dress.

"Christa, if I could make it stop, I would. I swear."

A shaking finger touched the tiny cut on my cheek from a ring on her finger.

"I did this. I keep saying you are the one destroying my

family, and I have physically harmed you more than you have ever touched us." A sob caught in her throat. "And Peter, I have hurt you too. I am so worried about other people leaving those I love alone, I am not even paying attention to what I do." She stretched her arm towards him, and he hastily took it.

He pulled her up into his arms and kissed her gently.

"She hurt you though." Christa was torn, so unsure of right and wrong. "Did it hurt, Mother? Did dying hurt?" Her hand traced a scar right above my collar bone. "Was it frightening, Mother? Is dying scary?"

She sounded like a tiny child, afraid of a monster.

"Christa, I haven't died yet. I'm not dead."

Her eyes floated around, without focusing.

"Of course you are. I saw it. It hurts. It looked like it hurts."

A bright streak of red hair sprang up in her bangs, and the rest sank to a dark brown, the curls relaxing into a loose wave. She jumped up and threw her arms around Peter, clinging to him.

"I do not want to be Rèлïǎ. I do not want this."

She sagged against him, and he easily scooped her into his arms, somehow managing to hold her, and support his cane at the same time.

"Let's go inside, Christa. You need a break." He tried to take a step back to the camp, and his leg nearly collapsed. The Captain reached out and took his arm. They hesitated for a moment, and the Peter handed his bundle over to The Captain, allowing him to take my daughter back to camp. Peter refused to let go of her hand though.

Without a glance at me the trio walked back to into the camp. I shivered and tried to keep up, but I glanced behind me in-spite of myself.

The General leaned against the tree again, and waved at me.

"I'll see you soon, Trophy."

Inhibited

Christa

He was carrying me.

The Captain was.

The man I did not trust.

Why was I letting him carry me?

Peter, do not let him kill me.

My fingernails pierced through Peter's skin, but I could not loosen my grip. My eyes drifted back to my mother. Her cheek was bleeding.

I did that.

I punched her.

"I told you. She walked back into my arms, no hesitation. You tried so hard, but still she came back." A man mocked me as he tortured her.

"Peter?"

His hand stroked my hair; his eyes full of concern, and the blood vessels on his green eye popped from my punch. I punched him, too.

My lover and my confidant.

Who could I trust?

I could not trust anyone. Not now. Not with what I knew.

But I loved him.

I could not look at either of them.

I was ashamed.

I hurt them.

I was in control two seasons ago. The visions were under control and I could think clearly.

Why was I losing control?

My eyes wandered over my dead trees.

They killed them.

My forest.

My home.

Mother stopped following us, and stared behind her into the forest.

"Mother? Do not dawdle."

She did not even turn. We stopped to watch her, and The Captain's arms tightened around me.

"Alice. Keep up, Dear." He took a half step towards her. I wanted to get down and allow The Captain to go back to his wife. Alice trembled, but still did not turn. I could not see what she was looking at, but slowly she turned back towards us.

Her eyes were wide, and she was too pale. Her hand was on her throat, massaging it slowly.

"Captain." She gasped. "Captain, I can't breathe." The Captain shoved me into Peter's arms, and took two steps towards Alice before she collapsed to the ground.

Peter also instinctively hurried towards her. The Captain held her. She was limp, eyes rolled back in her head. Peter checked her pulse.

What was wrong?

Screaming and chains and the scent of blood.

"You tried so hard. What's it like to fail?"

Cackling laughter.

"Christa. Don't blame yourself. It's okay." Alice was in *his arms. That wicked man. His hand stroked her hair. Her eyes held sorrow, but she did not wince. He laughed at me.*

"Why would you bring her here if you wanted to keep her safe?"

The Captain ran to the camp, holding her in his arms; his wicked traitorous arms. His murderous arms.

"Keep an eye on her. The closer you guard her, the more fun I'll have taking her away from you."

My head hurt.

Screaming and whips and blood.

"You're no match for me."

"Stay away from me!" I screamed at The Captain. "Stay away from my family, and keep your screwed up wife and screwed up life. I do not want it. I do not need it!"

I stopped her from walking out the gates three times that night, and each time she did not even know she was going.

She was Inhibited.

Maybe I was wrong about The Captain. Maybe it was not him betraying us. It was probably her the whole time.

"These will help." I clipped some shackles around her wrists and secured them above her head on the headboard of the bed.

"She doesn't need to be chained up, Christa!" The Captain tried to undo the locks, but he did not have the key.

Alice lay very quiet on the bed. She swallowed hard a couple of times, and tears danced in her eyes, but she did not move.

"I want to sleep! I will not sleep if she is wandering around my camp!"

"It's not your camp anymore, Christa. Let her go!"

"If she is chained up in here, he can not seduce her out there. Which would you prefer? If I let her go now, I will not go running after her again. She is not my problem."

She shut her eyes at that, and a tear streaked her cheek.

"She's not a "problem"!" The Captain was enraged. He shook the chains connecting her to the bed, but they did not break. Eventually, he would be able to break the chains.

I needed my powers. I could repress the visions if I had my powers back. The visions did not let me sleep. The darkness held me as I tried to stop the visions. It whispered dark promises in my ear and taunted me with a future I could not avoid.

I needed my powers back.

I would go insane without them.

I grabbed Alice's shoulders and shook her.

"Give them back to me!" I screamed. My blood pulsed through my head. "Give them back! You stole them from me!"

She would not look at me. Her body shivered under my grip.

"Christa, back off." The Captain placed one hand on Alice's forehead, and one on my shoulder. "This is too much for her."

"What do you mean? Too much? She has been the strong one through all this, 'oh look at me, I made it, I survived, you can too!' She told my kids about how strong she is. These are just two tiny chains. How can they be too much?" Her eyes were shut again, and her lips moved silently. "Give them back to me!"

She flinched and pulled against the shackles. I released one of her hands and watched it shake violently as her hand fluttered through the air. I guided her fingers, since her eyes were still closed, but I sighed with relief as her cold fingers pressed against my temple.

"Èɲèẓṭaviṭ."

My powers coarse through me, and the visions again were shoved into the closet I kept them in.

I smiled.

My anger was gone.

There was peace now.

I was free again.

I went to secure her hand again, but The Captain snatched the cuffs out of my hand.

"She doesn't need to be chained."

Her free hand reached out and grabbed his hand, still shaking.

Why did he keep interfering?

Could he not see?

I was doing this for good.

I pressed my lips together and glared at him.

"Fine." With my powers back I did not need the chains. I raised my finger to my lips, and the chains holding her disintegrated.

She rubbed the chafing spots on her wrists as The Captain slumped back in his chair, believing I finally listened. I smiled at him and raised a second finger to my lips as tree roots shot through the floor, twining around the bed, creating a cage around her. Her eyes widened as she stared at the roots, and one pale hand wrapped around one, testing the strength. She bit her lip as more tears fell onto the pillows.

"Christa!" The Captain pulled on the cage, trying the free her. "No, no, no, no, no. Not good. Please, don't do this to her." He, too, was crying as he pulled on the roots. Alice pulled a blanket up over her shoulders and covered her face with her hands. "The General kept her in a cage. People shouldn't be kept in cages. It messes with them." He pushed a hand through the cage and rubbed her arm.

"If I think this is the best way to keep the camp safe, who cares who goes in the cage?"

"Don't do this to her. She's your mother. Cut her some slack. You owe her that much."

"I do not owe her anything! She waltzed in here and ruined the life I built. She has only ever ruined things, Captain."

"What have I ruined, Christa?" She whispered through her hands.

"You ruined everything! Sound familiar, Mother? That is what you said to me after you sent Micheal away." I screamed. "You sent him away and he died and I liked him! My dad was not around when I was at home. I did not really have a dad. But I had a mom. I had a mom until the day she died and she was a lousy mom. I did not need another mom! But I never had a dad and I wanted one and you sent him away and you killed him! You ruined everything!" I slammed a hand into the wall and stormed out of the cabin.

Alice

Micheal asked me to move in with him. Not yet. He wants to wait until my birthday. But after that. Of course I said yes. He's such a sweetheart. I didn't even have to think about it. I have dreamed of him asking me to live with him since we met. Obviously, I still have to tell my parents, and I don't think they will be too thrilled, at first. I am their only child, and this is very nontraditional, but I think, eventually, they will be okay.

"**Y**ou love him? How could you love him? He's nothing! He's nobody! Our family has status. I've never even heard of his family. You cannot marry that boy!" My father was so angry. I didn't expect him to react like that, I thought he would be reluctantly happy for me. I thought he liked Micheal. "Your mother and I have already found

the man you're going to marry. We've already promised you
to him."

"You've never said anything to me!"

"We thought it would be assumed." He sputtered.

"Why would I assume that?" I couldn't marry a stranger.
I loved Micheal.

My father clenched a fist and slammed it on the table.

"Because that's what this family has always done. It's
always been arranged. That is how we keep our family line
separate from the human lines. I won't have your blood mix
with a human's blood. Not after everything we've gone
through to stay untainted."

"I don't want to marry someone I don't know. I want to
marry Micheal."

My mother had been quiet, but she now stood beside my
father.

"You can't marry Micheal, Alice. We've already
promised you to another man, and he's already excited
about it. His family is very prestigious, and very dangerous.
We don't dare cross him."

"I'm going to marry Micheal!" I spun towards the door,
but hesitated with my hand on the knob.

"You walk out that door, you're dead to us." My father
turned his back to me, but my mother watched me carefully.

"Please, think about it, Alice. Is Micheal worth all this?"
She gestured around the grand entry way, which was lined
with gold and topped with Firestones and WhiteStars. This
was the only life I knew. I glanced through the silk drapes
covering the front window, and saw Micheal waiting for me.
He hated Nalaise. He wanted to move to the Snartec
Region. For a moment I wavered.

Was he worth it?

He saw me watching, and smiled. His smile made my
heart beat a little faster, and I knew we would be okay if we
were together. It would work out.

"I think he is."

As the door clicked shut behind me, I heard my mother scream.

"What are they going to do to us? He's going to freak out! We had one job, raise her and hand her over. He's going to kill us, Eric! We broke our promise."

† † † † †

70th Day, The Season Of Living, 736-PW

I've been here for a few seasons. I'm passed from Rak to Rak and they put me through things I try not to think about when they're done. Last night The General bought me for the night. All night long he hit me and cut me, and then, once, my fingers turned blue and all my injuries healed. His eyes widened, and he ran from the room. Out in the hall he called the Rak in charge of buying people. They were talking prices. I don't want to belong to him. Of all the Raks, he's the worst.

"I finally have you. I've waited so long to find someone just like you. I can't believe I found you first." The General grabbed my necklace, studying it between his sharp fingers. "This will fetch a good amount of money."

I tried to pull the chain out of his hand, but he held fast.

"Please, let me keep this one thing."

"I let you keep the book, and your journal, Darling." He pointed to the worn book in the corner.

"It's your choice. Your family's heirloom book, or your

boyfriend's necklace."

"If you let me keep both, I'll do whatever you want."

He broke the chain, and held it in front of me.

"Oh, Baby, you'll do that anyway." He grabbed my hair and pulled my head back, running his sharp fingers over my exposed neck. "You're going to do great things." He pulled the chains holding my arms against the metal cage, yanking on it until the bones snapped and my arms started to fold. He laughed as I screamed.

"You deserve this. You know you deserve it. We can't move on until you've been punished. I will strip away all you have, all you know, until you have no shelter but me."

I pushed against the bars, but the chains held me close to him. I heard his knife click open, and the blade pressed into my stomach.

"You will be fully mine." He grabbed a handful of my hair and twisted it around his fingers, weaving it into an intricate braid.

The knife pressed into my neck as he kissed me over and over again.

"The more you fight me, the harder I press." He whispered as I tried to squirm away from the knife. "No shelter but me." His fingers twisted in my hair. "Cry if you like. Cry on my shoulder and hold me and beg me to make everything okay again."

I shook my head, closing my eyes, and his voice rose a level.

"Cry! Lean on me and cry!" A small tear slipped under my lids. "That's it. Cry. Trust me. I'm all you have. You need to feel free to cry." He shoved my head into his shoulder and wrapped his arms around me.

As much as I fought it, somehow his embrace was comforting, and soon sobs wracked my body. Gently, he rocked me and smoothed my hair.

"I'm going to go sell your necklace, and your book, and then you will know not to ask me for things. I don't owe you *anything. You won't need them anyway."*

I inhaled sharply, and the sobs ceased. Micheal's necklace. His arms tightened, and his fingers drove into my arm.

"You don't need anything but me now." He jerked the chains once more, and then let go, I retreated to the corner, cradling my broken arms. He swayed the charm in the air and then headed towards the door, pausing to turn and look at me.

"It wasn't supposed to go this way. You ruined everything. You know that right?"

I ruined everything. I couldn't breathe. Someone was talking to me, but I couldn't look away from the cage. Another cage.

I had been free.

"At least let me in there for the night?" The Captain yelled into the courtyard.

Christa hated me. She told me to my face that she hated me. As she slunk back into the cabin, she glared at me.

"Just let me in there with her. She can't handle this. It's too much."

A tiny opening appeared at the foot of the bed, and it was all I could do not to claw my way out. Christa wanted me in the cage, so I would stay in the cage.

"You'll never survive. The cage will eat you. I'm coming for you, Darling. The only shelter you get."

I couldn't stop shaking. For cycles I lived in a cage. Cycles in a cage, with no escape. I couldn't run away from him. I couldn't hide.

A strange wailing filled the cabin, and I frantically searched the room for the source. I couldn't find it. The Captain leaned over me now. The cage was small for one person, and with his huge frame there was very little room to move.

"Where's that noise coming from, Captain?"

He shifted onto his side, and eased one arm under me. "Honey, that's you."

I couldn't stop.

"Christa, please let her out. Can't you see what this is doing to her?" He pried my hand away from my neck and held it up. There was blood under my fingernails.

Christa squatted down on the other side of the cage and pressed her hand through the gaps. Her hand wrapped around my throat and I clawed at it.

As my hand wrapped around hers, my fingers glowed and the bright red seeped up her arm and spread out from her to the cage. The cage glowed for three seconds, and then the bars vanished. Her eyes widened and she snatched her hand away.

"How dare you! How dare you cross me! I want you behind bars!" Tiny sparks shot from her fingers. "You cannot be loose! You are Inhibited!"

"I would never harm you or your family, Christa!"

As she struggled to keep her hands at her sides, more roots rose up and trapped my arms to the bed. Roots wrapped around my neck, tightening slightly. It was so hard to breathe. The roots on my neck tightened for a moment, and then loosened enough for me to breathe.

"You killed my children, destroyed my house, and stole my powers! You are only here to take things away from me. You are preparing me for him. This was your plan all along. You adopted me so you could eventually turn me over to him! That is why you let that Rak disguise himself and teach me about the Àraid. You were preparing to turn me over! You never wanted me." She lost it. "And then you saw me getting close to Micheal, and he probably suspected what you were doing. He was probably going to tell me, and so you had to get rid of him. That is why you killed him!" She gasped, eyes wide.

"How could I not see it before? It is so clear now. No. No. Do not think I am just going to let you loose now. You are stuck in this cabin. I do not want to see you. I do not want to have anything to do with you. Stay away from us." She stormed out.

"I'm not going to betray her. Why can't she see that?" The lump in my throat was hard to talk around. "She hates me, Captain."

"I know." He hugged me close. "Here's your necklace."

I lunged for the chain as soon as it emerged from his pocket. As I clutched the charm in my trembling fingers he flinched.

"Careful, Babe. Don't strangle it."

I released my grip a little, and tried to relax in his arms.

Christa hated me. The roots changed to chains, and I gained a little movement. He pressed my head into his shoulder.

"Go ahead. You can cry. You have me." He was trying to be comforting, but all I heard was The General.

All the times The General tortured me and raped me, and comforted me after.

Go ahead and cry. I'm right here. Your only shelter is me.

Inhibited

Christa

Make it stop.

Make it stop.

Make it stop.

The screaming never stopped.

"Christa." Peter followed me back to our cabin, and tried to get me to look at him. "Christa, what do you mean Alice never wanted you?"

"She told me when she was very sick. She looked me in the eye and told me she wished she left me at the border."

I never told anyone that. It was not anybody's business.

I hated pity.

Peter pitied me now. I hated the way he looked at me.

"What? It is not a big deal, Peter. I never expected her to want me. It was not a surprise."

"Everyone is entitled to the reasonable expectation that mothers, fathers, spouses, and children will love you unconditionally. You must have expected her to love you. It must have hurt to learn otherwise."

"I do not expect you to love me. Why is she different?" I did not mean to say that out loud. I did not mean to let him know.

Peter took a step back, his face betraying his shock. "You... what?"

"Nothing. I did not say anything."

"You don't expect me to love you? Are you hearing yourself? Christa, I am your husband, I'm *supposed* to love you. That's basically a given."

"But I never asked you to love me. I am not lovable." I really did not have the energy to talk about this right now.

It did not hurt if I did not think about it. As Peter told me what I should be allowed to expect, I felt a pang of jealousy for people who could expect love, and acceptance, and go to sleep knowing that their husband would still be there when they woke. I looked at Peter squarely, and hoped he did not see the tears in my eyes.

"I walked into this marriage with certain expectations, that is true. I expected you to be a good father to my children. Which you have been, so thank you. I expected you to keep food on our table, and a roof over our heads. You have also done that." I glanced at the open sky above us, and thought of the remains of our house. "For the most part."

Peter stayed quiet, waiting for me to finish.

"Those were my only expectations. I did not plan on getting attached. I did not plan on you being able to make my pain bearable." I looked away as tears left my eyes, and whispered. "I did not plan on falling in love with you." Peter reached for my hand, but I moved just out of reach. "I did not want to fall in love, because I do not want it to hurt when you leave."

"I'm not going to leave, Christa."

"Not yet, but you will. They all do. Right now you say all the right things, and you make me believe you mean them, but you will get bored. I cannot keep you happy. And that terrifies me because I do not want to lose you, too. Every morning I get up, and count your clothes, just to make sure they are all still there. Just to assure myself that you are not packing. I know that day is coming, and I know that when you leave, I will not chase you."

Peter was crying now too, and it hurt so much to look at him.

"Why won't you chase me?"

"Because when you leave, it will be because I could not keep you happy. When you leave, it will be to be happy. I will not steal that from you."

Peter wrapped me in his arms, and I relaxed into his embrace.

"I'm not going anywhere, you crazy, battered soul." He whispered through my hair. "I'm going to prove you wrong. You can keep me happy, and I can keep you safe." His thumb brushed against the scars on my arms, and I knew he meant safe from myself.

Alice wailed in the cabin. The whole camp heard her. I hated what I said to her. I should not have said those words. I knew how much they hurt to hear. But they were necessary.

"You can't say those things to people, Christa." Peter whispered as we stared at the cabin. "Did you see how she looked?" He paced anxiously across our porch.

I curled into a ball on the ground and that always made him nervous.

"Didn't you see her, Christa?"

She had been clawing at her throat, which was already covered in blood. Her eyes were wide, and her entire body shook.

She was terrified.

Yes.

I saw her.

But it was necessary.

Peter knelt next to me. He knew better than to touch me,

but he inched as close as he could without touching me.

"Did you see her, Christa?"

"Yes! Yes, Peter, I saw her. It is the best I can do."

"What do you mean the best you can do? You can't leave her in there. It'll kill her."

"No, it will not."

"You have to let her out. You can't leave her like that."

He did not get it.

He did not understand.

"Let her go, Christa. Being right isn't worth this. Getting revenge isn't worth this. She's gotten the message. Let her go."

"I cannot!"

"Can't? Or won't?"

I did not like the way he looked at me. He looked sad, and angry.

He thought I was acting on emotions, not logic.

"I will not, Peter. I will not let her go! I cannot go through that again!"

"Again?"

I sighed, and sprawled on the ground.

"I cannot watch her die again. I have already been through it too many times."

"Then don't let that happen. Strike first."

"No! You do not understand!"

Nobody understood.

I thought about the Àraid Elders waiting for me in the woods. They brought who they could from their camps, but they did not support me yet. They were waiting for me to prove myself. They were waiting for me in the woods, but they were not safe out there. They should not be here. My forest was dead now. It could not protect them.

"Alright. Calm down." He tried to calm me, but the walls were closing in. They were getting closer. "I know you're good at what you do. Let's just put our heads together and figure out how to take them out." Peter grabbed my shoulders and held me at arms length in front of him. "Explain it to me, Christa. Explain to me why traumatizing Alice, and making her feel horrible about herself could in any way help this war. Christa, I signed up for your baggage. If you want me to handle it, then you can't carry it all."

I did not want to tell him.

He would not like it. But he insisted.

"Okay," I took a deep breath. The screaming got louder, I was letting it in. The darkness laughed at me. "When she stole my powers- she stole my powers, Peter! She took them from me. You saw that right? You were there. She stole them from me!"

He held firm to my shoulders, even though I was shifting anxiously now.

"Focus, Christa. Please, don't think about what she did. It doesn't matter."

"I could not stop the visions after she stole my powers. I had to watch them. I had to watch the Raks kill her, and maybe you, and the kids. I saw two paths to take for this war. I am choosing this one."

He nodded slowly and backed me against the porch steps, easing me down onto the wood.

"Tell me about both paths." His fingers pressed against my temples. "Show me both paths."

"Přǎv." I shut my eyes and the visions slowly came into focus. I chose first to go through the one I already chose.

"Let her out, Christa! It's too much for her!" The Captain begged me constantly now. She wailed in the cabin, but her cries were getting softer. It had been half a season since I chained her up in there. I thought he would have given up by now.

I was in charge of the camp again. The Captain was too upset to be a logical leader. It was all pretty fuzzy, but from what I could make out, the children were still training to fight, but no one attempted a war.

Seasons passed.

No one fought.

My condition grew worse.

I was bedridden.

The visions would not stop.

No one left the camp.

They were all happy and healthy and they rode out the war. The visions eventually drove me into the ground, and I died two seasons into it, but everyone else in the camp made it to Iceloch.

The General never crossed into Iceloch, and Alice was never found. The Raks were never defeated, but they did not need to be. Most of the world thought the Raks were fine. It was just me, and the Àraid, that the Raks were afraid of. Without me, they no longer cared about the people in my camp. The Captain went back to work as a Suit, and protected Alice as well. Eventually, hidden away in another city, they had a proper wedding ceremony. They were happy, and although she never recovered completely from the horrors of the Raks, she repressed them enough to live happy and die satisfied.

She was safe.

I blinked my eyes open, and stared up into his blue and green ones. They were filled with tears.

"You're going to die in two seasons?"

"Maybe. That is why I do not like the visions. There are some things that are better left to the imagination."

He rubbed the stubble on his chin, eyes wandering everywhere but me.

"Um, how... how does it happen?"

"I just die, Peter. People die. Everybody dies."

"And that's the path you chose for this whole camp, stuck behind these walls and then stuck behind more walls and the Raks rule the world forever. They win? What is your other option?"

"Okay, I will show you, but just know this one is really spotty. There are too many variables, so I cannot get a clear view."

"Let her go, Christa! This is too much for her!" The Captain screamed at me.

I was torn. I should not let her go. It could not end well, but her wailing was so hard to listen to. I walked towards the cabin. It grew spotty there. I could not make out what happened. I could maybe make out shapes, but it was too out of focus. When it cleared I was deep in the Rak camps. I sat in a hard metal chair, shackles digging into my wrists.

"Tell me where she is! I need her!" The General yelled. I saw The Captain looking through the door.

"Why would I bring her here? Into the midst of battle?"

"I know she's here." He held a crossbow to my head, and slid an arrow into place.

"I'm right here, General." Her tiny pale hand closed around the tip of the arrow, pushing it towards the ground. Everything clouded over again, and the next time it cleared Alice lay on the ground in a puddle of blood. The Captain held her in his arms, crying. Alice died, and The Captain was reemployed. I did not know where Peter or my kids were. A season later the Raks lost a major battle. The beginning of the end for them. Eventually, the war ended, but nobody ever managed to move past the horror of the war.

The suns shifted in the sky while I showed Peter the visions, and we were both quiet.

"So," Peter was thinking as he spoke. "Who eventually kills the Raks?"

"The King."

He stopped rocking.

"The King won't return until a child of a Hybrid and an

Ѐтѐгла is crowned."

"I know. I told you that prophesy would come true." I had been thinking about that since I got the vision. "Somehow, that will happen. That child is out there and the Raks know it. So, not only do I need to break into the Rak camps, but I also need to beat them to the Rѐхтаӱла."

"What does that name mean anyway?"

"It is what The King always called them. It is Àraid. It does not directly translate, but roughly it means high-rank or status. Translator. In the legend, the Rѐхтаӱла will somehow be able to translate what a person, or persons, need into reality."

"What does that mean?"

"No one knows, The King never explained, he just prophesied."

He went back to the visions.

"So either, we stay here, you die, but Alice lives out a long a happy life inside the walls of another city. Or, Alice dies, and the war is ended. Everyone is freed from this oppressive life."

"I cannot lose her again, Peter. I already lost her once, and I have to watch her die every night as I sleep. I cannot let it happen." Somehow, I ended up in his arms, crying onto his shoulder.

I never cried.

"But I still don't understand why traumatizing Alice is going to help?"

"Because, Peter. Because she came back. In the vision, she made it out, but she came back for me and that is what got her killed. You do not go back for someone who hates you. You do not sacrifice yourself for someone who so obviously despises you. I need to make sure there is no way she would ever want to save me. I need her to hate me so much that she is actually relieved if I die in the attack. I will partake in this war, but I cannot end this war if it comes at the cost of her life. Look at her Peter, look at what she has been through.

I cannot let her die at their hands. She deserves to die happy and that is what I am going to achieve, even if people say I am a coward. I am forcing another path. I choose the third option. Even if people talk about how rotten I treated her. I do not care what is going to happen to me because I know she is going to die happy. She has earned it. She needs to stay away from me because I kill happiness."

Peter frowned.

"What do you mean you kill happiness?"

"The longer people are around me, the more happiness I drain from them. Look at you. When we got married you were so happy. And then we had Jess, and you could not stop smiling. You rarely smile now. I did that."

"No you didn't." He shook his head.

"Yes I did! I failed to give you the children you want so desperately. That is my fault. That is on me. And now one of the children I did manage to give you has been murdered. Taken away from you too soon."

"That's not you fault. Don't blame yourself."

"But it always happens. Alice was happy when I moved in. And then bam, less than five cycles later she was as much as homeless, and she was not happy anymore. And my father was unhappy before he sent me away. And my mother. And now I have stolen your happiness, and my children's. I need to end the Raks, but I need her to be happy more. I need her to stay away from me."

Peter never stopped rocking me, and he did not argue.

I was right.

I was always right.

The screaming in my head deafened me. I could not hear myself think. I curled up on the floor and rocked slowly back and forth. As I listened to the screaming in my head, my heart broke, not because of the sound I could not stop, but because of the sound that rose above it.

The sound of Alice wailing in her cabin.

Inhibited

Alice

"Alice, stop pulling on the chains."

I couldn't stop.

I needed to get out of these chains. The Captain held onto my arms, trying to hold them still.

"Alice, I can see bone."

"I need out, Captain. Please. I know I'm safe here, but I can't handle it. He's here, with these chains, he's come back and I can't get him out of my head."

He quickly exited the cabin, and returned a few moments later with a flower bud.

"Here, Baby. Look, the first bloom is near."

My eyes filled with more tears as I studied the bud.

"You picked it before it bloomed. This flower won't bloom now." I didn't know why that upset me so much, but I couldn't stop the tears.

"I'm just showing you you have something to look forward to. Something to hang on for. You love the first bloom of the cycle." He tucked the stem into my hair and tried to smile. His fingers stroked the scar on my wrist, but he didn't press it.

"It's going to be okay, Dear. I'm here. Pretend it's like all those times he attacked you. I was there. I protected you right?"

I could breathe a little better now.

"Right? I was there the whole time. That made things easier right?"

I nodded, never breaking eye contact.

"I'm right here, Baby. He can't reach you here."

I started to notice how much my wrists hurt, and I regretted fighting the handcuffs so strongly.

"I'm going to go get someone to bandage your arms. I'm not leaving the cabin, alright? I'm right here."

But he wasn't. I couldn't see him anymore. I could hear him moving, and speaking to someone outside, but I couldn't see him. My heart sped up. My arms pulled at the chains, even though I knew I should relax.

"Don't worry, you'll be home with me soon."

He was coming for me.

Again.

"Alice, Honey, it's okay." His arms wrapped around me again, and Peter struggled to release the chains.

They popped off and I pulled my arms to my chest, rubbing them gently. They were both bleeding, and The Captain was right, I could see bone on the left one.

How could I have gone so far?

"Give me your hand, Alice." Peter set some bandages on his lap, and he reached for my arm.

"I know who you are, Majesty." He told me when I found him living in my daughter's closet.

Why had he been there?

"Peter?" He glanced up from my wrist. "Have we met before?"

He pursed his lips and shook his head.

"Don't believe so, Ma'am. Why do you ask?"

"No reason."

He finished bandaging the wrist I did less damage to, but carefully studied the other one. He looked reluctant to even touch it.

"Is Christa still upset with me?" I didn't really want to

ask. I didn't really want to know.

"She's not upset with you." He answered too quickly.

"Don't lie to me, Peter. That girl built walls around her heart before she was eleven. She's done everything she can to shut me out. And I didn't help much."

Peter's head jerked up from my wrist, and his eyes flashed, but his voice was cool and level.

"Have you ever thought maybe she didn't build those walls to keep you out?" He cut off my question. "She never built those walls to shut you out, or to shut anyone out. She built them simply to see who cared enough to climb over them." His fingers brushed the scar on my wrist, and then he pressed on it lightly and changed the subject. "How much pressure does it take?"

I forced a chuckle over my anxiety. It always came back to that. Everyone wanted to know.

"More than that, Peter. Do you want me to forget something?"

Nervously, he laughed along with me.

"How do you do it Alice?"

"Do what?"

"This scar represents cycles of horror and torture. And yet here you are, joking about it. Taunting me to do exactly what brings you so much grief."

The Captain paced nervously on the porch, and in my mind I saw him forcing his pliers into my wrist. He looked so sad as I screamed. That's what stuck with me while I ran away with him. How sad he looked. I watched Peter's fingers stroke the scar.

"How do you joke about it?"

I watched The Captain as I responded.

"I can't let it become me. I did, for a while. I got special treatment because I was the victim. And I allowed, and embraced that. Then one day it occurred to me that that was no way to live. I woke up everyday sad and scared and I wasn't allowing myself to live. That was the day I laughed for the first time in twelve cycles. It felt so good, so freeing, to laugh." I smiled and closed my eyes for only a second. "I survived the camps. I am not what I went through. Please, stop treating me like I am."

He withdrew his hand and stared at his lap. Clumsily, he rose, leaning heavily against his cane.

"Yeah, well, let's get you up and outside. A little fresh air will do you some good." He grabbed my arm, but I pulled it out of his grasp.

"I can do it myself. I don't want you to strain your leg." I pushed off the bed, but I wasn't as strong as I thought I was.

"Don't be ridiculous. My leg won't be a problem."

"Are you sure? It looks pretty bad."

He was defensive now, trying to shield his leg.

"It's not a problem, I can handle it." He spit out through clenched teeth. I smiled and nodded at him.

"It feels lousy, doesn't it?"

"What?"

"When someone assumes you can't do something because of what happened to you."

Slowly, understanding dawned in his eyes. He offered me his arm, and this time I took it.

"I would love to go outside, Peter. Not because it will 'be good for me', but because it's a nice day and should be enjoyed."

"Right, but you might want to keep a tight hold on the railing, just in case my cane fails me." He chuckled, waiting for me to laugh too.

"I don't understand."

He sighed.

"That was my first joke about my leg. I'm no good at jokes."

"Oh." I smiled as I replayed his "joke". "They get easier over time. Don't worry."

"Oh no, I got one. When kids play in my yard, I have to threaten them with "you kids better leave contact information because if you run there's no way I'll catch you!"

"Oh you're really are not good at that."

He shook his head, trying to explain.

"So I can contact their parents to complain about them."

"No, just stop. Please." I laughed, but not at his joke.

"I don't care that I suck at jokes. I achieved what I wanted to."

"And what was that?"

"I made you smile." We were outside now, and the sky was completely cloudless. Christa crouched on the other end of the courtyard, glaring at us.

"She's right you know." Peter pointed to his wife, noticing me watching her. "She said you deserve to die happy. I hadn't seen you happy until just now. She's right. You've earned it."

Inhibited

Cerynn

"**D**o you think he's okay?" I asked Josh for the third time. We were playing check with pieces we made out of different of rocks and leaves. Josh drew the board in the dirt, but we had to be careful not to rub the lines away.

"I mean, a few days ago he was following The Captain around and being his usual, arrogant self, but today he's just sitting there, in the dirt, staring into space." I took his queen, and placed him in check. "Do you think I should go talk to him?"

Josh sighed and crossed his eyes.

"You're right, Josh. I mean he doesn't have a great track record. But, on the other hand, he was Jaycobe's best friend." Josh nodded. "You make a good point, Josh. I should go talk to him."

"Talk to who?"

I jumped at the voice right behind me.

"Oh, Roland. Hello."

"I see you're talking to yourself again." He sneered as he scuffed through our check board. Josh frantically tried to save the pieces, but it was too late. "Who were you talking about, Sweetheart?" He pulled a makeshift cigarette out of his pocket, and lit it, blowing smoke in

Josh's face.

"We were talking about you. You look terrible." I gritted my teeth as Josh choked on the smoke.

"Of course I look terrible, Babe. I ain't had no alcohol since your house blew up, and all I got to smoke is these crazy weird plants growing on the wall."

"Roland! Those aren't smoke-able!"

He twisted the butt in his fingers, and then shrugged.

"It works for me. So what are you two dweebs up to?"

"We were playing check if you must know."

"Check! No, no, no. That's not a game. Here, get me six decks of cards and I'll teach you the game that won me my fortune." He pulled out his money pocket and held it open so we could see all three celets in it. Not much of a fortune. "Enough to entice a pretty girl to go out with me, no?" He winked at me. I rolled my eyes.

"By "pretty" you mean me?"

"Look around, Princess!" He gestured to our meager camp. "Your options plummeted when the city died. Why not give me a shot?"

"Because," I looked him up and down. "You're nothing. Marrying you wouldn't move me up in the world."

"Is that what you want? To move up?" He smirked. "Not love?"

"Why bother with love?" I shrugged.

"Well, I've heard The General is single, now that Alice is here." He chuckled. I thought for a moment, and sniffed.

"I don't think he'd look at me twice."

Roland stopped laughing and glanced my way.

"Wait... you'd want him to?"

"He's cute." I shrugged.

"He tortured Alice! He's a monster!"

"Maybe he had good reason."

"He's evil, Cerynn."

I didn't like sober Roland. I shot him a frown, and shrugged.

"How would we get six decks of cards?" I turned the conversation back.

"At the bar." His eyes narrowed as he watched me. "He's evil you know."

"I know." I blushed.

'She's a young girl.' Josh signed. 'Swayed by the power.'

"I am not!" I slapped his arm. "I didn't mean it anyway." The blushed creeping up my cheeks betrayed me. I hated The General. I did. But he had a castle and right now I was sick of sleeping on dirt. I'd be crazy to turn him down if he asked for my hand. Roland on the other hand was not an option. I'd still be sleeping on dirt if I married Roland. I just wanted to get off the floor. My prosthetics ached from the hard ground.

"The bar is outside our gates." I mumbled, desperate for a topic change. "That's not safe."

"Well, you've got to live a little. I think you'll be just fine. Let's go." He sauntered towards the gates, glancing back at us.

"Should we go, Josh?"

Josh rapidly shook his head.

"If you come with, I'll give you a sword." Roland called back.

"Josh, a sword. Come on."

He still shook his head, but reluctantly followed me out the gates. Mother would kill me if she knew I was outside the gates.

"So the princess is rebellious." Roland leaned against a tree, still smoking. "Oh, and your little sister's coming too, I see." He gave Josh a half wave. Josh didn't return it. "So here's your sword. You might need it, so keep it handy."

It was intricately carved, and the tip curved just slightly. It wouldn't just go in and out easily, it was made to rip people apart. Roland also handed Josh a sword, although Josh's looked more like a toy.

"Alright, Dolls, let's go." Roland put his cigarette out on

Josh's sword, and then hooked one arm around mine, and one arm around Josh's. "We're off to get a card set. A wonderful card set indeed." He sang, and half skipped.

What had my brother seen in him?

Josh reached around Roland and poked my arm.

'We're going to get caught.' He signed.

"What's the freak saying?" Roland directed his question to me, although he never looked away from Josh. Josh and I both knew Roland understood sign language. He was simply being rude.

"Doesn't matter anyways, we're going to the bar. Alcohol and cards, my beautiful mistresses."

I didn't really want to go into the dead forest, but Roland drug us through the black trees. He was giddy; fueled by the reward. I had not been back to the house since the night I blew up my brother. Since the night I decided the only option was to use my powers to blow up our home. I expected guilt when I thought about it, but I only felt a thrill that made me want to do it again.

We sent four or five scavenging groups back to get what they could, but Mother wouldn't let anyone related to her go on the trips.

"Roland, do you think this is a good idea? Mother doesn't want us to leave the camp."

"Ever again." He retorted. "Your mother isn't willing to go to war for us. We're just supposed to sit around until she dies, and then we're free to go to war. I don't know about you, but I don't want to live behind walls anymore. Why don't we just attack their camp? We could come back heroes."

"Because that's a stupid idea. We're just going to get the cards, and then go back to camp. I'm not just going to walk into their camp, we'd be slaughtered."

Raks shifted deep in the forest. I could see them, though they were a ways off. The trees thinned out. As we got closer to town it occurred to me that my brother was still there, and so were all the people he killed.

Nobody did anything about the bodies.

Our feet crunched on the ash coating the ground. Most of the buildings burned to the ground, and bodies were heaped in the middle of the street. Someone tried to burn them, but the fire burned out too soon. Flies buzzed around the smelly rotting piles, and we swatted the stragglers away. No one spoke as we picked our way through the rubble. The smell overwhelming us, and Josh bent at the waist and lost his lunch.

"The bar is over here." Roland whispered, leading us down a side street.

"But the bar is on Mainstreet. Why are we going down the alley?"

"Back door. You saw all the Raks in the forest. They'll be watching Mainstreet looking for stragglers."

"How do you know what they'll be doing?"

We stopped, and he looked slightly confused.

"I'm not sure."

Josh was at the back door, jiggling the handle.

'Locked.'

"Oh yeah, I can fix that." Roland reached into his back pocket and pulled out a key ring. "The owner gave me a key 'cuz I was his best business." He unlocked the door in seconds. "Oh sweet alcohol I've finally come home to you." He left us standing in the alley; his forgotten sidekicks.

The bar was dark, so we both stood just inside the door and let our eyes adjust. We could hear Roland rummaging around in the bar, and soon he was screaming again.

"No! No! No! No!"

"What's wrong?" I called into the depths of the bar.

"They drank the booze. Everything is gone!"

I heard shattering glass as he threw the bottles in frustration.

"Roland, let's just get the cards and get out of here. You're going to get a lot of attention with all that noise.

Where are the cards?"

He threw bottles against the bar, and then empty glasses. Josh tugged on my arm and pointed out the window onto Mainstreet, but I didn't have a chance to look. The window shattered behind us.

Roland launched over the bar and pushed Josh to the ground, reaching up to pull me down, too. He grabbed the sword from my hand and ran towards the broken window. Seven Raks braced their crossbows against their shoulders, and aimed them at the three of us. Roland disappeared into the midst of the Raks, and in less than a minute the Raks all lay, beheaded, at his feet. He cleaned off his swords on a Rak's shirt, and then straightened his own.

"Yeah. We should get the cards and get out of here."

"Roland, how did you do that? You're not even trained."

Josh still lay on the floor, arms over his head. Glass splattered the ground around us, and puddles of blood formed around the bodies.

"Okay. You have to swear you won't tell anyone, but I'm pretty sure your mom's right about The Captain."

"What?"

"When he "trained" us, he didn't actually train us, he blindfolded us and took us into his cabin, and then something held our hands. Whatever held our hands was very warm. That's all that happened. Something held our hands and now we all rock at combat. I don't know squat about Àraids, but if that's how you train, you would have done it by now. Humans don't train like that. So that leaves Raks. That's why I think we should just storm the camps. I freaking rock. I mean, I don't know how, but I know I can't lose. How handy would that be?" He ran over to the card table and stuffed six decks onto his pockets. "Now that I've really tested out my ability, I think I'm ready to tell your mom. Let's get going!"

What he said couldn't be true. Nobody just acquired skill. Roland scooped up two of the Rak heads.

"We can experiment on these, and maybe we'll be able to out-smart them. Plus, they might be kind of fun as pranks."

"Pranks?"

"Like, putting them in a cupboard for The Captain's wife to find. That could be pretty funny."

"You can't do that! Not after all she's been through." I tried to hide a giggle. I couldn't admit it would be a little funny.

"Trust me. It'll be funny. We need something to do since we're not going to war. Why did your mother start training us if she wasn't going to use us? All our lives have led up to war, and now she's called it off. Pranks are the only thing I have now. We better get back to camp, it's getting dark."

"Go." Roland taught us his card game, and although I hated to admit it, it was way better than check.

'Go.' Josh signed.

"Alright losers. All in, no discard. Let's get this show on the road."

"And I'll be judge for you. Okay?" Jess lay on his stomach and propped his head on his hands, watching the cards closely.

"Why is your baby brother here?" Roland tossed his cigarette into the dirt, crushing it out with his thumb.

"Mother's worried that his life has been 'too much routine and not enough play'. She's decided now that there isn't going to be a war, he should learn how to play."

"Well that definitely limits what I can talk about." Roland laid down his cards, picking up his next hand. "I pretty much only talk about women and booze, and beating everyone I know at games. I don't want your mom yelling at me if Jess learns some new... phrases."

"Okay first, I'm eleven and I know some phrases. And second, you don't need to talk through me. I'm right here."

"Mom told us to just pick new words to be our swear words. Mine is 'muffins'." I explained. Roland frowned at me.

"What do you mean your word is 'muffins'?"

"Aw, muffins, I think Roland is beating me at games. But he'll just have to get the ocean over it because I bubbling rock at trouncing people. At. Games. Boom."

"What are you even saying?"

"Words." I managed to keep a straight face, but I made up "bubbling" on the spot and was cracking up inside. I sounded insane.

"I know what those words stand for, Cerynn. Don't ya know what they stand for, Roland?" Jess wanted Roland to like him, because Roland was older, and so he must be wiser.

"Hey! Mrs. McCain!" Roland ignored Jess, shouting across the courtyard to where my mother was walking with The Captain. "Word on the street is that you put the k-bosh on the war. What's up with that?"

"The visions showed that everyone would be safer if we stayed here."

"And by "everyone" you mean Alice, don't you. One vision showed her living and one showed her dying and you picked the lesser of two evils, didn't you?"

Mother stopped, and glanced around at the townspeople who stopped to listen to Roland's question. Her eyes stopped on The Captain's cabin. She allowed Alice to be free during the day, but didn't like her outside the cabin. She was making sure she remained prisoner.

"Yeah, Mom," I spoke up. "You think you're saving us, but are you? Are we really free from them if the one person your trying to save will never truly recover from them?"

"She's recovered from them. She's just fine."

A piercing scream cut through Mom's excuse. It came from The Captain's house, and he ran towards the open door before it died. The entire crowd followed, curious. I elbowed my way to the front of the group, and peeked into the cabin.

Alice huddled in the corner, arms over her head, rocking slowly. The Captain wrapped his arms around her, and glared at the other side of the room.

I already knew what he was looking at, but I followed his gaze anyway. One of the cupboard doors hung open, and, hanging precariously out of the cupboard, was one of the Rak heads Roland brought back with us. Black blood dripped from the head onto the counter.

"Who did this?" The Captain's voice was barely more than a whisper. He was fighting the urge to yell. "Tell me who did this to her. This is a hateful thing to do and I swear when I find who did this, I will kill you. I will slit you navel to nose and I will make you beg for you life and I will laugh and deny it."

My mother picked her way through the pieces of what once was a teapot, and put one hand on the Rak head. Bracing herself with that hand, she pulled the three knives out and cleaned them carefully, and handed them to The Captain. Then she scooped the head into her arms and walked back to the door. Although she tried hard to conceal it, the flash in her eyes said she was about ready to kill over this, too.

"Let me deal with the prankster, Captain. You deal with your wife." Her eyes never left Roland as she spoke, and he ducked his head like a puppy in trouble.

She always knew who caused trouble. Somehow she could always pick them out, even with no evidence to convict them. She grabbed Roland's ear and pulled him aside. Somehow, she knew, from just a few seconds to observe, that Roland planted that head. Josh tugged on my arm, and poised his hands.

'If your mother is right about Roland, with absolutely no evidence, how could she possibly be wrong about The Captain. Is it still safe to trust him?'

Inhibited

Christa

"**Y**ou can't honestly tell me she's moved past it. She's never going to be better. Why prolong it?" Roland already spewed excuses before I could lay into him. "We need to go to war, Ms. McCain. You can't pussy-foot around anymore."

I shoved the mangled head into his face.

"Why did you do this, Roland?"

"To prove to you that this war is necessary. She'll never be over it, and that's the reason you chose not to go to war. In all your training sessions you told us not to allow our own comfort decide the world. But isn't that what you're doing?"

Was that what I was doing?

I always made the best decision for the group, regardless of my own comfort.

He had to be wrong.

Not going to war was the only choice.

"We stay here. No questions." I struggled to keep my voice calm. His mouth opened and closed, as he scrambled for a way to convince me.

"Is this the one that did it?" The Captain raced towards us, and grabbed the front of Roland's shirt, lifting him off the ground. He slammed the boy into the side of the cabin, and punched him in the face. "Why would you do that? How could you do that to her?"

"Captain." I reached out to stop him, but a cane landed on his shoulder before I could reach him.

"Step away from him and control yourself, Sir." Peter's voice was low, but commanding. Roland slid down the side of the cabin, holding his face as blood spurted through his fingers. "Beating him up will solve nothing."

"He can't get away with it! Make sure he's punished, or you'll find his body strung up in the courtyard!" He screamed, and the veins stood out on his neck. Alice hovered on the porch, watching.

"Captain, don't joke like that." She frowned.

"It wasn't a joke."

Alice clung to the railing as she made her way off the porch. She braced herself against the building as she went over to the boy. She wrapped her arms around him, hugging him like a mother hugging an injured child. Then she pushed back slightly, and eased his hands away from his face. Roland's nose was skewed, and blood ran down to stain his shirt.

"Captain." I never knew her voice could hold such authority. The bigger man shrank at her voice. "You know what I want you to do."

He glanced over at Peter and I, and then leaned closer to her, whispering.

"Here, in front of them?"

She shrugged.

"I don't see why it should matter. Apologize to this young man."

"He hid a Rak in our house to prove to Christa that we should be at war by traumatizing you. Why would you want to help this boy?"

Her eyes met mine.

"You're not going to war? You need to go to war."

Panic rose inside me again.

"Stop questioning me!" I collapsed to the ground, holding my head.

The Rèxtaÿла is with you. Crown them, and I will be able to return. This war will end.

The King's comforting voice was replaced with a gravelly laugh.

You think avoiding war will keep her safe, but that's where you're wrong. I know how to get her, and I will, just wait. I'll get her back. I'll steal your Rèxtaÿла. Your King will never return.

But then The King cut in again.

You know who the Rèxtaÿла is. All you have to do is crown them. Just think hard, Christa. Just think.

I cracked my eyes open. Peter leaned over me with one hand on my back. Roland and The Captain both looked as if I was possessed. But I focused on Alice. When everyone stared at me as if I lost my mind, she had the most overwhelmingly peaceful look on her face. A look that calmed anyone who saw it. I pulled myself to my feet, and then helped Peter up next to me.

"Will you please step aside with me." Peter whispered to me. "I have an idea."

Alice and The Captain went back to their discussion while Peter pulled me aside.

"I had a thought on how to change your vision."

"What do you mean?"

"In your vision, Alice was there. And that's what got her killed. What if I take her somewhere in the past where the Raks can't find her. She'll be out of the picture until you send someone back to get us. Then you can go ahead with the war, and she won't be there. Your third option."

You know who the Rèxtaÿла is. You have always known.

"Don't you think that will work, Christa? Tell me how that wouldn't work."

You have always known. Think. Just think. Who has the ability to trust me through all the bad? Who has proved over and over that they are not what they seem.

Slowly, I turned away from Peter, back towards my mother. She leaned against The Captain, relying on him to hold her up. She pulled his head down to her level, whispering in his ear. His face held consternation, but he slowly eased her to the ground, and knelt beside her. He cupped his hands and dug a small hole in front of her.

"I can keep her safe, Christa. Just say when." Peter twisted his cane in the dirt.

"What is he doing, Peter?" I did not look away from The Captain.

Just think. Just think.

"Are you even listening to me? Is it even a good idea?"

Just think. I'm coming back.

"Why is he digging, Peter?"

My husband threw his hands into the air, and stalked off into the woods. The hole was about a foot and a half deep, and now Alice stopped The Captain with a hand. He rocked back on his heels and watched her. Her hand shook as she reached out for the Rak head. She pulled the head into her lap and, gently, respectfully, closed his eyes. Then she ripped off a section of her skirt, wrapped the head, and laid it in the hole. The Captain pulled her into his arms, and she buried her head in his shoulder. He pushed the loose dirt over the head, and then wrapped his arms around her, shielding her from the mound.

Just think. You know who it is. Who has gone through the most, and yet forgives the most?

Alice

You'll never escape me. Your only shelter is me. There is nowhere to run. You've always been mine.

The General seemed to scream through the Rak head, and his voice faded as I scooped dirt back over the head.

"I'm sorry, Ma'am. I didn't know it would be such a shock to you. I thought it would just be a funny prank."

The Captain lunged towards the boy again, but I stopped him.

"It's alright Roland, you couldn't have known."

Both boy and man stared at me in surprise.

"What?" The Captain was incredulous.

"He couldn't have known, Captain. It wasn't his fault."

"This was exactly his fault! Don't just write it off!"

"He's a good boy, Captain. I'm fine. Really." I gave the boy's hand a comforting squeeze, and he smiled at me gratefully.

"Um, excuse me." Peter timidly tapped my shoulder. "I need to borrow you a moment."

The Captain started to stand, but Peter shook his head.

"Not you. Christa just wants Alice to meet her in the woods. No one else."

The Captain pulled me over to him, and held me against him tightly.

"Where she goes, I go. No way am I going to let her be alone with that psycho."

"My wife is not a "psycho", and she won't be alone. I will be there. But she specifically asked for you to not be there."

"I am not leaving her side." His hands squeezed my arms.

"I'll be okay, Captain." My curiosity was winning. His hands rose to my face and he tilted my head back.

"Are you sure?" I nodded. "I don't want to leave your side." He whispered, his face inches from mine. "I miss you just thinking about not being by your side. I've spent so much time watching you, what will I do if you're not here?"

"You'll just have to manage." The words barely slipped out before he kissed me.

"Don't make me stay behind." He kissed me again before I could say anything. Another slow kiss, and then I pushed him away.

"What's your name, Captain?"

His eyes closed off again, and his hands released.

"Go ahead and meet with Christa. It's fine. I'm fine." He groaned as he pushed himself off the ground and stalked into our cabin. Peter offered me his arm, and slowly I rose to my feet, although Roland had to put an arm around me to steady me.

"I think I should walk with you, just until you get out there, and then I'll leave. She won't make it on her own." He whispered to Peter, who nodded and led the way. My legs could support my weight, but I seemed to have lost the ability to balance, and leaned heavily on Roland, apologizing as he sagged under this new burden.

Peter eased the gates open, and the three of us hobbled out into the unprotected forest. I glanced back at my cabin, and saw The Captain glaring out the window, arms folded. He was upset that I wasn't including him. I hoped he would be done pouting by the time I got back.

"He'll be okay, Alice." Peter reassured me.

We walked in silence, and it was only when we were almost to the clearing that I recognized the path. This was the same path Christa and I walked the day I stole her powers. I was about to ask Peter where we were going, but then the trees parted and I saw Christa sitting in the clearing, watching, waiting for me.

Behind her stood the Elders who appeared the last time I was here. The others had gone, but these six remained. They stood in a semi circle, all facing me, as Peter led me to the center of the clearing. He pushed me down into a kneeling position in front of Christa, and then slowly backed back out of the clearing.

Christa's eyes closed, and she wore an intricately carved crown on her head. Her hair was blonde on top, cascading down to reds and blacks, rippling through uncontrolled loose curls down to her waist. An intricate crown glittered in her hair.

Slowly, she opened her eyes, which glowed violet, and studied me. Then, without a word, she stood and moved behind me, nudging her knees against my back. I twisted around to watch her as she eased the intricate crown out of the mass of curls. Then she motioned to me to look at the group, and they all stared back at me. Some looked skeptical, and some were in awe.

The crown settled onto my head, but no sooner had I realized what it was and the entire sky lit up in fire. Flames danced around the clearing, and up into the sky. The suns set rapidly, and the stars shown through the fire. The people gasped, and fell to their knees. Every single person still faced me, and now they placed their index finger to their chin. Christa came around in front of me, and also fell to her knees, mimicking the Elders. The flames ceased their dance, and as my eyes adjusted to the light, I could make out the words they formed.

"Lift your eyes to the hills. Your help is coming."

† † † † †

Christa fell to the ground and buried her face in her hands. The Elders came up to me, single file, and kissed my hands, and sometimes my feet. They kept mumbling how long they'd been waiting for me. The words were still etched in the sky. They sizzled and burned and yet they never faded. Peter and Roland came out from the trees, and stood beside me.

"That settles it, Mrs. McCain. We have no choice now." Roland spoke up.

"No choice for what?" I asked.

Christa lifted her head from her hands; her cheeks soaked with tears.

"No choice but to go to war, Mother. That message can be seen in all eleven regions."

"So?"

"So, the whole world now knows The King is coming back. The Raks will make a mad dash at anything that breaths to try to wipe out The King."

"But what caused him to come back now?" I was confused.

"You. You are what the world has been holding its collective breath for." She crossed her arms and glared at me. "You could not have just been an obnoxious woman who took me in. You had to be the Ȓèx̱ṭaỹла."

"What have you done? What did you do?" The Captain stood at the edge of the clearing. His eyes settled on me, and he stomped over to my side. His fists clenched at his sides, and then reached out and grabbed the crown off of my head. The crown hissed and he threw it from him, rubbing new burns covering his hands.

"Raks cannot touch The King's crown." Christa frowned and snatched the crown out of the dirt, stroking the intricate band. The Captain squatted before me and put his hands on both sides of my face.

"What did they do? What have they done?"

"We've started the end. We're finally taking back control on our lands." One of the Elders moved to my side, and the others stood ready for any sign of danger. The Captain shook his head.

"You don't understand. He'll come for her now. He will stop at nothing to get her back into his possession."

"I'm right here, Captain. I'm not invisible." The Elder helped me up as I pushed The Captain away. He tried to pull me back to him. The Elder raised his hand and lightning shot from his finger tips.

"My job is to keep The Rèχtaỹла safe. No one touches her until this war is over."

The Captain stared at Christa, waiting for her to step in, but she shrugged.

"You are going to be busy helping with the war anyway, Captain."

"So you are going to war?" Roland fingered the knife strapped to his leg. Christa chewed her lip for a few seconds, and then collapsed to the ground.

"The war is coming. The King is coming. The Àraid are scattered. We have no army." She mumbled as she rocked, and then she jumped to her feet. "This is going to happen. We need to prepare." Her voice was commanding, and everyone stood a little straighter as she spoke. "We need to take out the Rak prison. He has a few Àraid hidden up there. We need to get them out." As she spoke, she moved through her people.

"Cerynn." She called to her daughter, without looking around. Cerynn, and her silent friend stepped forward, waiting for orders. "You are now the oldest. I am sure you have realized that. I am going to need you and Roland to go out into the regions and convince the Àraid groups to bind together again. We need to be united if we are going to fight, so I need you to find each Àraid camp."

Cerynn nodded solemnly. Christa once told me how suspicious the Àraid were.

"They will not believe without seeing. They have been hurt too many times, Mom." Her tiny hands were held up in front of her, and above them hovered a cloud of smoke. The smoke twisted up into different shapes, before it settled into a coiled snake.

"The Àraid always say that even if a snake isn't venomous, it should pretend to be."

The smoke snake twisted its head to look up at its creator.

"It is a good idea, really. No one really knows what you are capable of. But at the same time, if even the harmless snakes pretend to be deadly, how can you trust them?"

"You are going to need this." Christa waved her hands slowly in front of her, and a tiny glittering charm began to take shape in her palm. She rubbed her fingers together and slowly a chain also materialized. She took the necklace and latched it around her daughter's neck.

"This will prove to them that you come from me." She paused, and tears sparkled in her eyes. She stared at her daughter, and blinked a few times. And then, slowly, awkwardly, she pulled the girl into her arms. Cerynn's eyes opened in surprise at the hug none of us expected, but her arms quickly wrapped around her mother.

Christa sniffed, and then pushed the girl out to arms length. She took a deep breath, and brushed a stray tear from her cheek, struggling to compose herself, suddenly embarrassed at this show of emotion.

"Roland. Josh. You both better watch out for her. She has my head, so she is probably going to do some stupid stuff."

Roland and Josh joined Christa in the middle of the circle. She hooked her arm around Josh's shoulders.

"You are like my son. You know that, boy?"

He swallowed hard and nodded, never looking up from the ground. She roughed up his hair with her free hand, and then he wrapped her in a bear hug.

"I-I-I l-love you." The silent boy stammered. Cerynn stared at him, and Christa looked away. She stared at the sky, at the words still burning there. Nobody spoke. We hardly dared to breathe. Christa nodded slowly, then she grabbed Cerynn's hand, and Cerynn grabbed Roland. Josh still clung to her, and she let him stay.

"Be safe. Come home soon. Please, do not die on me." She whispered, and in a burst of light and smoke, they vanished. Christa crumpled to the ground, and I ran to her side, but she smacked my hands away.

"Do not touch anyone." She hissed at me, and then she looked back out at the crowd. "And nobody touch her. Stay away from her until we understand what she is." She snatched the crown from the ground, and bolted into the woods.

† † † † †

"Wake up. I am coming." The whisper was comforting. It was not The General.

The cabin was dark, and I could barely make out the shape of The Captain in the chair beside the bed. I sat up and strained my eyes in the dark, trying to find the source of the whisper.

"Come into the courtyard."

I could see a figure, all in white, waiting in the dust. The bands around my wrists burned as I inched to the side of the bed away from The Captain. These were a new form of handcuffs that burned when I got too far from the key, which The Captain kept hidden in one of his pockets. I already tried to slip my hands back through the cuff, but the blood coating the silver told me to stop.

"Come out to me, and I will answer any questions you have."

I wanted those answers. I wanted to know what was

going on. The bed creaked as I stood. I froze and glanced at
The Captain. He shifted and raised his head, but his eyes
were still shut tight, and soon his breathing relaxed back
into a slow pattern.

"Come to me." The figure still stood in the middle of the
courtyard, but now his arms were raised, inviting a hug. The
handcuffs changed color as they heated up, but I no longer
felt the burns.

I ran to The King, and threw myself at his feet, burying
my face in my hands. He gently touched my back, and
smoothed my hair. We stayed like that for only a moment
before he pulled me into his arms, and I was finally home.

† † † † †

"You have been through a lot these last few cycles have
you not?" His voice was like a song winding around a
person, coaxing all the darkness out into the light. His
accent matched Christa's. I never noticed that before.

I could only nod. The King gave me my memories back,
but I didn't think I was ready for them. I felt like I was
drowning in the sorrow, but then The King would call my
attention back to him and all of that would fade. I watched
my hands twist in my lap, and suddenly remembered the
burning handcuffs.

Blood bubbled where it hit the white hot metal. My
mouth dropped open as I realized what it was doing to me.
Frantically, I grabbed the metal and tried to pull it off of my
wrist, but only scalded my hand.

"Hey," The King's voice was quiet. "Do you want me to
take care of those for you?" He held his hands up, and the
tips of his fingers frosted over.

I could almost feel the ice on my burning wrists.

"You only have to ask, and I will handle it."

"I need you to handle this, please." I whispered.

His larger hands circled my wrists, and instantly the

burning stopped. The handcuffs popped open and fell to the ground, and the damaged skin repaired itself.

"Have I ever not handled it, Alice?"

I shook my head. The King was my "imaginary friend." As a child he would slip back to this world, and keep me company. He always helped me.

When I was a child.

But that was long ago.

"I have never let you down? Are you sure?"

"I'm sure."

"Then why do you try to do everything yourself, instead of asking me for help? I want to help you, but you never even ask anymore."

"When I was a child I could hear you all the time. I rarely could see you, but I could always hear you. But in the prison, your voice was quieter. And after I got out, you stopped speaking to me."

He sighed and folded my hands into his.

"I never stopped speaking to you. You just stopped listening. When you were taken prisoner, you focused on surviving. You could not think about trying to breach a gap between worlds to speak to some banished King. And once you got out, you were safe for the first time in cycles. Suddenly, you did not need me to comfort you, so you shut me out."

I frowned.

"I didn't shut you out. I kept trying to find you, but you weren't there." Tears flooded my eyes as I hastened to explain myself.

"I never left. And I never will. My people just stopped seeing me. The humans do not see the Raks scales, or their patchwork skin, because they do not want to. And they do not see me either. I once roamed this world welcomed by the humans. They would run out and greet me, and I always helped them. But once the Raks came into the world, they swayed the humans. 'The King cannot protect you from losing your loved ones, he is not as powerful as he seems.' They would whisper in grieving ears.

"And, as The Collector collected more souls, more people begged me to bring them back. And when I did not, they began losing faith. No one is meant to return from death. They do not understand that. That is what created the Raks; by returning from a land that is meant to be the last stop.

"As people lost faith, I lost touch. I cannot stay where I am not wanted. Unless someone wants me here; I am not really a part of this world. I am but an observer, trying to help ease your pain. But people do not listen to what you say, they listen to their own opinions in a different voice."

"Alice?" The Captain awoke and now his gruff voice cut through The King's gentle one. The King folded his hands in his lap and leaned back against the porch as The Captain approached. "Why are you outside? Without any guards?"

"I was talking to The King."

The Captain tried to follow my pointing finger, but his eyes didn't focus on The King. He knelt beside me and felt my forehead.

"Are you okay?"

"I'm fine, Captain, why?"

"There's no one here."

The King smiled sadly at me, and shrugged.

"My people stopped seeing me."

"You know where you are supposed to be right now, Captain." The King whispered, and The Captain frowned and straightened. His eyes slowly focused on The King.

"How?" He sputtered.

"You know where you are needed." The King repeated.

"I don't want to go. I'm needed here."

"I will take care of her. You need to go. Now."

The Captain stood shakily. His face blanched white, and his hands shook. Then his eyes clouded over, and he reached for my necklace.

"Why do you keep that dumb thing? Give it to me." He held out a hand expectantly.

"I can't, Captain. Please." I looked at The King, hoping he would defend my necklace, but he only looked down at his feet. This was my battle.

"I need to sell it. We need the money."

"No."

"It's the only thing of value we have. Give it here." His fingers brushed my neck as he undid the clasp. "Trust me, Baby. It's better for you if you don't love him anyway." His sneer didn't mask the pain in his eyes as he dropped my necklace into his pocket.

My eyes stung, but I was out of tears. The Captain knelt in front of me, and traced my jaw. Then he pulled my head down and kissed my forehead.

"I am sorry, My Love." He whispered.

"Say goodbye." The King prodded.

"No." The Captain shook his head.

The King's eyes blazed with fire, and soon his hair, too, was a mass of flames. The Captain jumped up and took a half step backwards. His eyes were filled with tears as he looked at me.

"Goodbye, Alice. I love you."

Questions flooded my mind.

Why are you leaving?

Where are you going?

I love you, too.

I couldn't speak them.

"What is your name?" That was the only thing that seemed important. It niggled at the back of my mind, and would not let up. He looked like he was about to answer, and then he clamped his jaw tight, spun on his heel, and stalked into the night.

"Why did he have to leave?" I turned back to The King.

"That is none of your concern. You need to focus on what is happening to you. You are my greatest creation. You have my greatest abilities."

"I don't have any abilities." I corrected.

"You are the Counselor. I have given you the most of myself. I created you to figure out and understand what people need. When someone touches you, if they have a need strong enough, you will do it. If someone touches you, and they desperately need water, their thirst will be quenched. It was meant to be a gift used only for good. However, it is an easily manipulated power. You have healed people, have you not?"

"Yes, but not everyone. When Ginny died, I didn't heal her. And when Jaycobe died I didn't heal him."

"Because when Ginny died, the strongest need Christa had was to accuse The Captain. Her primary thought was not to heal her dead daughter, and so you did not heal her. And when Jaycobe died, Christa needed to keep the rest of her family safe, not heal her son, and so you protected the rest of the family. The General figured out how to use your powers. He would beat you nearly to death, and then he would heal you. He understood how to manipulate it, and that is a very dangerous thing."

I remembered only too vividly begging for death and being denied.

"There is more I want to tell you, but we do not have time."

"Why?"

"Because I need to tell Christa something."

"Mother?" Christa stood directly behind me. I hadn't heard her approach, so her voice startled me. She seemed to be trying to understand why I would be out here alone, and then her eyes widened and she gasped. "Your Majesty!" She fell to her knees at his feet. "We have waited for you for so long!"

"And now I am here, but not for long, I have a lot of other things I need to do." Christa rocked back on her heels, and wiped tears from her face. "Christa, I need you to listen and obey. Can you do that?"

She nodded slowly, biting her lip.

"You are going to attack the nearest Rak camp. Send Peter to the past to keep him safe. Your daughter is where she needs to be, so good job on that. Gather The Elders and the townspeople, and attack the Raks. I will let you know when to pull your people out. There are many Àraid inside the prisons. If you can get them out, they will trust you. The Àraid in hiding will not yet trust you. But know this battle will end with death. Sometimes you need to accept losses in order to win." His voice was stern.

"Can you not attack them? You are much stronger than I."

"Not yet. I still cannot be here. Not completely."

"Then when will you be here? Completely?"

"Alice needs to unite the Àraid Objects. They cannot work independently. Until then, I need you to be their Rèлïă."

"But, Majesty, they do not trust me. They do not want a Rèлïă." Christa argued.

His eyes softened, and he smiled.

"Dear, they will. You will convince them. I know you, and you are persuasive. Now go get things in order." He took my hand in his, and I relaxed. Finally. Finally I found peace. I was not afraid. Christa's eyes flashed as she looked at our hands.

"And what about Alice, Your Majesty?" She tried to sound strong, but her voice cracked, and she wouldn't meet my gaze.

"Do not bother with her. She will be okay."

Christa frowned and stood. She whirled away from The King, and took a few steps towards her cabin.

"Peter!"

Peter poked his head out of his cabin, where he'd obviously been eavesdropping, and then, reluctantly, stepped out onto the porch. His cane thumped on the wood as he made his way over to us.

"Yes, Dear?"

"Come here." He did so reluctantly, his eyes never leaving The King. "I am going to send you, and Alice, into the past. You are to wait until I come for you. Okay?"

"Christa," The King spoke up. "I said not to do anything with Alice."

"No! Option three. I'm going to save her!" She hissed, grabbing Peter's hand, and then mine. With a bright flash The King disappeared. Then the little town, and Christa, too, disappeared. Peter and I were in a new forest; alone.

"She sent us into her past." Peter said, looking around the woods. "We should go that way." He pointed with his cane.

We didn't speak. There was too much to think about. We were both preoccupied with the thought of Christa, riding into war that we knew she couldn't win. The leaves cracked under our feet. Peter cleared his throat.

"Alice?"

"Yeah?"

"May I? I mean, could I, maybe, try to use your abilities?" He ducked his head shyly.

"Peter, I don't think that would be a good idea. I'm not even sure how it works yet."

He nodded.

"I understand."

We both stopped. Ahead of us, we could make out the side of a cabin. It seemed familiar somehow.

"Wait a minute."

"*I know who you are, Majesty. And I'm sorry.*"

I'd met Peter before, late one night, in Christa's room.

"Peter, that's my cabin."

"What?"

"I own that cabin. I'm inside that cabin, and I'm going to meet you in there, hiding in Christa's closet."

"Okay," Peter didn't understand where I was going.

"Peter, I met you, I didn't meet me. I wasn't there."

Again he nodded.

"You need to get out of here, then." He whispered. "But Christa will kill me if I let you out of my sight."

"Shouldn't we be helping her?" The thought of my daughter, fighting all alone, put a knot in my stomach that wouldn't go away.

"She doesn't want help. She definitely doesn't want you there."

"Why does she hate me so much?" I could still see her smoldering eyes as she screamed at me the day her house burned down.

"She doesn't hate you, Alice. She wants to save you but she doesn't know how."

"Save me?"

"She has visions; of what's to come, of what has been. And in the vision of her fighting the Raks, you are there, and you die."

"So she's trying to change what's already set in stone?"

"She's headstrong."

"I said not to send you away. You are needed in that camp." The King's voice filtered through the air. *"You will save her. Only you."*

"I can't be here when Christa finds you, Peter. You need to send me somewhere else."

He didn't want to, I could tell that he was trying to think of another way. Slowly, he tapped his cane against the ground, and then he sighed.

"Okay," He held my hands tightly. "You're right, of course." He worked his jaw, and seemed to be contemplating what to say. "Okay," He cleared his throat. "You need to focus on a place, any place. I won't be able to tell where you've chosen, so choose wisely."

I already had a place taking shape in my head.

"I'm ready."

He tightened his hands, and a light flashed again. Familiar smells crowded my nose as his hands disappeared.

Mold and dust and blood. I didn't want to open my eyes. I didn't want to see this room again. I heard fighting in the streets. Slowly, I opened my eyes. My memory hadn't failed. It took me exactly where I wanted. Back to that room, and that horrible cage.

Back inside the Rak camps.

The dark room looked as if The General hadn't touched the it since I left. Only one thing was different. There was a boy, half reclining, on the bed. As he shifted his face into the moonlight I gasped. The boy smiled, a leering cynical smile.

"Hello, Mother. I'm not dead. Surprise."

Christa

"Christa." The King whispered.

I should not have disobeyed him.

No one ever disobeyed him.

But I needed to save her.

She could not be there when I attacked the camp.

I could not lose her.

Not again.

"Do not tell me I should listen to you. I have lost her too many times, Majesty. I am sorry." He pressed his lips together, and did not say anything, but he was disappointed. "Tell me what to do now, Majesty." My disobedience made things awkward between us, but I tried to move past it.

"You do what I made you to do. The Àraid are here to protect. So... Protect."

I still was not comfortable heading into a battle I could not win. That was not logical.

I am logical.

I could not do something illogical. But I already disobeyed him. I could not afford to do so again.

"I have no army." I pointed out.

"You will. By tomorrow morning you will have a big enough army. I will take your townspeople to Iceloch find them a safe home while you attack the prisons."

"Why can you not attack them? You are much stronger than I."

"I was kicked out of this world. I am not welcome. Until I am invited back in, I cannot help." He reminded me.

"But-"

The King held up his hand to cut off my protest.

"I have been gone for a long time, Christa. There are other things I need to see to. You will do fine. You were not chosen as Rèлïǎ for nothing." He stood, and the pine-needles at his feet swirled around him. When the needles settled back onto the dirt, the King was gone.

When he left, the screaming returned.

It grew louder, and more insistent, and I collapsed to the ground, holding my head.

Make it stop.

Make it stop.

I needed to focus. I needed to shove the visions into the corner of my head. I could not think about them.

The Àraid Elders were in the woods. I needed to think about them. I needed them to support me, or I would be alone in my war. I could not afford to be alone.

Make it stop.

Please.

"Stop. Leave now. I'm going to kill you."

"Darling. I'm already dead."

Stop!

The voices echoed in my head.

Taunting me.

I could not push it out.

I could not handle it.

I needed an escape.

I pulled out a small knife, and watched the blade glint in the meager light.

So sharp.

So freeing.

I pressed the blade against my wrist. Not very hard. Just hard enough to bring small beads of blood to my skin. Just enough to find relief.

I should not.

But I did.

I stared at the tiny red drops, and, as they began to run down my arms, my stress ran with them.

I had been doing so well.

All of my cuts healed, yet here I was opening them again. It was so freeing, and so imprisoning. It eased my pain by causing more.

Pain wakes you up.

Pain keeps you going.

I added another cut to my arm. This one was only slightly deeper. It felt better. Another cut. And then another. And another. I could not stop. With every cut, the screaming got quieter. I just wanted to be free. I was just freeing myself. I should be building an army. I should go to the Elders. My knife stopped mid cut.

I wanted to finish that cut.

I did not have time.

I was running out of time.

I knew where to find the Elders now. When I first found the clearing, I could not remember where it was. I got lost several times returning to them.

But not tonight.

I was there in minutes, but it was empty. All of the Elders were gone. I paced for a moment in the clearing, and then sat in the middle of the clearing. I pulled out my knife and pressed it against my arm again. But I was interrupted.

"Your Majesty?" One of the Elders stayed. He had been hiding in the forest, so I did not see him. The one with fiery hair. Now he came over to me, eyebrows furrowed. His long robes were made of coals that smoldered and flared in the breeze.

He was Jðɼðïл.

An element Àraid.

He came and knelt next to me, taking the knife from me. But he did not say anything. He did not even look at my bleeding arm.

"I am Elder Vǎrẓ. What do you need me to do?"

"Where are the others?"

"They refuse to follow you until you prove yourself, Ȑѐлïǎ." He kept his head bowed as he answered my question.

"Why are you still here?"

"Because you are Ȑѐлïǎ. You were chosen." He pointed to my cartilage piercing. "It is not my place not to trust you. You were chosen to rule. We were chosen to follow. What do you need?"

I did not like trusting those I did not know. But I needed help, and he was holding his loyalty out to me.

"I need an army. You get me enough people to attack the Rak camp, and I will trust you."

He seemed to expect my response, and rose immediately. He saluted me with the Àraid salute, and then the ground opened up and swallowed him whole.

† † † † †

He did not return for six hours, but when he came back, he led a small army.

"I went to Wellwald. I believe you told me to go into hiding there once, so I thought it would be fitting to get your army there." He whispered to me. My plate could barely pick him up, but I could read his lips.

"Not many people are willing to risk their lives for an unknown Ȑѐлïǎ, but these people decided to take a chance." He brought back maybe eighty people, but they gave me their full attention. Of those people, there were only five Àraid.

"Elder Vǎrẓ did explain to you that you might not come

back from the prison, right?" I asked them. Some of the eager looks faded, but they all nodded. "Once we start out on the mission. I need you to obey me without question. Even if I ask you to do something that you know you will not survive. If you do not think you can do that please leave now."

Only seven people returned to the forest, but the others began shifting uncomfortably. There were not enough people for a proper army, but it would have to do.

"Alright. Let us go take down the Raks." I spun on my heel, and hoped they would follow me.

The Rak camp was several miles away. I did not want to walk that far. I called down my dragon, and climbed onto his back. Four more dragons he brought with him landed near me, and scooped some of the humans in their claws. They would need to make several trips to bring everyone, but it would be faster this way. The dragons dropped us right on the edge of my woods. From here we could see the prison, but it was still a ways off. A tall round building towered above the other buildings, and Raks paced in front of it.

They would see us coming.

The human's eyes did not see it, but I could see a dome covering the Rak camp, protecting them from the suns.

Today the Icy Sun won.

Good for Àraid, bad for Raks.

"Z̃ũÿð."

No going back. The ground began to tremble, and the dome protecting the Raks cracked. Elder Vǎr̥ʐ chanted, and the trees twisted at his command. The Raks noticed us now. Lightning shot through the sky, crashing against their shields. Holes ripped through their shield, and the Raks were exposed to the Icy Sun. They fell to the ground, powerless.

"Stay here, and keep the shield down. I am going in." I told Elder Vǎr̥ʐ.

He nodded, never ceasing his chant. The humans and I stole into the Rak camp. The fence lay in ruins on the ground thanks to Elder Vǎṟẓ, and we stepped over it. The Raks could not fight us. The Icy Sun was killing them. They ignored us, and dragged themselves into cabins, and under porches; anywhere to get out of the sun.

I won without even trying.

Using my powers was more freeing than my knife. I no longer denied who I was. I raised my hands in the air as power surged through me.

"Ÿvị̇tè ṭalðṟï. Ṛaҳ vïẓṭÿ ʌagèṭ ṛavïʌħa. Ƶvaṯħè ҙuÿð ṛavïʌħa. Ǎṟaïd èʌṟèẓṭavïṭ þèṛšðʌè, ṛavïʌħa. Óvèl ṛavïʌħa."

Their houses crumbled at the words that poured from my mouth. Any Raks inside the buildings were smashed by the concrete. Finally, I could wipe out the Raks like I always wanted to.

They killed Micheal.

Ginny.

Aurora.

Jaycobe.

"Always outnumbered. Always right." I muttered to one of the Raks as I pushed my knife through his ear, into his brain.

The whole Rak camp was at my mercy.

I was Ṛèʌïǎ.

The screaming was deafening, but it no longer bothered me.

"Call your people back, Christa. You made your point." The King whispered to me.

I was not ready. There were still Raks alive. They needed to pay for what they did. I motioned for my army to proceed deeper into the camp.

"Why do you refuse to listen?"

My way is better.

My people listened without question.

I was Ṛèʌïǎ.

I found the third option.

My mother was safe, and I was killing the Raks. Wiping them out. I smiled and glanced back at Elder Vǎɼʐ, expecting him to smile back, but his eyes were wide, and the blood drained from his face.

"Your Majesty! The Hybrids."

"You will attack. And you will lose." The King warned me in my dreams a few days ago.

How could I forget?

The Hybrids would not be affected by either sun, because they were Àraid and Rak.

"You got too cocky, young Ʀèлïǎ." A voice whispered behind me. I whirled, knife poised to sink deep into whoever stood behind me, but they grabbed my hand and twisted away the knife.

"I don't feel like dying today." The General laughed at me as he pinned my arms to my side. One of his fingers traced the scars down my neck, and he sneered. "I remember giving that to you. You should have died that day. Why did you not?"

"I did not feel like it." I spat at him. Four Hybrids stood behind him, waiting for permission to attack my army. I led my people into a trap.

Their lives were in my hands.

Their blood was on my hands.

Elder Vǎɼʐ managed to keep the Rak shields down, waiting for me to call our people back. I waited too long. I cost them so much.

"Look to the sky, young Ʀèлïǎ."

I did not want to, but my eyes followed the General's pointing finger.

The Hot Sun was fighting to take back over the sky.

We needed to get out of the camp before it won. But even as I watched the suns, the Hot Sun won and I slumped in the General's arms. He laughed and smashed his hand into the plate behind my ear. Feedback and flashing lights and total, complete silence.

No screaming.

No Raks.

No wind.

He nodded briefly at the Hybrids, and they were released to feast on my people. Again. The Àraid lost again. Elder Vǎrʐ collapsed outside the camp, and the shields went back up.

We were trapped.

The Captain

I twisted her necklace between my fingers, and tried not to listen to The General. He was killing the prisoners they captured from Christa's attack. He was killing them slowly; savoring it. I rubbed the charm, and felt it in my heart.

It still worked all these cycles later.

I heard the snap of bone, and a low growl, and my head shot up to watch him. The General broke into a sickening, toothy grin.

"She's come. She's finally come home to me." His dark eyes locked on mine. "I told you she would come back to me."

A lump rose in my throat as my mind recalled the images of what he'd done to her.

"Go fetch her for me, Captain." He ordered. I had no choice but to obey. "And when you bring her back to me," he already headed down into the prison. "Bring her down to cell V. She'll want to see what I'm doing to her daughter." He laughed as he disappeared down the corridor.

Run, Alice. Get out of here.

I couldn't think anything else. She didn't understand what she was walking into. Roboticly, my feet led me out of the door, and down into the streets. Arrows clanged on the streets, and sank into the humans while they tried to escape. The Raks were concealed in buildings made for battle. Bodies littered the streets, some dead, some dying. In the sky, the burning message from The King was still visible.

The General sent me to get my wife, and although I dreaded doing it, I had to obey him.

More bodies were heaped outside The General's house. The paint peeled away from the building, and blood splattered the white. His windows were barred, and the door had four locks on it. A jail within a house. There were no lights on, and the house looked abandoned, but I heard Alice talking to someone up in The General's bedroom.

Run, Alice! Please.

I wanted to yell to her, to warn her somehow. Then Christa's voice echoed in my mind.

You are going to kill her. How can I trust you?

I had been so sure I wouldn't harm her. I'd defended myself to no end, but now I wasn't so sure. I heard a boy laugh, and something thudded against the window. Alice yelped.

I can't stop, Alice. I can't help you.

My fingers knew the combinations to the front door, and soon it creaked open on rusty hinges. The General's house was littered with beer bottles, and bloody chains piled on the ground. He used to bring Alice down here and chain her up again.

There was another thump upstairs, and everything in me fought against going up. But my legs wouldn't listen to me, and soon I stood right outside the door.

Why would she come back here?

To the place where so much of her pain started.

"That's right, Mommy." The boy's voice filtered through the door. "You should have given me a proper funeral, instead of leaving me in that cabin to rot. You knew better, too. You told The Captain to bury me. He really let you down didn't he?"

Collin.

He died.

I watched him die.

Alice cried behind the door. I wanted to go to her, to make everything better, but that wasn't why I was here.

Run, Alice. Please, run.

I undid the locks, and the door creaked open. Collin stood in the middle of the room, and Alice lay at his feet. The door squeaked and they both turned to see who came in. Alice stumbled to her feet and ran to me; clinging to me.

Run, Alice. Stay away from me. It's not safe.

My mouth wouldn't form the words.

"We should have buried him." Tears streamed down her face as she glanced back at her son. My heart broke. I tried to hug her, but my arms wouldn't obey.

"We should get her back to my father, shouldn't we?" The boy stood right behind Alice, reaching out to grab her arm. She shied from his touch, pushing harder against me. "Come on, Mother. Don't be shy. We've all known this was how it would end, didn't we?"

Her hands twisted in my shirt. She was waiting for me to rescue her like I always did.

"I was free." She whispered. "I was trying to recover."

My hand wrapped around her arm. I squeezed it too hard, but I couldn't let go. She squirmed, and walls flew up behind her eyes. She was beginning to understand. I could see black veins pulsing through my hands as I tried to release her, and I knew she could see them, too.

"Captain?"

Run, Alice.

She tried to twist free and I threw her against the wall. She gasped and clutched at her side, slumping over. I grabbed her shoulders, slamming her against the wall.

I couldn't stop.

Her head lolled to the side, and I just wanted to get her out of this horrible camp. I wanted to get her away from me. She was limp in my arms, but her eyes met mine slowly.

"Run, Alice."

I spit out through a clenched jaw. Her hand shook as she caressed my face.

"I'll never be free until I face my demons. I need to do this, Captain." She didn't understand what he was going to do.

I wrapped her long hair around my hand and yanked her out into the hallway. Her hands clawed at mine, trying to free her hair. I pushed her in front of me, and her feet missed the first step. I grabbed the railing, and let go of her hair as she tumbled down the stairs. She didn't move once she hit the bottom.

Don't be dead. Please, don't be dead.

For only a second, the poison let up, and I was free to go to her. The stairs creaked as I lumbered down them and knelt beside my wife. Her hand clawed at her neck, searching for her necklace, and her eyes were shut tight. My hands ran over her quickly, checking for any broken bones. I didn't find any.

Collin laughed at the top of the stairs as Alice moaned and opened her eyes. She smiled at me, and for a moment, it was just us, just like we always were. And then the poison took over my system again and I pulled her roughly to her feet. My hand found one of the knives I'd given her, and I pulled it out, pressing it against her neck. I kept her ahead of me as we stepped out into the battle.

Alice cried when she saw how many died in this battle they already knew they would lose. The prison loomed in front of us, and Alice shivered when she saw that's where we were headed.

"I forgive you, Captain. I know you aren't in control right now." She whispered.

My hands loosened on her knife as I fought to let her go.

My hands shook, but wouldn't release. I pressed her against the front door of the prison, and her hands scrambled to find the door knob, and the door swung easily inward.

Chains rattled and whips cracked, echoing through the cement corridors. Screams also echoed down the halls, and each one chilled my blood. Those screams would soon be Alice's; and it would be my fault.

We passed twenty-two doors as we headed towards The General. Each door had a window. Through some, we could see Raks breaking recruits, and behind some of the windows, we saw the recruits that didn't survive the process.

"Are you out there, Captain?" The General's voice came from the next cell. "Do you have my trophy?"

"I have her." I answered reluctantly. Alice's face filled with horror.

"Good. Then I don't need Christa anymore."

We both heard an arrow click into place in his crossbow. I didn't even notice that I released Alice until I saw her opening the cell door; rushing in to confront The General.

"Don't harm her, General, please!"

I peeked around the corner, and inadvertently met Christa's eye. She glared at me, and then sharply looked away. The General chained her to a chair in the middle of the room, and her ears were bleeding.

"Why are you here, Mom?" Her voice slurred as she struggled to form the words.

"Because it's not your time yet, Christa." Alice faced The General as she spoke, and Christa sighed.

He raised his bow again, and aimed it at Christa's head. Alice positioned herself between the bow and her daughter.

"Don't harm her. She's *my* daughter." The vehemence in Alice's voice surprised me.

The General laughed and stepped forward to balance his bow on her shoulder.

"You know... I don't care." He smiled, and then roughly wrapped her in his arms.

Anger coursed through me, but I couldn't save her. Her arms flailed, and pushed against his shoulders, trying to push him away from her. He finally broke away, and Alice glanced back at her daughter.

"Let Christa go, and I'll stay with you... without a fight."

"Alice!" I could finally speak. "Don't say that. He'll hold you to that!"

The General turned to glare at me, and suddenly his bow trained on me, and two of his Suits grabbed my arms from behind.

"I don't think that I have your full loyalty anymore, Captain. I don't think I need you anymore."

Alice bit her lip, fighting any hasty responses.

"I'll tell you what, Alice." He said as one of his Suits pressed a knife to Christa's throat. A cold tip of an arrow also poked into my temple. "I'll give you a choice. Your daughter's life. Or your lover's."

Alice's eyes filled with tears as her hand scratched at her neck.

"That's not a choice, General."

He smiled at her, and nodded to one of the guards. They grabbed Alice, and The General lunged at Christa, pushing the chair over. Her head slammed into the concrete, and she didn't fight as The General unchained her. He dragged her over in front of Alice, and forced her to kneel. Alice screamed and cried as The General put a knife in each of Christa's ears, and dragged them down to her neck.

"Don't hurt her! Please."

"So you choose Christa, then?" He nodded to the guard next to me, and he wrapped a length of barbed wire around my throat, slowly pulling it tighter.

"No! I don't. I mean I haven't decided yet."

The wire loosened just a little.

"Oh, you need more time to decide?" The General put on his gentle voice; his soothing voice that made it sound like maybe he was a nice guy. Alice nodded and bit her lip as tears dropped from her face onto Christa's head.

"Okay. I can do that." The General threw Christa back into the chair, and the Suits pushed me towards the wall, and locked me in the shackles waiting there. "I'll give you time to think about your choice as you come make up for lost time. You will kill one of them though, Dear. You know that don't you?" He laughed and pulled her to him again, running his sharp fingers over her neck.

He bent and kissed her neck as she stared at me. Her eyes begged me to help; begged me to save her, but I couldn't. She bit back a whimper, and averted her eyes. She was too embarrassed look at me now.

The General sneered at me and reached around my wife, clicking off the box at the base of her back. Her legs went limp, and she clung to him for support. That's all he wanted. He winked and dragged her out into the hallway. The door slammed behind them, but didn't stop the screams of agony he soon coaxed from her.

"This is your fault. You are a Rak. I always said it. I was right. Was I not right? I knew I was right but no one believed me." Christa muttered in her chair. She didn't even try to escape, just sat there, ranting. "Why did you pick that face, Captain? Why pick the only face she would trust?"

"This is my face, Christa. I didn't steal it from anyone."

Her eyes widened.

"You mean you-"

I cut her off with a sharp nod.

"Yeah. I am. I thought you knew that. That's why you hated me so much. For leaving you as a child."

"It cannot be yours. It just cannot be yours."

The screaming in the hall stopped abruptly, and Christa and I both watched the door, tried to see through it, just to make sure Alice was alright. I shut my eyes, and tried not to think about what he was doing to her on the other side of that wall.

Seconds ticked by.

Those turned into minutes, and, if I counted correctly, those minutes turned into two and a half hours.

Not a sound had been heard in the hall for about an hour, and Christa drifted into a fitful sleep. Then I heard a key in the lock, scrapping the rusted metal. A guard appeared, different then the ones that had been there before. This guard was small, not well equipped for battle, and she hurried over to Christa's side.

"You need to pull your people out and leave here as soon as possible. He will come after you again, so get out and get gone." The girl whispered to Christa as she undid the chains. Christa barely glanced at me as she left the room, but she smirked.

"She chose me."

The door slammed shut, and I was alone. More minutes ticked by, and then the poison seized my body again. This must be it. My fight to the death. My hands clenched and released without my bidding, and the muscles in my legs coiled, ready to strike. The door creaked open, but I couldn't see who opened it.

"Well then, here to finish me off?" I taunted my killer. I would not go down without a fight.

Timidly, Alice walked into the room. The door slammed shut behind her, and The General grinned through the window. My arms fought to free themselves from the shackles. Alice came over to me, and started in on the chains; trying to break them.

"Alice, get out of here." I pleaded with her. She shook her head, but wouldn't look at me. "As soon as you let me go, I will kill you. The General will either make me kill you, or have you kill me. There's no way we're both walking out of this room. Run now or I'll kill you. Please."

Fresh bruises covered her arms and neck, and a deep cut along her jaw was still bleeding.

"Darling," she sighed. "I am already dead."

All the progress I made, the strong woman I built up

since saving her from these camps, was gone. I would never hear her laugh again. And I would never see that special flash in her eyes.

"Get out of here, Alice." My hands already tried to reach for her, but the chains held them back.

She watched my hands trying to break the chains, and her hand stroked the handle of the dagger on her side.

"Yes, Dear." I whispered. "You promised me you would use that on anyone. You *promised*, Alice."

She slowly pulled it from its holster, and braced it in her hands, looking back at me in horror. The last shackle broke, and fell to my feet as The General stepped into the room. His smile didn't hide his anger. I was free, and I was fighting the orders trying to control me, but I was getting weaker as he strode over to me. My veins no longer pulsed black, they were solid black, and The General laughed in my face.

"Go ahead, Captain. Do it." He spit at me.

"I will not." I could barely form the words, but I did, and that was enough.

A small smile danced in Alice's eyes, but faded as The General's smile turned to a sneer. He chuckled, and placed a dagger in my hand.

"You think you have a choice, and that's cute, but it's time for you to take that knife and do what I created you for." He stepped back, and gestured towards Alice.

She should be running. She should be safe back at the camp, but here she stood, unflinching, in front of me.

"I picked you specifically. I knew you'd love her. I knew she'd love you. I hoped that would be enough to break her, but I am willing to start over with a new project."

I lunged towards her as he explained. Alice halfheartedly raised the blade, nicking my arm, but it wasn't enough. I twisted the knife out of her hand and turned it on her. The knife slashed through the air and caught her cheek. I was losing the battle inside me.

"Run, Alice." I hissed, but she shook her head.

"Not without you." Her hand rubbed her cheek, but she didn't move.

My other arm swung up and punched her, right beneath the ribs, sending her into the wall.

"Why do you want me to kill her, General? She's your "trophy"."

He only smiled at me.

"I can find another trophy. They cannot open the gateway to The King's world without her. The Àraid will come out of hiding for her. They need her to bring The King home. It's better for her to be dead."

I couldn't fight the poison anymore. I could only watch as my body moved without me. Alice pushed herself up off of the floor, and cupped my face in her hands. Tears shimmered in her eyes and her lips moved silently as she tried to pull me out of the poison. My hand wrapped around her throat, and I lifted her easily, pinning her to the wall. She didn't struggle as I held her there and reached around to switch off the box on her back. Her legs went limp.

It was over.

She knew it.

As my knife came up and sliced through her abdomen, memories of her laughter flashed through my mind. Blood splattered my hand and her laughter faded.

The poison released me.

Alice was slumped on the floor when I understood completely what I'd done. I knelt beside her, and eased her onto her back.

"Baby, it's going to be okay. Hang on. I'm going to get help." I whispered as I started to get up.

Her hand stopped me, and one look at her stomach told me that it was already too late. Her smiling face paraded across my mind, but was drowned out by this nightmare before me. Blood soaked through my pants, and pooled on the concrete around us. Her hand massaged her throat, and I pulled her necklace out of my pocket.

"Here, Baby. Here."

Her fingers wrapped around the charm, and squeezed my heart. But her body relaxed. She was happy to have it back. Her body trembled in my arms, and her lips could barely form words.

"I'm so cold." She whispered.

I pulled off my jacket and wrapped it around her. The jacket dissolved into ash.

"Let her have a coat, General." I pleaded as she shivered in my arms.

"She hasn't earned it."

"She has earned a thousand coats!" I screamed at him.

Her hand was gentle on my shoulder as she tried to quiet me. She tried to speak as her hand twisted the necklace now red with blood. Blood spurted out of her open mouth. The General laughed.

"I told you I needed someone I could control completely. You just proved you'll do just fine."

"Leave us alone!"

"No."

Black fog filled the room, and a whisper echoed with it.

"Let them have this, General."

But The General stood stubbornly, and watched the life drain from my wife. The black fog thickened, and soon I could only see her. It was just the two of us. Just like we always wanted.

"Do you remember the flowers?" Her eyes were hopeful as she whispered her question. I nodded as tears clogged my throat.

"I wish-" she gasped, and coughed, "I wish I could see a flower once more. I loved flowers."

"Here you go, Love." I held out a tiny blossom, and she scooped it out of my hand eagerly.

"The first bloom of the cycle!" Her eyes lit up, and she cradled the delicate flower between mangled fingers. "I

love the first bloom."

Her face softened, and she looked back up at me.

"Thank you." She whispered, and pulled my head down. Her lips brushed against mine as I wrapped her in my arms.

Another gasp pulled me out of the memory.

"You'll see flowers again, Alice. The first bloom is right around the corner. You have to see it."

"I loved flowers, Captain. Will you grow a flower for me? An orchid? To remember me?"

"Of course." I lied.

No. I wouldn't grow a flower for her.

It would hurt too much.

"I wish I could see it." A tear streaked her face, and her eyes widened.

"I thought I was ready, Captain." She shook her head and pressed her lips together. "I'm not ready. I want to see the flowers bloom."

I pressed my fingers against her scar. If I pushed hard enough, she would slip into sleep, and she would go peacefully. I started to press, but she pulled away.

"I'm not ready, Captain. Please, please don't let me go."

"I won't. I'll hold on to you so tight you won't be able to go anywhere."

"I'm so very scared." Her lips quivered as she spoke.

I hated the tears in her eyes. I wrapped her gently in my arms as she shuddered. Her eyelids drooped, and she struggled for breath.

"It's time." The Collector knelt beside us, and pulled a jar out of the folds of his robe.

Tiny grey fragments rattled in the jar. He dumped the fragments onto Alice's chest, and they flared blue and absorbed into her body.

Alice's eyes widened briefly, and she smiled. The Collector retreated slightly, giving us this moment. Alice's hand raised up to my face, and she slowly ran her fingers along my jaw, pausing at my lips. Briefly, she smiled, and pulled my head down next to her.

"I love you." She whispered, her voice constricting with the pain I caused her.

Her hand fell away, and her eyelids drooped, and then closed one last time. Her breathing slowed. She was gone. Just like that. I couldn't cry. I couldn't scream. I couldn't comprehend what happened. All I could do was hold her body, and rock slowly back and forth.

"She needs to come home now. " The Collector poised his jar over her body, ready to collect her soul, but he gave me this one last moment, while her soul was still here, to tell her goodbye. I slowly kissed Alice's forehead, and bent to her ear; finally answering the only question that mattered.

"My name is Micheal."

Inhibited

Character and Pronunciation guide:

Christa McCain
Human Pronunciation= kris-tah
Àraid Pronunciation= shry-sta
Job: Healer, Leader of The City Of Purple Coal, next Àraid Queen.
Age: 30

Peter McCain
Human Pronunciation= Joe (Just kidding why are you looking up how to say Peter?)
Àraid Pronunciation= pet-ra
Job: Book-keeper, Negotiation Monitor.
Age: Unknown

Jaycobe McCain
Human Pronunciation= jay-cub
Àraid Pronunciation= jah-show-be
Unemployed.
Age: 19

Ginny McCain
Human Pronunciation= jenny
Àraid Pronunciation= guy-na
Job: Inventor.
Age: 18

Cerynn McCain
Human Pronunciation= ker-ren
Àraid Pronunciation= shraw-yen
Job: Healer.
Age: 17

Jess McCain
Human Pronunciation= Jess
Àraid Pronunciation= juh-ease
Job: Child.
Age: 11

Quartnee McCain
Human Pronunciation= court-nee
Àraid Pronunciation= que-rot-ah-nee
Job: Child.
Age: 8

Aurora McCain
Human Pronunciation= Uh-roar-uh
Àraid Pronunciation= eh-ruh-rah

Job: Child.
Age: 2

Josh [Last Name Unknown]
Job: Mail Sorter, Stable Boy.
Age: 18

Roland Drap
Job: Trade Runner
Age: 23

Alice Avens-Tallante
Human Pronunciation: a-liss
Àraid Pronunciation= eh-lye-shuh
Job: The General's Trophy, Former Healer.
Age: 42

The Captain
Job: The General's Suit
Age: 51

The General
Runs the Regions
Age: Unknown

Elder Vảŗẕ
Àraid Pronunciation= feh-ross
Job: Element Àraid Elder
Age: Unknown

† † † † †

Seasons:
Àraid Season=Human Season
Cycle=Year
The Season Of Life=January 1st–March 31st
The Season Of Living=April 1st–June 30th
The Season Of Dying=July 1st–September 30th
The Season Of Death=October 1st–December 31st

† † † † †

Àraid Race Pronunciation:

Àraid: air-aid
Aлṯvaŗ: ahnt-far-ah
Face-changers and mind-readers
Çvïl: shuh-fil

Time-changers and age-freezers
Jǒṛđïл: yor-dine
Earth-shifters and element-controlers
Èṭèṛла: e-tern-a
Royal race. Have abilities from all lower races. Rare. Ŗèлïǎs will always be
Èṭèṛла

† † † † †

Àraid Word Guide:

Læҳlïezè= lay-eek-lie-easy
Special Meaning: "Undo damage inflicted by stupidity."
Àraid For: alleviate, doctor, dress, heal, make healthy, make well, make whole,
medicate, mend, minister to, patch up, regenerate, rejuvenate, remedy, repair,
restore, revive, soothe.

Vïẕṭÿ= fie-st-ya
Àraid for Life.

Vÿđðẕïҳ= fya-dose-ike
Àraid For: beg, beseech, bid, cause, command, compel, crave, demand, desire,
feel necessity for, have need, insist upon, instruct, need, order, request, require,
want, wish.

Bǎл= bon
Àraid For: I, me, mine, my.

Ŗaҳ= rek
Àraid For Rak.

Ŗèҳṭaÿлǎ= reek-teya-na
The King's promised one. A mix of Hybrid and Èṭèṛла blood.

Ŗèлïǎ= ren-eye-ya
Àraid for: empress, female ruler, female sovereign, queen.

Ҳǘša= koo-za
Special Meaning: "All together."
Àraid For: as one, collectively, combined, in sync, together, united.

Ẕvaṭhè=s-feht-he
Àraid For: ambiance, atmosphere, domain, province, realm, world.

Ẕṛaлǘla=sreh-nuh-leh
Àraid For: abduct, divert, hold For ransom, make off with, remove, steal, strip,
swipe, take, take without permission.

Z̧r̩ïèl'vÿz̧t̩= sra-eye-eel fyast
Special Meaning: "Fire."
Àraid For: attack, barrage of projectiles, bombardment, crossfire, fire, sniping.

Z̧лаv= *sn-ehf*
Àraid For: blizzard, frozen vapor, snow, snow flurry, snowfall, snowflake.

Z̧èr̩t̩= sea-rot
Special Meaning: "Go away."
Àraid For: dematerialize, disappear, dissolve, evaporate, fade, go away, melt, vanish.

Z̧űÿð= sue-ya-oh
Special Meaning: "Break down."
Àraid For: demolish, destroy, dismantle, eradicate,   extinguish, gut, mutilate, raze, shatter, wreck.

P̧r̩åv= prahf
Special Meaning: "Open the visions for review."
Àraid For: anticipate, envision, foresee, foretell, predict, prophesy.

P̧æχa= p-ayee-keh
Special Meaning: "Put an end to."
Àraid For: block, cease, discontinue, end, halt, stop, terminate.

P̧èr̩šðлè= peer-zone-ee
Àraid For: intimate, personal.

Лagèt̩= neh-jeet
Àraid For: deny, disallow, discard, disclaim, discredit, disown, nullify, refuse, reject, revoke, turn down, withhold.

Лèÿçű̃= nee-ya-shuh
Special Meaning: "Burn to a crisp."
Àraid For: consume, devour, dissipate, drain, eat up, monopolize.

Å̇= ah
Àraid For: on, in contact, with.

Å̇r̩aïd= air-rad
Àraid For Àraid.

Èлr̩èz̧t̩avït̩= een-ree-steh-fight
Àraid For: bring back, improve, mend, rebuild, reconstruct, recover, renew, repair, restore, revive, refresh, rejuvenate, touch up.

Ǫ́vèl= oh-feel
Àraid For: expose, reveal, unmask, unveil.

Ÿvi̯tè=ya-fight-e
Àraid For: authority, authorization, command, domination, supremacy.

Ðŗavằŗ= draw-fara
Special Meaning: "Trust that day will come again."
Àraid For: assurance, belief something is true, certainty, certitude, confidence, conviction, credence, entrust, expectation, faith, hope, reliance, trust.

Ṭalðŗï= teh-low-rye
Àraid For: convey, declare, make public, pitch, say, sermonize, speak, talk.

62545126R00302

Made in the USA
Middletown, DE
28 August 2019